4-13-2012 ♡ W9-AKO-652

SORRY

To Dave & Cheryl
With my blessings.
Don Costolos

THE SCORPION

A Novel

A prequel to "The Brotherhood"
and "Operation Infidel"

Dom Contreras PhD

ARCHWAY
PUBLISHING

Scripture quotations taken from the New American Standard Bible® (NASB), Copyright © 1960, 1962, 1963, 1968, 1971, 1972, 1973, 1975, 1977, 1995 by The Lockman Foundation Used by permission. www.Lockman.org.

Archway Publishing books may be ordered through booksellers or by contacting:

Archway Publishing
1663 Liberty Drive
Bloomington, IN 47403
www.archwaypublishing.com
1 (888) 242-5904

ISBN: 978-1-4808-4062-1 (sc)
ISBN: 978-1-4808-4064-5 (hc)
ISBN: 978-1-4808-4063-8 (e)

Library of Congress Control Number: 2016919643

Print information available on the last page.

Archway Publishing rev. date: 1/5/2017

Prologue

"Senator Richards here, what can I do for you?"

"Tyree this is Isaiah Hamilton; sorry that I had to call you on your private line can you talk?"

"Yes I can Dr. Hamilton, what a pleasant surprise. It must be important, otherwise you wouldn't have called, especially on my private line."

"Tyree, I know you are very busy so let me get to the point. I recently received from a dear friend of ours, a letter that was written in the fourteenth century. It was written by our founder, Count Fernando Joaquin De La Cruz, a letter written to his son passing on the mantel as head of Twelfth Knight's. But there are some facts that I was not aware of. I will read the letter to you. There is another matter that has also come to my attention. Our two staunch enemies, Heilman and Fenneman. My concern is that if there is any truth to what the Count entrusted to his son, we must act as soon as possible. Oh; one more thing before I read the letter to you, I was also informed that a well-known drug king pin named the Alacran aka Scorpion has been hired by Heilman and Fenneman."

"This is very serious regarding the Scorpion, one of our fellow brothers who I am recommending as a candidate for a Twelfth Knight. He is currently head of the FBI, but has stated to me in private that he would like to resign and serve full time for the Lord. Gregg Johnson is the fellow I mentioned to you a few months ago. What is in the letter that is so earth shattering?"

"Let me read you the letter then you can see why it is so imperative we act as soon as possible. The letter reads as follows."

12 of June 1330   Place, Innis Austria

Diego my son; please put another log in the fire, it is chilly for an early summer night. Also, come close to me my son. I have thought long and hard about a vow I took over fifty years ago concerning the guarding of the robe and parchments entrusted to me by my best friend Alberto de La Vega. He was instructed by our Lord in a dream to guard these artifacts from the wolves of the world. As I think back to that day in Jerusalem when the king of Spain, King Ferdinand, issued orders to arrest all the remaining Knights we ran for our lives to protect what we were instructed to do, by De La Vega. Now I am ready to meet my Lord and feel I have met my obligations.

My son Diego I have prayed to God almighty over whom to leave in charge. God answered my payer and selected you. I have written a letter of trust and hope that you will accept the responsibility as I have outlined in the letter. Come close to me my son, my sight is not what it used to be, so I may read the vow to you as you kneel before me and God; and accept this sacred vow. Please repeat after me."

"I Diego De La Cruz do hereby accept this pledge to guard the secret manuscript and the robe belonging to our Lord. I have taken a sworn oath that I will give my life if necessary to guard these artifacts. They will be hidden in a secret vault at my discretion to guard its secrets after my father's demise. I believe that in the hands of the wrong person they could cause much harm. At my demise, I will pass on the mantle to the next Knight selected as successor by the leading of the Holy Spirit."

"As Paul the apostle wrote to Timothy I Count Joaquin Fernando, likewise instruct my youngest son Diego. "You therefore, my son, be strong in the grace that is in Christ Jesus. The things which you have heard from me in the presence of many witnesses, entrust these to faithful men who will be able to teach others also. Suffer hardship with me, as a good soldier of Christ Jesus. No soldier in active service entangles himself in the affairs of everyday life, so that he may please the one who enlisted him as a soldier" (2 Tim. 2:1-4 NASB-U).

"My son; my fellow Knights have succumbed to the inevitable, death on this earth. I alone am left, but I am passing the mantle to you. Prayerfully you will select eleven other Knights of good character to guard what is entrusted to us. I also warn you my son to be on the alert for those who would try to steal the manuscripts and especially the robe. It is believed to have healing powers because of the blood stains; which is the blood of our Lord. I now take the sword that has helped guard my life long pledge to Christ my Lord and God, do hereby pass on the mantle to you. As Paul, the apostle entrusted Timothy I now entrust you. I crown you head Knight."

"I now ask my Lord to bless you and keep you always with a pure heart. Thank you Lord Jesus the Christ. Amen"

"I Diego pledge my life to faithfully keep this vow. Father; I have one question, where shall I store the artifacts?"

"My son Diego, it is your choice to select. You should inspect them on an annual basis as you gather with the other Knights once a year and replace those knights that pass on to be with our Lord. Remember being one of the twelve is a lifetime commitment. We are called to serve the 'Brotherhood' and mankind to spread the gospel of Jesus Christ. I have one last request my son, before I pass on from this life. I ask that you bury my remains close to where you store the artifacts."

"Father I will do as you have instructed me. You can rest in peace that you have given me this responsibility and that I will do my best with God's help to oversee all that you have commanded me. Christ my Lord shall be my witness" Amen!

Signed June 12th 1330 in the day of our Lord and attested and signed by me Diego De La Cruz.

Count Fernando Joaquin De La Cruz so witness this letter by my signature and seal! Count Fernando Joaquin De La Cruz."

"Isaiah I have known you many years. If you say the letter is authentic, then we must act without delay. I have read second Timothy many times and felt that there was more to what Paul the apostle was saying. There have been rumors of all sorts, but this find in the wrong hands, especially like Heilman a former Nazi and a man with an incurable disease of the skin could control the world, which has always been his aim."

"Tyree I'm scheduled to speak in a few weeks at your place Lords Land, perhaps we can persuade one of our brothers to go in search of the manuscripts and cloak. Oh; I almost forgot there is a map held by one of our brothers in Europe that has the location where the artifacts are located. He will release the map to the person we select to go on our quest. I will let you know if I hear anymore on this matter, God speed."

"Isaiah, I will be praying to the Lord that somehow Gregg will accept the challenge. I can think of no other man that is equal to the task. God, bless you my brother. I look with great anticipation when we gather at our home. Good bye."

Chapter 1

Glancing at my watch as I drank my first cup of coffee I knew I would be late to the office. My wife Bev refilled my travel cup and handed me the cup and my jacket as I headed out the door, while jumping behind the wheel of the car I buckled up my seat belt; all in one motion. While pushing the garage door opener at the same time, I backed out of the garage, glancing over at the 57 Chevy, a work in progress thinking I needed to get busy on restoring this classic beauty still hoping the boys would help after they graduated from the Point.

Having to drive the expressway would be a nightmare because of the summer traffic. Weaving my way through side streets to get onto the Virginia expressway was bad enough, thinking what a beautiful day as the sun shone brightly in the eastern ski---- a joy for those who enjoy the commute. For some reason, there was a clear stretch of expressway open, allowing the traffic to speed up. While pressing on the gas pedal to accelerate something was drastically wrong with the car. This auto is highly classified as to what it can do. It is fully armor plated and built with all the latest technology available. Glancing from side to side; I noticed that further ahead cars were coming to a complete stop then starting up again. When I pushed on the brakes the engine started to exhilarate more. I continued to apply pressure on the brakes, causing the car to reeve up the engine more. It was doing just the opposite it is designed to do. The computerized engine had been tampered with, causing a high-powered car to be out of control on the expressway. I dialed 911 on my cell phone and told the dispatcher my predicament. She in turn notified the State Police.

I was headed for the thickest part of the traffic, even the steering wheel would not respond without all my strength. There was a computerized backup safety system, but it too had been somehow compromised. Again, glancing at the speedometer, the car was approaching eighty miles per hour. I also tried the horn, but it too had been dismantled.

I've been accused of having ice water in my veins, but this time fear entered my heart, fear of what a car out of control can do to innocent people. I started praying and saying. "Dear Jesus I need your help and protection." I knew there was an off ramp about three quarters of a mile ahead. Thinking if I could make it to this spot---- there was a renovation project going on. During the construction, the company placed large plastic drums full of water for trucks and cars that have a difficult time stopping their vehicle, for whatever reason. They are there as a safety precaution to slow down the vehicle as it hits the drums. Knowing this, it was useless to hit the brakes, because they would not respond, making it worse, as the engine increased its speed. If I could just make it to the impact area, hitting the drums the car would stop and the pod would save me from a violent death. The pod is a device that inflates the inside of the front seats and cushions the impact. It is designed after the Indy 500 cars. They hit the walls at over two hundred miles an hour and walk away from the accidents. I was counting on this.

Looking ahead and seeing a school bus full of kids, I had to figure a way out of my dilemma, knowing that unless I stopped this runaway auto, numerous people were in jeopardy of being critically injured or even dead. I could imagine the carnage as the image flashed before my eyes of young children's bodies littering the expressway. Suddenly! spotting a break in traffic, knowing God had answered my prayer and relying on my early days as a hot rod racer suddenly came in handy. It was a maneuver that we called sling shot-ting. It was a risky move, but felt I could execute it. As I went around the bus hitting the divider and bouncing off the center wall it would sling shot me around the bus in mini seconds and thus diverting a tragedy. With most of my strength fighting the steering wheel, I executed my plan as I hit the wall and careened of the wall throwing me around the bus I hit the first drum full of water as it exploded; then the second and the third drum until the car finally came to a stop. The impact of the car hitting the drums sounded like bombs going off in unison. The built-in pod held as the air bags inflated while the car hit the water cans bam, bam, bam.

I sat there for what seemed like an eternity then popped the door to the pod and looked around and saw all the people that thought I had been killed. The only thing I had was the ringing in my ears and shaking as I tried to get out of what was left of the car.

I dialed Mary my secretary and told her what had happened and to please send a car for me. Feeling very lucky to have her as my secretary, now married to one of my best friends Burt Smith a CIA agent. Making my way over to where the troopers were directing traffic. I showed them my credentials and told them what had happened. One of them said; "The big man upstairs must have His hand on you from the looks of your car."

"He sure does, I was praying all the time while trying to get the car in control. Something similar happened to me a few years ago in the prototype of this car, but this accident was much tougher because of the consequences." One of the officers said, "Mr. Johnson; are you alright? You don't seem hurt or in a state of shock?" "Thanks for your concern officer, but other than thanking God for His intervention in saving that bus load of children, I'm truly blessed." One of them asked me if I thought I knew what had happened.

"We won't know until we examine the car in our lab. My first thought is that somebody deliberately tampered with the built-in computer so that when you hit a certain speed, the car would automatically speed up. The brakes froze up as well. Do me a favor men until our guys come to pick up the car, we need to secure the accident scene. People are souvenir hunters and like to take parts of a wrecked auto. They could compromise the evidence." My ride arrived as I got into the agency auto, I thanked the troopers for their dedication and for their service to our state.

After arriving at my office, Mary wanted to know if I was alright, and well enough to work? I told her I was fine and would be tied up most of the day going over personnel records and mail and didn't want to be disturbed. I asked Mary to get me my morning usual bagel and coffee. While I waited for her to bring me my breakfast, I thought who was trying to blow me up and why? I would find out shortly.

While eating my bagel, and enjoying the taste of the flavored coffee, my mind wandered to the past three years and how we had routed Heilman and Fenneman, both Nazi's who wanted to control the world by controlling the Gold and Diamond commodities. They were still lurking in the shadows; like Praying Mantis.

I also thought about my friend Buck Burns our former president, saddened that he did not seek reelection. The new president was an extremely liberal woman. Not that I have a problem with a woman president, but her socialist agenda caused me a lot of pain. Her successor in waiting the Vice President was an African American male with the same agenda. All this weighed heavily on my mind. I was seriously contemplating resigning, and perhaps I would soon. I was mildly surprised that the new president had asked me to stay on as director of the FBI.

Mary interrupted my thoughts on the office intercom and said, "Mr. Johnson there's a call for you sir from an agent from the DEA, he says it's extremely important? I can't pronounce his name, it sounded like Vasquez or Velasquez. He said you have a mutual friend; a drug and fire arms officer from Mexico; named Anthony Bustamante. He also said he wouldn't take no for an answer, it sounds extremely urgent, Sir."

"Put him on." "Gregg Johnson here; what can I do for you, agent Velasquez?"

"First, it's Vasquez and the first name is Manny, Manny Vasquez."

"Sorry Manny, but you would be amazed how many calls I get from disgruntled agents, especially from other federal agencies wanting to come to work for the Bureau. What's so urgent that you wouldn't take no for an answer?"

"Mr. Johnson, I know you're a very busy man, but I don't know if you are aware of it, but do you remember the Mexican drug Lord and terrorist that you thought you put away a few years ago named el Alacran, the Scorpion?"

"Sure do. We caught him and his cronies almost three years ago about this same time as part of Operation Infidel. Has something happened to him?"

"I'll get right to the point. One of our liberal judges for some unknown reason claims El Alacran was denied due-process. This judge claims that we violated his constitutional rights."

"Manny, excuse me but didn't you and I work a case together a few years back?
I believe we met when I was a field agent. We were after some guys that had smuggled large amounts of heroin through Texas. It was a big bust as we worked the case together, DEA, ATF and the FBI. They also tried to smuggle weapons in for a local skin head group who had purchased them from a European arms dealer that just happened to be Russian Mafia. I'm that same Guy. Sorry Manny, go on continue."

"It turns out this guy is a U.S. citizen and has dual citizenship from Mexico. I received a call from a mutual friend in Mexico Tony Bustamante. He alerted me to what transpired. It seems they released him from a federal facility in New York, where he was being held. There were other charges pending against him for a crime he committed in the federal prison. He had killed another inmate in a fight. The court was so backed up with older cases, they thought because he was an alien they could hold him if they wanted. He somehow could retain a lawyer, and of course the lawyer got him sprung. My main purpose in calling you is that he was making threats that he was going after you and a D.C. cop named Butler! He also said he would initiate a 'Venganza'. I know a lot about this guy and have been working with Tony on how we can nab him. By the way, a Venganza in Latino Circles means they go after the entire family, aunt's uncles and immediate family until your entire line is wiped out."

"Manny, I saw this guy's eyes when we caught him and felt I was looking at pure evil. He still gives me the creeps thinking about him. When we worked that case together I was amazed at how confident an agent you were. I'm sorry I'm trying to remember what you looked like. Ah, you were a sergeant at that time, about 6'4" and weighed in at about 230 lbs. Why I remember you is that you were the first Hispanic I had ever seen with blue eyes. What are you doing now, besides chasing drug traffickers?"

"I've been working undercover the last three years. I finally had to resurface because my wife threatened to leave me. Listen, I would like to see you right away about our boy El Alacran. I have some other information that if he carries out his threats, can threaten National security. My boss said I should get this to you right away. What does your schedule look like for the rest of the week? It's that important that I get with you."

"Manny, can you be here in the morning at 9:00 o'clock?"

"Yes Sir Mr. Johnson, nine-AM sharp."

"Its settled then I'll see you in the morning."

As he hung up, the first thing that hit me was, where do all the evil people come from? I was still feeling that I would rather be a field agent any time than being a paper pusher. Was I ready to hand in my resignation to the president as head of the FBI? Senator Richards my mentor knew my feelings, he said I should pray about it, and if it was God's will, God would give me peace of mind. This job took far too much time away from my wife. The boys only had a year to go before graduating from West Point. I wanted to spend more free time with Bev and work on the boy's car that we had bought to restore, a father son project. The one we had prior was burned beyond repair in the bombing of our home. We later found this 1957 Chevy Bellaire on the internet that needed a lot of work and bought it for the boys, but now they were gone, I suppose it was my dream as much as theirs.

I thought; how crime had not quieted down since we uncovered the plot to kill President Burns. Even though we had broken the back of one of the largest terrorist cells on the East Coast, along with exposing Heilman and Fenneman the leaders of organized terror. We felt we were still very vulnerable, especially along our borders and open ports. The Russians were rattling their swords again and China was upping its arms production. Pakistan and India were beefing up their borders as well. It seemed like the World was on the verge of exploding, and of course certain parts of the Middle-East seemed intent on an all-out war! I pondered; were we living in the last days? Were Heilman and Fenneman still a threat by being involved in something more heinous, more immoral? How far will the moral decay contribute to our downfall?

The phone startled me as it rang on my private line. "Gregg Johnson here"

The voice on the other end laughed, but then he spoke. "How are you Gringo? Remember the last time I saw you. I told you your puny jail could not hold me. Yes, it's me; El Alacran in your language 'The Scorpion.' I'm sorry I didn't send you a Birthday Card. You should expect a belated one any-day. My secretary will get it off right away---He had cupped the phone, but not enough so I couldn't hear as he said: 'Hey Beto, don't forget to send that gift to his Excellency Gregg Johnson.' He then spoke-up in a highly sounding sadistic voice. "You will hear more from me again. Oh, I almost forgot, your friend Tony Bustamante has been dispatched, ha, ha to his ancestors. Adios, Gringo."

I sat there listening as he spoke these words, and thought what was he up too? His voice sent cold shivers down my spine. Knowing with all my heart; he was a servant of Satan. I will never forget how he stared at me the last time we met face to face, with his cold empty green eyes glaring at me, emanating pure evil. I was interrupted by my thoughts as Mary came in and said that Captain Butler was here to see me. I glanced at my watch it was 4:00 o'clock.

"Hi Gregg; it's been a couple of weeks since we last talked. I thought I could use a little advice about a couple of things. Can you spare the time?"

"My brother; I always have enough time for you. How's the new promotion coming? Like being a Captain? It should be a piece of cake for you. You deserve to be police commissioner, one day you will. What's on your mind?"

"Gregg, the job is okay, but the----forgive me, 'it's the butt kissing' that is hard for me. I must be a man of integrity, not someone's lackey. I don't want to do anything that my wife and kids aren't proud of, but especially my Lord. Why does it seem that the higher we go in our jobs the more you are asked to compromise your principles? I'm having a hard time with this aspect of the job. I thought you might give me a few pointers, you know I think of you as an older wiser brother."

"Look Short Stuff, you are a man of principle and God fearing; allow God's word to guide you in being the best that He alone can be proud of. May I ask you a question; does this pertain to taking a bribe?"

"How did you guess Gregg? This guy wants me to turn my head at what is going on. It comes from a city official concerning a new type of drug that has hit the streets. This guy handed me an envelope with fifty grand. It's in the precincts office safe. He knows I won't accept it, but I believe it goes higher than him. My gut tells me it goes high up on the food chain, clear to the Mayor's office. I want to break the case and catch the entire bunch. I think it involves some cops with a lot of years on the DC force. Remember the former Mayor who was caught in a FBI sting? We don't need any worse publicity in DC. At this juncture, I don't know how far it goes, but it may also involve child prostitution and slave labor as well."

"Have you discussed this with any of your superiors?" "No Gregg, you're the first person I have said anything too. I don't feel I have enough to go on and I don't know who else is involved. Oh; one other thing, remember the guy we caught in New York, what was his name? Ah---yeah the Scorpion, he was released a few days ago."

"Yeah I know, I had two calls this morning, the first call was from an agent from DEA who said that this guy was intent on killing me and my family. I'm going to meet with the agent in the morning. Then El Alacran also called my private line and tried to be cute with me no threats though."

"Gregg; I believe this guy they call El Alacran, AKA Scorpion may be connected in this new drug, child prostitution ring, and other illegal enterprises."

"You could be right my brother, but I sense that something else is bothering you?"

"There is Gregg. A friend of my son was found dead in the bathroom at his school. A 15-year-old boy is dead because of an overdose of this new drug. Its street name is called 'Euphoria,' It's a mixture of methamphetamine and another substance that our lab people are still trying to ascertain its chemical makeup. We looked at several police reports from the south-west mainly Texas and Arizona. I suspect there are other areas where the drug is being sold. Several young kids have died from the drug along with known drug addicts. The high is like Crystal-Meth. The main difference is the high, the intensity is stronger and lasts much longer than regular crystal-meth.

But when the drug starts to wear-off, the user overreacts and ups the dosage causing the heart rate to accelerate three to four times its normal rate, then the heart literally explodes. Am I concerned? You bet Gregg."

"Short Stuff my brother, do you think the Mayor is tied into the distribution and sales of this drug?"

"Well; at this point I'm not sure. Again, because he is a high-ranking City official, I need to be darn sure he is involved up to his eyeballs before I move on him. One thing I know for sure, corruption is destroying this country."

"Why don't we do this? Be here at nine o'clock in the morning for a meeting with Manny Vasquez. We will both ask him about this new drug and its current effect on law enforcement."

"Great my brother, I have a very important meeting. Sorry but I need to go I'm meeting with the police commissioner. I'll see you in the morning, God bless."

As he walked out the door Mary handed me a note stating that Charlie Wong had called. He said that it was urgent that you call him right away.

I dialed Charlie. "Dr. Wong speaking how may I help you?"

"Hey Charlie; what's so urgent?"

"Hi Gregg, why I called; I have a problem with some bodies. I thought maybe you could come and see the remains? By the way when are we going to play poker, I miss getting together like we used too. How's the wife and boys?"

"Everyone is fine Charlie. How's your wife Charlie? Give her my love, and hug the girls for me. It has been a long time since we got together for a game of poker."

"I called you Gregg because I know you can get results right away.

Could you come by the morgue right now? I think it's important? We have a couple of bodies that might interest you. I just finished the autopsies on them, but I found something very strange, it's the way they died. I really feel you need to see the bodies and see what I found during the autopsy."

"Ok Charlie, I'll see you in about an hour." After he hung up, I thought, what's so strange about people dying? It had to be important if Charlie felt I needed to see the bodies. I cleaned up my remaining paper work and headed for the morgue."

I got to the morgue and walked to the back office looking for Charlie. As he saw me he came over and gave me a big hug. I had never witnessed to Charlie, and thought perhaps the Lord would open the door for me to share my faith with him.

"Charlie what's so important that you needed to see me right away?"

"Gregg; let's go to the back-dissection room. It's kind of slow right now, but it will pick up later. It's easier to have a conversation away from the noise. Follow me, I don't know what we're dealing with so we better suit up. It's just a precaution, you never know."

We made our way to a back room where they autopsied the contagious corpses. After we had put on the special suits, Charlie walked over and pulled out one of the slabs on rollers where they place the bodies after a performed autopsy. Charlie uncovered the first one. I was taken back at how young the boy was. He couldn't have been more than fifteen.

Charlie spoke up. "Gregg; notice the discoloration around the mouth and look at his teeth. Notice that some are missing and most of them are rotten and discolored. You would think he had been using Meth for years, but not so. Meth will destroy other organs, but I checked his liver and it's completely healthy, want to see it? I thought not, but you must look at his brain and what happened to it along with his heart. Both his heart and the central part of his brain turned to mush, literally. The sad part of this scenario is----this kid is not the only one we have that this has happened too. I've got at least another half a dozen in storage, all with the same symptoms. Gregg whoever is pushing this stuff is intent on murdering young innocent kids. I don't have enough words to describe what I feel about this drug."

"I feel the same way Charlie, but you know this is not part of the FBI's turf. Have you called drug enforcement people on this?"

"No; I felt you might have more clout with them. I want to show you why I think this thing involves the FBI as well. We can take off the suits and go to another part of the morgue."

We put our clothes back on after being decontaminated and made our way to the dissection room. "I said; Charlie where are you taking me too this time?"

As we stopped at one of the tables Charlie spoke up. "Notice this gentleman, anything peculiar about him?"

"I don't know Charlie what am I looking for?"

"Let me show you Gregg. Help me turn the body on its stomach, notice the strange Tattoo on his back. It reads, 'Viva El Alacran,' but also notice what has been scratched on his back. 'Muerte para el traidor y Venganza.' Gregg my Spanish is a little rusty but I believe it says, 'Death to the traitor; and vendetta.' I've sent his prints to the locals, but nothing has come back yet. He was brought in here a few days ago. Maybe you may want to find out who killed him and why? He apparently is Hispanic. My guess is he's Mexican. I found residue of heroin and cocaine in his liver what they call speed-ball. What killed him was, get this, highly toxic bites from a scorpion. Notice he has several puncture wounds on his torso. Gregg, they stung this guy to death. One more thing, he is tied to the Nuestra Familia, a well known Hispanic gang. You can see by the tattoos on his arm and torso."

"Charlie; do me a favor. Keep this guy on ice until I check with Interpol, also under no circumstances release this info to anyone, especially the press. The last thing we need is a snoopy reporter looking for a story, okay?"

"Gotcha Gregg, you have my word on it. Do you think this death might be tied to the drug deaths? I know it's a stretch, but you never know."

"I don't want to say too much until we have more info. Thanks for alerting me. Oh, before I go why don't you get the guys together for a poker party, say this Friday night. Today is Wednesday and we can catch up on old times."

"Sounds great to me Gregg, can we meet at your home my wife has something going this Friday. Do you realize it's almost three years, since we last got together?"

"Yeah I know. It's settled then my place at seven this Friday."

I called the motor pool and spoke with the agent in charge to assign me another vehicle. They would have one waiting for me in my parking space.

As I made my way to the parking lot, ever on the alert looking from side to side to see if I was being followed or someone lurking in the shadows to do me in. I noticed a couple of guys eyeball me. I thought, am I becoming paranoid as I made my way to my car? The keys were on the visor as I had been told. I started the engine and made my way home without any surprises.

CHAPTER 2

I weaved my way in and out of traffic as I made my way home. I kept looking in the rear-view mirror out of habit. I knew in my gut that I was being followed. I no longer had a driver, since I felt it signaled me out. I broke with Washington protocol when I did, but when it came to my own safety, I felt I could drive as good as any agency driver. After what had happened this morning I didn't trust many people except my close friends.

As I settled in for the half hour drive home; I thought about the July 4th surprise with Fenneman and Heilman and their attempt to control the worlds gold and diamond markets. Time had whizzed by so fast. I felt that we had not finished the job because Heilman and Fenneman were still free; plotting their next vial plan.

I was brought back to reality when I glanced out of my rear-view mirror. I saw one of the biggest scorpions I had ever seen crawling on the back seat, making my skin crawl. I quickly pulled over to the side of the parkway, barely stopping the car and jumped out. I opened the back door to see if I could kill it. It was jet black with a fat tail! It had crawled between the armrest in the back seat. Thinking to myself; how do I kill this thing? I was afraid to stick my hand down between the seats, so doing the safest thing, I called the Bureau decontamination department and asked them to come and see if we could catch it alive.

I stood by the side of the road for what seemed like hours, but they responded quickly and were on the scene within twenty minutes. It took them about half an hour to extract not one but at least six of the deadly stingers.

One of the men spoke up; "Mr. Johnson, somebody must really want you dead. These things are not local to our country. They are from another part of the world; North Africa and I might add, the most-deadly of the species. The ones in the southwest of our country have some highly toxic venom, but the ones we caught are called the fat-tailed scorpion, or Fattail. They grow to about four inches in length. They were most likely brought into this country by ship. There is anti-venom for all species because for some people it can kill them within minutes, especially if they go into anaphylaxis shock. This species is illegal in our country because of its highly toxic bite."

"I never knew these things could kill you. I have heard horror stories about them. I understand they are very common in Arizona and New Mexico. I was led to believe that they are very shy and stay away from humans. Oh, one more thing, do you think you got them all?"

"Mr. Johnson if you don't feel secure driving home we can take you home and take the car in for fumigation and get it back to you in the morning?"

"Good; let's do that. Can you deliver the car to me by eight in the morning? Oh; one more thing, can you get me one in a jar after you put them to sleep. I want it as a reminder how close I came to either dying or getting very sick." "No problem Sir."

I got into one of the vans as we made our way to my home. I had a lot to share with my wife, how I was brought to my knees over a Biblical Arachnida. I thought about the movie the boys loved to watch a few years ago; the Scorpion King. And now my experience with the same type of Scorpion was featured in the movie. I would be kept busy relating my experiences to my friends and relatives.

———————

As they dropped me off, I couldn't help thinking about what had been attempted. I started to laugh as I thought about what the headlines would read; "FBI director killed by scorpion bite." It was not funny, but there are various scriptures referring to this spider. Man, was I glad they were extracted from my car.

As I opened the door, Beverly was standing in the doorway looking ever radiant. I walked into the house I reached over and put my arms around her and hugged her as she looked at me with those blue eyes and that wonderful smile. We kissed in the middle of the kitchen and I prayed out loud thanking God for bringing me home safe to my wife.

"Dinner is in the oven and we can eat now or you can shower first, it's your choice?"

"Shower it is Honey."

———————

I came back down stairs after showering and changing into some casual clothes, I was eager to sit down with my wife and enjoy our evening.

"Food looks great, Rib-eye steak, baked Potato's a great lettuce

and tomato salad and warm French rolls. You made my day honey.
I'll bet you bought some Mango-Peach ice-cream?"

"Did you forget what day this is?"

"Oh my dear Lord; it's my birthday! How could I forget.

"Surprise, as the Senator and Maw-Richards came into the dining
room along with Rachel and Cash, Mary and Burt and of course Short
Stuff and his wife. All of them chimed in singing Happy Birthday
Gregg."

I wondered where they had been hiding when I came into the
house. Everyone came over to hug me when the doorbell rang it was
John and Kathleen, as they walked into the dining room. An added
surprise, were my twin sons James and John. I was overcome with joy
as I started to weep tears of gratefulness to my God.

As we all sat down to a great meal and fellowship in Christ, giving
thanks to our Lord, who made all this possible. I was further blessed
by all the funny cards and small presents I was given. I felt it an honor
to be part of God's family. Everyone went home near midnight. After
they left, we made our way to bed. For some reason, I kept waking
up every hour.

I got up at three in the morning finding it difficult to sleep.
I decided to go down stairs and make a cup of tea. Our new dog
Buster, who was an exact replica of Butch his sire, followed me into
the kitchen. As I was warming the water; Buster growled and went for
the back door which was adjacent to the garage. He kept sniffing and
carrying on. The alarm system was set; or so I thought. I walked over
to the master alarm box and found it armed, but with all the modern
technology available it could have been compromised. I would have
it checked out later today. Buster started barking, so I made my way
to the den and pulled out my 7mm-glock and pulled the hammer

back as I heard that familiar click; a sound made by a weapon armed for action.

My adrenalin sped-up as my FBI training kicked in. Armed with my hand gun and a flashlight I eased my way back to the kitchen. Buster was still making funny growling sounds, but at what? I didn't have a clue. I decided to be brave and turn on the garage lights and open the door. I looked at Buster and noticed that the hairs on the back of his head and shoulders were bristled as his instincts had also kicked in. He was ready for battle! I almost laughed as I gently opened the lock to the garage door. I didn't know what to expect as I proceeded to push the door open. I was startled and taken back as I quickly closed the door, along with grabbing Buster and pulling him back into the kitchen. The garage was full of scorpions of all sizes and shapes. There were black ones, yellow ones and grey colored ones. From what I saw, it would take a professional exterminator to capture or eradicate all of them.

I was about to contact a twenty-four-hour exterminator we had used in our old home, when the phone rang. I knew as it rang it was El Alacran. "Good-morning Senior Johnson did you like my birthday present? My pets needed a new home so my friends and I decided to send them to you. Oh; before I forget, be careful if you try to pick one up. I understand their sting can be fatal!"

"Listen maggot or the cockroach that you are. You should change your name to 'Cucaracha, instead of Alacran. One day soon you will be exterminated just like your little pets in my garage will be. We have a special cage waiting for you at Leavenworth, unfortunately we don't have a better place for social deviates. It's a specially designed cell where you will be on display 24/7. Good night Cucaracha" As he hung up, I heard a faint profane word uttered from his mouth.

By this time the boys and Beverly came downstairs, they said in unison, Dad; honey what's going on?"

"All of you calm down, we have a slight problem. Our garage is full of deadly scorpions. I'm going to call the exterminators right now. Under no circumstances will you open the door to the garage until they have given us an all clear; okay? Now I want all of you to get a flashlight and go through the entire house and see if you can find any more. Start upstairs in the bedrooms and closets and work your way through the bathrooms. I'll start downstairs. If you find one; take your shoe off and whack it, I'll explain it all later."

We had to leave the house for an entire day as the experts cleaned up the garage. None of the creatures were found in any other part of our house, but I knew this guy the Scorpion was determined to eliminate me and my family. I went to the office and the boys went back to West Point. Beverly spent the day with Rachel, whose second baby was due in a couple of months.

I called the motor pool and asked them to deliver my car earlier than I had instructed. I was assured that I wouldn't find any surprises. Even at six am there is traffic on the expressway. I made my way through traffic thinking how I could catch this guy. I had a meeting with Manny Vasquez and Short Stuff and was running late after driving Bev to Rachel's house who insisted I eat some breakfast. I called Mary and told her I would be in the office in about twenty minutes and to let my two friends know what had happened. I got to the Bureau building without any trouble and made my way to my office. As I walked in, Short Stuff and Manny were already waiting for me.

Short Stuff spoke up; "Gregg; I understand this guy the Scorpion infested your car, then your home with the critters. How did he get them into your garage? Do you have any ideas? I've got my whole family on alert until we catch this guy, since he made threats about me. Manny and I have been talking about him and how bad a dude he is!"

"Guys, come on into my office. Listen I haven't had breakfast yet. Cash's wife Rachel insisted I eat, but I only had a cup of coffee with her and my wife, so if you want something now, you can join me. I buzzed Mary, and said: can you get me my usual and whatever Short Stuff and Manny want; oh, and thanks Mary."

CHAPTER 3

As we sat down in my office we all exchanged pleasantries during our quick breakfast and coffee. I spoke up first, "Thank you both for coming this morning. The reason for our gathering is that we all have a mutual enemy, El Alacran. Manny, since you know this guy better than any of us please tell us what were up against?"

"Thanks Gregg, first thanks for seeing me on such short notice, and of course for a new-found friend, Capt. Butler, or as he likes to be called Short Stuff. Let me begin with what I know about El Alacran. His real name is Jose Mace Caulfield Juarez. He was born to a Mexican mother in Prescott Arizona. His father was a retired career Army Sergeant, who died in the local VA hospital when Jose was around twelve years of age. His mother took him back to Mexico. His uncle his mother's brother was a leading drug and arms lord. He was killed by a rival drug lord when Jose was in his late teens. He then enrolled at the University of Michigan and graduated with a major in business and a Masters in economics. When his uncle died, he took over as head of the drug cartel. This was about thirteen years ago."

"My first contact with him was about six years ago when one of our agents was ambushed by him and his men. What they did to the agent is very painful for me since we started together with the DEF. We were like brothers in fact I am Godfather to his eldest son. I have a personal reason for seeing this guy brought to justice. About three years ago he made an alliance with the oil mogul Russell Fenneman and a close friend Max Heilman, the Nazi billionaire."

"Here's the corker, the job that he agreed to do for these two lunatics failed, blowing up the diamond exchange offices in New York. He was so upset that he beat up a couple of cell mates who crossed him. One guy is in a vegetative state. I recently found out that the alliance he made with Heilman and Fenneman is a permanent one. My guess is if it suits his purpose. One more thing, he is a sadist, his mother would beat him mercilessly as a boy. I suppose she took out her frustrations on the boy after the death of his father. That's it in a nut shell guys."

Short Stuff spoke up: "Manny where did this guy get the nickname Alacran?"

"Great question; I'm told that he picked it up because of where he lived, in Durango Mexico, where they have a species of scorpion that is highly toxic. Somehow he started arm wrestling with guys with a scorpion tied in the center and the first man whose arm hits the scorpion and gets stung is the looser. He got the idea from a movie starring Marlon Brando, called the "Appaloosa." I've never seen the movie, but those who have seen it told me about a scene where Brando arm-wrestles the bandit; who stole the horse. The scorpion of course stings Brando, but he doesn't die. Our guy's people started calling him El Alacran, which inflates his ego. Sounds sadistic to me, does this answer your question?"

I spoke up. "Manny, I've got a question for you. It concerns a drug that I just found out about, it's called---'Euphoria.' What's your take on it?"

"Guys; this is the second part of the equation. El Alacran and his cartel introduced this scourge on humanity almost a year ago. Our agency got involved when we found out that he started trading 'Euphoria' for arms. ATF is also working on this case. He has gone International as well. We received a wire from Interpol asking for information on the drug. My friends, we are dealing with a drug that if it becomes available worldwide we will see a plague worse than the one the killed thousands in the middle ages."

"Manny; what can we do to help?"

"Gregg; first and foremost, all law enforcement agencies need to be alerted about this drug and what we are faced with. Trading drugs for arms is a great concern to me. Just imagine a terrorist group trading drugs for a nuclear weapon? The horror of this drug is they can't isolate the second drug mixed with the methamphetamine. DEA has a cadre of chemist working around the clock to try and isolate the second chemical. We will eventually do it, but look at the havoc it has unleashed!"

Short Stuff chimed in. "Manny; where is, the drug being manufactured, or do we know who discovered it?

"Short Stuff we don't know. Like I said, it hit the States near the end of last year, but thought that the handful of Meth freaks who died was because of speed-balling. We also thought that it was Meth that had been cut improperly, but we later found out, not so. I have an idea that it may be manufactured in South America. I don't have any proof, just a gut feeling. Maybe Venezuela because of the tie-in to Heilman and Fenneman"

I believe like you Manny, Heilman and Fenneman are close to the dictator Chavez. It would not surprise me. I should alert the President and let her know what we are up against. I rate this problem top priority. Let me see if we can get in to see the President right away.

'Mary will you call the President's office and see if she can see us right away.' Guys it will take a few minutes for her to get through; can I get you some more coffee?"

"By the way, I went to the morgue yesterday and saw the effects of what this drug can do. I suggest that you both go and see the effects it does on our young. I have never seen anything like it in all my years in law enforcement."

Mary came in within a few minutes. "Mr. Johnson, the President is on the line. She said she would like to speak with you."

"Stay where you are guy's let me take this call. Good Morning Madam President, how are you?"

"I'm fine Gregg; How's the wife, is she okay? I haven't seen you for a couple of weeks. I understand we have a problem; what's up?"

"Madam President my wife is fine and yes we do have a serious problem that could become a crisis issue. I don't know if you've had time to read my entire report regarding Operation Infidel?"

"As a matter of fact I did, what does this have to do with the problem at hand?"

"In that report, I wrote about a man they called 'El Alacran' in English it means 'The Scorpion.' It seems that he was released from prison because it turns out he is a US citizen and his civil rights were apparently violated during booking. He is behind the sale and distribution of a new street drug. Several deaths have been caused by this new drug called Euphoria. I have one of the DEA agents and Capt. Butler in my office as we speak. I believe our old nemesis have resurfaced along with this guy they call, El Alacran."

"Gregg, you know that I respect your judgment on our Nations security. Why don't I call a special meeting for the first of next week, say Monday at ten AM, if that's okay with your schedule. I'll get

Maggie my secretary to send out a memo for the meeting. I'll also have the head of ATF and the DEA at the meeting. What's the agent's name that is working the case?"

"His name is Manny Vasquez, Lieutenant Vasquez. Madam President"

"I want him here as well since he has all the information. Also, have Capt. Butler here. I believe he has a lot of potential, see you Monday."

"It's all set guys, be at the White House Monday at ten AM. If you don't have any more to add to this I have a lot of paper work to do. I almost forgot, while I was at the morgue the other day, Charlie Wong called me and showed me the body of a thug that was bitten several times by scorpions. We don't have a lot of leads yet, but what does bother me is that this guy had scratched on his torso in Spanish, 'death to the traitor and revenge.' My question is, why did they kill this guy? Do we have a gang war going on at the same time? These are questions that need answering, sleep on it and get back to me, okay? And if you have time, stop by the morgue"

Manny answered and said; "I may have an answer by this evening, do you have a private number where I can reach you Gregg?"

"I sure do here's my card. Hope to hear from you manana. That's one of the few words I know in Spanish." Manny and Short Stuff were both laughing as they walked out.

I had a thought about who should be at that meeting. One of my police science professors was an expert on drugs and alcohol, I decided to call him. I asked Mary to get Dr. Sergio Calderon on the line. He was a Ph.D. in Bio-Chemistry. He is one of the leading experts on street drugs and their effects on the human anatomy.

Mary walked in and said that he would call me back in a few minutes.

My private line rang. It was Dr. Calderon. "Good morning Gregg; it's been awhile. How are things going with you and your family?

"We are all doing well sir. The boys are in their last year at the Point. Beverly is doing well she recently got a clean bill of health as to the breast cancer. As for me, other than being shot at and fighting terrorists, life is normal. I know you're busy so I won't keep you very long. Dr; have you heard of a new street drug called; Euphoria?"

"As a matter of fact I was having a heated discussion about this very drug with a colleague when you called. What do you want to know about it?"

"Dr; we are seeing a rise in teen deaths attributed to this blight on society. The reason I contacted you is that the President is having a meeting on this problem; this next Monday at 10 AM. I was wondering if you would accompany me to the meeting. I can get you top clearance right a-way."

"Yes Gregg; I would like it very much. I have a late afternoon meeting? Ah---yes I can make it. You know I don't drive, so you must pick me up here at the institute. I am in the process of examining this drug and its contents, I may have an answer for you by next Monday."

"That's great Dr. I'll pick you up at nine thirty sharp."

"One more thing Gregg; I have a special interest in this case. A nephew of mine recently died because of this drug. He was only thirteen years old. I'll be ready, and looking forward to this meeting. God bless Gregg."

As he hung up, I told Mary and told her to contact the Presidents secretary and have them add Dr. Calderon's name to the list for the meeting.

I looked at my watch and saw that it was almost one in the afternoon. I decided to take a walk and grab a bite from one of the mall vendors. I needed to do some thinking and pray for some guidance.

I made my way along the D.C. mall and noticed how many young people were strolling and enjoying the sunny day. Being a very observant person, I noticed out of the corner of my eye a couple of guys dealing drugs. You can always tell a deviate individual by their actions, always glancing behind and sideways to see if anyone is watching them. It's nothing but guilt and the fear of being caught as they spotted me they quickly put the drugs back into their pockets. There were two young kids in their early teens that were making the buy. I thought, were they hustling Euphoria? I prayed to God that they weren't.

I continued my stroll intent on watching and taking in the wonderful day along with the thousands of people visiting the mall. I never felt as lucky being an American as I did at that moment. As I walked along, I thanked the Lord for my walk of faith in this wonderful country. I became so engrossed in what I was observing and praying, when I was knocked to the ground by a skateboarder! The guy kept going and never stopped to see if I was all right, then I noticed the blood on my pants. A young couple came over and asked me if I was alright; as they helped me to my feet. The young man said; "It looks like you skinned your knee mister, perhaps you should go to the emergency room?" The young woman said; "I can call an ambulance if you like sir?"

I responded and said; "Thank you both, but I think I'm okay." I noticed that there was a slice in my pant leg, like it had been purposely cut. "I think you should call 911 if you don't mind." I felt myself feeling woozy and looked for a place to sit down.

CHAPTER 4

While I waited for the ambulance and police to arrive I called Mary and filled her in as to what had happened and asked her to notify Bev. By the time the ambulance and police arrived I had cut my pant leg to look at the wound. I saw that I had been cut deep, the wound would require several stitches. The ambulance arrived and the paramedics quickly loaded me into the ambulance and hooked me up to an IV while on the way to the hospital. I started to perspire profusely along with the shakes. When they got me to the ER, I told the doctor on duty what had happened. He examined my leg and immediately ordered some blood work done. Somehow I knew that I had been poisoned by a contaminated surgical knife, laced with Fattail scorpion venom by one of El Alacran's men. When the results came back positive, he ordered some anti-venom to be administered, by this time my heart rate was starting to accelerate dangerously high.

While I was waiting for the anti-venom to counteract the poison Beverly walked in with Rachel. I had been given an IV a standard procedure. She along with Rachel came over to where I was laying on a gurney.

Bev leaned over and kissed me as she said; "What am I going to do with you. Perhaps it's time you thought about another profession? Oh; honey, how many times have I prayed to Jesus asking to protect you? What happened? Did they catch the perpetrator! We should pray for his soul."

Rachel came over and put her arm around Beverly and reassured her I would be okay. She turned to me and said; "Gregg do you believe this is the work of El Alacran?"

"I have no doubt that it was. He has vowed to exact vengeance on me and my family. I am going to assign agents to watch Bev and the boys 24/7."

"Oh how I wish I were back in action, but I want this baby so bad. It will be my second and Cash is so excited about being a new father again. He wants a boy, but if it's a girl we are still blessed. Rachel junior is almost two, but I must admit I enjoy being a mother. Cash said to tell you he has been waiting for you to call him for a new assignment."

"Rachel; you tell Cash that I will contact him either later today or in the morning."

"Beverly said it must be tomorrow. When he gets out of here I'm going to take him to dinner, then home."

There you have it Rachel, my wife has settled it. Please tell Cash to come to the office in the morning around eleven, ok."

After several hours, the doctor on duty said I was set to go. He affirmed that I indeed had been poisoned by scorpion venom. He didn't feel that I had absorbed enough to kill me----because of the bleeding, and felt that the anti-venom would suffice. He stated that if I started feeling nauseous again to bring me back to the emergency room. Beverly had brought me a new pair of pants, since Rachel had driven her here----She would drop us off at my office.

As we walked out the front door, one of the nurses caught up to us and said; "Mr. Johnson there was a note addressed to you delivered by a special messenger."

I thanked her as she left. I opened the envelope with a lot of caution. I instinctively knew it was from my enemy, El Alacran! I read the note that said; "Mr. FBI director, you are warned. My sting is usually fatal, but I will not fail the next time. This is only the beginning. Signed El Alacran. P.S, who is the attractive pregnant woman with your wife? Is she related to you?"

I didn't want to scare Beverly and Rachel, but they had to know what we were up against. Rachel dropped us off at my office to pick up my car. It was almost six thirty in the evening. I alerted my DC director and had him assign a squad 24/7 for Rachel and my wife. We were under siege. Rachel was like a kid sister to me and I would die for her if need be. She also was a great law enforcement agent as well.

As we made our way to the agency car I had this feeling that we were being watched, by unfriendly eyes. Eyes full of hatred and wrath. Getting into the car, I said to Beverly; "Honey; where do you want to go for dinner?"

"Gregg dear you pick the spot; besides you rarely get to pick the menu."

"Okay; I will. How about a steak? I heard of a new place that just opened its south of here about a thirty-minute drive, ah what's the name? Ah yes; Clancy's Prime Rib."

She said; "great let's go." As we made our way to the Virginia expressway, I glanced in the rear-view mirror and saw a foreign make sports car weaving in and out of traffic. It was silver in color and from the looks of it, one would be hard pressed to outrun it. He didn't know what this Jaguar prototype could do. It could outrun almost any vehicle in production. I started to laugh for some insane reason.

I thought of the fictional character 007, James Bond who is always outrunning and outgunning his enemies.

Beverly said to me. "What's so funny dear? Did I say something funny?"

"No; I was thinking about James Bond agent 007 how he is always being chased, like we are being chased right now. Don't worry honey this car is armor plated with a classified engine that can outrun most any car made. I don't want you to panic. I dialed a code into the computer with our destination and where we were at this moment. They would be here soon. You could hear the soft ping-a-ping as the bullets bounced off the driver side. I glanced over to see if I could see inside the vehicle as he passed by. I hit the positive traction specially designed breaks and came to an almost instant standstill. I was surprised that my leg didn't ache when I accelerated. He went flying by me, as I slowed then speeded up again. We saw a huge fireball explode in front of us as I made my way to the next off ramp. Our killers had been cremated in the fiery inferno. My car phone rang. "Mr. Johnson; they have been eradicated, anymore vermin you need exterminated?"

"No thanks guys," as we made our way to Clancy's.

Beverly spoke up with tears in her eyes. "Dear, doesn't this bother you? Two human beings were just wiped out with an order from you?"

"Honey; this is the third time in three days I have been personally attacked. This is not a movie or a television program. These people were intent on killing you and me. I couldn't take the chance and try to outrun them. I did it to protect you. I'm sorry you had to be exposed to this." As we pulled into the parking lot of the steak-house, I said; "honey if you don't want to eat we can go home. I knew when I signed on with the Bureau that I would be exposed to extremely dangerous situations. I would have given anything not to have exposed you to this. I am so sorry, please forgive me dear."

She reached over and grabbed my hand and wept and kept kissing my hand saying she was glad she had been exposed to evil, but knew she was safe in my hands and our Lord Jesus Christ. She also said that we should go ahead and eat, as we made our way to the entrance.

As we sat eating a delicious steak and making small talk, I glanced over and saw a couple of guys I recognized as CIA ops. One of the guys came over and sat down. I said; "Hi Harry Stewart long time no-see, what's it been, five years? Forgive me Harry this is my wife Beverly."

"Hi; Mrs. Johnson, it's my pleasure. Forgive me for the interruption, but Gregg and I go back a long way. We started out together with the Bureau. I left after a couple of years and went to work for the Agency. Gregg; congratulations on your appointment as director, you earned it. I need to get with you; I have some info that if true, could compromise national security. What's your day look like tomorrow?"

"Let me check my schedule." I pulled my cell phone and opened my calendar. I scrolled down to June 14th. It looks like we could get together tomorrow, how's ten AM?"

"Sounds good Gregg; I'll see you tomorrow, ten sharp nice to have met you Mrs. Johnson. God, bless you both."

Beverly said; "What a nice guy. He works for the CIA as a covert op?'

"Yes he does and yes he's a nice guy. Harry, John and I ran around together when we were all starting out with the Bureau. The reason he changed to the CIA was that he loves the challenge of being on the edge as a secret op. He would have made a great FBI agent if he would have stayed with the Bureau." I glanced at my watch and said;

"Honey we need to go, it's after nine and I have a busy day tomorrow, but the weekend is free for a change."

We made our way to the parking lot when out of the corner of my eye I spotted a guy that gave me the creeps. He sneered at me as our eyes made contact. Instinctively I knew he was one of the Scorpions henchmen. The attendant brought our car around as we both made ourselves comfortable for the ride home. I felt a little more at ease, knowing that I had a couple of agents following close as backup.

"Honey; I noticed an evil looking man as we got into the car. I noticed how he stared at you. He made my flesh crawl."

"Dear; you're not alone. I believe that he is following us, but I want you to enjoy the fastest ride you will ever experience." As I stepped on the throttle and accelerated to over eighty miles an hour when I hit the expressway and was cruising at over a hundred miles per hour."

"Gregg dear; I can't hear the engine on this car. How fast are we going?"

"Honey; I don't know the specs on this baby, but I can assure you it will outrun and outgun any auto built today. It's even better equipped than the Presidents limo. See that blinking button next to the built-in computer? Turn it twice to the left. Notice the screen is lighted up, now push the button in. You will hear a voice that will ask you what you want."

The voice came on and said. "I don't recognize the female voice, shall I run a scan Mr. Johnson." I responded affirmative.

The voice came back on in a few seconds. "The female voice is Beverly Johnson married to the director of the FBI. Is a homemaker with two sons who are attending West Point in their senior year? Beverly Johnson is a graduate of Harvard Law School. She had a partial mastectomy over four years ago to remove a cancerous tumor. Her parents died when she was attending the University of Ohio. Her blood type is," I reached over and turned it off.

"Honey; because of 9/11 our Country has been under attack from within and outside. The information gathered is not to harm us, but to help us keep the peace. That's why it's so important that we keep a close watch on those whose intentions are not honorable."

She kept silent for the next few minutes as we made our way into our driveway and into our garage. I turned the engine off and sat there for a few seconds. She reached over and touched my hand. Assuring me of her love, we made our way to our bedroom and went to bed wrapped in each other's arms as we drifted off to sleep.

CHAPTER 5

I arrived at my office knowing I had a full schedule and an important meeting set for ten o'clock, with Harry Stewart. Mary greeted me and knew that I needed my usual, strong coffee and a toasted bagel, buttered with jam.

I sat down at my desk and tried to read my mail, when I finally gave up and called Mary to come into my office.

"Yes Mr. Johnson; what can I do for you sir?"

"Mary; grab a cup of coffee and join me for a few minutes." Mary came back with a cup of coffee and sat down." I want to ask you something. Mary, you know that it's been over three years since I gave my heart to Jesus. I want to make sure that I'm still in His will. I have been praying to God for some sort of sign for guidance as to what He wants me to do. Part of me says one thing and another part says another. I know I'm not making sense Mary, but I don't think I'm cut out to be director. I miss being a field agent, where I can devote my total efforts to one case. As director, I must account for security for the total Nation. They also decided to do away with the Secret Service and place them under the leadership of the FBI. This happened under the Preachers watch. Do I make any sense Mary?"

"Mr. Johnson; may I speak frankly?"

"Of course Mary, that's why I called you in. I've hinted to Beverly about resigning, but as I stated, I'm torn as to what to do?"

"Mr. Johnson; why don't you take a few weeks off and pray and fast about what you think God wants you to do? While working, you have too many distractions."

"I think you're right Mary. I will do that. What's my schedule look like for July?"

"Sir; since the Congress and Senate are not in session it would be a good month to take off. Why don't you and Beverly go on a cruise or go to Europe. You've certainly earned it."

"Thanks Mary; I'm going to talk it over with Bev and see what she thinks about a long vacation. It could be the honeymoon we never had. Oh, my, it's almost ten and I have a meeting with Harry Stewart. Thanks, Mary, I appreciate your advice"

As she walked out of my office, I said a short thank you to God for my friend and secretary, a true woman of God. I heard voices in the outer office and walked out to greet Harry and another agent named Raul Castro. We exchanged pleasantries as I escorted them into my office, and said to Mary to hold all calls, unless three people called, the President, Senator Richards and of course my wife.

"Harry; it's good to see you again, you too Raul it's been awhile. Let me see; almost six years since I last saw you. You are married as I remember and were expecting your second child. How many do you have now?"

"Gregg, I have four children. Since I saw you last my wife had a set of twins. Two identical girls, Rachel and Ruth, they are almost six years old. The oldest is a boy named Raul Jr. who is ten years old and Maria eight years of age."

Harry spoke up and said; "It's been over seven or eight years since we worked together and currently we're on a case chasing a guy they call El Alacran."

I said; "That's great guys, I had a run-in with the same character almost three years ago. Now this guy is making threats against me and has tried to kill me a couple of times."

Raul spoke up; "We have a mutual friend Cash Cameron. I understand he is a Christian now. We were on a men's retreat together last time I saw him. Say Hi to him for me when you see him."

"That's great, how about you Harry are you a believer?

Harry responded. "Gregg; I was raised in church. My Dad was a street preacher with a small evangelical church in Albuquerque New Mexico. I went to a Christian University in New Mexico. While I was there, one of the outreaches we conducted involved handing out tracks in the streets of the city. I dealt mostly with drug addicts and alcoholics and led a lot of them to the Lord. I felt I could do more to further the Gospel than being a minister. So here I am. I have never looked back or regretted my decision."

I said. "Each one of us needs to do what he feels God has called him to do. I respect your decision to serve Him in law enforcement.

Guys, I have at lot to do so we need to get down to what our meeting is all about. What do you know about this guy El Alacran and his involvement with this new drug; Euphoria?"

Raul spoke up. "Let me say this first. He is the most sadistic killer I have had the displeasure of having met. He has a well-organized gang of thugs, with a network that stretches all over the globe. He has one weakness----women, but when he tires of them he hooks them on heroin. Most of them wind up as hookers or are found dead or overdosed victims. He has a couple of sons. One in his early twenties and one in his late teens, he has a couple of daughters from another wife. Get this; they live here in the States. He has homes all over Mexico and South America. His uncle was a Don in one of the Mexican Cartels, but when he died he took over. Rumor has it that he killed his uncle, using the arm wrestling technique. Gregg; are you familiar about this game he plays?

"Yes as a matter of fact I do. You know Manny Vasquez from DEA, he told me about this game he likes to play. Go ahead continue."

"He had a chemist develop this killer drug so he can knock off his enemies. The Russian Mafia has joined forces with him to bump off the Columbian Cartels. I just found out that he is also in cahoots with Heilman and Fenneman the two multi-billionaires. They are planning to meet in Caracas sometime next month."

"What about the drug distribution here in the United States, you guys have any leads?"

Raul spoke up. "Gregg; this is what is giving us fits. We don't know how they are getting it into the States. We have followed leads all over the US. We have added agents to both borders, but still it manages to hit the streets. We are working closely with DEA and ATF because it is being shipped from out of the country. I believe that it's coming in on ship containers. As far as I'm concerned it is all our responsibility, especially while the deaths continue to mount because of the drug. We understand that the deadly chemical that was added to the drug was to kill their competitions users, then blame them and discredit drugs sold by them. It serves a dual purpose. It can also fool the sniffing canines. They don't care what the effects are if they can keep the flow of distributing the drug openly. Can you see why this guy needs to be caught? We haven't caught a break yet."

Harry spoke up. "Man what kind of human debris is this guy? I have seen some of his work in the morgue. Young kids who would never have a chance in life to reach their potential, solely due to the drug."

I responded by saying. "I have alerted the President on this scourge. She has called for a meeting for certain agency heads. The meeting is scheduled for next Monday at ten AM at the White House. Since you guys are working this case, why don't you have your boss bring you in? I think we have discussed this enough. You have the weekend to think about the meeting, maybe you will come up with some good ideas on how we can trap this guy. Hope to see you guys at the meeting."

Harry spoke up. "Gregg the reason I alerted you to what this guy represents is that he has placed a bounty on you. He wants you and your family dead. My boss said he would try and find out more as to who may be the hit men he assigned."

"Thanks Harry, I'm aware of his threats. Oh; before I forget. We are getting together tonight for a game of poker at my house. We only play for pennies and the most you can lose is around twenty bucks. Some of my old cronies will be there. Charlie Wong, John Kelley, Cash Cameron and even Burt said he would come and a couple of other guys I went to college with. Why don't you guys come? Here is my card with my home number and address."

Both said they would try and be there. As they left I looked at my watch, it was around eleven thirty. I decided to call the Senator and see if he would have lunch with me.

I dialed his private number. "Hi Senator; how are you? Have you got time to have lunch?"

"As a matter of fact I do Gregg. Guess who is here? Calvin Duckworth, Sheriff of Natchez County. You remember him? Why don't you meet us at my club? I have a proposal I need to run by you.

I can't get over how you called at the same time I was talking to Cal about you. We'll see you at noon. God bless."

As I hung up I cleared my desk of a couple of pressing letters and left my office and made my way to where my car was parked. I drove to a swanky club where a major portion of the Senators are members. The attendant parked my car as I made my way to the dining room. I spotted the Maître-d' and asked him where the Senator was? He led me to a private room. The Senator stood up and motioned for me to come over to their table.

The Sheriff stood and greeted me. "How you doing; good ah hope."

As he shook my hand; I said, "Fine Sheriff Duckworth; how's the fishing down your way?"

"Great my boy when yah-all coming down my way so we can go fishing together, besides you need to take some time off son. All work and no play is not good. Here sit-down son we just got here ourselves."

"Thank you sir; it's a pleasure to see you again. We saw each other about this same time last year. About the fishing date, how's the fourth of July weekend suit you?"

"You're on son. When we fish; it's like hunting we usually have a side bet, largest fish, or the biggest buck. Looser must buy dinner for the other one. I'll start making plans. Before I forget, how's that pup that my bitch sired doing? He sure looked like his father."

"The dog is just great sir."

The Senator chimed in and said; "about a fishing derby, we always have a big barbeque on the fourth. We'll call it the first annual Lords Land fishing derby, how's that sound? Let's order lunch I'm hungry."

After we finished lunch I spoke up and said. "Senator; I need some advice. I feel that I---ah. I won't beat around the bush Sir; I am seriously thinking of stepping down as director. I have a hard time dealing with the politics that goes on in Washington DC. The paper work takes most of my time. The bickering between the other agencies drives me crazy. Above all, I miss the action of being in the field. I feel I can't use my special talents as director when I should be helping solving cases. And with a new President a liberal socialist goes against everything that I believe. I need to step down."

"Gregg; I guess I'm partly to blame. When you exposed the plot by Fenneman to control the oil market, we may have over-reacted by placing you in charge and stifled your expertise. It was on my recommendation to Buck----ah I mean the President that he promoted you to director. I also influenced the Senate. I'm sorry son, but I felt that you were the right man for the job, but how can I help you now son?"

"Senator; I say this without reservation, I love you more than my own father. You know how he was with me. I cherish you and Maw Richards Sir. I am sorry; that I didn't speak out before I accepted the position. I have a couple of people in mind that I think would make excellent directors."

"Son; I'll speak with the President about replacing you. What do you want to do? Before you answer let me ask you a question. Do you know how the Brotherhood got started and when?"

"No sir; but I have wondered?"

"Gregg; have you ever heard of a man named Count Fernando Joaquin De La Cruz; most likely not. He was a crusader from Andalusia Spain. Along with being a very devout Christian, he was also a 'Knights Templar.' He and other knights apparently incurred the wrath of the sitting pope. They had challenged him about his being the Vicar of Christ. The Pope had the approval of the king of

Spain as well. He then started the first of many inquisitions. De La Cruz was accused of heresy along with his brother Knights. He and his wife with their three sons, Fernando Junior, Diego, and Martin managed to escape to a small village nestled in the Austrian Alps, now called Innsbruck. Everything that he owned was confiscated by the church. He managed to take enough gold and some ancient manuscripts. It is also said that he had the robe that belonged to our Lord. Count De La Cruz and his family settled in with their new beginning in the Austrian Alps. De La Cruz being somewhat of a biblical scholar found a passage that hit a cord in his memory. Peter the apostle in his first letter wrote; "Honor all men; love the brotherhood, fear God, honor the king" (1 Peter 2:17 NASB).

The count was responsible for reforming the "Brotherhood" and that we follow Biblical inerrancy in teaching the Bible, not a man's ideology but God's theology.

"By the way this has been our motto. What caught his eye was 'Love the Brotherhood?' He went back to some of the manuscripts and found some letters written by second and third century Christians that had founded a highly secretive group, called the 'Brotherhood.' He felt that based on a letter by Peter and the apostle Paul that they were to protect the integrity of scripture, scripture being the final say in all church matters.

The manuscripts would prove this. He realized why the Papacy was trying to kill him and other knights who were fortunate to escape, the inquisition."

"The Papacy was afraid of losing control of the people. Scripture was for the priesthood only, not laity based on to the Papacy Ex-Cathedra. While living in this small Austrian village some other ex-Knights Templar's joined him and took an oath to guard the robe and the manuscripts along with doing everything in their power to preserve the teachings of the Bible." Are you still with me?"

"Yes sir; I'm all ears."

"Good; stay with me. The Count decided, along with the approval of the other Knights to form a group of twelve men all ex Knights Templers. One of them would be the 'Final Knight'. In Jewish theology, the number twelve is considered the number of organization and authority. Since then our group became a worldwide organization with several hundred men as 'Knights'. Notice this ring that I wear? A ring with a Cross of Loraine; made famous by the Crusaders. Notice that the stone is a ruby and the cross is inlaid Gold. Along with the symbol of the crusaders; it is our symbol, because the founders were Knights, men of honor and integrity. Today; once every seven years we gather for a week in various countries. This year we will gather in Innsbruck in honor of our founder and will visit Dom Zu St. Jakob, known in English as St. James Cathedral for a special meeting.

We gather for prayer and discuss what we can do to stem the tide of liberalism within the church. We normally gather the week of Easter. We recently have had a rash of member Knights dying in strange circumstances. Because of these deaths, we will be meeting in mid August. Let me add another thing about the robe, it is said that it is still in existence along with healing powers. If this is true, can you imagine what would happen if this robe fell into the wrong hands."

"Now as to why I wanted to talk with you about; we recently held a meeting to add other knights. I have recommended you to this high honor. Part of the oath for this elite office is that the candidate must have proven that he has shown faithful service in serving our Lord. I don't know how to put this to you other than being blunt. Would you be interested in serving? Oh; one other piece of vital information, legend has it that the robe and the manuscripts are hidden somewhere in a cathedral in Europe."

"Senator; this is something I would have to pray about. I took an oath when I first joined the Bureau to protect this Country. I love the Lord more than I do my own life, but to work in a secretive group bothers me sir!"

"Gregg; secrecy is of the utmost in maintaining integrity for being a Knight. I don't believe in secretive organizations or acts either. It certainly goes against everything I believe in as well, but we are at a crossroads in our way of life. Washington is controlled by a bureaucratic machine that wants socialism to replace our current form of government; a representative republic. I look at my own career and service. The Knight's are the ruling body of the Brotherhood; it is how we protect the Brotherhood. My original intentions when I went to Washington were to serve the maximum of two terms; it's now going to be my sixth term. This will be my last. I'm tired of the corruption and immoral attitude of some of my colleagues. As to the Brotherhood, we always strive to work within the laws of the United States and God. I want you to pray about this and then get back to me. It is a lifetime commitment."

"Absolutely sir, it would be an honor for me to keep the faith alive, but I will pray and seek God's will."

"Good my boy, I will wait for your reply."

The Sheriff spoke up and said; "Gregg; if you do become a Knight, just remember you will be saving lives and preserving the truth."

"Gentlemen, I need to get back to my office. I have a lot of praying to do and speaking with my wife. We both need to agree with this decision. I'll see you all later." I got up and started to leave as I heard the Sheriff make a statement to the Senator; "why didn't you tell him more about the robe?" As I made my way back to my car I thought I had over twenty years of service with the Bureau and a comfortable pension. I could walk away and do the Lords work, but I needed to pray, fast and read God's word for direction. I also thought about the faint comment Sheriff Duckworth made to the Senator. I wondered what he meant by his comment?

As I left the club, I decided to head home and drove to the expressway. I called Mary and told her I wouldn't be back in the office till the first of next week. Ever vigilant as always I looked all around and saw my too guys following me when the next thing I know I start to blackout as the last thing I hear; is the screeching of metal and tires being blown out.

CHAPTER 6

I woke up with a familiar face staring at me. It's one of my assigned body guards, saying, "Mr. Johnson can you hear me? We need to get you to a doctor."

"Except for the ringing in my ears I think I'm okay. Let me try and get up." I got up with the help of the agents who had been following me. I checked all my moving parts and decided that I was all right. "Do you guys know what happened?"

"Sir, it came from out of the sky. It was a chopper bearing down on you. The next thing we see is a missile headed straight for you. As you can see the built-in pod saved you, but I'm afraid the car needs a lot of repair. Somebody upstairs must be looking out for you.

"You bet; He has stepped in on several occasions. His name is Jesus Christ my Lord. Oh, and this is the third time the pod has saved me and now I know that the pod works. God at times uses mans inventions as well."

One of the men said. "We had heard that you were a Christian. Do you really believe that there is a God and Christ was His Son?"

"I believe it with all my heart. Are you guy's non-believers?"

One said. "I was raised in church, but I slowly drifted away from my faith. My dad was a minister, but he died rather young so I blamed God. I recently started going to church again."

The other agent spoke up. "Well I think there are all sorts of beliefs, why do I need to go to a church. If God is everywhere like you guys believe, why can't I just worship in the forest or by the ocean or in the confines of my own home?"

Just as I started to answer him the State Troopers showed up. After they called a tow truck to take the car to our crime lab; they closed off the area to allow the crime scene people to search the area for evidence. I called Mary and told her what had happened. I told her I was all right, other than the ringing in my ears. My two agents drove me home.

The guys came over for the long anticipated poker game. Charlie was the big winner as he took home a whopping seven dollars and sixty-five cents. We mostly talked about our current president. A couple of the guys were very frank about their feelings. They felt she was far too liberal. They were seriously thinking of taking early retirement. Short Stuff took us all by surprise by speaking about our current drug problem and how we could stop this scourge on humanity. I shared with the men the several attempts on my life this past week. Charlie said I was like a cat with nine lives. (I knew better)

"Guys one of my main concerns regarding drugs, is the availability of street drugs and prescription drugs. You can buy almost any drug on the street if you can afford it. Legalizing drugs is not the way to go, but intervention and education is sorely lacking in our Country. Another concern of mine is what happens to a person who is faced with a life of addiction. It must be a nightmare for them. I recently read up on methamphetamines and was amazed that the Japanese developed it for their soldiers before World War II condemning many to a life of hell. Gangsters and thugs seem to be the ones that profit from illegal drugs. Now you can make meth in your home. If you want the formula for meth and how to manufacture it, just go on the web. Gentlemen; we are dealing with Satan himself. Paul the apostle wrote in his letter to the church at Ephesus that our battle was not against people."

"For we are not fighting against people made of flesh and blood, but against the evil rulers and authorities of the unseen world, against those mighty powers of darkness who rule this world, and against wicked spirits in the heavenly realms" (Eph. 6:12 NLT).

"By this scripture we can see that we are fighting an unseen enemy. We must be shrewder than the dark-one. Our number one weapon is the power of prayer and guidance from the Holy Spirit."

Charlie jumped in with both feet. "Gregg, I disagree with what you just said. We need more agents on the streets, not God."

I saw my opening so, I gently put it out as a question. "Charlie; do you believe we are born with a soul?"

He responded by saying, "My definition of the soul is what you are inside."

"Charlie; that's a good answer, but a person's soul is what goes to heaven when he dies. It is your mind, emotions and your will along with your spirit. It is where the conscience lives. It is the seat of morality in all humans. An atheist of course does not believe this."

Charlie shot back. "If this is the case, and what you say is true, all my ancestors are in hell because they were all practicing Buddhists. I have been toying with the idea of studying the bible. I have never had anyone explain its meanings. Perhaps you can share it with me some time?"

"Charlie; I'll do better than that. Beverly and I will come by your home Sunday and take you and your family to our church. We would love to have you as our guest. As to your ancestors, perhaps they asked Christ into their hearts before they died"

"Gregg you have a deal, we will go to church with you this Sunday. You are the first person who has ever invited me to a Christian church. Come by and pick us up."

"Bev and I will pick you up at nine AM Sunday morning. We'll be there my friend; you won't be disappointed. Where were we? Ah----we were talking about the drug problem. Any of you guys have any solutions to the problem or ideas?"

Manny Vasquez spoke up. "Yeah, I've got a solution. It would require that all drug related crimes carry a much heavier penalty. For the addicts, I would place them into a rehab program, based on biblical principles using the AA format. The incarceration would last for a minimum of two years. A second offense would double their incarceration time. Third strike would bring a life sentence. For the dealers, a minimum of five years for first offenders and the second double the time. The drug lords would receive a twenty-year sentence and if any death occurred because of their actions, life without parole. Special prisons would be strictly for crimes related to drug trafficking and dorms for drug rehabilitation."

"Addiction to Drugs or Alcohol is a moral social issue so I would also ask for the death penalty for those who caused the death of any minor, eighteen and younger. I would have drug and alcohol specialist in our schools as intervention and prevention counselors. There have been pilot programs in a handful of schools, they work, but the schools don't have the finances. Remember, kids will always experiment. Most parents are not equipped to deal with a kid who is fooling around with drugs. We also have many parents who are addicted. What kind of role model are they for our kids? They would lose their kids for a second offense if they are caught using or dealing."

"Wow Manny, you have this thing well thought out. Do you have any idea what it would cost to initiate this program?" Short Stuff said.

"It wouldn't cost us hardly anything, we would use the money confiscated from the arrest of those involved in dealing and trafficking, which amounts to billions. Most of the money confiscated is tied up in litigation or has already lined the pockets of corrupt cops and politicians. They would receive thirty to fifty year sentences if caught miss using these funds." Manny responded.

I jumped in and said. "I think your idea is fantastic Manny, but based on how the political climate is, the liberals wouldn't go for it; sad to say. Perhaps our Lord would intervene on our behalf for such a plan. His word says we are to pray for our needs. I glanced at my watch. It was midnight. "Guys; the time has passed by quickly, thanks for coming. The hour is late. We must do this again soon. Don't forget Charlie I will see you Sunday morning."

I made my way upstairs and found Bev still awake. She was reading a Christian novel, but ever the radiant one. She wanted to talk, so I suggested we go down to the kitchen and have some hot tea, besides we could sleep in because it was Saturday. I took a quick shower and made my way downstairs. Bev had made a great Banana Cream pie, so we both had a slice and talked about the two new guys that had come to our gathering. And of course, wanted to know all about Charlie Wong going to church with us Sunday. It was almost three AM when we finally made our way to our room. As we both drifted off to sleep.

—————————— ——————————

I was awakened by a growl from our dog. I keep a loaded Glock G17C 9mm compensated pistol handy. I reached over and firmly gripped the pistol as I slowly rose from the bed. Bev was sound asleep as I placed my slippers on my feet. We had an intruder in the house. I glanced at the clock it was getting close to half past four. Buster was at my side as I made my way downstairs ever watchful, stopping and straining my ears and eyes. I was just about to step into the kitchen when Buster went into action. He had his jaws tightly locked into a guy's arm. I had my hands full fending off blows from the other guy. He had a vice-grip around my throat, but he made one fatal mistake, he had left my left arm free. I had a firm grip on my Glock as I fired it into his leg. The instant he was shot he released his grip and bolted towards the front door. Buster was still biting the other guy, which seemed like an eternity. Buster finally released his hold which gave the other intruder an opportunity to bolt towards the front door a well.

By this time Bev had awakened and realized what had transpired as she called the local police. I turned on the kitchen lights and noticed a lot of blood on the floor leading to the front door. I grabbed a flashlight and made my way to the front door as I heard the roar of a car engine speed away. I got to the curb only to see his tail-lights turn the corner. I shined the light on the curb and noticed a man's body lying in the gutter. I made my way to him, but just as I got to him he was trying to say something but the life went out of him. I checked his pulse and knew he was dead.

Within a few minutes a couple of squad cars pulled up as they shined a light on me. They knew who I was as they approached me. One of the officers asked me what had happened. I told him how I had been awakened by my dog. I said that I had hit one of the assailants. "As you can see he's lying in the gutter and sad to say is stone cold dead. My shot hit him in his main artery on his left groin, thus he bleeds to death within minutes. I don't know who they are. This one looks Hispanic. I know that a drug kingpin has a contract out on me, and I suspect this was another try to complete the contract."

One of the locals asked me if I would come down to the station later today and fill out a report on the incident. I said that I would. Bev and I made our way back to the house. We would have to replace the carpet in a couple of rooms. We finally went back to bed after the police left. I felt saddened that I had killed a human, but also thanked God that Bev and I were spared. My last thoughts were where---- would all this end?

We slept until after eleven in the morning. We showered and ate a great breakfast of ham and eggs, fried potatoes with homemade rolls. After breakfast Bev and I made our way to the police station to file the requested report of last night's incident. The same two officers were just coming on duty. They had a make on the dead culprit. He was a Mexican national with a rap sheet a mile long, and a distinguishing tattoo of a scorpion on his back. I wasn't surprised, in fact I had a hunch it would be one of El Alacran's men.

We decided to take a trip to a close by mall. I needed to pick up a few clothes and Bev wanted to look for a new dress. I told her about what I wanted to do as to retirement, along with considering the Senators offer. I explained to her all that the Senator told me about the Brotherhood and being a Twelfth Knight.

As we made our way to the shopping mall I couldn't shake the feeling of being watched. I thought about some of the new technology that is available to the Bureau. The space age made it possible to follow citizens and subversives from space with high-tech cameras carried by satellites circling the Earth. I thought; how this new high tech could determine the outcome of modern warfare. With new weapons, such as smart bombs that can penetrate deep bunkers to kill our known enemies. All this being done from outer space. They also have a way of x-raying the earth from space to see if there are tunnels. I blurted out-loud; "Why Lord?"

Bev said. "Honey, are you ok?"

"Yes dear; I was thinking about how our world has changed. Sorry to say, not for the best. Honey, let me ask you a question. Do you think we are entering the last days?"

"I sometimes think we are when I read and hear of all the lawlessness here at home and abroad. Based on what Jesus said in the scriptures, I would say yes."

"I asked Christ into my life four years ago, but whenever I can I read the Bible. Thank God I was blessed with a great memory, which has helped me to memorize scripture. I know that our Savior the Lord stated that there would be all sorts of testing's. Remember Whitey, the Angelic being. I believe he was the first horseman of the Apocalypse. I believe that the rider on the Red horse is here on earth. I don't have any proof other than a gut feeling." I started to say----ah. When my cell phone rang as I said, "Gregg here."

"Gregg; this is Manny Vasquez. I need to see you right away; it's a break on our enemy El Alacran. I can meet you anywhere, within twenty minutes."

"Manny; Beverly and I are on our way to the Empire Mall. We are about five minutes from the parking lot. Do you know where the restaurants are on the west side of the mall?"

"Yes I do; I can be there in fifteen minutes."

"Ok Manny, see you in a few minutes. Honey; I guess we must table our discussion for later."

CHAPTER 7

(Sat, June 14ᵗʰ)

As we reached the mall parking lot and started looking for a parking space. Bev found one when she said; "that fellow over there is pulling out" I pulled in and was taken aback as I realized it was Saturday and thousands of kids would be at the mall. We made our way to the fast food court. We spotted a pretzel shop, and each of us ordered one. Bev ordered a cinnamon flavored one and I a cheese flavored one.

We found a table and sat down to wait for Manny and enjoy our coffee and pretzels. I looked up and saw Manny smiling at me as he said; "you both look out of place here today with all the kids in the mall." As we started to sit down a couple of kids dressed in black; both with all sorts of chains dangling from their bodies passed by. Both had their heads shaved. Manny commented, 'see what I mean? 'Let me get a pretzel and a cup of coffee.' He came back with a cup of coffee and a plain-pretzel and sat across from me.

"Manny what's so urgent that this couldn't wait till Monday? Oh; I'm sorry, this is my wife Beverly. Honey this is Manny Vasquez. He is with DEA.

"My pleasure Mrs. Johnson, sorry we have to meet in this place. Gregg, can I speak freely in front of your lovely wife?"

"Yes you can. Honey what you hear must not be repeated under any circumstances."

"Gregg dear let me make it easy on you. I'll go do my shopping and see you back here at 3:30. It's now a few minutes past 2:00. This should give you both enough time to chat and discuss business." She leaned over and kissed me as she went off to look for a dress.

"Gregg; let's find a table away from all the noise"

As we moved I said; "Is this spot ok?"

"This is fine Gregg. Man; you could get hooked on these pretzels."

"You bet; "Before you start, let me tell you what happened early this morning." I related to him my encounter.

"Sounds like you had your hands full. Why don't you have some of your men guard the property? After all you are the director of the FBI."

"I have a couple of men who watch me during the day, but I suppose I must use them twenty-four hours a day. I didn't want to alarm the neighbors, but I guess I will have too. What was so important about El Alacran that couldn't wait?"

"I received a call from one of our agents stationed in El Paso. He said that they had arrested one of El Alacran's top men, Raul el Gato (the Cat) Acosta. He was caught in a drug bust where they discovered a massive tunnel coming into the USA from Juarez Mexico. This tunnel ran four city blocks long. This guy is a three-time looser so he copped a deal. He gave us some information that may lead us to our main character. As we speak."

"El Alacran is operating close to us in Virginia Beach. He recently bought a yacht which he likes to show off and hobnob with the rich and famous. In the past he has been known to rent a villa, or may even own a place in the Hamptons. He is supposed to be there sometime next week. Per my informant from Mr. Gato, El Alacran has a couple of politicians in his payroll."

"Manny; did he give you their names? Also, do you have any people assigned to see if your source's info is correct? If el Alacran has connections with some of the DC elite, he will be difficult to catch. My take is we must be very discreet. Let me see if I can get Burt Smith and Cash Cameron and see if they are available to do some snooping. Perhaps you can get your boss to let you go with them? I would not say anything in our meeting on Monday. Also, find out if any teenagers have been found dead by overdose. Just a hunch, but I believe that El Alacran's ego is his Achilles Heel based on his open defiance of the law."

"I verified the info with a couple of my snitches and they confirmed what the Cat said. As to the two guys you mentioned, I normally work alone Gregg, but if this guy is smuggling in this new drug I can sure use some quality help. It will take a concerted effort by all law enforcement agencies to arrest him. Have Cash and Burt contact me. I'm sure they are good men; besides I know Cash and have heard great things about Smith."

"Many; I trust these men with my life. Both are Christians and true patriots. Our Country has changed drastically in the last twenty years. I would love to get personally involved, but as director I can't. I would enjoy seeing his face when he goes down. I would love seeing him squirm when we place the handcuffs on him."

"I've heard a lot about you as man of character. I concur with you about being able to trust people. I am blessed and honored to be able to work with you. Let me know if Cash and Burt are available. I need to leave so have Burt and Cash give me a call, you have my cell number."

After Manny left, I called Burt and Cash and told them that they were on special assignment to work with Manny Vasquez. They were to keep me informed of their progress. They were also to meet me at my office at three Monday afternoon. Just as I finished my call with Cash I looked up and saw Beverly coming back to where I was sitting. She looked so radiant. I thought how blessed I was to have her for my wife.

"Did you find what you were looking for?"

"Yes I did. I can't wait to get home and show you how cute they fit and what a savings I made. I would like a cup of coffee I didn't finish it before. I see a Starbucks over there. Honey do you want a cup?"

"I guess I could have a Latte. Do you want me to get them?"

"You stay put. You need to rest and enjoy your day off." As she got up and made her way to Starbucks.

I noticed that Bev was taking a long time getting our Latte's. I also noticed that a large crowd had gathered in front of the coffee shop. I decided to make my way over as I got up I saw a couple of paramedics rushing into the now large crowd. As I approached the crowd there were a couple of mall police officers restraining the people. I saw my wife talking with an officer. I noticed that one of the paramedics was also attending Beverly. I told the officer who I was and showed him my ID card. I made my way over to Bev, as she looked up and said, honey "I'm ok." I rushed over to her side as I heard the paramedic say, "Ms. You'll have to get that arm set I believe it is broken."

The officer in charge asked. "How did this happen; Mrs. Johnson?"

"I was standing in line when the next thing I know I'm lying on the floor. I remember just before I hit the floor a man came up beside me and said something that sounded like Spanish. He was so close I could smell his breath that reeked of stale beer. He said; "tengo un mensaje para tu esposo, espero su muerte." The nearest I can figure what he said. "I have a message for you. I await his death." Then he shoved me, causing me to fall as I fell I tried to catch myself, this is how I believe I broke my arm."

The officer said; "one more question Mrs. Johnson? Do you feel you could identify the man who shoved you?"

"I don't believe I could, it happened so fast. I am so sorry. I will never forget his voice; it was the sound of pure evil."

"Ok Mrs. Johnson thanks for being so cooperative. Do you want the ambulance to take you to the hospital or do you want your husband to take you?"

I spoke up. "I'll take her to our doctor's office. I have already called his exchange. He will meet us at his office within the hour. Honey if you are ready let's go."

"Not until I get my latte," she said.

As we both laughed. The paramedic had given her a sedative for pain and it had just kicked in as the manager came over and handed us both their biggest Latte's, "With our compliments sir."

We made our way to the doctor's office as I was ever vigilant looking in both the rear-view mirror and side mirrors. I was so glad that I was driving an agency vehicle not a prototype. As an agent over the years I have developed other senses as well----to look for danger in unsuspected places. Some call it intuition, but I call it my sixth sense discernment.

After the doctor set Bev's left arm and placed it in a cast, he gave her some pain pills and sent us home. It was a clean break, just above the wrist so it would not require any surgery. We went home and spent a restful evening. Bev slept most of the time. I called and ordered a

Pizza and a salad and went to bed relatively early after trying to watch an old John Wayne Western.

I had a rough night trying to sleep. My mind wandered back and forth thinking about being asked by the Senator to take a giant step of faith, along with making plans to get El Alacran. Sometime during the night, I finally dosed off to sleep, but was awakened by my alarm going off.

I went downstairs, and found her toasting Bagels and had the table set with cream-cheese and blackberry-jam.

Bev was already up trying to cook with one hand. I might add she was doing great. We had to leave early because Charlie my friend and family were attending fellowship with us.

CHAPTER 8

(Sunday June 15th)

"Good morning angel, how did you sleep?"

"Not so bad, the pain pill worked great, it aches a little bit, but not all that bad. The cast the doctor placed on my arm allows me to use my arm with limited movement. What time do we have to pick up the Wong's? We are still planning on picking them up, aren't we?"

"As far as I know we are still on for today. I'd better call them right now and confirm it. I told it was seven thirty. I told her I had told Charlie we would pick them up at nine." I dialed Charlie's home number and confirmed that they were going to church with us. It was all set. Charlie's daughters were all excited that they were invited.

We finished breakfast and got ready for church and were on our way to Charlie's home. We picked them up and made our way to our gathering place. The minister came over and met us as we introduced Charlie and May his wife and two daughters.

The sermon dealt with what it means to be born again. The Ministers text was out of the third chapter of the gospel of John. One point he stressed in his text, was; are you searching for the truth? You will find it in Jesus Christ. When he told the congregation, it was time to take a stand for Jesus and faith in Him. Several people went forward for prayer. Charlie and his family all went together and asked Christ into their hearts. I thought how awesome a God we have. Four souls gave their heart to Christ, a friend and his wife and two daughters were added to those who would live in security for eternity.

As we drove back to Charlie's home, Charlie and his wife asked us to join them for lunch. They wouldn't take no for an answer. Charlie's family would be joining us for a Chinese dinner at his home.

It was one of the most memorable days I have ever experienced. I thought it was a small group that would be gathering. There were at least thirty to thirty-five people. I have never seen so much food being brought to a family gathering, with all sorts of Chicken and Duck dishes with sweet and sour pork and different types of soups and rice dishes. We ate so much I was stuffed. Then Charlie stood up and spoke for about twenty minutes about his new-found love---- Jesus. Then he turned to me and said that I would tell his family about Christ being God. My mouth fell-wide open as he asked me to stand.

I looked around the room and saw their faces, but with great anticipation in their eyes. I thought; Lord what shall I share about you and my love for you? I heard this little voice within me say give your testimony and go with your heart. I felt like Peter must have felt when he delivered his message to Cornelius and his family in the book of Acts. I spoke for almost an hour. I told them how I had been closed minded to the truth and how God had placed Godly people in my path. How I knelt at my bed and asked Christ into my heart, while sensing His presence in the room. I shared that I had poured out what was on my heart, all my thoughts and the forgiveness I felt when I did. I shared how at times He has intervened in critical situations by saving my life. When I finished, I saw the expression on their faces they had been touched by my testimony. I decided to gamble and asked if anyone would like to ask Christ into their heart. I no sooner got the words out of my mouth when over half of the people responded and knelt and prayed the sinner's prayer.

I was overwhelmed by the response, but even more that God would use me to share His love and grace with my new-found brothers and sisters in Christ. I stood there for a couple of minutes, when all of them came up to me and thanked me for sharing the plan of salvation. All who accepted the call stated they would be in church this coming Sunday. The rest of the evening Bev and I answered questions for a couple of hours and got to know them better.

I looked at my watch and glanced at Bev and knew it was time to leave Charlie and May's home. We thanked them for the great day and evening and left. We were both ecstatic and overwhelmed by what God the Holy Spirit can do. God had showed us how important His grace is. We made our way home laughing and singing Christian songs.

Chapter 9

(Monday June 16th)

I arrived at my office bright and early in preparation for the meeting I had scheduled with the new president. There would be experts on drugs in attendance, especially Dr. Sergio Calderon and Manny Vasquez DEA agent.

The morning passed without any prank calls or suspicious packages. My private line rang just as I started to ask Mary for a certain folder, a folder that I had started on the Scorpion. "High Senator, what a nice surprise; what can I do for you this fine morning?"

"Gregg my boy I called to see if you had any time that we could get together today?"

"Let me look at my schedule. I have a meeting with the president and a handful of DEA agents and the new National Security advisor. I have some free time around three this afternoon."

"Good, can we meet at my apartment, we can talk in private and not feel we are being bugged. I recently had the apartment updated with the state of the art de-bugging equipment. Does this sound ok with you?"

"Yes sir; I'll see you at three."

It was time to head for the White House and meet with the new president. I hadn't been to the great office since President Burns left office. The new president, President Gloria Blankenship was a graduate of Harvard Law School. She had been the Governor of New Jersey for one term. She had risen to the post of attorney general of New Jersey, and prior in private law practice. She has never been married and is noted for her candor, some would construe her demeanor as downright rude. She is also known for her contempt of our military. She will use profanity when she is angry and dressing down a subordinate. We arrived at her office with about ten minutes to spare, after picking up Dr Calderon.

We were asked to wait for a few minutes. The other men and women who were invited started arriving at the same time. The president came out and shook hands with all of us. I had only met with her a couple of times, but never felt at ease when I was in her presence. We were asked to go to one of the conference rooms where a small buffet would be served for those who needed a snack. She also asked to see me in private after the main meeting.

The professor and I were asked to sit next to the President with her National Security Advisor to her left and the professor and me on her right side. Short Stuff and Manny sat next to each other. The head of the DEA was not at the meeting which made me suspicious if he was on his way out. I found myself thinking perhaps she would ask me to step down? After all it was a new administration. My only concern was that the FBI should not be politicized, but it has been from its inception. There were still rumors floating about certain classified files about everyone in DC going back to the Clintons.

The president stood up and brought the meeting to order. She thanked us for attending on such short notice and promised that we would be done by one thirty at the latest. We were to eat while the meeting progressed. She had one of her aides show a slide on how drugs were on the rise again. She ran on a platform of getting rid of the illegal drug trade. Most of the report was based on what all of us knew. She then turned to me and said, "Gregg Johnson has brought to my attention that there is a new type of street drug that is killing our young people. I'll let Gregg tell you about this new menace! Gregg."

I stood and thanked those in attendance for coming and thanked the President for calling the meeting together on such short notice. "Ladies and gentlemen, I am not an expert on drugs, but I have invited one of the world's leading pharmacologist Dr. Sergio Calderon who will give us a run down on what type of drug has hit the streets, it's called 'Euphoria.' From what I have learned about the drug, it brings shivers up and down my spine. The problem is that it's a new type of methamphetamine replacing crystal meth as the drug of choice. Dr. Calderon will explain to us what we are up against; Dr. Calderon"

"Thank you for inviting me and I pray that I will be able to answer some of your questions if you are not familiar with the dangers of this drug. I brought along a few slides to show you what we are dealing with. Please show number one. This drawing of the brain is what we call the reward system of the brain. As you can see it is a combination of structures in the brain that are activated when an individual fulfills some emotion or feeling that came about, such as hunger, thirst, or sexual desire. The principle parts are the ventral tegmental region, the nucleus accumbent septic, lateral hypothalamus and prefrontal cortex. Within this section of the brain are also the Amygdala, the Hippocampus and the Substantia nigral. Forgive me for boring you with this slide, but bear with me a couple of minutes. What you see right now is a picture of a normal healthy brain, now show the next slide. Notice any difference? Notice the Hippocampus, it looks like mush, and so it is. This new drug damages part of the brain that is beyond recognition. I have dissected the brains of several young people who show the same results. It destroys the brain and kills the user as it rapidly eats all the brain tissue, while the addict craves more of the drug. They go insane unable to distinguish objects, blinded and begging for more of the drug. The drug's base is a high grade of Meth, but the killing agent has not been identified yet. I hope to have a breakthrough very shortly. I will take questions at this point."

One of the Presidents staff members asked a question. "Dr. Calderon why is this drug different than crystal Meth. Doesn't crystal damage the brain beyond repair?"

"To answer your question; no Crystal destroys your teeth and can destroy other organs, but generally takes years. What you see before you are the effects of less than three months' usage of this new drug Euphoria by a teen. It takes a few weeks longer for an adult user, but the results are the same, death!"

I interceded and thanked Dr. Calderon and asked for Manny Vasquez to stand and explain how the drug is coming into the country. "Manny Vasquez is a veteran DEA agent with over twenty years' service and an expert on drug cartels. Manny"

"Thank you Gregg for the opportunity to share a small part of my expertise. Ladies and gentlemen, we are facing a scourge on our streets. This drug we suspect is being cooked in Mexico or Venezuela and being sold and distributed by one of the large drug cartels. For us to stop this drug from being sold in our streets, we need to devise a workable plan. We need to seal up our borders, especially the drug lanes and alleys that are used for trafficking illegal drugs. We need stiffer sentences and parole boards that are not paid off to allow drug thugs back on the streets with early release. We need a mass scale intervention plan to keep our youth from experimenting with street drugs, along with prevention programs making the public aware of what lurks in the shadows in our society. Finally, we need more trained agents to catch the scum and put them behind bars. That's all I have to share; I will take questions now."

The president asked a question. "Agent Vasquez; I have a question do you have any leads now as to the person or persons behind this heinous drug?"

"Madam President, yes there is a drug lord that I and several others believe is behind the sale and distribution of the drug. His street name is Alacran, in English the Scorpion. His real name is Jose Mace Caulfield Juarez. He is half Mexican and half Anglo. He is a sadistic killer and runs one of the largest drug cartels in the world. Mr. Johnson has had a few run-ins with him and knows how maniacal he is. I hope this answers your question Madam President."

"Yes it does agent Vasquez, thank you for your input and dedication. Gregg, do you have any other guest that can give us vital information? I'm sorry the head of our DEA was unable to attend; unfortunately, he had a death in his family. If we have no more questions, we will disperse the meeting. Thank you all for coming."

We all stood up and started out the door when Short Stuff caught up with me. "Gregg have you got a minute I need to see you in private, it's urgent. How about having a cup of coffee at 4:30 this afternoon at the mall in front of the Lincoln Memorial, if you can get away?"

"I need to drop Dr. Calderon off at his office, then I'll swing by and pick you up. Sorry brother; I forgot I have a meeting at three with the Senator at his apartment. Maybe we can squeeze it in say five thirty?"

"That's fine Gregg I'll see you at five thirty in front of the Lincoln Memorial."

I thought to myself what was so important it couldn't wait?

I also asked Dr. Calderon to wait for me a few minutes. The president wanted to see me in private. He said he would catch a cab, so he went on his way.

I walked over to the president's office and spoke with her secretary. She said the president would see me right away and to go on in.

"Come on in Gregg. Take a seat. Can I get you anything?"

"No madam president, I'm fine."

"Gregg let me get right to the point. I have given our law enforcement structure a lot of thought. Most of my bureau chiefs are over worked with paper, as you well know. I am thinking of restructuring the FBI, Secret Service and the other law enforcement agencies. Not under one directorship; but like our military more of a fast response unit for each agency. I want my directors to be able to spend more time in the field. I want you to give me some input as to how we can streamline all our agencies. I understand you have some backed up vacation time. I want you to take your vacation and when you come back we will get together with the other agencies. There are far too many threats placing our nation at high risk."

"May I respond to what you are trying to accomplish and where I fit in?"

"By all means, I want your frank and honest answer."

"I personally like the idea of being in the field, although being director gives you certain privileges. I have seriously thought about early retirement, but am open to something different."

As I said before, take your vacation time or if need be a three-month sabbatical, and when you get back I can hear your input as to what your ideas are. Today is June the sixteen, we will meet in late August or early September, now get out of here."

I left her office with a new perspective on our madam president.

I called Mary and told her I was on my way to the Senators apartment. I thought what was so important that he asked to see me in his home away from home. My mind wandered back to the night I asked the Lord to come into my life. It was almost four years ago. The boys were in their fourth year at West Point. The current president was my sixth president that I swore to protect with my life, but I felt that my life was about to change drastically. I was fifty-two years old and had spent all my entire adult life in service to my country as a federal agent. I thought about the death of William Sullivan the Preacher the president and Sling Shot McGovern former CIA agent. Also, the death of a fine policewoman Tashanna Brown and the impact she had made on all of us. The positive was when we saw Cash Cameron FBI agent and his wife a former Israeli Mossad agent Rachel become one in marriage with Cash and now she was expecting their second child. I thought about Mary and Burt exchanging marriage vows and becoming Mr. And Mrs. Smith.

I was startled and brought back to reality as a huge semi truck without the trailer rammed me from behind. I noticed I was close to a freeway onramp and accelerated to get ahead of the huge truck tractor that caught up with me and proceeded to ram me again. I pressed on the gas pedal and decided I was going to outrun my antagonist. I knew he couldn't keep up with me, but the next thing I know I'm being chased by a high speed supercharged Mercedes. He came up along side of me and decides to ram me. He undoubtedly knew my vehicle had an armor piercing body, so they rammed me. At this point I accelerated and was approaching speeds close to 90 miles per hour. Because of the heavy traffic I knew it would be easier to lose myself. I saw an opening in the truck lane. I sped up and pulled in behind a vehicle hauling all sorts of metal pipe. I thought most likely on the way to a construction job. I noticed that I wasn't fearful, but felt a huge adrenaline rush I hadn't felt since I was a teenager! I decided to get off at the next exit and saw that it was still a half-mile ahead, just as I started to get off, another truck pulled over and blocked my escape. I found myself between two mammoth trucks. I knew I had been lured onto the expressway for this very purpose. I said a little prayer to the Lord and heard myself saying Holy Spirit show me the way; just as I got the words out of my mouth both trucks moved closer to me to crush me between them. Just as they moved over I hit the brakes as they had to move away from me or the one on my right would have jackknifed his truck. I found myself driving on the side of the expressway lawn. I saw my chance to exit as I stepped on the gas as the supercharger kicked in and I was heading for the exit. I know in my heart God had to intercede on my behalf for me to evade sure death. I saw a parking lot and pulled in and parked the car as I sat there not shaking but spent emotionally, yet thankful to God for His intervention and grace.

I arrived at the Senators apartment a few minutes after the incident and made my way to the front door. This apartment had been our home for several months, when our home was bombed. I rang the bell and the Senator came to the door.

"Come on in Gregg. Did you run into some traffic problems? It's after three."

"Yes I did sir; in fact, it was an attempt on my life!" I told him what had transpired. I also found myself saying, "Sir, why all the secrecy for our meeting?"

"The last time we gathered for lunch with Sheriff Duckworth you said you were seriously thinking of leaving the Bureau. I also shared with you the history of the "Brotherhood". I purposely left out a few key points, especially the part of you becoming one of the twelve. Let's go into the living room. Can I get you a cup of coffee?"

"Yes sir: That would be fine."

"Go on into the living room. Calvin come on into the living room, Gregg is here."

I walked into the living room as Calvin Duckworth entered at the same time. He walked over and gave me a big hug. He said, "How are you Gregg. You look like you need a cup of Southern Coffee. We generally add chicory to ours. You Yankees drink yours rather weak. Would you like to try some of our Southern style?"

"Why not, it would be a nice change."

He went into the kitchen and he and the Senator came back with a tray of hot steaming coffee with the aroma of chicory and a platter of Southern pastries. We sat and chatted for a few minutes. The Senator finally spoke up and said. "Gregg; Cal and I have been praying about you for a long time. But before I get ahead of myself I need to share with you what is transpiring in the White House. First, I need to ask you if the President has spoken to you about your future as head of the FBI."

"Yes Sir, she asked me to come to her office right after our meeting today. She wants to restructure all law enforcement agencies. She told me to take a sabbatical or the vacation time I have accumulated and when I return I am to give her my recommendations on streamlining all the agencies."

"I have it from a very reliable source that she will ask for your resignation. It's not that you aren't one of the best directors we have ever had, but she wants a yes man who will do as she wills. Without knowing it, she may have inadvertently did you a favor."

"It may have been a smokescreen what she said today. My guess is if she replaces me, she will name as my successor, Betty Webber agency chief in Florida."

"I don't know if she is the one, but be extremely careful with Madam President. She is mean and vindictive, especially if you try to show her up. The other issue I wanted to discuss with you deals with the "Brotherhood". As you know from our last meeting we briefly stated to you about working full time for the "Brotherhood." It will be doing the Lords work 24/7. You will be asked to travel a lot. You will be able to take your wife along with you on many assignments. I told you we are gathering in August in Innsbruck Austria for ordaining the Twelfth Knight. There are one-hundred and forty-four of us who wear the ring of Twelfth Knight worldwide. We work close with all free police agencies throughout the world, like Interpol and MI6 and the CIA. We try to work with only those countries that believe in freedom of the individual. Under no circumstances do we believe in usurping local governments and taking a life. We will protect ourselves if provoked and if need be; we retaliate when attacked."

"Sir; I have been a career FBI agent for most of my adult life. I used to love what I did, but I don't know if I am ready for a drastic life change. If what you say is true about being asked to step down, it means my career with the Bureau will end abruptly. I have a question, based on what the president asked me to do today. I would like some time off to respond to your question, as to me becoming a Twelfth Knight. Bev and I were planning on going to Europe for a much-needed rest. She even bought the plane tickets. Our tickets take us to Madrid and from there we will rent a car and tour Europe for several weeks and then fly back to the US. We may want to extend our time if what you say is correct. Senator when is the big gathering in Innsbruck?"

"We had to change the time frame again it's the last week in August. The meeting wouldn't coincide with your vacation time frame. I don't want to rush you. Talk it over with Beverly, and oh I almost forgot. I'm throwing a surprise party for mother Richards 75th birthday this weekend. I want you and Beverly to come, it would mean a lot to her. The boys are welcome as well. I have also invited a special guest to speak at our gathering, Dr Isaiah Hamilton, noted theologian and his lovely wife."

"We will be gathering this coming Friday afternoon at Lords Land. Today is Monday, four more days, then a well needed rest and some great biblical teaching by Dr. Hamilton."

"Sir I feel that we need to pray about what is about to transpire that will impact all of our lives. Sir would you pray that the Holy Spirit would guide our minds and hearts? I am also concerned about this new drug Euphoria and the drug king, El Alacran. Pray that he would be brought to justice here in our Country."

CHAPTER 10

(Tuesday June 17th)

After a second cup of coffee I left the Senator and Sheriff Duckworth and decided to head for home. I remembered that I had an appointment with Short Stuff and reached him on his cell phone. He said he understood and said perhaps we could get together in the morning. I said that would be fine. I started to call my office and realized that Mary was not there as I looked at my watch and saw that it was almost six thirty.

I drove the remaining miles to my home and was pulling into my driveway. Just as I was about to get out of the car, I instinctively hit the ground as that familiar rat a tat and ping zing hit the cement! I had pulled my revolver out of its holster while falling, unfortunately I landed on my shoulder. I heard something snap as I hit the ground, I knew that I had broken it. Beverly came out of the house as I lay there in a lot of pain! I screamed and yelled out, "Beverly go back into the house and call the police!"

The attack lasted only a few minutes. Because of the quick response team from our local police department, they arrived within ten minutes, along with an ambulance. Beverly came out when the officers arrived. They attended to me and helped get me to the gurney as the Paramedic attended to me and gave me the bad news. "Mr.

Johnson we must get you to the hospital. You may have to have a pin placed in the clavicle. X-rays must be taken and possibly an MRI. I just gave you a shot for the pain. It should be working in a few minutes. The officers would like to ask you a few more questions, then we will be on our way."

After I explained to the officers that I didn't see a car or the person or persons that shot at me; I started to drift off as the shot started to work. Beverly would follow the ambulance to the nearest hospital which would take about ten short minutes. It was a small local neighborhood hospital with about forty beds that was close by.

I woke up lying in a hospital bed with a lot of pain and my shoulder and arm wrapped in a sling. I looked around and saw Beverly sitting in a chair and my old friend Short Stuff and his wife all sitting and talking. My first thought was, both of us with broken bones, Bev with a broken arm and me with a busted shoulder. I managed a weak laugh.

Short Stuff blurted out: "Hey bro, what's so funny? You couldn't stand it that your wife has a broken arm so you are looking for sympathy. What a way to get a day off. Hey man, you're the director of the FBI you can take off anytime you want too."

Beverly came over to the bed and gave me a big kiss. "Honey how do you feel, the doctor said it was a bad fracture the way you fell on it. I suppose the good side is it's one of the most common fractures. It is painful but will heal in time. It will be awhile before you will be able to play golf. He said your fracture necessitated inserting a pin because you splintered the bone. He said the pain would go away after a few days, but in total it would completely heal in about twelve to fourteen weeks. We may have to cancel our vacation plans."

"Not on your life honey we are going as planned and we are also going to Maw Richards birthday party Friday. Even if I must load up on pain pills, I won't miss her birthday. Enough said."

The phone rang in my room it was Mary, asking how I was doing. Beverly had called her and told her what had happened. I took the phone and told her I was ok and would see her in the office in the morning. As I hung up the phone I overheard Short Stuff say something to Bev. "Should I tell him?"

"Tell him what?" I said.

Honey, "It's all over the evening news."

"What's all over the evening news?"

"The late news is on right now let's hear what they are saying?" As she flipped on the television, the guy was talking about how I had broken my shoulder and had to have a pin inserted to help it mend properly. He also said that they had it from a reliable source that I had a falling-out with the President and that she had asked for my resignation.

I sat up in bed and was furious. "That's a bold face lie. I had a meeting with her this morning. It was a very productive meeting. I also met with her privately. Short Stuff was there, isn't that so my brother? I don't know where they got their info, but all she said to me was that she was pleased that we were on top of the new drug problem, and hoped for a fast solution to this latest scourge. I can't believe how rotten some people are, but when it comes to politicians I can't believe anything they say, she is a piece of work."

"Now, don't get so upset, you need to rest. We are all going home. I'll be back late tomorrow morning and pick you up. You get your rest, come on guys let's let him get some sleep." As she ushered Short Stuff and his wife out the door. She came over and kissed me and said good night. She always smelled great; like she had just stepped out of the shower. I closed my eyes and soon drifted off to sleep.

(Tuesday June 17th)

It was sometime in the middle of the night that something woke me up. It was an evil presence. Someone or something was in my room. I found myself saying, "who's there?" while ringing for the nurse. She came running in and turned on the lights. She screamed when she saw all the scorpions crawling on my bed and on the floor. She went running out of my room calling for whomever. It took a cadre of people to kill all the pesky critters. I managed to get out of bed without getting bitten. I stood on top of a chair while all this was going on. They had been meant to kill me, but the Lord had intervened. I thought, I'm getting real tired of the attempts on my life.

The security staff and the local police department were dispatched to the hospital, but by the time they arrived all that was left of the attack was the cleanup needed to restore order. For some reason, I started laughing. One of the cops asked me what was so funny. I told him that this was the third time I had been attacked by arachnids, but for whatever reason it struck me funny as to the reaction of the nurses and staff.

I thought of a scripture in the New Testament: "And they were not permitted to kill anyone, but to torment for five months; and their torment was like the torment of a scorpion when it stings a man" (Rev. 9:5 NASB).

There are only two other scriptures found in the New Testament referring to scorpions. Jesus used it to make a point about prayer while dealing with His disciples, about persistence and the grace of God. "Now suppose one of you fathers is asked by his son for a fish; he will not give him a snake instead of a fish, will he? Or if he is asked for an egg, he will not give him a scorpion, will he?" (Luke 11: 11-12 NASB).

The other scripture is found in Luke chapter ten. "Behold, I have given you authority to tread upon serpents and scorpions, and over all the power of the enemy, and nothing shall injure you" (Luke 10:19 NASB). I found myself telling the officer that I was a Christian and knew that God would protect me. I also told him that I wasn't going to run around the country picking up snakes and trying to kill them. This verse was directed at the seventy when they returned from a ministry outreach. The officer concurred with me, it turned out he was a believer and knew his bible----

After all the excitement subsided, I was moved to a more secure room and a guard stationed in front of the room. It was after three in the morning when I went back to bed. As I lay there for what seemed like hours thinking about how persistent my nemesis, El Alacran was. I awoke startled as my doctor came in and told me I would be allowed to leave around noon. He wanted to take a few more x-rays to make sure all was in place, without complications. I would be allowed to leave, if I didn't do anything strenuous. He said he felt it was ok if I went on our trip to Europe.

I called for the nurse and asked if I could get some coffee and a bagel along with some strawberry jam. "I think I can get it for you in our snack shop. The kitchen is closed for breakfast and lunch is a couple of hours away. I'll be back in few minutes."

She came back with a tray with a great cup of coffee and a bagel along with several little cups of jams. "Thank you so very much nurse Sarah. How much do I owe you for this great food?"

"Mr. Johnson, it is my treat and won't accept anything. I know all about you; my brother was with the FBI for several years and was killed by a terrorist. His name was George Clements. I'm his youngest sister and what they did to him was horrible. He used to mention you a lot. God, bless you for what you did for his little girl. The little boy that they took was never found." She at this point was in tears as I thanked her for her dedication and for being a light to those who are suffering.

I found myself asking her. "Sarah; what happened to the little girl, who is raising her?"

"Thank you for asking Mr. Johnson. I have her along with two of my own. Enjoy your breakfast, sorry but I must make my rounds, and Jesus bless you and your family. I must go," as she left to fulfill her nursing duties.

I flipped on one of the cable network news channels as they were talking about me being sacked. The channel was a liberal one and so what they had to say was a spin on why Madam President had decided to make the change. I found myself getting angry and turned it off. I no sooner turned the television off when my phone rang. "Yes; this is Gregg Johnson." The voice on the other line said please hold Mr. Johnson, the president wishes to speak with you."

"Gregg, this is President Blankenship. Are you feeling ok? Sorry to hear that you broke your shoulder. Can I do anything for you? If not, the other subject concerns the story that was leaked to the press. I wanted you to hear it from me why I decided to make a change in the directorship of the Bureau. You have been a model director, but after our meeting yesterday I received a report that your religious beliefs have gotten in the way of your decision making. I have had a few complaints about your eagerness to share your faith, which violates separation of church and state. If you want you can still come in and see me when you return from your sabbatical, but since it's been leaked to the press, I feel no further discussion is needed; do you?"

"No President Blankenship, it's your call. I only have one question? Do you want me to stick around for an easy transition?"

"I don't feel it's necessary. Betty Webber is a career agent and well versed on Bureau procedures. What I need from you Gregg is a letter of resignation, can I get that right away? I like to move quickly."

"I'll have it on your desk tomorrow morning, and be out of my office by the end of the week, if that's all right with you?"

"Sounds good Gregg, I'll expect the letter no later than noon tomorrow then, Betty can move in by Monday of next week."

As she hung up. I thought what a piece of work. Bad thoughts about her exploded in my mind. Then anger was starting to well-up inside. I then composed myself, how crude and inconsiderate she was. I thought about the oath I had taken almost twenty-five years ago, to give my life if necessary in protection of my Country the United States of America. It would be hard for me to stop a bullet for this woman. I found out how ruthless she was and how the men and women in service of our government would be hard pressed to work for her. I couldn't believe she had set me up after our meeting yesterday. I stopped and asked God not to allow me to let bitterness become a problem because of her.

I decided to change into my street clothes and rang for Sarah my nurse. She came into the room and asked what I needed. I told her I wanted to get dressed. She asked me if I wanted to take a shower, or a sponge bath and a shave. She no sooner got the words out of her mouth when in walked my wife Beverly and Cash Cameron.

Beverly came over and gave me a big kiss. "Hi sugar, how do you feel this morning? Are you feeling a lot of pain?"

"Not much Honey, how about you, your arm is also broken? One of the reasons I love you, always worrying more about me and less about yourself. I just got off the phone with the President. She is a piece of work. She wants my letter of resignation in her office by noon tomorrow. I think I will wait until Monday, or perhaps mail it in. There will be no transition. Cash, I'm sorry I sound angry, but I am. Not because of the dedication I have given my country in service as a FBI agent, but the lack of dignity given me for my years of service. I am also saddened by how our great country has slipped into the garbage pit and how slimy people hold entrusted offices. I'm sorry just blowing off steam."

Cash spoke up. "Brother what are you going to do?"

"For now, Beverly and I are going to take a long vacation in Europe and enjoy our lives together. I will probably go to work for the 'Brotherhood,' but I'm praying about it. What about you Cash? What are your plans?"

"Gregg, Rachel and I have been thinking a lot about our lives. I feel the Lord is calling us to full time service. We are both tired of chasing evil people. We have one child and one on the way. Our home church wants to expand and start another church in Las Cruces, New Mexico my home town. They are willing to send me to seminary and pay our expenses for two years. We are still praying about it, but we want to be sure this is what God wants. Oh, before I forget, I hooked up with Manny and it will be my last assignment."

Beverly spoke up. "I think that's fantastic. I think you will make a great minister, and with Rachel at your side and the Lords help you make a great team."

"Great my brother, that's the best news I have heard in a long time. It makes me proud that I am your friend and brother in Christ"

"I called Manny and he said Burt had backed out. Burt said something about going on a long trip. Manny and I will be heading for the Hamptons next week."

Short Stuff walked in about this time. "Hey Brother what's up? Are you still goofing off? You know I'm just kidding you, Bro. How do you feel; do you have a lot of pain?"

"I've got some pain, but I have a higher tolerance to pain than most. I'm waiting for the doctor to write the release so I can get out of here. And before you ask, I am going to take a vacation and then decide what I'm going to do, but not until I get back. We will be leaving at the end of next week."

I no sooner got the words out of my mouth when the phone rang. Bev answered the phone and said it was the Senator. They exchanged pleasantries; then handed me the phone.

"Hi pops, uh Senator. Sorry for the slip."

"Gregg; you are my spiritual son and you can call me Pops any time. I heard about your ordeal; how are you feeling son?"

"I'm doing fine sir, but having a difficult time suppressing my anger towards the new President. She didn't even give me the courtesy of me coming in and telling me in person, very uncouth. A fancy name for jerk, forgive me Lord."

"Gregg my boy, what you are feeling is righteous anger. Just don't let it become bitterness. Ask the lord to take it from you; otherwise it will blind your judgment. Ask the others to hold hands and we will pray for you for a speedy recovery and that your anger will subside."

"Thank you Senator, I already prayed to the Lord asking for bitterness not to take hold. Sir, are we still on for this weekend, Mother Richards birthday party?"

"Yes son, I'll send my plane for you Friday afternoon.

"Sounds good to us Sir. Senator please pray for me for a quick recovery."

"We look forward to fellowshipping and sharing some thoughts with you." He prayed for me before he hung up.

As he hung up, I had tears in my eyes. Bev came over and hugged me as she whispered in my ear. "I love you honey, this is one of those times that our Lord is stretching us. We will be fine."

The doctor came in and said he wanted to look at the incision. So, he asked everyone to go out into the waiting room.

"The shoulder and incision look fine. I'll need to look at the incision by the end of next week. Say around Thursday or Friday?"

"We were planning on being gone all of next week, but we can be back here a week from Friday."

"The dressing needs to be changed every couple of days. Have your wife check the incision to make sure it's healing, while she's changing the dressing."

"Thanks Doc; I'll come in a week from Friday afternoon if that's alright with you?"

"Good, you are fine to leave----see you next week. Call my office for a set time."

Beverly and I said our goodbyes to Cash and Short Stuff and headed for my office.

CHAPTER 11

(June 18ᵗʰ AM)

After leaving the hospital we decided on a late breakfast. There was an IHOP close by. Beverly had to drive; even with her small arm cast she could maneuver the car well as we pulled into the IHOP parking lot.

We sat down to order. Bev wanted a Cheese omelet and I decided on French toast. We gave our order to our waitress and thanked her for her promptness.

"Dear, forgive me if I sound a little testy. It's my ego that is wounded. I never dreamed my years at the Bureau would end like this. I'll get over what happened this morning, but I understand that we are living in some trying times."

We sat for a while making our plans. Our former president Buck Burns could get a philanthropist friend of his to build us our home at no cost to us. I had a good size pension coming from the Bureau, so we were well fixed, money wise. I stopped talking and asked my wife to join me in prayer. Thanking God for our food and His great financial blessings as the waitress delivered our food.

Bev spoke up and said; "Honey do you know the women that is coming over to our table?"

"No dear, I don't. I have seen her before. I thought so, she is a co-anchor from WSB the local TV station."

"Mr. Johnson, I'm Hillary Gould, could I speak with you regarding your resignation as the director of the FBI?"

"Please, sit down Miss Gould. This is my wife Beverly we are just finishing up our late breakfast. Could we order you some coffee or tea?"

"No thanks Mr. Johnson. Let me get right to the point Mr. Johnson, the President fired you I was told by her chief of staff; so, what are your plans for the immediate future?"

I started to respond to both questions when there was a tremendous blast in the room! It rocked the whole building and filled it with smoke. After the blast subsided I pulled out my little pocket flashlight to see if the three of us were alright. I asked Bev if she was ok as I heard a meek; "I'm fine dear."

I shined the small light on the reporter and saw her slumped body in the chair! The way her head was positioned, I knew she was dead. To make sure, I reached over and felt her pulse and reaffirmed she was dead. It was difficult for me to do anything further because of my shoulder. I told Bev that we needed to exit the building. As we reached the outside, I noticed that many of the people were walking or running out of the building and some were walking like they were in a trance! I recognized that they were in a state of shock.

By this time there were police on the scene and several firemen running in and out of the building. As I looked around there were a couple of other buildings that had been hit harder. I stopped a police officer who wore the rank of captain. I told him who I was as I showed him my badge. I asked him what had happened. "Mr. Johnson, a bomb went off next door to the entrance to the metro! We are sure that it was a terrorist attack. There are people trapped below under tons of rubble! Preliminary reports are still filtering in. Some estimate that the death toll may reach several hundreds. Listen I have to run, sorry that you won't be director anymore, but may God continue to bless you and keep you safe."

I turned to Bev and said, "Isn't it amazing how God has people who love Him spread all over the world? My agents would be investigating as to who set the bomb off if I was still the director. I prayed for my successor that she would be successful in catching the culprits.

"Oh honey; I feel we need to pray for all the souls that are trapped and for the soul of the young woman who was trying to do her job. I don't know what killed her. The way she was slumped over, I believe that her neck was broken."

"Bev Honey, when I checked her pulse there was a sliver of glass that had penetrated her temple which caused her death. There is a bus bench across the street. Let's go over there and sit. Let's pray that God's grace would reign for those who survived and for the families of those who didn't. For the rapid response people who will place their lives on the line. Pray for the firemen and the hospital staff that will be stretched to the limit, along with the paramedics and search crews who must crawl into dangerous places trying to excavate the living and the dead!"

We sat there praying together. People who were in a daze and looked lost stopped and asked us to pray for them and their lost loved ones. What started out as a fifteen to twenty-minute prayer lasted almost two hours. I asked Bev what time it was and realized it was almost four in the afternoon. We got up and made our way to where we had parked our car. There were several cars with a lot of debris strewn on them. I started to get into the driver's seat and realized what I had done, as we both broke out laughing.

"Sorry Honey; I forgot about my shoulder. Let me move over." As I slide over to the passenger side of the seat.

We dialed Mary to tell her why we would be late.

"Hi Mary; this is Gregg, how are things going this afternoon? Bev and I were eating at the IHOP close to where the bombing took place!"

"Oh Mr. Johnson; I am so glad you are both alright. Your phone has been ringing off the hook. I must ask you a question if it's ok? Did you resign for personal reasons?"

"Mary, you have been working for me for a long time, between you and me, no. I was asked to resign by President Gloria Blankenship, effective immediately, but for publication tell them it is for health reasons."

"I suppose it will affect me as well. Even though I am a civil servant the new director will want their own secretary. I don't know if I could work for someone else Mr. Johnson, besides Burt has been after me to resign. He is well fixed financially and is not in debt to anyone. I still owe money on the house that my former husband left me when he died in Vietnam. All these years I have been working so I could pay off the debt. I think I'll discuss it with Burt, it would be nice not to have to work anymore and just spend my time with that big lug of mine and my grandkids."

"Mary; God will show you the way as to what you should do. We will remain friends, and of course brothers in Christ. Listen Mary, I'm on my way in, but won't stay long. I need to dictate some letters; see you in a few minutes."

CHAPTER 11

(June 18th evening)

As we drove along, Bev broke my silence as she said, "Honey I've been thinking. Why don't we ask Mary and Burt along for our trip to Europe, God knows she deserves it? What do you think of my idea?"

"I think it's fantastic, but I thought you wanted this to be our vacation?"

"At first I did, but I will have you all to myself for a long time now that your' unemployed, unless you take the Senators offer right away."

"Bev honey you can ask her when we get to my office. There's the parking lot; pull into my spot. Wow, can you beat that, their changing the name already. I don't care pull into it anyway."

Mary was waiting for us as I walked into my office along with some of the other people who I had worked with over the years. Mary had been busy calling fellow agent's personal friends who were dedicated to our Country. Men and women who would sacrifice their lives for our Country. Even Burt was their along with Charlie Wong and Short Stuff. There was a huge cake and cards of appreciation from the local people. I also noticed a large pile of telegrams and another stack of e-mails from people I had come to know over the years. One that caught my attention was a telegram from president Buck Burns. It would take me several days to answer them all. They all started to sing for he's a jolly good fellow, when in walked Cash and Rachel Cameron. It was well after six in the evening when people started to leave. Only Burt and Mary along with Cash and Rachel were left. Short Stuff would have stayed but he had a baseball game to attend as his son was playing Pony League.

"Thanks for hanging around gang. What say we all go out to eat at my favorite Italian Restaurant? I know it's on short notice, but I am springing for the dinner. Cash and Rachel, can you get your baby sitter for a little while longer?"

"I think so, let me call Marie Luisa, Mary's daughter and ask her if she minds staying for the evening." She came back with a big smile and said, "It's all set. She said her husband was out of town and would love too."

"Bev honey would you call the restaurant and make reservations for us for seven thirty."

She dialed and came back smiling and said it was all arranged. I found out later that Beverly had called to see if the Senator was still in town and had asked him to join us. She also called John and Kathleen our dear friends. John could relate to what had transpired with me, being my predecessor. We all decided to take our own cars, as we made our way to the parking lot.

It took us about thirty minutes to get to Georgetown. I glanced in the side mirror and noticed that we were being followed, about four or five cars behind. As Bev drove into the parking lot, followed by Burt and Mary, along with Cash and Rachel I noticed a dark color sedan with tinted windows park behind us. I waited for Cash and Burt to get out of their cars. I noticed that Cash and Burt had both spotted the car. They gave me the high sign that they were watching my six. As we made our way to the entrance of Casa de Italia the doors on the dark sedan opened. Four big burly guys that I knew were thugs got out. I also knew that they were packing heavy artillery. One of them I knew I had seen recently, but I couldn't put my finger on where? I shrugged it off as we were escorted to a private room by an old friend and owner named Papalino.

In his broken English, he said; "Ha Mr. and Mrs. Johnson; what ah nice---ah saprizah for Papalino. It---ah has been many months' ah---since we have---ah the pleasure you're---ah presence. Please, all of---ah you sit-ah. Marcello bring---ah the most---ah expensive---ah wine for our guest. I Papalino will order for all of you Familia style. I will go to the cocina (Kitchen) and speak-ah to the cook."

We all looked at each other and smiled. I started to relax and felt my shoulder throbbing. It had been several hours since I had taken a pain pill. Bev saw that I was becoming uncomfortable as she handed me one of the pills the doctor had given me. I no sooner swallowed the pill; when the Senator came in along with John and Kathleen.

The Senator spoke first. "Gregg my boy, how are you feeling after such a trying day. The pain in your shoulder must be almost unbearable. Mother Richards sends her love and looks forward to seeing you this weekend. All of you are invited to Lords Land. We have a special treat this weekend. My plane will be here late Friday at the small private airport in South Virginia, so if you are there with your luggage. I will assume you are going. I didn't realize how hungry I was until I walked into the dining room and smelled the aroma of the Italian food cooking. What's on the menu for tonight?" Gregg; what kind of food did you order?"

"Sir; the owner is bringing his own specials, I'm sure you will love it. And thank you Senator for the invitation to all of us for this weekend. Beverly and I are going. We wouldn't miss this gathering, unless the Lord returned. What about the rest of you folks? If you don't know it, it's mother Richards seventy fifth birthday. As to the food I can guarantee you will all love it.

All of them said they would try and make it, and thanked the Senator for his hospitality. After giving thanks for our food the plates of succulent Italian dishes started gracing our table. Starting with a family style Antipasto, a dish filled with all sorts of olives, fresh garlic and various Italian cheeses and Roma tomatoes and a spinach type lettuce. Then a dish of "Three World Known Lasagna," stuffed with Italian hot sausage and all sorts of juicy mouth watering mozzarella cheeses were served. Next on the feast, plates of hot spaghetti with several different types of sauces and battered egg plant were served. Papalino was not through. He then brought in chicken- cacciatore and chicken-parmesan. Hot Italian bread and finally the house specialty, small fillet steaks smothered in a wine sauce with mushrooms. I thought there would be no end to the food. Wine was served for those who wanted a glass; but most of us declined, some of us ordered espresso coffee. To top off the meal a great dish of Italian Ice Cream for desert.

Everyone was blessed with our meal. During and after dinner we all talked about what our plans would be for the rest of the year. We went around the table starting with the Senator. He said that this would be his last year in Congress. He wanted to devote his remaining years working full time for the Lord. Next to share were Cash and

Rachel. Cash was enrolling in a very conservative seminary and felt God wanted him to go into full time ministry. Rachel stated that she was looking forward to being a minister's wife and mother. She was excited about being pregnant with child number two. Cash's daughter was also expecting her first child. So along with being parents, Cash and Rachel were going to be grandparents as well. We all found ourselves saying, awesome!

Kathleen and John shared their testimony of how after John served his time for his part in the Fenneman Oil fiasco. They had just celebrated their second year of reconciliation. John was working for a large pharmaceutical corporation as head of their security division. Burt said that Mary was going to take early retirement and that they were going to go on a long vacation. We hadn't had time to ask them to come along with us on our vacation, but would later.

I was the last to speak on what I was going to do. I told them that we were going on a long vacation to Europe and felt that I would not rest until the Scorpion was brought to justice.

"I haven't taken care of what God called me to do, and that's bringing to justice this new enemy of God, El Alacran, or Scorpion. I have had numerous encounters with him so far. I was even attacked last night by a horde of black scorpions in the hospital. It scared the living H out of the hospital staff. I want to bring this man to justice even if I must go out of the country to do it. He is a menace to God and society. Thank you all for coming, and I hope to see you all at Lords Land this weekend. It's rather late and I'm tired. I need to get some much-needed sleep."

The Senator motioned for me to stay behind for a minute. After everyone left, only the Senator, Bev and I were left. "Gregg I won't keep you too long. I need to know if you have thought over our offer to work for 'The Brotherhood?"

"Sir we are still praying about it and want to make sure it's the Lord's will. I will have an answer for you this weekend; if that's ok with you?"

"Good Son, it's what I wanted to hear, that you are praying about this decision and that it's God who will give you guidance. We will talk some more this weekend."

We walked out together to our respective cars. We both hugged the Senator and said we would see him Friday afternoon. I noticed that the same car that followed us was parked near the back of the lot. I also noticed as we pulled out of the parking lot another car pulling out which I knew was an agency car. They fell in a few cars behind our shadow. We made our way to the expressway and noticed that our shadow had exited after a couple of miles. We finally made it home as we pulled into our very secure system. It was new state of the art equipment. I shouted out, thank you Lord for providing this security.

All we had to do was punch in our code from inside the car and a pin would activate a voice and arm the system. It would say, "Intruder in the house, or intruder in the yard." It would let us know where our security breach was. It also tells you all is safe inside. We made our way to our bedroom and both of us barely said our nightly prayers. We both fell into a deep sound sleep.

CHAPTER 12

(June 19tham)

I was awakened from a sound sleep by laughter coming from the kitchen. It was Bev and my two sons. I glanced at the clock and was shocked that it said it was ten after nine in the morning. I got myself out of bed and went down stairs to join my family. "Good morning everybody; boy did I sleep like a rock."

James and John came over and gave me a big hug and simultaneously said; "we love you Dad, and were sorry about you losing your job. What are you going to do? Have you got another job lined up? How's the shoulder feeling, do you have a lot of pain?"

Bev said; "Boys give your dad a chance to answer your questions after he sits down and has his first cup of coffee. Honey, are you still in a lot of pain?"

The boys started laughing. Bev asked; "What's so funny? Boys."

"Mom, you told us to let dad answer and the first thing you did was ask him how he felt? So, it hit us funny."

Then she started to laugh, and soon we all were laughing. It was a moment to cherish. It was a great family moment.

I finally said; "The shoulder feels stiff and a little sore, but as you know I have a high tolerance for pain. I guess I'm lucky in some respects. Boys what are you doing home so early? I thought you both had finals this week?"

"We did Dad, but we took them all last week and scored in the top ten at the Point. We have one more year to go; then we will be assigned to our special units. James and I asked to go into Special Forces training when we graduate next May."

James spoke up and said, "Yeah Dad, John and me have been thinking about making the Army a career. We were talking about it with Mom. She said it was our decision and whatever we decided after talking it over with you. Ah, what do you think?"

"I think you have your minds set on being Delta Force; and of course, you have my blessings, with one condition. Pray to our Lord Jesus Christ and ask His blessings"

John answered: "Dad we didn't tell you the rest of what we want to do. We want to go to theology school and become Army Chaplains along with being in Special Forces, either Delta Force or Green Beret. We believe they need spiritual guidance also, don't they? They have a special program offered in our Sr. year at the point where we can take extra classes dealing with religion and becoming a military chaplain. Seminary is two years and then another year in Special Forces training and prayerfully we will be assigned to a unit. What do you think?"

"I am so proud of you both. You are both what being a Godly father is all about. Seeing his children being servants of Christ, of course you have my blessing and I know your mother is just as proud of you both as I am. I am reminded of a passage of scripture. "Children, obey your parents in the Lord, for this is right. Honor your father and mother which is the first commandment with a promise that it may go well with you and that you may enjoy long life on the earth. Fathers, do not exasperate your children; instead, bring them up in the training and instruction of the Lord" (Ephes. 6:1-4 NIV).

"This is one of those moments that I get to see and hear the blessings of God. "Let's eat, I'm hungry what's for breakfast?"

"Fresh baked biscuits with chicken fried steak and eggs with plenty of honey for your biscuits and good strong coffee. Do you boys want milk or coffee? Bev said."

"Honey you amaze me. You have a broken arm. You get up early and have your time with the Lord. You cook a fantastic breakfast. I am so blessed by God for you as my helpmate!"

Both boys like always said, "Amen. Now please pass the milk."

We spent the next hour talking about some of our vacations that we had spent together as a family. Laughing about some of the errors I had made; while on a camping trip.

James said; "Dad, remember the incident with the bear?"

"How I forgot to put the cheese and lunch meat in a special metal box and a bear came and tore-up the entire camp looking for the food. Then we all had to sleep in the car all night because of my error; do I remember, you bet I do." We all laughed until my stomach ached.

My cell phone rang, so after several rings I picked it up and answered. "Yes this is Gregg Johnson who is this?" As I heard the heavy breathing coming from the cell phone, this distinct voice came on the line."

"Hey amigo, how are you feeling; my last surprise didn't do anything for you. You are worse than the cat with nine lives. I am truly sorry you lost your job, but that does not even the score Gringo. You are like a wounded tiger, more dangerous than ever. I will be watching for you, when you come out of your lair, then you will finally feel my sting." As he hung up, I thought I could hear a familiar voice speaking in the back ground, a voice out of the past, Mathew Hopkins.

I decided not to say anything about the call to my family, but told them it was a prank call. As we finished eating breakfast I noticed the time and it was almost noon. I asked Bev to help me dress and asked the boys if they would take me to my office. Of course, they were ecstatic to be able to drive their old-man to work. James won the toss and he drove the car to the Bureau. I sat in the front seat while John sat behind me. We decided to drive on the expressway. James was a good driver and made no mistakes as we drove along. I noticed in the side mirror that we were being followed, as our tail slowly got closer to us.

I said, "boy's make sure your seat belts are on. James, we are being tailed by some seedy characters. I hope you are up to loosing the tail using evasive tactics." I no sooner got the words out of my mouth when I heard a loud bang, as they hit us from behind. James shouted out, "Don't worry Dad, watch me out maneuver these guys and loose them." As he accelerated and maneuvered in and out of traffic he saw our exit, but passed it as he shot behind a slow-moving truck then passed him on the left and got in between the flat bed truck with a full load of potatoes. He then maneuvered right behind a moving van as we exited the off ramp. It was a slick piece of driving. "Son I said; where did you learn to drive like that?"

"Dad; I'll come clean. The last two summers John and I have been taking race car driving for fun. We paid for the lessons out of our summer jobs. It paid off today."

John spoke up. "Dad; who were those guys. They were shooting at us. I could hear a couple of pings as we outran them."

I decided to tell them about the Scorpion and his quest to kill me.

I told them that he was trying to get even because I arrested him a few years ago for conspiracy against the United States.

We arrived at the Bureau parking lot and had to get temporary clearance for the boys. We made our way to my office and a lot of Bureau employees stopped me and wished me the best, some said they were truly sorry I was no longer their chief. Mary was speaking with a group of people whom I recognized as long time government employees. Mary looked up when she saw me and came over and ushered me into my office.

"Mr. Johnson, these are the people that will oversee the Bureau office. I understand that the new director has ordered a complete change of office staff. Her secretary will be here Tuesday of next week; so, my last day will be yours as well. Here's the directive, signed and approved by her and the President. We were all offered a severance package for early retirement. What do you think about all this, Sir?"

"Mary, I'm sorry about this. The new president ran on a platform of change and cleaning out the old bureaucracy. Good honest employees will be asked to leave their jobs. With the national unemployment rate at over 10% I don't know how firing employees with fifteen to twenty years' service will help. It will damage our ability to function smoothly as a nation. You and I are considered antiquated and no longer useful to the FBI. When you walk out of here today hold your head high. I will walk out of here also regardless of who takes over. We can be proud for the service we gave our country."

"I have the resignation letter all set for you to sign Mr. Johnson. I have worked with you so long I knew what you would want to say."

I picked up the letter and read it. It was very sterile and to the point. I signed it and had Mary run off a couple of extra copies for me. One to stay in my personnel file and one for me personally, the original would be hand delivered Monday by courier."

I cleaned out my desk of all my personal belongings. I didn't turn in my badge or ID card on purpose. After saying goodbye to the staff, I then thanked Mary and told her that Bev and I would be honored if they would go on vacation to Europe with us and let us know right away. She would love too and would ask Burt if they could go. I rounded up the boys and headed for our car.

⸺ ⸺

John got the honor of driving as we made our way home on the expressway without incident. I; the ever-watchful agent kept looking in the side mirror. My eye caught a glimpse of a state of the art motorcycle. It was a model I had never seen before. It was a James Bond type of vehicle. He stayed far enough behind so that those that he was tailing would lull into a false sense of security. I said nothing to the boys as we made our way home. We were about two miles from our exit when the guy on the bike does a wheelie. He stood it on one wheel and pulled up right next to us. The flames along the side of the engine and a painted head of a black scorpion hiding what this bike was designed to do, kill with its rocket stinger. He fired one off target to get our attention. Along with its blue flames along the body made the bike look just like a scorpion with its tail ready to strike. The small attack was not meant to kill us, but to warn us that I was the priority hit. I surmised it would travel over two hundred miles per hour. Just as he passed us, he looked back at us and shook his fist at us, as he sped away.

James spoke up and said. "Dad does this happen to you every

day? With all the power, you have I'm sorry you couldn't have this guy blown up?"

"Listen to me both of you. I have had this power, but I honor it by using it only when necessary. Lord Acton once said; 'Power corrupts. Absolute power corrupts absolutely.' Jesus said that all power and authority had been given to Him, yet he never abused His power. Evil men given power will use it for personal gain, remember this lesson well. Some day you both will be given power and authority, how you use it will be how much you love our Lord. Let's get home, your Mom and I are leaving tomorrow in the afternoon for Lords Land and we need to shop for a gift for Mother Richard's birthday. Do you want to go along with us?"

James and John said in unison, "Dad we had other plans. We are going to our cabin for a weekend of fishing. Some of our friends from the Point will be with us. You know us----Dad, we only invite guys with the same morals as us."

I said "Ok. What about Buster?" John said. "We planned on taking him Dad, if it's ok? "It's settled, you are going to the cabin, mom and I, Lords Land.

CHAPTER 13

(Friday June 20ᵗʰ)

Late Friday evening the Senators plane picked us up at a private airport near our home. Burt and Mary also went with us. This was Mary's second trip to Lords Land. Cash and Rachel had other plans. Short Stuff and His wife couldn't get away. Short Stuff was up to his eyeballs with the problems he had as a Captain on the DC force, due to the rise of the drug Euphoria and its related deaths in D.C. The new presidential administration was hosting a "Save the Planet March" in Washington, and security had to be beefed up.

We arrived at the small airport where the Senator kept his private jet and were met by the man himself, and as always smiling and ever the optimist. How are yah all. I pray that you had an enjoyable trip? I have a surprise for you when we get to Lords Land. My man will get your luggage. How are you feeling Gregg? Is the shoulder bothering you? I and some of the other Elders that are here will anoint you with oil later tonight, which is very biblical. Scripture states; 'Is any one of you sick? He should call the elders of the church to pray over him and anoint him with oil in the name of the Lord. And the prayer offered in faith will make the sick person well; the Lord will raise him up. If he has sinned, he will be forgiven" (James 5:14-15 NIV). This is one of my favorite passages of scripture in the New Testament. I believe that praying for the sick and ailing is a duty for all Christians. You will see this evening when we gather at Lords Land."

"We are nearing my home, and mother Richards has a great feast prepared for us. It's a special Southern Style meal. It is a surprise for you and our special guest. It is now six thirty and dinner will be served in about half hour. Mother Richards has assigned you all your rooms. If you need to freshen up, you still have time.

———————

After arriving and freshening up we made our way to the main dining room. The table was set for twelve people. The table had name place settings carefully placed by Maw Richards. I sat next to our surprise guest, our former President Buck Burns. Bev sat next to Joyce Burns the President's wife. Next to me on my left was Calvin T. Duckworth's wife; sheriff of Natchez County, Mrs. Bernadine Duckworth. Across from me was Burt and next to him was Mother Richards. Next to Mother Richards was a man I knew as an icon in religious circles. He was a renowned theologian Dr. Isaiah Hamilton an African American and his lovely wife Matilda who sat next to the Senator. Mary was placed on the other side of Dr. Hamilton

After every one sat down the Senator rose and asked us all to bow our heads as he asked for God's blessings for the meal and for our speaker Dr. Hamilton. During dinner, I had a chance to speak directly with Buck Burns a man of great character. He leaned over and said to me. "I will never forget how you and Lt. Butler saved my life. I will be forever in your debt. I am truly sorry that you were asked to resign. It is a great loss to our country. Men like you are hard to find. I have a scripture for you, please receive it in love. "And we know that

God causes everything to work together for the good of those who love God and are called according to His purpose for them" (Romans 8:28 NLT).

This scripture has helped me understand certain things that have impacted me during my life; I pray that it will guide you also when you face difficult decisions. I also consider you a friend. Here is my card and private number in case you need to talk."

"Thank you Mr. President, it means a lot to me to be your friend and thank you for the scripture."

At the end of dinner, the Senator rose and said that it was time for us to go to the chapel. He said that Dr. Hamilton would be speaking at a private session after chapel services to the men billeted here at the house and that he would share at chapel services as well. He also stated that there would be a service in the morning at ten thirty AM. Breakfast would be served buffet style at the chapel dining room. A local church would be hosting the services.

We all got up and made our way to the camp grounds located about two hundred yards from the main house. While walking to the chapel, I noticed the amount of Secret Service agents deployed to guard the former President.

As we made our way to the chapel the Senator said to me, "Gregg hold-up a minute. Could you and Beverly meet with Mother Richards and me for breakfast in the morning? We have something very important to discuss with you both."

"Of course sir, what time?"

"Nine is fine son. Now go and sit next to your wife. You don't want to miss any part of Dr. Hamilton's Sermon."

I motioned to Bev to catch up with me. She was walking with Mrs. Hamilton along with Mary. We all sat in the front row. I looked around and was amazed at how many people had arrived to hear the great doctor speak. He had a deep voice that sounded like Earl Jones the great actor who played Darth Vader in the movie series, Star Wars.

The service started with a wonderful praise and worship group, playing a selection of contempory music while everyone joined in. An elderly gentleman sang a special song called "Oh Lord You're Beautiful." He played his own guitar accompaniment, but what struck me about his solo was----you could feel his love for Jesus our Lord. It was etched into my brain as I recall that flock of white hair and deep baritone voice ------

Then the Senator stood and introduced Dr. Hamilton. I was amazed at his resume. A Ph.D. in theology, and earned a doctorate in Archeology and a Doctorate in Biblical studies and is fluent in Biblical Greek, German, French, Hebrew and English along with Spanish.

When he stood to speak, I could see the love in his eyes for God's people. He chose as his text the parable of the Good Samaritan which gives us three examples of the philosophies of life. Luke 10:30-37. His text dealing with the Good Samaritan was the first time I had ever heard it preached. He illustrated that there were three major points, he wanted to expound on. What the robber's philosophy was. "What you have is mine, and I will take it." "The priest and the Levite's philosophy was, "What is mine is mine and I will keep it." The Samaritan's philosophy was "What is mine is yours, and I will share it with you." Jesus philosophy was the same as the Samaritan when He said to the one who had asked Him who was his neighbor; He said Go and do the same. His entire sermon emphasized that we are to help our neighbors, regardless the cost. It was the way he delivered it to us is what amazed me with God's special anointing on this man.

After the formal gathering at the chapel was over we made our way back to the Senators house and were directed by mother Richards and the Senator to our respective gatherings. The men went with the Senator to his large study and the ladies retired to the family room with mother Richards.

Those who were asked to join the Senator were the six men who ate dinner together. The Senator asked if anyone wanted any of the refreshments that were sitting on a huge credenza. Coffee and cookies and for those who needed more, there were some finger sandwiches. I chose a cup of coffee and was asked by the Senator to sit next to him on his left side, and to my left was Sheriff Duckworth. President Burns sat in a large easy chair next to Dr. Hamilton. Burt sat next to the President.

The Senator stood up and asked Burt if he would please close the door as he began. "Gentlemen; thank you all for coming. It is with great pleasure that Dr. Hamilton accepted my invitation to speak to you. You are all members of the Brotherhood. All of you have had top clearance from our government, so what you will hear from Dr. Hamilton is something we have heard mostly from second and third hand hearers. Under no circumstances will you repeat what you hear this night. Dr. Hamilton. You have the floor."

"I am deeply honored by your presence. I have been part of the Brotherhood for over thirty years and am still amazed by the caliber of men who make up our organization, which I might add is worldwide. Tonight, we will be awarding a new ring to one of our own. He has only been a member for about three years, but he has earned the honor of wearing the same ring that I wear. He will also be anointed in Austria later this summer. Before we honor our brother, I have something of vital importance to share with you all. Is this all right with you Tyree?"

"Of course; you have the floor Dr. Hamilton; please continue."

"Thank you Senator. Let me take you back a few years. It was the first time I had heard about a legend that drew my attention. Remember when the Vatican allowed a bunch of historians to examine the Shroud of Turin. The Shroud supposedly belonging to Christ, the problem was they placed so many stipulations on the specialist who were to examine the shroud, that the results were inconclusive as to its authenticity. I don't feel we will ever know if it is authentic. My own feelings are that it is not." He took a sip of water and then continued.

"At about the same time the Shroud was being examined I was in Israel working on a dig, near the town of Bethel, a dig that to most was very insignificant. One day while excavating a site, my colleagues and I came upon a crude tomb that belonged to one of the Spanish crusaders. A certain knight had been buried with all his armor. We found remnants of his sword and a metal vile which was his drinking cup. As I continued to brush away dirt from the site; I came upon a badly decomposed leather pouch. Because of its fragile condition and what might be in the pouch, I took it home with me so that I could do a deeper analysis. I just recently reconstructed the letters that were in the pouch. I have been working on reconstructing the letters for fifteen years. A monumental task, thank God I have had others helping me."

"There were four letters in the pouch. Three were written about the same time frame, the thirteenth century, in Latin and Aramaic. But the last one is the one I want to talk about. This one was written in Aramaic, which made it more difficult. It is supposedly a letter written from John the Apostle to the brother of our Lord, James, at Antioch. John was concerned about the Lords Robe. It appears that Demetrius in John's letter supposedly delivered the Robe to James. It also states that if anyone touches the robe, they are healed instantly, regardless of who they are. It seems when Paul wrote his last letter to his beloved Timothy he also stated, "When you come, bring the robe that I left with Carpus at Troas, and my scrolls, especially the parchments" (2 Tim. 4:13 NIV).

"I have many questions to answer if what Paul wrote to Timothy to bring a specific robe and certain parchments. We know that Count Fernando Juan De La Cruz a Knights Templar buried some parchments, even a robe, perhaps the very one that belonged to our Lord?"

"Gentlemen, our dilemma and concerns are of the utmost. Somehow or other it has been leaked that I have in my possession this letter. I believe it to be authentic, but suppose the cloak is still in existence? Can you imagine if it fell into the wrong hands what a charlatan would do with it? One more thing and I will open this up for discussion and then at the end we will anoint our new Knight. Two days ago, I received a letter from a man you all know, Russell Fenneman. It reeks of vileness. This man offered me a king's ransom if I would sell him the letter. The offer was well over a billion dollars with an added offer of name your own price. Yes Mr. President your question."

"Isaiah; you and I have been friends for many years. Can you say without a doubt that the letter is genuine?"

"Buck; I would stake my life on it. One more thing, there are clues to the whereabouts of the parchments. I believe the key to the whereabouts to the robe will be found in those parchments."

"Calvin; you had your hand up last."

"Isaiah; what can we do to find the parchments. We need someone young enough with the stamina to go on a quest in search of the artifacts, a quest what some would think a wild goose chase."

"Excellent question Calvin. This leads me to the next point. Senator Richards, President Burns and you and of course I agree that the man to try and find the robe and manuscripts should be our dear brother, Gregg Johnson. Gregg; I know it's like dropping a hand-grenade in your lap that might be a dud. Our by-laws state that a Twelfth Knight must be the individual chosen for this quest. Before you say anything Gregg, we will now install you as a Twelfth Knight. Senator Richards has the longest tenure of those who are here. He along with Buck and Calvin will administer the oath to you and I will present the ring and scroll."

"Dr. Hamilton, I am overwhelmed by the honor of being selected as a Twelfth Knight. I feel totally unworthy. I can see God's hand in all of this. I was uncertain about becoming a Knight, but am not sure I can live up to the honor."

"Gregg; you have proven by your commitment to our Lord that you are deemed honorable to carry the mantle of Twelfth Knight." The Senator said.

After the Senator read the creed, they all signed the scroll then Dr. Hamilton placed a gold ring with a large Red Ruby depicting the blood of Christ on my index finger on my right hand. The Gold for its purity and the Cross of Lorraine a symbol of dedication to duty. Then the four of them laid hands on me. Cal Duckworth read out of the book of Acts. "While they were worshiping the Lord and fasting, the Holy Spirit said, 'Set apart for me Barnabas and Saul for the work to which I have called them.' So, after they had fasted and prayed, they placed their hands on them and sent them off. The two of them, sent on their way by the Holy Spirit, went down to Seleucia and sailed from there to Cyprus" (Acts 13:2-4 NIV).

When they had finished Dr., Hamilton asked me. "Gregg, let me assure you, we have no authority other than the one given to us by the Holy Spirit. What we have done is Biblical and in no way, makes us an elite group. The Bible says 'From everyone who has been given much, much will be demanded; and from the one who has been entrusted with much, much more will be asked' (Luke 12:48b, c NIV). You have been given a great responsibility, yet the only authority you have comes from God, but we are confident that you will succeed. We will help you all we can if it is under the laws of this government. Our prayers will be with you daily. One more thing, I must emphasize, we always work within the laws of nations that allow us to exercise the authority that God has given us. You are also considered an agent of God with His full authority, even to investigate criminals and their actions."

"Dr Hamilton, Mr. President, Sherriff Duckworth, Burt and Senator Richards I am overwhelmed that you found me worthy to carry this mantel, I pray that the Lord will sustain me. My shoulder will take a couple of weeks for it to feel up to par. Also, Bev and I are planning on a vacation in a couple of weeks."

Dr. Hamilton spoke up. "Gregg; do you believe in divine healing?"

"Yes sir I do, but I have never seen anyone get instantly healed."

"I am going to ask the Lord to heal you. I believe that if He wants to heal you now, He will. Let us pray. 'Oh omnipotent Father, we ask on the behalf of your one and only Son our Lord Jesus Christ that said. That if we laid hands on the sick, they would recover. I now place my hands-on Greggs shoulder per your words. I ask in faith that he be healed, and thank you. Amen!' How does your shoulder feel now Gregg?"

"It feels warm all over and the pain is gone."

"Let's see if you can move the arm? Let me help you with the sling. Now try moving your arm."

I lifted my arm and found I could rotate the arm without any pain. I let my arm hang to the side and knew that a miracle healing from the Lord had taken place. I started to weep with joy and the other men were ecstatic! They even got vocal about what had taken place, so much so that the women came running to see what had happened!

Bev came running up to me and saw that I had my arm hanging at my side. "What happened to Gregg? Mother Richards said, "why all the fuss? Praise be to God," when she saw that my arm was no longer in the sling and that I could move it freely without pain. She was rejoicing in Christ.

Senator Richards spoke up. "What we have seen is nothing compared to what God can do. Gregg is an instrument of God. He has chosen to heal him now for a purpose. God does things to honor Himself. Gregg will be on a mission for the Brotherhood and the Lord. I don't attempt to speak for God, but He knows that Gregg will need all his strength for what lies ahead. Let us give thanks to God for His mercy. Join me in prayer, and let us all join hands as we thank Him."

He led us in a prayer of thanks and adoration and said that the hour was late and that we would be hearing Dr. Hamilton again in the morning. We all made our way to our respective rooms.

CHAPTER 14

(Saturday June 21ˢᵗ)

We got up at seven thirty in the morning. We showered and dressed then made our way to the kitchen, to meet with the Senator and Mother Richards. We brought along the gift we had purchased for Mother Richards since it was her birthday. We wanted to present it to her in private. It was her favorite perfume along with a lovely card we had both signed. While she got up to get us a cup of coffee; we placed the card and gift on her plate.

She said, "oh my, what a lovely surprise." As she wiped a tear from her eye, while struggling to open the card and gift, as she read the card. "Oh thank you both, thank you for remembering my birthday. You are both very dear to us, since we have no living children, you have become our children." She reached over and kissed both our hand's as the Senator patted her on the back. We would all cherish this moment.

While eating breakfast the Senator spoke up and said; "Mother Richards and I have spoken about what I am about to say to you both. We have decided after much prayer that we want to leave a major portion of our estate to you. You are the only family we have. We know you are mature in your thinking and know that you will maintain Lords Land after we are gone."

We were speechless, and started to cry. Bev spoke up. "You are the only grandparents our boys have ever known. You both are like the parents we always wanted. We love you dearly and are overwhelmed by your generosity. Bless you both and we pray that you will both be around to see our sons' children."

I said. "Amen and amen." We both got up and hugged them and kissed each one on the cheek.

The Senator said: "Gregg, along with wanting to tell you of our wish's, I also wanted to alert you to a problem we are having. There is a highly secretive organization that we believe is killing fellow knights all over the globe. I received an urgent message yesterday from a fellow Twelfth Knight. Dr. Reynaldo Juan Cabrillo. He is a church historian. You will meet him when you and Bev are in Europe. He lives in Madrid, Spain. The gist of his letter is his concern that two men we all know of, are behind the killings, Russell Fenneman and his compatriot Max Heilman. Apparently, they have knowledge that the Robe and parchments may exist. As you heard last night, the Robe supposedly has the power to heal. So far the death toll attributed to these scum is five Knights, all of them were poisoned. The doctors have not been able to trace the type of poison that killed them. From what the toxicology reports state, the poison is like a scorpion's venom. When I read this part Gregg, I thought of this guy you arrested and has now openly attacked you on several occasions, the Scorpion. What's your take on this? Do you think he is behind this along with Heilman and Fenneman?"

"I most certainly do Sir. Now I know why he is so intent on killing me. He knows that I am a fellow Brother and now Twelfth Knight. My guess is Heilman has a personal interest because, as you know, he has a rare disease that affects pigmentation of his skin and is unable to venture outside during the day because of direct Sunlight. I might add, like the rat he is, he is pure evil and cannot stand the light."

"What kind of a plan do you have in mind Gregg?"

"The Scorpion is like a Zebra; he doesn't change stripes. He likes to be in control and may have joined himself to Heilman and Fenneman to use them and their fast sums of money. I am going to get Manny Vasquez involved because he knows the Scorpion better than anyone alive. I also have a friend in Italy named Mauricio Grabaldi. I know people worldwide that I can trust and I can rely on. Burt is my friend and like the Bible states, he is an Armor Bearer."

Mother Richards spoke up. "It is time we made our way to the chapel. I don't want to miss the worship group and Dr. Hamilton's message.

Those of us who were staying with the Richards sat in the front row. Senator Richards opened the meeting with prayer and then introduced the worship group. I knew them by reputation only, but it would be the first time I would personally hear them. They didn't disappoint anyone; they were awesome----as teens say.

Then Dr. Hamilton was introduced by the Senator. The crowd was silent as he made his way to the podium. After all the accolades bestowed upon Dr. Hamilton by the Senator, the good Dr. stood for a few minutes and just looked out at the standing only crowd, staring out at the people. Then in that great voice he articulated his message----stopping to smile and to stare at those of us who waited in great anticipation for the next part of his sermon. His text was taken out of Acts chapter eight, "Revival in the Desert." The Lord sent Philip to evangelize one man, the Eunuch. The emphasis of his message was on the importance of one soul being saved, despite the location. He tied Jonah into his message. Jonah did not want to go to Nineveh and ran from God. Philip obeyed the Lord and went gladly, while Jonah went reluctantly. His message lasted about thirty-five to forty minutes, but seemed like a few minutes. After he finished his sermon he offered salvation for those who were seeking the Lord. About thirty souls gave their hearts to Christ. The services ended about twelve thirty. Everyone stood waiting for Mother Richards to come forward.

The Senator called Mother Richards to the podium and everyone sang a happy birthday song to her. They gave her cards and gifts with a cake that read in red and blue letters; 75 more. The barbeque was also in her honor. Everyone who knows Mother Richards knows she is a Godly woman.

Lunch would be served at the campgrounds. It would be a great barbeque. We spent the entire afternoon fellowshipping and talking about the Lord, and singing worship songs to our Lord. We also heard short testimonies of what God is doing in people's lives.

Then someone asked a question of President Burns and our conversations turned political. He was asked why he didn't seek a second term. His answer shocked us all. He said, "As you all know I was a lifelong Democrat after the model of John F. Kennedy, but I felt that to be President of the United States a President had to put aside his political affiliation. My party would not support me and asked me not to run. I couldn't get a war chest because I lost a couple of key supporters. Sad to say, but money is the main factor for a successful run for the Presidency. I prayed for guidance from the Lord, He kept saying to me not to run now, but to perhaps try again in four years. I will need to get a lot of support from conservatives and independents.

My ex-party will do everything to try and discredit me. God will tell me if He wants me to run again."

I asked Dr. Hamilton a question regarding the second coming of Christ. He was very frank. He felt that we were living in the end times, based on what we see so far in world conditions. There would be a sing along and special music later in the evening. There was still enough food for those who needed more. The entire celebration ended at nine that night.

(Sunday June 22nd)

We all slept in and would eat a late breakfast. Bev and I made our way to the main dining room which was a ranch style room. A large long table sits in the middle of the room that could easily sit twenty people. Mother Richards along with the Senator plus Mary and Burt were all sitting, drinking their first cup of coffee. The Hamilton's and Sheriff Duckworth and his wife had left earlier. Dr. Hamilton had to catch a plane and Sheriff Duckworth offered to take him and his wife to the airport. They would see us in a couple of days before I had to leave for D.C. President Burns and his entourage left early.

Senator Richards was the first to greet us. "Good morning yah-al. There are no services this morning, but there will be an early afternoon service at two. Come, sit next to us."

As I took my seat my cell rang. I answered it and was somewhat surprised at who was at the other end. "Hi Gregg are you able to speak?"

"Yes Madam President I can."

"Can you meet me this evening in Houston, Texas at the Houston Hilton say six?"

"Just one moment Madam President" "Senator, can you get me to Houston this afternoon."

"I sure can. What does she want from you my boy?"

"Excuse me Senator, I'll know more after I meet with her."

"Madam President, yes I can; six this evening is fine. Can I ask a question as to why you want to meet with me Madam President?"

"Gregg, I have a new position that I want to offer you. I'll also explain why I asked for your resignation. You can turn me down if you wish, but at least hear me out. I'll see you later today. Bye."

I said a weak "ok; Madam President, by."

The Senator was the first to speak up. "Gregg; what was that all about. Is she having second thoughts about the way she fired you?"

I decided to share the call with everyone. "Dear ones, the call I received was from the President. She wants to see me this evening in Houston. She wants to explain why she fired me the way she did and has a special position she wants to offer me. I haven't got a clue, but out of courtesy, I need to hear her out!"

Bev spoke up; "Honey what about our trip to Europe?"

"Dear; I promised you this trip and we will keep it. I have a feeling that it will involve going overseas. But let's wait and see what she has to offer."

Burt and Mary both spoke up and said; "Gregg is right, wait and see what she has to offer. The aroma of bacon, eggs, and flapjacks are making me hungry. Let's eat; I said.

"Mother Richards got up and said, so am I. Even though I cooked the meal, they do smell good. The flapjack recipe came from my mother. Tyree honey, please pray for our breakfast."

I remembered I needed to call my doctor and tell him what had happened concerning my shoulder; but then remembered it was Sunday. Besides I would be in to see him Friday. I'm sure he would be very skeptical concerning my healing.

We arrived in Houston about five in the evening and caught a cab and went right to the Hilton. Bev, Mary and Burt decided to come along for the ride. The Senator and Mother Richards stayed at Lords Land. They would fly us back the next day. We had time to check in before my meeting with the President. Bev, Mary and Burt would eat dinner while I met with the President.

I made my way to the second floor set aside for the President and her entourage. As I approached her suite of rooms there were several Marines and secret service men and women mulling around outside her room. I approached two secret service people who knew me. They were people who I had worked with for years. I said; "Conrad, Dorothy, good to see you both?"

Conrad answered; "Gregg what a surprise, I never expected to see you here. Go on in the President is expecting you. But before I let you in, I need to see if you are packing. Hey I thought you broke your collar bone?"

"I did, but the good Lord healed me. He did a miracle on me, last night."

"Yeah; sure, go on in."

I walked into her living room, as I noticed she was dictating a letter as she motioned for me to sit down. I sat down right in front of her as she glanced up. After she finished her letter; her secretary left the room as the President told her she wanted to be left alone for the next hour.

She started out by saying, "Gregg, may I ask how you got here?"

"No not at all, Madam President. Senator Richards flew us here in his private plane. My wife and a couple of friends are here also. They are having dinner as we speak."

"Gregg, I'm sorry the way I forced you to resign. Of all the men who uphold the laws of our country and wear a badge, you without a doubt are one of the most deserving. I consider you to be a real hero, a man of character. I have a proposition to make to you. As you know, many of my supporters want us to trim back our military. They also want to cut back on our law agencies here at home. The FBI and CIA are also agencies that they want to trim. I am not so naïve to think that we need good intelligence agencies here and abroad. My plan is, to start a small special security unit that works directly under me. This unit would deal with domestic and international situations. I want you to be the head of this unit that reports to me, but has oversight and funding from Congress. I have spoken with ranking members of Congress and they concur that because of the size of the FBI and the CIA, these agencies are vulnerable to infiltration from domestic rogue agents and foreign subversives. Once they get in they can undermine our security. This was why I had to make it look like you and I were not in agreement on how the Bureau was to function. What do you think, would you be interested in such an opportunity? By the way your pay grade would remain the same."

"Madam President, I am overwhelmed by such an offer. I have a few questions I must ask. How many agents did you have in mind? If you want a rapid response unit, it would have to be mobile, so a private jet would also have to be part of the deal. If you want it to remain secretive, a secret mobilization location would have to be set up. A closed small airfield close to D.C, but highly secure would be a necessity. You're going to have to hire highly trained language specialists. I believe that we must keep it a small cadre of men and women. We can always add people if need be. I concur with what you have in mind, but I will need to think about this for a few weeks. My wife and I are planning a vacation to Europe. We are supposed to leave this Friday. I have your private number, so I can get back to you with my decision."

"Gregg; by all means take your vacation and when you come back contact me at this new number and I'll make arraignments to meet with you. I have not mentioned this idea to any members of my cabinet except for my National Security advisor. Oh; one more thing, I thought you broke your collar bone?"

"Yes Madam President I did. I was healed miraculously after a group of elders prayed for me from our church. I go back Friday to my doctor and see what he is going to do with the pin." (I thought to myself, she didn't bat an eye about my healing.)

"Well; I'm glad you're all right. Take your time on your decision. Congress will be going on break, but it's a good time for terrorist groups to try and do something big here at home."

I walked out the door and thought about her offer. I still loved my Country and would do anything to keep her safe, but I didn't know if I could work under this President. I would ask Bev what she thought along with Burt and Mary. I would depend on the Lord first as to what our new President had offered me. I also felt that she was holding something back. She didn't bat an eye when I told her that the Lord had created a miracle by healing my shoulder. I would be able to prove the healing by the x-rays taken of the collar bone that showed the break. I looked at my watch and decided to see if my wife and friends were still in the dining room. I made my way in and spotted Burt as he motioned for me to come over to their table."

"Where are the girls? I suppose you guys finished dinner?"

"Burt said; "they went to the lady's room and we just ordered. How did the meeting with Madam President go?"

I related to Burt what she planned on doing and that I was seriously thinking about accepting her offer. I told him I needed to pray about this for a few days and see if this was what God wanted. The girls came back and of course they wanted to know what the President wanted. I had to explain the entire scenario to them. Bev said something that caught my attention. "Why do you think she went through all this trouble if she wasn't serious, but also worried about her un-loyal so-called follower's? I think she is covering her back, in case her new FBI director flops. She also has concerns about the rise of crime and terrorist being involved with the drug trade!"

I said, "you make a good case honey for me to turn her down. Most likely you are right. I need to order. Let me get the waitress attention." After taking my order, the others waited for their food, after it arrived we sat and enjoyed our meal. We talked about our trip to Europe and what country we wanted to visit first. We would be gone a total of six weeks.

Mary said; "This will be my first time out of the Country. I am so glad and happy it will be with Burt and both of you, I am truly blessed."

We all looked at the time and decided to go to bed. We were all tired and had to be up early for the Senators plane to pick us up at nine in the morning.

CHAPTER 15

(Monday June 23ʳᵈ)

I was startled by the ringing of the phone next to my side of the bed. I hesitated as I stumbled to find the light so I could answer it. As I picked up the phone I expected the worst, a call from the Scorpion. The voice on the line was Short Stuff. "Sorry to call you at such an early hour my brother, but I just got a call from Cash. He said that the twins were in a car accident on their way back from your cabin. James is in critical condition and John has two broken legs and a broken left arm. We have been trying to reach you, when I thought about the Senator and called him. He gave us the name of the hotel where you're staying. He is sending his plane for you and will pick you up at six O'clock. It's now six thirty here in DC, four thirty Houston time. I'll see you at Walter Reed when you get here, and fill you in as to what happened. The early report stated it was a hit and run accident. I was told it may have been intentional! Again, I'm sorry for the bad news, but we now need to trust our Lord more. God bless my brother; we are praying for you and the boy's lives."

As he hung up, I told Bev what had happened to the boys. I called Burt and Mary's room and filled them in. Bev came over and said we need to pray to the Lord to spare their lives and that He showers us with His peace. We sat there as I prayed for our two sons, asking God to intercede for their lives. After dressing and making our way down to the lobby we met Mary and Burt, then hailed a cab and made our way to the airport.

The Senator and Mother Richards were the first to meet us at the airport and offered their deep condolences as we all boarded the plane and flew to DC. We arrived in the Nation's capital near noon. We had a limo waiting for us courtesy of the Senator who drove us directly to Walter Reed hospital.

When we arrived at the hospital we went directly to the intensive care unit. Both of our sons were in beds next to each other. James with all the wires and life supports hooked up to his torso, most of his injuries were to his head. I thought back when he was a little boy and how inquisitive he was. I could not contain myself from crying, thinking if he would have permanent brain damage due to his type of injuries? I thought of my other son John. With two broken legs and one being shattered which would possibly need more extensive surgery. He was the quite one of the two, as I looked at each one I began to weep and sob. Bev and I held each other asking God for divine intervention as we wept for them. I knew that God was feeling our pain.

We made our way over to James's bed and started speaking to him, encouraging him that we were there with him. While we were speaking, and praying we heard a weak voice from the other bed. "Mom, Dad, James will be all right, the Lord spoke to me in a dream." We went to his bed and leaned over and hugged him as best we could. We reassured him that he would be all right also. We asked him if he had a lot of pain.

"Mom; Dad, I do have a lot of pain, but they are giving me pain medicine when I ask for it. I don't like taking pain medicine. I don't like the side effects. I can't remember much, but the last thing I remember was seeing bright lights coming from my side of the car. The next thing I know I wake up in the hospital." He started to say more, but drifted off to sleep.

He would be in and out of consciousness for the next few hours. One of the doctors came into the room and was checking James then John. I asked to speak with him. I told him who I was. He stated that he was an internal medicine specialist, one of four doctors assigned to the care of our sons.

"Mr. and Mrs. Johnson; I need to speak with you in private. There is a room just outside the ICU we can go there. First to ease your minds, the prognosis for both boys is good. James has some internal damage; he lost his spleen, but will function ok with medication. Our concern right now is to his head; he has a lot of brain swelling which is normal for brain trauma. The next twenty-four hours will tell us a lot. John, on the other hand has a bigger problem, his right leg. The femur was broken in several places, but we feel he will recover. The left leg has a clean break and his left arm is broken above the elbow. I must add that I have never seen such fine specimens of health, which will help them recover more quickly. Then of course I understand they are both going to be divinity students after they graduate next year from West Point. It has been my experience that people of faith always seem to recover at a faster pace. Are there any questions that you might have regarding their conditions?"

Bev asked, "will you keep the boys in the same room when you take them out of the Intensive Care Unit?"

"I will make sure they are in the same room next to each other. Oh, one more thing, we may have to draw some fluid from James cranium to release the pressure. I'll keep you posted every four hours with updates on their recovery. If you don't have any more questions I need to return to my rounds."

As he left, Bev and I looked at each other and knew that the boys were in good hands. We went looking for Mary and Burt and the Richards. We found them in the hospital cafeteria drinking coffee. We filled them in as to what the doctor had told us.

Mary spoke up, "I guess this wipes out our vacation; I was so looking forward to going."

Burt said; "I know dear but, perhaps when the boys are out of danger we will be able to go."

"Bev Honey, we can go as soon as James is out of danger. Let's just wait and see how they progress. God is in control and he will allow us to go on our quest. My concern is; will they be able to stay and finish school next year, and graduate as officers? God says he won't give us more than we can handle, Amen."

Senator Richards spoke up; "I will do everything in my power to see that they can stay in. I know they want to be Army Chaplains, which warms my soul, but what does God want from them. They may change their minds. Remember it is their lives not ours and as such, they must make their own decisions. Folks; I'm hungry I haven't eaten since dinner last night. Most likely all of you are too, why don't we go get a bite to eat. After dinner, we can come back here and see how they are progressing." "That's a great idea, let's go." I didn't get the words out of my mouth when my cell rang. I recognized that evil voice as I said, "how are you doing cucaracha? I was beginning to think you didn't love me anymore."

"How are your two sons? Next time they won't be so lucky. I told you I will eradicate your entire family."

"Listen maggot; hear me good. I make a pledge to my God. I will squash you like the vermin you are. You have gotten as close to my family as you ever will. I will search the entire world if it takes me the rest of my life to catch you and the rest of your cucarachas. Why don't you change your name to scumbag or cucaracha since you only come out at night then run and hide? I make you a promise; I will get you dead or alive."

He hung up swearing at me. All those at the table knew who I was talking too. "Let's go eat, I'm mad and hungry."

We returned to the hospital after dinner and went straight to the ICU unit where the boys were. John was awake and motioned for us to come over. He was much more talkative when we got to his bed. He said he had eaten half a sandwich and sipped part of a soda. Both his legs were in a cast, the right one was in a special sling to keep the swelling down."

A nurse came over and said that James was showing signs of coming around. Most likely he would wake up sometime within the next twelve hours. She said we should go over to his bed and speak to him and tell him how much we loved him. We spent a few minutes with John and told him how much we loved him; he had tears in his eyes, and reached over and held my hand. He soon drifted off to sleep. We went over to James bed and started talking to him when he started to stir and opened his eyes. He saw me first and said in a barely audible voice; "Hi Dad, where am I?" Bev took hold of his hand and said; Hi son, you're at Walter Reed hospital. You were in a car accident; do you remember anything about the accident?"

"I'm sleepy Mom," I----as he drifted off to sleep.

The nurse had heard us talking to him and she saw him open his eyes and was as excited as we were about the recovery of James and John. She said, "why don't you folks go on home and get some rest. It looks like your boys are going to be all right, thanks be to our good Lord Jesus Christ. When I graduated from nursing school, I prayed to the Lord that He would get me a job where I could be a witness for Him, so I wound up here. That was over ten years ago. Now go on home and rest, your boys are in good hands."

We looked at each other and decided to take her advice and found the rest of our group. The Senator had offered to loan us his car till we could get ours. We said our goodnights to all and started home. As I got into the car I told Bev to buckle up tightly because we were in for a ride. I told Bev that we were being followed as we made our way to the express way. Traffic is not very heavy at night, as I glanced at the dashboard clock that read ten thirty PM. It would take all my wits to get us home safely. I said to Bev, "Honey dial Short Stuffs cell number and tell him we are under attack on the Virginia DC expressway." I no sooner got the words out of my mouth when we were hit from behind. As I hit the accelerator. I said; "thank God this Cadillac SUV has a V8 engine with a lot of power."

There were two dark colored autos after us. The one that hit us was a Chrysler 300. The other one that had pulled alongside us was a dark maroon Mercedes. I anticipated their next move, they were going to try and sandwich us between them. I purposely sped up as the supercharger kicked in. We started outdistancing my two adversaries. I allowed them to get real close to me almost totally alongside when I hit the positive traction brakes and brought the SUV to a dead stop. I had used this maneuver when I was racing cars as a youth. The guy driving the Mercedes tried to stop also, but one of his tires must have been worn thin, as the front left tire blew and caused the driver to over compensate as he inadvertently flipped the Mercedes causing it to roll at least half a dozen times. I quickly took advantage of the situation and exited and drove the remainder of the way home on surface roads. They meant business, but I was just as determined as they, and besides I have God on my side.

I called Short Stuff on his cell and told him I wouldn't need his help after all. He said that the car he had dispatched saw the wreckage on the expressway, but that there were no fatalities, but a car full of thugs. They were taken into custody because they were undocumented aliens and the police found some Cocaine and Mexican Brown (Heroin) in the car. They were bruised up and one guy would need his arm set. I thanked my friend and said I would see him tomorrow.

We hit the sack tired, and exhilarated, due to the adrenaline rush we had experienced after the attack on us. We took time to thank God for His covering and Grace, and so thankful for His sparing our sons.

(Tuesday June 24th)

We drove to the hospital after a quick breakfast. We would meet with Mary and Burt later in the day. Mary had to clean out her office, but would call me, later after they went back home. We made our way to the intensive care unit and were led into their room by a nurse. There was a doctor attending James. He looked up and said, "You must be the Johnsons. I have great news; James is in and out of consciousness and states that he is hungry, which is a great sign. He still has some brain swelling, and is complaining about headaches.

It looks like he will be here for a couple more days. We are going to move John to the orthopedic ward. We took some more x-rays of his right leg and we may not have to do anymore surgery. So, I guess this is all good news."

"Its great news and we are truly blessed." We said.

I pulled the Dr. aside and asked him. "Doctor, do you think you could pull some strings and get James a bed in the orthopedic ward next to his brother. As you can see they are identical twins, they have been inseparable since they were toddlers so it would be nice if they could still be together."

"I'll see what I can do. The problem is James has some internal bleeding, and trauma to the head, but John needs to start therapy on his legs right away. I can't promise you anything, but I will try."

We went back and forth to both boy's beds and was blessed that they were getting such fine care. It was Tuesday and from what the doctor said it would be a couple of more days before the boys would be moved. Friday, was the day we had originally set to leave, but we felt that we could possibly leave the first of next week. We would talk with the boys if they thought it was ok. We went to the hospital chapel and knelt in prayer holding hands, thanking our God for keeping our boys alive and on the way to recovery. We stayed in the chapel until my phone rang, it was Mary. I filled her in on the status of the boys. I told her that we would talk with the boys and ask them if it was ok with them about us still going to Europe. She thought that was a good idea.

We started back to the ICU unit. My phone rang, this time it was the Senator wanting to know how the boys were. I filled him in as to what the prognosis was.

"Son, Mother Richards and I were talking. The boys will need some care after they are released from the hospital. We have a fine VA hospital right here close to our home. Since John will need therapy and James will be more mobile, I felt they could stay here with us at Lords Land for if they need care or till you get back. The errand we are sending you on is a dangerous quest. It's vital that we consider the existence of the artifacts, and if they truly exist, we want you to try and bring them back with you!"

To set your minds at ease, we can hire a house sitter to watch your home while you're gone. This may sound selfish, but I just received a call from Germany, another fellow Knight has been found murdered. I need you to investigate what is going on. The boys will be spoiled rotten by Mother Richards. Talk it over with Bev and get back to me. Our prayers are with you Son. God bless."

I said I would and would let him know our decision, which I knew would be to leave Monday of next week. We would be gone over the Fourth of July. I discussed it with Bev and she said it was fine with her.

We walked into the room and saw that they were talking to James. He was awake and alert as we made our way to his bed. John was teasing him saying he was acting about his head aching to get better treatment from a cute nursing student. I again thanked God for the fast recovery for our boys. The accident had happened Sunday night, three days had transpired and my sons were on their way to a speedy recovery.

We hung around until eight in the evening, then said our goodnights to our sons. We would be back the next day which would be Wednesday. We would discuss our plans with the twin's the next day, and made our way home without incident. With one exception, out of the corner of my eye I saw a jet-black custom chopper with the body shaped like a scorpion, as he passed he waved his arm. We

were still being watched. I felt we would be watched as along as the
Scorpion lived.

When we got home I realized we hadn't eaten dinner, so we
decided to eat something. I was hungry for waffles, so we both pitched
in as Bev made the coffee I prepared my special recipe and totally
enjoyed the first one so much that I had two. Bev had one. We sat and
talked about when the boys were small and how they kept us busy
trying to keep up with them as toddlers. We both missed the years we
were learning how to be parents. We discussed the offer from the new
President and the special unit she wanted to set up. I remember that
the preacher had wanted a secret unit, but never got it off the ground.

"Bev Honey; you know that if I accept this new position I will
still be in the loop in DC. I'm in my early fifties. It's not the money,
since the Senator has made our lives secure, but as good stewards.
God wants us to use our future inheritance for His kingdom. We are
well set, but I have always wanted to see my Country stay free and
be a place of safety. Can you understand why I think I should accept
her offer?"

"Gregg, you're right. Besides she may need your expertise more
than she realizes. I think the Senators idea about allowing the boys
to stay with them during the time we are gone would be fine. I also
believe that its God's will they will be allowed to stay at the Point and
graduate with their class."

"Honey let's go to bed I'm tired, oh I almost forgot. How is your
arm since it's only been a couple of weeks since you broke it, does it
still hurt?"

"It barely hurts, and besides, I can take off the cast when I want too. Did you have something in mind?"

We made our way to our bedroom and did what married couples do. After we held each other until we fell asleep.

(Wednesday June 25th)

I awoke and looked at the clock and saw it was after seven. Bev was just getting out of the shower as I made my way into the bathroom. After I showered and shaved Bev came over to me and hugged me. She smelled so good and fresh that we felt breakfast could wait, as we climbed back into bed.

We ate a wonderful breakfast of biscuits and gravy; a recipe Mother Richards had given Bev. I was finishing my second cup of coffee, and started on the last bite of a biscuit when the phone rang. I got up and answered it. "Gregg here, what can I do for you?"

"Gregg; This is Manny Vasquez. Sorry to call you at home, but when I dialed your cell they said it was no longer in use."

"The cell was government issue so I had to turn it in. How are you doing Manny? Oh; before I forget let me give you my new cell phone number. So, what's up my friend?"

"I'm doing great Gregg. I wanted to keep you up to speed about the new drug Euphoria. Cash and I followed el Alacran to his yacht. I might add a luxury yacht and an expensive condo in the Hamptons close to the Kennedy compound. I think he has a couple of Senators in his grimy hands. The drug is coming in on other yachts and transferred to smaller crafts. They transfer the drug as many times as necessary to evade the Coast Guard. I also think he must be paying off some of the Coast Guard people as well. I've been studying this guy real hard. I think his Achilles heel is his ego. He prides himself as the number one drug lord in the world. I know that you are no longer the director of the FBI, but still have an interest in finding this guy and arresting him."

"Manny; I am still an officer of the law and always will be. I was offered a new position by our new President. You know how all presidents have czars to advise them. She wants me to head-up a new agency that answers only to her, Czar of a quick response team that can be used on any crisis in the globe. If I take the position, would you consider coming to work for me?"

"I would in an instant. The DEA is so hindered by political correctness we can no longer do our jobs as we should. As a Hispanic, I have been passed over for promotions because I didn't wear a skirt and am not ethnic enough."

"Listen Manny; keep this under your hat. My wife and I and another couple are going on vacation most likely next week. We were going this weekend, but my sons were in a traffic accident and were both injured. They are out of danger now, and will be well enough by the end of next week for us to leave on our trip. You have my new cell number, so we can keep in touch. If anything breaks on El Alacran, call me anytime. Good hearing from you Manny; talk to you soon."

———

We drove to the hospital without any glitches, and went directly to the ICU unit. When we got there, we found out that the boys had been moved to the orthopedic unit. They had made an exception because they were twins. James brain had completely been normalized. But because he had a small fracture of the skull he would be kept in the hospital a few more days, strictly for observation. They had also started him on medication that he would have to take the rest of his life because of losing his spleen.

John's leg was healing as expected, but he would have to remain with his leg in a special cast, with the leg elevated to keep the swelling down for a few more days. When we walked in, they both saw us and called out, as always in unison, "Hey, mom and dad were over here."

As we made our way to their beds, I thought how young people recover so quickly. We asked how they were. As both in unison stated they were ok. James said he could get up with help, but said his head still ached, but seemed to be getting better. John was the one who was agitated because he couldn't get out of bed. We told them they would be going to Lords Land next week. Mother Richards and the Senator were making arraignments to keep them at the ranch. They were excited about going. They considered the Richards' as their only grandparents. We told them that we were still going on our vacation with Burt and Mary. They were happy for us and told us that they would do fine. John would be able to get around in a wheel chair by the end of next week.

We spent the entire day with the boys. We talked about their goals for life and what they would do if they were unable to stay in the Army. Both said they would cross that bridge when they came to it. I was impressed with how much they had matured over the last three years.

I was a very proud parent because they had turned out as they did, clean healthy young men. I prayed to the Lord that He would find them two Christian girls that would marry them and give Bev and I grandchildren.

CHAPTER 16

(Monday June 30th)

The next four days passed peacefully, but when I got up on Monday I felt very uneasy. I felt a strange premonition----I couldn't shake. I decided to go through the entire house to make sure there were no bombs planted. Bev and I started in the attic then worked our way into our bedroom. I was even looking for scorpions as I remembered what happened a few weeks ago. Bev motioned to me that she had found something, a strange looking wire. I motioned for her not to speak, but to make signs. The wire was under the carpeting behind a dresser close to a heater vent. We could trace it to a telephone pole. At this point when we were outside I called a friend who knew how to debug houses. He would be out later in the day.

Bev and I called the boys and told them we would visit them later in the day. We decide to have lunch. My friend arrived just as we were sitting down to eat. I went to the door to let him in, but he motioned to me not to say anything until we were outside. We went outside and explained to him where the wire was laid throughout the house.

"Gregg, in most cases one wire is a decoy; we will need to find the main wire. Most likely it's in a place where we generally spend a lot of time daily. I have a hunch; let's go back into the house to the family room and see what's behind your TV and sound system."

"Larry; I have a question concerning the decoy wire. Is it a sound wire or one that would detonate a bomb?"

"Gregg; it is used for both wire tapping and setting off bombs in buildings. It's the newest type of wire in planting bugs and bombs. With today's technology, it makes it difficult to stay ahead of the competition. As to a bomb being planted in your home, I'm not sure. Let me see what I come up with. I'll have a better answer for you after I go through the entire house."

We went back to the family room. It was the biggest room in the house, with every piece of furniture new. The TV was the newest HD type on the market, a 54-inch picture screen with the latest in sound equipment. We had been in this house for a little over two years since our former home had been blasted to nothing but rubble.

Larry motioned for me to come over to the TV. He showed me a small device that had a small camera and sound attachment by the speakers, placed to look like part of the sound unit. He also showed me what had been planted underneath the DVD player, a bomb the size of a DVD that would pulverize the entire house and parts of my neighbor's homes. We went back outside as Larry spoke up. "Gregg; I don't have the equipment to neutralize the bomb. I have a gut feeling that it's tied to one of the miniature cameras. Let me call Mike Murphy head of the Agency Bomb Squad. They have more sophisticated equipment than I, besides there may be more cameras and bombs in the house and if I accidently trigger one, my wife would be a widow." He dialed Murphy and he would be here soon.

"Larry, I understand. I have a few favors I can call in. Thanks for coming, I owe you one."

As he left Bev looked at me and said; "Honey, when does it end. I'm not afraid, but I am getting tired of feeling like a punching bag!"

I couldn't call the FBI, because I didn't want the notoriety and to alarm my neighbors. It was close to three in the afternoon when they arrived. I laughed because they arrived in a carpet cleaning van. They unloaded all their equipment and within three hours they were finished. One of the guys came over and talked to me. "Mr. Johnson; your home is as sterile as a hospital burn unit. We found a lot of bugs, but one thing that bothered me, we noticed that some of the wires were tipped in poison. We are taking a sample of the wire with us to our lab to analyze the substance. These people who are trying to harm you, they did a good job in turning your house into a large bomb. You don't have to worry; you can feel safe now. God bless. Oh; one more thing, you should contact these people to give you a state of the art alarm system. The one you have now is obsolete. Tell them Murphy sent you, they'll give you a break on the cost. Goodbye and good luck."

As he left, I made a note to call these people in the morning---- "State of the Art Security Systems".

Bev had called the hospital and told the boys that we were running late. We drove to Walter Reed and spent the rest of the day with our sons.

(Tuesday July 1st)

It was now Tuesday morning as I sat at my desk reading my Bible and meditating, thanking God for the fast recovery of my sons. I had taken the advice of the agency that had debugged my home and contracted "State of the Art Security Systems" to have the system installed. They were to finish the work in the morning. They guaranteed me that they have a five-minute response team, regardless if we are home or not. If we are gone they have access into my home and the slightest noise or movement is being monitored and they respond. The installation would cost us considerable dollars, but we felt it was worth it.

I was startled as my phone rang. My gut feeling told me it was not a friendly caller. "Gregg Johnson here, what can I do for you, Cucaracha?"

"Hello Gringo; how does it feel not to be the guy in charge, perhaps I can remedy it, by sending you to see your maker! I called to tell you I have dispatched a friend of yours to your heaven. Harry Stewart a CIA agent. He was interfering into my business. This awaits you Gringo."

"Hey Cucaracha, before you hang up, I swore that if you ever touched one of my family members, I would search you out and step on you like the maggot you are. Do you think you are the only one who can follow people? You better start watching your back." I hung up on him to make him mad. I thought----Harry was dead, a man I had known for many years. I thanked God he was a believer.

Bev and I were going with Burt and Mary to a travel agency to finalize our plans for our trip at two this afternoon. The men were finishing up the work on the security system for the day and would be done by noon the next day.

We made our way to the travel agency to buy our tickets and set up our itinerary. I told Bev about Harry, my friend. We both said a prayer for his family. Burt and Mary were waiting for us and acted like a couple of kids with a new toy. I truly loved this couple, thanking God daily for giving them a chance to live as one when they both had lost their spouse.

We were to fly to Madrid and be met by Dr. Reynaldo Juan Cabrillo a Twelfth Knight. He had information on the antiquities we were searching and a list of the Knights that had been murdered. He also would give us more names of Knights that could help us. We would rent a car and spend a week in Spain, then drive to Lisbon, Portugal, spend a few days seeing the country, then on to Italy. First Rome then Venice and other cities. While in Rome I planned on seeing my old friend Grabaldi with Interpol. Then drive to Belgium and spend a couple of days there, then on to Paris, France, where we would spend a week, then on to Germany. While in Germany, we would be met by a fellow brother from the Brotherhood, then travel on to Innsbruck Austria. Innsbruck would be our main objective and meet with one of the Twelfth Knights a descendent of Count De La Cruz. He would have more information on the manuscripts and the robe. He also may have some leads as to why Knights were being murdered. I would eventually have to tell the others, but for now, I felt it imperative that I not say anything to Burt and Mary, as I didn't want to alarm them.

When the travel guide gave us our itinerary we all looked to our trip with great anticipation. If we had time we would visit some of the Baltic States as well. It all depended on the progress of our quest. I was sure that the killings were related to the discovery of the artifacts. I knew that my nemesis the Scorpion was involved up to his eyeballs. I prayed to God for the arrest of the Scorpion, Heilman and Fenneman.

All these things were running through my mind; along with the safety of my friends and Bev.

We were set to fly out at eleven PM next Saturday the fifth of July on Iberia airlines and arrive around six AM on Sunday morning. International flights can mess you up, but with all the flying Burt and I have done we were used to it, but not so with Mary and Bev. As we made our way to our cars in the parking lot next to the travel agency, I caught a glimpse of a familiar motorcycle, with a guy staring at me as he started his bike up. I waited for him to pull out, but he changed his mind. I noticed that his leathers were black with a blue scorpion painted on his jacket. He resembled the Scorpion, but was much younger. He could have been the Scorpions son or a younger brother. Bev spoke up; "Honey who is that man in the strange looking outfit, He acts like he knows you."

"Bev, that guy is one of the henchmen that works for the Scorpion. I hope you caught a good look at him. Remember if you see him again and I'm with you let me know right away. If he's anything like his mentor, he is a sadistic killer."

"Gregg dear, how can decent people live frightened all the time. You had better pack my weapon as well for our trip, besides my permit is international and most countries will honor it. I would use it only to defend my life and those whom I love. I am sure glad you showed me how to use a firearm. Honey lets go, he makes me feel like I need a bath."

We pulled away from the parking lot and made our way to Walter Reed Hospital. The boys were ecstatic to see us as we were.

We spent a great evening with our sons making plans about their lives and us as their parents. We felt so blessed that they had grown to be mature young men. The plan was to release them to the Senator and Mother Richards this coming Thursday the third of July. The Senator had decided to have his private plane pick up the boys. A special hospital bed had to be rented for the care of John. A nurse was hired to help transport him to Lord's Land. He would be taken for therapy as needed. I explained all this to the twins and they were ecstatic. John would have to spend another week with his leg suspended an immobilized. We prayed with them just before we left, and told them we would see them off Thursday July the third. We had a lot to do in preparing for our trip on Saturday.

Friday being the fourth of July we would spend at home getting ready for our trip. We went to a special service held at our church and told our minister we would be gone for a few weeks. He and his elders prayed for us for God's protection and peace.

CHAPTER 17

(Saturday July 5th)

Saturday the fifth of July arrived. The Senators plane had come and taken the boys to Lords Land. They were set on fishing with the Senator and Calvin Duckworth. I had to beg off for the fishing derby because of our leaving for Spain. Our sons would be in secure hands with the Senator and Mother Richards.

———

We had spent the entire fourth packing and repacking. If you have ever gone on a trip, you know you always pack far too much. We were so excited that when we got through with the first packing, then repacked a second time, we looked at each other and started to laugh. We laughed so hard we didn't hear the phone ring until about the eighth or ninth ring.

I picked up the phone; "hello, Gregg Johnson speaking"

The voice on the line was a big surprise, "Mr. Johnson, this is a fellow brother and Knight; Dr. Reynaldo Juan Cabrillo. We are supposed to meet sometime in the morning, here in Madrid. I was calling to verify what time your plane would land. I also need to know how many are in your party, so that I can drive a large enough vehicle to transport you and your luggage."

I responded and told him there would be four of us. I also asked how I would recognize him.

"You will know me when you see me if you look for a tall white haired man in his seventies. I usually wear a large gold cross. I will have on a black jacket, a grey pair of slacks. I will also be wearing a black turtle neck shirt. I have a mustache and a goatee. My wife and I look forward to meeting you. We will be praying for a safe flight for both of you."

"Thank you Dr Cabrillo, it will be our pleasure to meet you. I think our flight is scheduled to land between six and seven in the morning----Madrid time. Before you hang up, could you give me an answer, how many Twelfth Knights have been murdered?"

"At last count there were six men who have been assassinated. Interpol believes that there may have been more, because of the different countries worldwide where we have Knights living. There were one hundred and forty-four, now a hundred thirty-eight. At this rate, we will be decimated, good honest dedicated men of God killed! Sorry; but I need to hang up, I am meeting with a dear brother in a few minutes. I will see you on the sixth. Day Madrid time, we will discuss the problem when we see each other." Bye."

"Good bye Dr. Cabrillo, see you soon."

As he hung up, I thought that he sounded like a nice descent man whom I looked forward to meeting. Little did I realize what awaited us?

We arrived at the airport three hours before our flight departure. We checked in all our baggage, as each piece was opened and inspected. Since 9/11 all luggage had to be inspected then weighed. We were over the limit so we had to pay for the extra pounds. Burt and Mary were right on the money when they weighed their luggage. Of course, we had to prove we had special permits for our guns. After we checked in and were assigned our boarding passes, we decided to have a cup of coffee and a piece of pie.

We found a nice table and looked at our watches and realized that we had over an hour and a half before we would be seated in the plane. While sitting, and sipping my coffee I glanced at a table and saw an individual that I had seen before, but couldn't recall where?

I said to Burt, "Burt, do you see those two guys sitting in the back row of tables?"

"Yeah Gregg: Why?"

"Have you seen the one staring at us before, or do you know who he is?"

"Let me think; ah yes. His name is Harry Blackman and the other guy is Marv Wilson. They work for the Agency."

"I just had a strange feeling, but I felt that we were being targeted, by them."

"Wow man, that's a pretty strong feeling to get about a person."

"Burt; it was the way the guy looked at me, with a sneer on his face."

"You may be right. They know me, yet they didn't acknowledge me as a fellow CIA agent, especially, Blackman. We go way back; we worked on a couple of cases together. I know this about the guy, if he must kill he won't hesitate. Just watch your back. Let me see if I can find out what they're up too?"

I watched as he walked right up to the two agents. Blackman motioned for Burt to sit down. As Burt sat down, the other agent got up and walked to the men's room. I thought that it was a strange action. I returned to my conversation with my wife and Mary.

After a few minutes, Burt returned to our table and chuckled as he sat down. "Harry told me that they were on a covert operation in Europe. He wouldn't say what for, but I have a suspicion that they are involved in our mission, Gregg."

"Why did the other guy get up and leave the table?" I asked."

"He said he was sick to his stomach and felt like he had to throw up. He still hasn't returned to his table. I see Harry has gotten up and perhaps has gone looking for his partner."

After a few minutes Harry came back alone and asked Burt if we could join him in the men's room. We got up and followed him to the men's room and found Marv his partner in one of the stalls slumped over, dead.

Harry said, "Notice on the side of his neck puncture wounds, they are either a snake bite or some other highly toxic type of bite."

"I know that bite, I would bet a month's wages that it's a scorpion bite."

Burt said: "Ditto Gregg."

Harry said to me: "forgive me for staring a while ago. I was thinking what a raw deal you got as head of the Bureau and laughed at how low it was to fire you. My facial expressions were not meant towards you."

"Apology accepted. We need to call the airport security along with sealing off the crime scene until they get here. Harry, you should call it in and leave Burt and me out of it."

"Your right, Mr. Johnson, I'll get on it right now."

———

The D.C. police also were called in for the investigation as well. They arrived shortly after the airport security showed up. I was taken back that my friend Short Stuff was with his men. He came over and gave me a big hug, as he said; "Hey my brother, what a surprise. I caught you just as you were leaving on your great vacation. I wished Mattie and I was going with you."

"I do too." What brings you here with your detectives, can't they handle this."

"It's not that easy Gregg; unfortunately, the murder was committed in an international area, so we have to notify the airport security people and the Spanish Embassy. It will take forever for them to show up. Since I was on call as Captain on this night, its tag----I'm it."

"My brother I believe this was a hit taken by our mutual enemy, the Scorpion."

"Gregg: why do you say that? Did you find evidence that warrants it?"

"Short Stuff; have the coroner's people check the back of his neck, and do a toxicology exam for scorpion bites. Trust me my brother, I have seen plenty in the last month. Listen; I must leave. They are calling us to board the plane. I'll give you a call when I get back. I have something I want to ask you. God bless and keep the faith."

We boarded the plane with two empty seats, the two CIA agents. We had splurged and bought fist class tickets. Burt had enough traveler miles saved up that Mary could afford first class as well. As I took my seat, Bev took out a book she had brought along to read. My thoughts returned to the victim----a man whom I did not know anything about. I thought about where he would spend eternity. I was taken back to reality when Burt leaned over and said, "Gregg; I was thinking, where was Marv Wilson when he was stung? Certainly, not in the dining area, the killers are still out there, perhaps on our flight?"

"Your right Burt, we had better keep our eyes open." I looked around at the people who were seated in first class. If the killer was going to come after me or Burt, he would have to have access to the first-class area where we were seated. As I leaned back in my seat the pilot said we would be taking off in about fifteen minutes, and that we should have great weather on our flight. I soon drifted off to sleep. Bev told me later I had a smile on my face as I slept.

Bev tapped me on my shoulder and said; "Honey, there is a man who is acting rather strange. I have been unable to sleep, but he keeps coming by our seats and tries to touch me. I have had to lean closer to you. He gives me the creeps."

"I'll go tell the flight attendant to keep an eye on him, I'll be right back."

As I got up I noticed that the guy got up also. I made my way to the rest room, but as I did I motioned to the flight attendant and got between the Steward and this character. I told him what Bev had told me. He said he would keep an eye on him.

After using the rest room, I went back to my seat. As soon as the guy saw me exit the rest room he got up from his seat and started for the seats where we were sitting, but the Flight Attendant stopped him and asked him to please take his seat. The guy got belligerent. He was screaming profanities at everyone in the plane. The next thing I know the guy pulls out a plastic knife from his shoe. He started hacking at the Flight Attendant, so Burt and I went into action and tackled the guy and finally subdued him. The flight attendant had several small cuts, but one was deep on his forearm. It needed stitches. There was a doctor on-board who came over and stitched his arm and attended to the other wounds.

The Copilot came out to see what was going on. As he came out of the cockpit we had already handcuffed the culprit, someone brought a piece of rope. We then tied him to his seat; all the while he was using all sorts of profanities. By his accent we surmised he was Hispanic, most likely Mexican. The doctor on the plane had something in his bag to knock the guy out, so he obliged.

After everyone was settled in their seats, the Captain of the plane came back to our seats and thanked us for restraining the man.

I thought the guy was on drugs, most likely speed. The way he kept going to the bathroom to self medicate himself was my reasoning. I thought of all the people who use abuse street drugs as well as mind altering prescription drugs. OxyContin being number one.

CHAPTER 18

(Sunday July 6ᵗʰ)

I tried to go back to sleep, but my analytical mind kicked in. I thought, what was this guy's original intentions towards us? Was he one of the Scorpions henchmen, or a lunatic or both? We would know after we landed in Madrid after the Spanish police arrested him and had a chance to interrogate him.

We finally landed at the Madrid airport and waited on the Tarmac for the police to arrive. We sat on the tarmac for almost three hours. While waiting, I walked over to see this guys arm, my suspicions were right, he had a tattoo of a scorpion on his bicep. He was a killer, and one who had blown a fuse. I glanced over to where he was seated. It was next to a very attractive Hispanic looking woman. She caught my eye when I glanced over. She turned away; but I saw the hatred in her eyes. I thought; how foolish I was not to think that some woman can be just as vicious and cunning when it came to killing for hire the same as men.

The police questioned all of us who were involved in subduing the man. After we were through with the police, we finally went through Spanish customs. I spotted the gentleman whom we were to meet. I recognized him immediately, a tall and very distinguished gentleman with the cross that he wore and the clothing, along with the white hair and goatee.

He walked up to me and said; "Are you Gregg Johnson?"

"I am; you must be Dr. Cabrillo; it is my pleasure to meet you sir. This is my wife Beverly and Mr. Burt Jones and his wife Mary."

"It is my pleasure to meet you all. Come, leave your luggage. My people will carry it for you. 'Ignacio, Martin, levanten las equipajes (pick up the luggage)'. I have taken the liberty of cancelling your hotel reservations, I will not take no for an answer, you will all stay at my home while here in Madrid. Your carriage awaits you.

We made our way to the parking lot. As is my habit, I glanced around and saw the woman from the plane. I knew for sure that she was one of the Scorpions killers. She paused and looked my way as she was getting into a SUV. I felt a chill run through my body as I knew we had dodged a bullet for the time being.

Burt spoke up and said; "did you pick up on the gal? I think she is part of the Scorpions gang, what do you think?"

"Burt, you and I are on the same page about her. We must be on guard 24/7. She may have been the one that killed Marv Wilson. Let's keep it to ourselves for now"

Dr. Cabrillo spoke up as we made our way to his hacienda. "Tell me Gregg, what do you think is going on regarding the killings of my fellow Knights. Do you have some ideas about how we are going to trap this maniac and his henchmen?"

"Dr! We are fighting an enemy that wants to destroy the "Brotherhood!" We must be extra vigilant. It is evil against all that is holy and righteous. I believe that the killings are being ordered by a man they call, El Alacran. He is the head of one of the leading drug cartels in Mexico. He somehow has developed a new drug called

Euphoria. It is the most dangerous drug on the market. It is highly addictive and lethal. An unsuspecting young person will take it and after a few times of usage; their brain literally turns to mush and soon death. I believe the Scorpion is testing the drug in the U.S.A. Dr. Cabrillo----you and I need to talk in private. Perhaps after we get settled in; we can discuss a plan to catch these killers. Like any snake or lethal spider, you cut its head off and it dies. The question is how do we catch it to cut its head off?"

"Gregg that sounds great to me we will be at my home in about fifteen minutes' sit back and enjoy the ride."

I thought about Euphoria and how the drug had gotten on the market. I believe it was designed to kill a handful of people sending us a message that we were being targeted because we are Americans and envied throughout the world, or perhaps some other evil scheme concocted by the Scorpion. I also believed he was being financed by Heilman and Fenneman.

I was shaken by my wife Bev. "Gregg honey, we have arrived."

"I must have nodded off, friends forgive me. One thing about me I can sleep through just about anything. Wow----what a gorgeous home. It is truly a Spanish Hacienda. I feel like I woke up and found myself living in the 18th century."

Dr. Cabrillo spoke up, "my friends, we are celebrating one of our holidays, thus the reason for the costumes. You will see tonight when the fiesta begins. It lasts through the balance of the week. As for the Hacienda, my forefathers built it almost four hundred years ago. We grow crops in our acreage, such as figs and oranges along with apples. Our main crop is raising hogs for ham and bacon. Spain is one of the world's largest distributers and sellers of ham. In fact, the Spaniards introduced pigs to your continent, along with the horse. Further south of here is where my countrymen grow and harvest cork trees; and the raising of fighting bulls. I will give you what you call a chef's tour."

We all laughed when he said chef's tour.

"Did I say something funny?"

I spoke up and said, "Dr. Forgive us, but it was the last statement you made. Chefs tour should be a Cook's tour."

"Ah----now I see why you all laughed. In my culture, it is impolite for us to laugh when a person mispronounces or misquotes a proverb. I must be on guard with my English. Let us go into the house. My wife will show you to your rooms. I'm sure you all would like to get some sleep and rest for a few hours. Here comes my wife now. Magdalena let me introduce you to our guests."

"Welcome all of you. It is my pleasure to serve you. I have been looking forward to this meeting for a long time. Let me see if I can name you all by the description Senator Richards gave me over the phone."

She approached each one of us and named us each. She was a beautiful woman with jet black hair and creamy white skin with deep blue eyes. She looked much younger than a woman who was in her middle sixties. She took us to our rooms which were modestly furnished. And of course, with a door that exited to a Spanish garden, with all sorts of roses, camellias and bougainvilleas growing over the aged trestles. The garden truly brought out the Spanish cultural motif. I could smell the pomegranates as they ripened on the trees.

Bev said to me, "Honey, I am so glad we came on this trip. This place looks like what I imagined as a little girl when we studied about Spain in school. I brought my digital camera with enough film for a lifetime. Now all we need is guitar music." No sooner did she get the words out of her mouth, when we heard in the background softly piped into our rooms, Spanish guitar music. We both showered and went to sleep.

We were awakened in the late afternoon after sleeping about five hours, by a soft knock on the door. Martin the male servant told us that an early dinner would be served due to the fiesta. We had about an hour to dress and make our way to the Jardine, (the garden). We made our way to where there was a long table filled with all sorts of cheeses and breads. There were cold cuts of all sorts and olives of every variety, one could imagine. The main course would be two kinds of meat. A quarter of a beef was being cooked on a barbeque along with a large pig being roasted. All the servants were dressed in early native costumes. I knew that Dr. Cabrillo and his wife had added the costumes for our benefit.

Our host and hostess were dressed in early Spanish garb. Magdalena had a traditional gorgeous red Spanish dress with a black mantilla. The Dr. had on a beautiful blue black suit with a red sash around his waist and red tie. We all felt somewhat out of place since none of us was dressed in the local garb. I thought we needed to apologize to the Doctor for laughing when he flubbed the colloquialism.

The Dr. motioned for us to come over to his table. There were two other couples that were personal friends or relatives of the Doctor. They were not Evangelical Christians, but had been raised Roman Catholics. One was a lawyer named Domingo Montoya and his lovely wife Christina, they were from Barcelona, the other couple, were from Toledo, Augustine and Rebecca Villalobos.

After the Doctor introduced us to them; He prayed for the meal and the fiesta. We were asked to go to the tables where masses of succulent Spanish dishes were spread. When all of us had gone through the line filling our plates, we sat down to our assigned seats.

I was asked to sit next to Christina Montoya and Bev was asked to sit next to her husband, Domingo. Mary sat next to Augustine and Burt was placed next to Rebecca. They also served wine that had been cultivated from grapes grown right here en el Rancho Escondido, "The Hidden Ranch."

During dinner Christina Montoya turned to me and said: "I understand that you are a born again Christian?"

"Yes I am, I gave my heart to Christ in Zurich during a difficult time in my life. I was always an agnostic, but my dear wife and her friends at our church were praying for me. While in Zurich Switzerland on a special project for my Country; I was in my room after a very trying day. Something urged me to kneel and ask God to forgive me. I awkwardly asked Christ to forgive me and change my life. I have never been so happy because of it. Since then after a lot of study of the scriptures; I now know it was the Holy Spirit who convicted me. John the apostle wrote, "And He, when He comes, will convict the world concerning sin, and righteousness, and judgment" (John 16:8 NASB). Jesus was telling His disciples that He was going to send the Holy Spirit, the third part of the trinity. I was of the world until I asked the Lord for forgiveness and to be my Lord."

"May I ask you another question?"

"Of course you may Mrs. Montoya, what is your question?

"Please call me Christina. Now----as a practicing Catholic, do you believe that Mary is the mother of God?"

"Yes I do, but I am an Evangelical Christian and we do not believe that she is equal to Christ. Scripture is very clear about this. The gospel of Luke explains her role as the vessel God used to bring His Son into the World."

"I must study these passages of scripture. Perhaps while you are here you can instruct my husband and me."

"I would be honored too Mrs. Montoya, I mean Christina."

Now, all the rest of those at the table, stopped and listened to what I had been saying to Christina.

Domingo spoke up. "Gregg my friend, I would like to know if you are the same famous FBI director that has two times taken a bullet for a sitting President?"

"I am. I thought that Dr. Cabrillo had told you who I was. I am no longer an active agent of the United States. We are on a sabbatical and want to see your wonderful country and get to know the people and their customs."

Rebecca said; "Gregg you are a hero to us as well, we keep up with what is going on in the rest of the world. Our government is rather; how do you say ah---wish-wash." She continued. "We did not know that you would come and visit Espania, (Spain). We welcome you and your lovely wife Beverly and of course the Smith's, Mary and Burt. We hope that you would come to Barcelona. It is very different than here in Madrid. Even the language is different. We speak Catalonian; it is a language not a dialog. We hope to be our own country some day, but that is a different story"

We would love to visit Barcelona, time permitting. As to your liberty from the rest of your country I suppose I sympathize with your plight, Rebecca

Augustine said, "You must come to our home in Toledo. The scenery is very beautiful. We know you have a schedule to keep, but if you can squeeze in a couple of days, we would be highly honored. Thank you for coming to our country."

"I know I can speak for the others, we are so glad we came. I thank the good Dr. and his lovely wife Magdalena for opening their home to us. I generally do not drink alcoholic beverages, but I would like to drink a toast to them."

As I was about to lift my glass, I heard a familiar ping-ping! Directly across from me was Magdalena. The bullet hit her in the left front shoulder! I saw the crimson stain as it flowed from the wound. I knew that the bullet had been fired from a distance. Everyone scrambled for cover, except Burt and me. I jumped over the table and covered her with my body! It was a natural reaction for me because of my training I heard a few more pings hit the table. I hollered out. "Stay down everyone, whoever is shooting may not be done firing!"

Domingo had used his cell phone and called the local authorities as we hid from the assassin. We stayed down for what seemed like an eternity, but actually a few minutes. I got up and reassured the rest of the people, all was well. As we all stood up, the ladies rushed over to see how Magdalena was. She was very pale looking, being in a state of shock, but thank God the bullet had gone clean through her shoulder and had come out the other side of her back.

The police and ambulance arrived at the same time. First aid was administered to Magdalena to stop the bleeding. She would be transported to a hospital in the city. The ambulance left with Magdalena. Her husband Dr. Cabrillo would follow later. The police wanted to know who we were and why we were here in Madrid. Dr. Cabrillo spoke to them at length and told them we were his guests and that I was the former FBI director from the United States. I told them what I knew about the attempt. I acted like I didn't know very much. I was asked how many shots were fired; I stated that I had heard a total of four. While I was talking to the Captain of Detectives, Burt and

Mary were being interrogated by another detective. They also asked Bev a few questions along with the other's present.

After the detectives finished their interrogations they searched the patio area and the surrounding property where a spent bullet was found. It was found near a pomegranate tree. The Captain stated that there was not much more they could do at night. We were told we could leave for the hospital. I told Dr. Cabrillo that I would go with him to the Hospital. He thanked me and said he was glad I would go with him. The rest would stay. Augustine and his wife Rebecca offered to take charge of entertaining Bev, Mary and Burt, while we were gone.

Burt came over to me just as I was getting into the car. "Gregg; after the cops leave, I'm going to do some snooping around. I may get lucky and find out where the shots came from. Be careful when you and the Dr. drive to the hospital. My gut feeling is the attempted killing was aimed at the Dr. not his wife, watch your back"

CHAPTER 20

(Sunday July 6th PM)

After a twenty-five-minute ride, we finally arrived at the hospital and asked where is Sr. Cabrillo's room was? We were told she was in the emergency room being attended to. A young doctor came out of the room after about a twenty-minute wait. He said Magdalena would be kept overnight, and would be allowed to go home in the morning or early afternoon. They wanted to make sure that she didn't get an infection in the wound. Dr. Cabrillo was allowed into the room to see her. He was back within a few minutes. He said she fell asleep while he was trying to talk with her, so he said he would see her in the morning.

As we left the hospital, Dr Cabrillo said, "I believe the shooting was meant for me. I did not tell the police, but they will figure it out when they see where the bullets hit the table. I think the first shot was a test shot, to try and kill my wife first, but the next three shots were aimed at where I was sitting. Most likely the shooter was a professional assassin. He had to be on higher ground. The only high ground is the hill just before you come into my driveway and entrance. There is a grove of trees where he could have parked his car and be totally hidden from the road and from us."

"Dr Cabrillo how well do you know each one of your staff?"

"I know most of them. I only have a couple who are new. Let me see there is Joaquin and, ah yes Feliciano. They both came to work for me about nine months ago. We checked their references and all checked out with one exception, Joaquin's. The main one did not come back. I thought it minor, but I should have been more careful. In fact, when I asked him why I got the letter back, he had an excuse. He claimed he had given me the wrong address. I let it slide and did not follow up."

"Let's keep it under wraps. Let's see if we can get a response from the people he supposedly worked for and the validity of the reference. You can ask him in a casual way so if he is lying, he will try and tell another lie. If he is a killer, he will try again."

"Gregg; that sounds like a good plan, we will put it into play immediately. I have something else I need to share with you. It concerns your quest in Austria, the artifacts that were supposedly hidden by my ancestor Count Fernando Joaquin De La Cruz. I am a De La Cruz on my mother's side. His son left a partial map of where he hid the parchments and the robe. There is also a note that he wrote stating that they belonged to our Lord and Savior. I gave the note and map to Victor Van Heisdorff, who supposedly is a distant relative. I believe they are authentic. Paul in writing to Timothy in his second letter instructed Timothy; "when you come bring the robe which I left at Troas with Carpus, and the books, especially the parchments" (2Tim.4:13). Gregg, I have seen the letter from Paul to Timothy stating this very same thing. As to its authenticity, a friend of mine who is a Doctor of Anthropology believes it is authentic. If the letter is authentic. Can you see what could happen? The whole story would make men search for the originals. Like the Holy Grail, people believing the grail has healing powers. This would be applied to the robe."

"Dr Cabrillo, I concur with you. We need to find the artifacts and the robe. Can you imagine some sadistic power hungry despot wanting to get his hands on the Lords robe? Imagine if there is dried blood on it? With today's technology with what they can do with D N A. Some nut case would try to create another Christ. Suppose it has healing powers? Can you even fathom what a maniacal greedy human would want to charge for the use of the garment? There are so many scenarios, and let's not forget the parchments. They are priceless if they are authentic."

"Gregg; I am told that the ancient artifacts are hidden somewhere in St. John's Cathedral. This Cathedral is in Innsbruck, Austria. The Cathedral was built on the site of an early Christian church. The site is where my ancestors are buried. I am told that there is an ancient graveyard situated near the entrance to underground catacombs. A fellow Twelfth Knight, Duke Van Heisdorff had a map and letter, but unfortunately he was one of the Knights that were murdered. His son Victor Van Heisdorff is in hiding, he now has the map and letter, or supposedly knows the location where his father hid the map. He is in a private mountain home well hidden in the Alps, near Salzburg. It is only accessible by skis during the winter. There is a road to this hideaway during the summer months for easy access. I will give you the person who can guide you to the location. You must promise not to reveal his name or his number, his name is Dr. Gutierrez Ph.D. in Wien, Austria."

"Thank you Dr Cabrillo. It looks like we are nearing your home. I suppose the rest are still up. I could use a cup of coffee. We also need to reassure your friends by telling the truth. They will understand, and they are searching for enlightenment. Perhaps the Lord will let us witness to them about Jesus our Lord."

As we walked into the house we made our way to the living room where Bev, Burt and Mary were sitting with the other two couples having espresso coffee. Burt was explaining to them the importance of believing in the Holy Spirit and His part of the Trinity. When they saw, us they wanted to know how Magdalena was. Dr. Cabrillo explained that his wife was resting and doing well. She would be coming home tomorrow. The Dr. and I sat down to have espresso with the others. I had a piece of Spanish sweet bread with my coffee. I spoke up and said, "what have you been discussing while we were gone?"

Domingo spoke up; "Burt has been explaining the importance of the Holy Spirit in the life of a person who follows the teachings of Christ. Christina and I were also wondering what this group you call the Brotherhood is all about. Is it like the Catholic Churches Knights of Columbus?"

"You have asked a very important question. The Brotherhood is not like the Knights of Columbus. We believe that any believer in Christ belongs to the Brotherhood, based on the teachings of our Lord. The Knights of Columbus is like the Masons. They do a lot of charitable work like the Masons. Both organizations have rites and rituals. The Brotherhood is open and has a handful of men who protect all Christianity. We believe that the Bible is the final authority in church matters. We believe that all scripture was inspired by God per second Timothy third chapter sixteenth verse. We try to live our lives as Christ taught His disciples."

I continued; "I don't know how much you know about the New Testament, but Jesus was asked a question about eternal life by a lawyer. Jesus said to him, how do you interpret the law? The lawyer answered by quoting the correct scripture. 'You shall love the Lord your God with all your heart, and with all your soul, and with all your strength, and with your entire mind; and your neighbor as yourself. Jesus said, you have answered correctly; do this and you will live.' 'The lawyer wanting to justify himself said; 'who is my neighbor? (Luke 10: 26-29 NASB). Then Jesus told the parable of the Good Samaritan. If you don't know this story I would suggest that you read it, it is found in the gospel of Luke the tenth chapter. The hour is late and we all need our sleep; I suggest we go to bed. We can discuss this in the morning if you wish?"

We all made our way to our respective rooms. Bev and I went directly to bed and slept very soundly.

(Monday July 7th)

We awoke to voices outside our door. I looked at my watch and saw that it was eight in the morning. The voice's I was hearing was Dr Cabrillo's and one of the maids. My Spanish is not very good, but it had to do with the health of his wife, Magdalena. Apparently, she had turned for the worse during the night. She was now in the intensive care unit. The doctor was trying to find out more about his wife from the maid. She had taken a call from the doctor who said Magdalena had gotten worse. Dr. Cabrillo was preparing to leave for the hospital, but was concerned about us since we were his guests. I opened the door and asked Dr. Cabrillo, how his wife was responding to her gun shot? "Dear brother, something has happened. She has turned for the worst. I couldn't get all the information from our maid. I have placed a call to the hospital, but the doctor who is attending her has not returned my call."

"Dr. Cabrillo, I have a hunch. I will go with you to the hospital and speak to the attending physician. Let me get dressed and we will be on our way."

"Thank you my brother, I am deeply grateful."

Bev had heard our conversation and said let me say a prayer for you and your journey to the hospital. "We will be praying for Magdalena."

CHAPTER 22

(July, 7ᵗʰ 9:00am)

We made our way to the garage and this time we decided to take his sports car. It was a Lamborghini made especially for the Doctor. It took us less than fifteen minutes to get to our destination, as we hit speeds of close to one hundred fifty miles per hour. When we arrived, we went immediately to the intensive care unit. I asked to speak to the head physician in charge. Within a few minutes a very distinguished looking doctor who was a leading Internist came and introduced himself. "I am doctor Machado----you are? I did not catch your name."

"I am Gregg Johnson; former head of the Federal Bureau of Investigation in the United States."

"What can I do for you Mr. Johnson?"

"I am a friend of the patient, Mrs. Cabrillo. She was shot last night. I suggest you contact your local police and ask them if they have the spent bullet? I believe that they will find that the bullet was laced with the venom of the highly toxic sting of the Black Scorpion. I suggest that you contact the hospital toxicologist. Have him do some blood work on Mrs. Cabrillo to substantiate my words and get some anti-venom of the Fat-tail Scorpion right away. If my hunch is right, you will need to treat her with the anti venom ASP."

"If you are right Mr. Johnson, we will save her life. We will do a blood analysis immediately. We have some anti-venom on hand. Excuse me I will attend to this personally. I will let you know just as soon we get the test results."

I went over to where Dr Cabrillo was standing talking with a nurse. "Gregg; What did the doctor say?"

"He is personally doing a special test for scorpion venom in your wife's blood. It will only take a few minutes." I then explained to him my hunch, he concurred with me that what the Internist was doing was right.

I hadn't had a cup of coffee yet so I asked Dr Cabrillo to come and get me when they had the results of the test. I made my way to a coffee bar and ordered a piece of sweet bread and a cup of plain coffee, with lots of cream. Spanish coffee is very strong. I spotted a table and sat down next to two doctors. They were discussing the politics of Spain, as to how intrusive their government was. They were speaking in English so I tried not to let on that I was an American. One of them leaned over and said, "You are an American are you not?"

"Yes I am, I'm sorry that I overheard what you were saying, I didn't mean to eves-drop."

"What is this eves-drop mean?"

"It's a saying that we use in the United States. It means to listen to another's conversation without being part of the conversation."

"Thank you for telling us. We are both physicians here at the hospital. May I ask why you are here?"

"Not at all, I am here with a friend to see his wife. She is a patient who happens to be very ill. I have a question for you both, how do you deal with the issue of government run health care?"

"We are sorry to hear about your friend, but as to your question on health care, it can be very frustrating at times, but it is better than no care at all."

The other one said; "You look familiar to me, have we met before?"

"No, I don't think so. This is my first time here in Madrid."

"Ah; yes----you are the former FBI director. We saw your picture on our television. It is an honor and pleasure to have met you. Enjoy your stay in our country."

They both got up and shook hands with me and said that it was an honor to have such a distinguished person in their midst. They each gave me their personal business cards. I returned to my coffee and pastry. Dr Cabrillo found me and said that Dr Machado wanted to see me.

We went back to the intensive care unit and were both let into Magdalena's room. "Oh, Mr. Johnson, thank you ever so much for your hunch and your expertise. You were right. The spent shell is now part of the evidence in an attempted murder plot. She would have died of scorpion venom since we normally don't do this type of test, unless we are told that they were bitten by a scorpion. We will be able to let her go home by tomorrow. She was lucky the bullet didn't have a lot of venom in it. You may stay and visit with her for awhile. We will transfer her to another floor after you leave. Once again thank you for your help."

After visiting with Magdalena for a couple of hours we decided to go back to the Hacienda. As we were heading out of the city and reaching the suburbs, the Doctor said; "Gregg we are being followed. Look in your side mirror. There is a black Mercedes gaining on us"

"I spotted him in the parking lot; Doctor. They had a chance to hit us on the first expressway, but didn't. One way to find out if they plan on taking us out, is to pull over and see what they do?"

"Gregg; isn't this a bit risky? I am not a trained peace officer, and really not much good when it comes to this sort of thing, how you say in your country, cops and robbers."

"Don't worry Dr. Cabrillo. Let me drive, since I have much more experience at evading killers. I carry a weapon, as I have an international permit, but the police may not recognize it here in Spain. I will use the gun if need be, but only to protect us."

He slid over after I got out of the passenger seat. I got behind the wheel just as the big Mercedes pulled up behind us. Two men got out and came over to the car. One of them spoke up. "Are you Gregg Johnson/"

"I am, why do you ask?"

"I'm sorry we scared you guys, but the Senator sent us to keep an eye out for you Mr. Johnson. He was afraid that you might be put in a compromised situation, like having to shoot someone. Go ahead and go back to Dr. Cabrillo's hacienda. We'll stay far enough back that you won't know were even around."

"Thanks guys, I didn't get your names? Oh; and tell the Senator thanks"

"Sorry Mr. Johnson, Frank and Harry Smith, see you later."

I laughed as I got back into the car and kept laughing. The good Doctor wanted to know what was so funny. I told him that they had been sent to guard us and that their names were aliases. The Doctor still couldn't understand why I was laughing. I tried to explain it to him, but he couldn't grasp American humor. We drove the rest of the way in silence.

I stopped just outside the entrance to the hacienda and saw a well constructed fence and gate surrounded the property. As I got out of the car I looked around to see if we were being watched from a distance. Only Frank and Harry were way back. I thought we were alone as I spotted a flash in the distance assuring me they were on the job. I walked over and examined the area where the shots could have been fired. There were some thick bushes and several full leafed trees that lined the area just next to the entrance. I walked over to where I felt I could see the patio with a night vision scope and tables that were still set. Even with the naked eye you could see where the assassin fired and missed in his attempt. I determined that most likely this was the place that the assassin shot his rifle from. There were some scrubby bushes where I found four spent shell casings. I picked one up with my pen and immediately saw that it was a favorite caliber with hunters, a Winchester 30/06.

"Dr. Cabrillo would you do me a favor. Please drive the car to the house and call the police. I will stay here and protect the scene of the crime."

"Yes right away Gregg. I will tell your lovely wife that you are all right."

I watched him drive down the small hill to where his home was and thanked the good Lord for protecting him from harm. He was a very nice man and a dear brother. He had earned a Doctor of Theology from the University of Madrid. He had written a few commentaries on the General Epistles, James, then Second Peter and was currently writing one on the Gospel of John.

I waited for about twenty minutes when the Doctor came back

with Bev. She said that Burt and Mary were discussing the Apocalypse with Domingo and Christina. Rebecca and Augustine were listening very intently, but hadn't joined in yet. I knew Burt would be gentle in his explanation about God's word.

"Bev honey, how are you holding up, I'm sorry this all had to take place on our vacation."

"I am enjoying every minute of my stay, and because I am part of what is going on. I also found out that Augustine is Dr. Cabrillo's second cousin. Rebecca and Christina are sisters."

I started to say something when the police arrived. I purposely stood by the area where I had found the spent shells. I had also found a button from a man's jacket. I had marked the tree with my handkerchief and had covered the footprints in the softer ground. I also found some Cuban cigar butts. These were clues that the locals could use.

The inspector said that their crime scene investigators were on their way and would be here shortly. He thanked me for protecting the crime scene. I told him I had found the four spent shell casings and the button along with some suspicious shoe prints. There are also a lot of cigar butts. The cigar butts intrigued me because they were Cuban.

The inspector spoke up; "Mr. Johnson you did an excellent job of protecting the integrity of the crime scene, you wouldn't be interested in coming to work for us, would you? I am only joking with you. I am very happy that we have a man with so much expertise about crime visiting Espana. We are honored----Sir."

"Thank you inspector for your kind words, it has been my experience that many crime scenes have been compromised by well meaning people, thus have negated the use of good evidence because they thought they were helping us solve a crime. I tried to take every precaution when I did what I did. If I can be of more service, please feel free to call upon me. I will be here a couple of more days with Dr. Cabrillo."

We went to the house. The Doctors people had prepared a meal for us. When I looked at my watch I noticed that it was two thirty their time. I didn't know I was hungry until I saw what we were about to eat. A table was prepared in the garden by a gorgeous fountain, where several species of birds would come and bathe. What amazed me was that the birds were not afraid to come so near to humans.

During lunch Christina asked me if I would finish the parable of the Good Samaritan. I said; "did all of you read the passage of scripture in the Bible?" To my surprise all of them said that they had. "First, why did Jesus tell the story in the first place?"

Rebecca responded: "Because a lawyer challenged Him as to who was his neighbor."

"Good answer" I said. "Jesus was trying to show us who our neighbors are. What about the rest of you, do you agree with Rebecca's answer?

In unison, they all answered yes.

Domingo asked me, "Why did the Levite and the Priest ignore the man and walk on the other side of the road?"

"There are many reasons for the actions of the two zealots. The main reason for them both was based on the Levitical law. The law said that if any one touched a person who was unclean, they would be contaminated for a limited time. Both the Priest and the Levite would have been disallowed from serving in the temple for a short period. But they failed to use compassion to a neighbor. The Samaritans were scorned by the Jews because of their mixed Jewish and Gentile ancestry. It is ironic, then, that a Samaritan helped the half-dead man, dressing his wounds, taking him to an inn, and paying his expenses. Jesus ended the parable by asking the crowd, "who was the neighbor" (Luke 10:36 NASB). The Samaritan was the one who proved that he loved his neighbor."

Bev said; "We should all be careful about ignoring a person in need, regardless of his position in life we are to offer help as Christ did here on Earth. Amen!"

"Thank you all for taking the time to read the parable of the 'Good Samaritan. I said. "One more thing, ask God to show you how you can be a Good Samaritan."

We all decided to go to our rooms and take a Siesta after we finished our meal.

CHAPTER 21

(July 8th AM)

We were all asleep when we were awakened by a horrific loud sound! I jumped out of bed along with Bev and ran outside of our rooms. Dr. Cabrillo came up shortly, along with Domingo and Christina. Burt and Mary had not come out of their room. Augustine and Rebecca were nowhere to be found. We looked across the garden and patio, to the rooms that were supposed to be theirs. We saw nothing but rubble. All sorts of thoughts ran through my head. Had I lost two valuable friends whom I loved dearly, Burt and Mary? Had a couple we had just met, been killed by a mad bomber?

I found myself running to the rubble and crying out the names of our dear friends. I heard a familiar voice. "Mary and I are ok. We went for a walk. We couldn't sleep so we decided to see the entire Hacienda. We heard the loud explosion. Are you guys all right?"

Bev said; "We are, but we don't know what happened to Augustine and Rebecca."

The Doctor said, "I am sorry, but they asked to be excused and said to say good bye. They remembered they had another pressing engagement, but stated that they would love to host you if you come to their home in Toledo."

"Doctor, what kind of work does Augustine do?" I asked.

"He is an engineer with a large demolition company that implodes buildings. Even as a boy his interests had something to do with tearing down old buildings. He goes all over the world where old communities are being torn down. I don't remember the name of the company. Its headquarters are in the city of Vitoria in Northern Spain. It is a Basque company. He is half Basque and half Castilian. His father is from Bilbao and his mother is from a town north of here. I'm sure you noticed that he is rather moody and not very interactive with others. That's all I can tell; oh, one more thing. He spent some time in a mental rehab hospital. He was hooked on methamphetamines, but I was told that he no longer uses the drug."

"We need to call the authorities concerning the bomb blast. Burt and I will go and examine the scene. The rest of you go into the house until they get here." As they went back into the house, I told Burt that we needed to examine the entire premises. If this guy Augustine had placed bombs all over, we were still in danger. I started with the empty bedroom next to Domingo and Christina's room. I saw nothing that aroused my suspicions. Then went into their room, I felt it was clean and then went into our room. I stopped when I noticed a suspicious package hidden under the dresser. I then went to the Doctors room and felt it was clean. Burt had checked the servant's quarters and felt sure that there were no more bombs. The police and their bomb squad showed up. Burt called me over and said that one of the servants had skipped.

"Gregg, some guy named Joaquin also skipped."

I said. "The Doctor told me that he was the last hire. He also said that the references did not check out, but hired him anyway. I've got a gut feeling that Augustine and this guy Joaquin were responsible for the bombing. Burt don't mention this to anyone----ok"

The head of the Bomb Squad came over to me and in perfect English said, "I understand that you are the head of the FBI. Could you give me your take on the explosion?"

"Sorry, but I'm no longer with the FBI. I would be more than happy to offer my expertise. Forgive me, but I have one question, where did you learn to speak English?"

"That's easy, I was born in the States. My parents were born here in Spain; which is now my adopted country. I graduated from the University of Southern California. I received a Masters degree in criminology. I went to work for the CIA, but after five years I decided to move to Spain. They snatched me up when I told them that I was a munitions expert and specialized in disarming live bombs."

"I'm sorry, but I didn't catch your name?"

"My name is Ignacio Beto Vendrell de Ybarra. My friends call me Beto."

"My pleasure Beto, call me Gregg. Listen, we did a search of this side of the Hacienda. I found a strange looking package in my room. I left it for you guys, the experts."

"Show me where it is and I'll call one of my guys. 'Raphael, I need you right away'. Thanks, Gregg, I suggest that you go back to the rest of your party. I'll talk with you after I check everything out. Thanks for your help."

I went inside where my group was gathered. They all wanted to know what the Bomb Squad found. I said it would take a couple of hours to check the entire premises. No sooner did I get the words out of my mouth when the police came in and wanted to talk to all of us. They and the two detectives who were checking the crime scene where the shots were fired also showed up as well. The two who I gave the evidence to, said that they were all done. They said that if they had more questions they would contact us. Most of the questions concerning the bombing were directed to Dr. Cabrillo. They wanted to know about Augustine and Rebecca and where they could be reached. He said they had told him they were in a hurry to get home to Toledo and he would give them their current address.

I sat there wondering how people can live their lives saying one thing, but living another life style. I was almost going to sleep when, when one of the inspectors said, "Mr. Johnson, what is your take on the bombing. I understand that there was an attempted killing last night, a shooting."

"Yes to your question, but as to my opinion, I believe the bombing and the attempted killings are related. Let me ask you gentlemen a question? Have you ever heard of a drug lord that they call in your language, El Alacran?"

One of the detectives that spoke English said that he had read a memo from Interpol about him. It had just come in a few days ago. He said in very broken English. "Forgive me esteemed Sir; but you are saying that a drug lord has risen to being one of the most wanted men in the world!

I responded, "He is a sadistic killer and would stop at nothing if someone gets in his way. I have another question for you gentlemen. Do you have a drug problem here in your country?"

The one who spoke English said, "I am not in that specific unit, but like most major countries I would say yes. As a matter of fact, a friend of mine's son died of a drug overdose, we believe, ah como se ah, how do you say ah----meth. Perdon, my English not so good. But to answer your pregunta (question), yes we have a drug problem, like any other country especially among our youth?"

I said; "This man called El Alacran is selling Meth that is laced with a drug that presently we do not know its chemical makeup, but we hope to have a breakthrough any day. Methamphetamine is the worst drug on the market. This new drug causes the drug users heart to literally explode. Some drug pushers have been known to lace the drug with rat poison, but a life committed to selling drugs as far as I am concerned is an abomination to God, especially when they sell their poison to kids."

Burt spoke-up and said; "I lost my only son in a car accident, because he was using drugs and alcohol. Even though I am a Christian; I have very little tolerance for drug pushers."

Mary said, "Burt my dear, I know you are still hurting and it is painful whenever you lose a loved one. I became a widow at a very young age. The only thing that kept me going was my relationship with my Lord Jesus Christ. He sent you into my life to fill the vacancy the loss of my first husband. I am to fill your void for your loss. It's how He works dear. I'm proud of you as my husband and a father image to my children. They have come to love you as their own father. They were all small when he was killed in Vietnam. But the plus is, you are also a grandfather to their children."

Burt stood there, then got up and said; "Oh Mary dear it's my way of hating sin. I don't hate people who traffic in drugs, forgive me for being so crude at times." Mary hugged him as both sat there holding hands.

Beverly my wife said, "Inspector, how much longer are we going to sit here and answer questions. I don't mean to be rude, but Burt and Mary lost all their clothing in the bombing. We need to go do some shopping for what was destroyed. Also, report to the United States embassy and get duplicate passports. Thank God Burt and Mary have photo copies of their passports. It is too late today for passports, but they will need clothing for the rest of our trip. We can get the passports tomorrow."

The inspector said. "Forgive me, but we are done with asking questions. Our bomb expert----is just finishing up. We will be leaving now. I'm sure he will tell us what type of bomb was used and where it was located when it exploded. Good evening to all of you. We are done here, but our work is just begun, trying to catch the people who did this horrible deed. Enjoy the rest of your stay here in Espana, and accept our deepest apologies for the inconvenience you have had to put up with. Adios." Oh, senior; the package in your room was not a bomb it belonged to one of the maids who had left it by mistake."

I shook their hands as they left and told them they could call on me any time for advice on cases. I offered my services out of protocol. I called the good doctor over and asked him where the nearest department store was. I had completely forgotten that Burt and Mary had lost all their clothing and toiletries, Bev had reminded me when she spoke to the police.

He said; "there is a Cortes Ingles department store, about ten miles from here." I will drive you there and we will take the limousine. We can go out to a nice restaurant after shopping. Let me get the servants started in cleaning up the mess. Martin my man in charge must hire a few more men and women to get rid of the rubble. Since the hacienda has been in my family for several decades, it will be hard not to notice the new construction. But thanks to God, my father left me with a debtless home and a rather large fortune. I have always prided myself in being a good steward as well. Excuse me for a moment----let me instruct my people where to start there cleanup. I will be back shortly."

As he went off to give instructions to his people, I couldn't help notice how easy it was for him. Here he was----almost killed by an assassin, then his home is bombed with two rooms and a bathroom turned into a pile of rubble, and his wife almost killed. I thought, he had truly learned to be content with what he had, even under stress caused by a crisis. I thought about a scripture, in the book of Romans. "And not only this, but we also exult in our tribulations, knowing that tribulation brings about perseverance; and perseverance, proven character; and proven character, hope" Romans 5:3-4 (NASB). He was truly a man of Christian character"

Senator Richards had told me that he was one of the wealthiest men in Europe, but also a great humanitarian. He knew God had given him wealth to help others in need worldwide. Christ our Lord said; "Give and it shall be given unto you" (Luke 6:38 a. NASB).

CHAPTER 22

(Monday July 8th pm)

As we drove to the famous department store, Domingo and Christina seemed the ones who were showing signs of trauma. I said; "Domingo and Christina, what are you feeling right now." They looked at each other as Christina told Domingo to go first.

He said; "I am angry at my brother in law Augustine and want to hurt him. I did not know that he was involved as a terrorista. We have been on many vacations together. Our children have played with their children. I feel betrayed by him; he was like a brother to me."

"How about you Christina, do you feel like talking about what happened today." I said.

"I don't know I am so confused. I feel like crying and another part of me wants to hurt my sister and her husband. Like Domingo said, we are all very close. But just suppose they are not guilty, it is not like them to leave without saying goodbye."

"Listen to me both of you." I said. "The God we serve states that vengeance is His, 'He says, I will repay' He also says to forgive. I know it's hard to understand what you're both feeling right now. I believe that Jesus Christ is holding out his hands to both of you. He is calling you and wants you to know that He loves you very much. Would you like to ask Him into your hearts; He will unload your burdens and take them upon Himself?" As we all held hands in the limo and prayed.

Christina cried out----saying; "yes, as tears of joy overwhelmed her."

Domingo very reserved, said "I suppose I do." As he choked back tears, tears of joy.

Dr. Cabrillo pulled over to the side of the road as all of us were praying in the car while Domingo and Cristina were added to the Lords kingdom. Both were overjoyed with the living water given by Christ, and the gift of the Holy Spirit.

After we rejoiced and thanked God for His mercy and grace, we resumed our trip to the department store. Domingo spoke up and said a very prophetic word. "I believe that I just heard a word from God. He said I would be used to bring people into His kingdom. I remember my great grandmother said to me when I was a little boy. 'Little Domingo, you will be used of God someday and lead people back to the promised land, Israel. My grandmother was Jewish, but had accepted Jesus as her Savior. Gregg; do you think she was right?"

"Domingo, the Bible says; 'Above all, you must understand that no prophecy in Scripture ever came from the prophets themselves or because they wanted to prophesy. It was the Holy Spirit who moved the prophets to speak from God' (2 Peter 1:20-21 NLT). God has used this time to affirm His word spoken by your great grandmother. When she asked Christ into her heart she became a Messianic Jew" I said.

Domingo said, "my bisabuela (great grandmother) was a hundred and two years old when she spoke these words over me. I always used to think she was senile, but now I know better."

Bev spoke up. "Domingo and Christina we have all been affected by a catastrophic incident. Thank God no one was hurt. God's word states, 'And not only this, but we also exult in our tribulations, knowing that tribulation brings about perseverance; and perseverance, proven character; and proven character, hope;' (Rom. 8:28.' NASB) God has allowed calamity in your lives, to bring you both into His kingdom. I am always amazed by how God can take something meant for bad and turn it into something good."

Dr. Cabrillo interrupted and said, we are approaching Cortez Ingles. Start looking for a parking space, dear ones."

Mary spoke up, "there's one right there almost in front of the entrance."

I said, Domingo and Christina would you be so kind to accompany Burt and Mary. Both of you can interpret for them in buying what they will need to replace what was burned. Bev and I and the good Doctor will meet you here around nine. Is this all right with you?"

Burt said; "sounds great Gregg, see you in a couple of hours."

After going through almost the entire store, we made our way to the designated spot we had chosen earlier, and waited for the rest to show. I spotted Burt as they all came carrying two large pieces of luggage. Domingo and Christina were loaded down with packages as well. We made our way to the car, and noticed a person whom I had seen before. The gal on the plane was with a man who I didn't recognize. I decided not to say anything to the rest of the group, but I knew that Burt had spotted them as well. As we got into the car, Bev leaned over and said to me, "Honey isn't that the woman we saw on the plane?"

"What women dear?"

"You know, the woman that was with the man who went berserk on the plane. She even smiled at us, but it was more a sneer.'

I love you dearly, but don't try to keep danger from me. I know you want to protect us, ok? If she is a killer I want to know."

"Sorry dear. I promise you I won't try to keep things from you. I leaned over and kissed her and told her how much I loved her."

I whispered in her ear and said: "We need to stay alert all the time."

For some reason, I felt a cold chill on my back, like an evil presence. This feeling was nothing new, having had this feeling before.

The good doctor was treating us to an authentic Spanish Flamenco restaurant.

Doctor Cabrillo spoke up, "Ladies and gentlemen we are at our destination."

As we got out of the car I could hear Flamenco music coming from inside the restaurant. Ironically it was called, El Matador. We made our way inside and were met by a large Spanish woman named Mama Victoria. "Welcome to el Matador, Doctor Cabrillo and I are long time friends. Come; I will give you a large table right next to the small dance floor, so you can see the Guitarista (Guitarist) and the Flamenco dancers."

Dr Cabrillo said; 'Thank you Victoria, please bring us the specialty of the house, your famous Paella, fresh baked bread, antipasto and of course you're great Sangria. The wine is a deep red wine mixed with fruit juice and carbonated water, sugar and brandy"

The first dish they brought out was a great soup called albondigas. It is a meat-ball soup and vegetables. The Paella is a dish made with saffron flavored rice with chicken, shellfish, and a variety of other ingredients cooked together. The wine, called Sangria can knock you down if you are not careful. Because it is so flavorful you need to be on your guard. For the wise, they will sip it. It was a fantastic authentic Spanish meal. For desert, they of course served a fantastic flan, a custard desert with a caramel topping. We all ate our fill and I must admit, I had two glasses of the Sangria, but promised I would never touch the stuff again. It gave me a tremendous headache.

The Flamenco Guitarist and the Flamenco dancers were outstanding. I asked the Doctor about the origin of the music and dance. He said, "the style of music has a unique beginning. Its origin, is part Gypsy, Moorish or Arabic, and Jewish and the indigenous Andalusian's. It started around the middle of the nineteenth century with the poor people. The dance and clapping of hands to the melodic guitar players rhythmic playing and tapping on the guitar. The music is not in written form, but learned from one another passed down from generation to generation. One of the most renowned players, now deceased was Carlos Montoya. Let us sit back and enjoy the dancers and Guitaristas."

I leaned over to my wife and told her how beautiful the gowns the girls wore, along with the black suit that the male dancer wore. "Bev honey, I wish I knew what the dance meant?"

"Bev said, I'm sure we can find a book that gives us the description and meaning of each dance."

"Honey you're right, when we get home I'll see if I can get one either on line. Borders or Barnes & Noble we may even find one here in Spain written in English."

We sat and enjoyed the rest of the evening dance show, it lasted until after midnight. We said good bye to Mama Victoria. It would be a night we would long remember. We made our way to the hacienda and arrived without incident. We all decided to go to bed. Burt and Mary were given another room on our side of the garden, along with Domingo and Christina. We all said good night and would see each other at breakfast.

CHAPTER 23

(Tuesday July 9th)

I awoke with a start, because of the silence in the room. I looked at the clock and saw that it was almost five in the morning. I knew that something was not right so I slowly got out of bed when Bev said in a whisper, "honey what's wrong? I don't know honey I felt that something is not right."

"I have that little pocket flashlight, so I'll look around and see what's going on." I slowly opened the door to our room and stepped out into the early morning. The next thing I know I'm laying on the ground as I almost blacked out, but was only stunned. I smelled a strange fragrance that I had smelled before. I looked up to see a dark figure hurry to the garden gate and exit. I thought that I had heard a woman's voice and a male voice, in the distance. As I got up to chase the intruders, I heard that old gravelly voice of my friend, Burt.

"Steady Gregg, get your mind clear, it looks like you got conked on the head."

"I was, and yes my head is still very foggy." I no sooner got the words out of my mouth, when we heard motorcycles roar away. "I think our intruders made their getaway on motorcycles."

"Your right Gregg; But I did find something that our friends dropped, it's a wallet. I think it might be a woman's wallet. It has that smell of perfume that only a woman's wallet will have."

"Listen Burt; remember the gal that was on the plane with us, when the guy went berserk? When she passed me on the plane, I got a whiff of the perfume she had on, it was the same fragrance I smelled as I went down. I'd bet a week's pay that it was her and another character we ran into in D.C., wearing a strange costume and riding a motorcycle painted like a scorpion. What confirmed it for me was the roar of the motorcycles we just heard."

Bev and Mary came out of their rooms about this time. They both said they wanted to know what had happened. I told them both I was all right. I said, "let's go into my room, I have something I need to run by you three.

As they came into our room I asked them to sit down. "Guys, I need to share a dream that I had last night. I believe it was a message directed to me from God, to make haste to Austria. In my dream, I meet Victor Van Heisdorff, who supposedly has a map of the phantom catacombs. Legend say's they are under St John's Cathedral in Innsbruck, Austria. I have never had a dream so vivid. Doctor Cabrillo told me his friend has a map that could lead us to where the robe, parchments and manuscript are hidden. The voice in my dream said, 'hurry, hurry' several times. This man lives in Salzburg, Austria. I have a private number where I can reach him. I will call him when we get to Salzburg. I called you together so that I could tell you what I believe God wants me to do, not what Gregg wants. It means changing our plans and devote or time in finding the artifacts. What do my friends say?

Burt and Mary spoke up and said; "were with you one hundred percent Gregg."

Bev said, "Honey I go where you go, besides I'm having fun with all the intrigue that we're exposed too. Now I know what living on the edge means. I know it's dangerous, but now I can relate to people who live this type of life daily."

"It's settled then, we'll leave right away. I'll tell Dr Cabrillo. He's supposed to pick up his wife this morning; he can drive us to the train depot. We can go straight to Austria, and when we get there we can rent a car and drive to; Innsbruck."

"Great," they all said.

Bev said, "It's now six thirty in the morning. The servants are starting their day and besides, the good Doctor is an early riser and usually gets up at six each day. I just saw the lights go on in his room. He most likely wants to get an early start to pick up his wife. Gregg honey; why don't you go and thank the Doctor for his hospitality and about your dream and our change of plans, I'll start packing."

"Ok Sugar I'll be back in a few minutes."

While Burt and Mary packed, I went to Dr. Cabrillo's room. He asked me into his room and asked me if I would join him for a cup of coffee. I welcomed his hospitality and told him the whole story about the two characters who were trying to cause us harm. I suggested to him that he contact Interpol and tell them what has happened here in his home the last three days. I told him that Burt would give him a name of an agency that will guard his home, at a reasonable price. We would eat breakfast and go directly to the hospital and pick up Magdalena, then go to the train depot.

I went back to our room and showered and shaved, dressed and went to the dining room. Domingo and Christina were sorry we were leaving, but they understood. They insisted that on our way back we visit them in Barcelona. I said we would try if all went well. They still had a lot of questions about their new faith and belief in Christ. We enjoyed a Spanish dish that they generally eat at breakfast, it is called a Torta. It is an egg dish with potatoes mixed with the eggs and baked in the oven. It can also be made with sausage. It was served with rolls and ham on the side and all sorts of fresh fruit. We relished the meal and all of us ate with lots of gusto.

After loading the car and saying good-by to Domingo and Christina we drove to the hospital without incident. I don't know if I'm becoming paranoid, but every time I get into an automobile, I start looking around, glancing out the side-view mirrors, a strained look in the back window. This time was no exception, but that little voice inside said to keep ever vigilant.

We pulled into the hospital parking lot and all of us decided to go with Doctor Cabrillo. We got to Magdalena's room and she was dressed and ready to leave. Dr. Cabrillo told her that we had changed our plans, but we would try to come back on our way home, time permitting. She understood and wished us well, and wanted to pray for us. After she prayed I extended an invitation to them to come to our home when they could get away. They promised to visit us in the future. Senator Richards had invited them on several occasions to visit Lords Land. They then drove us to the train depot.

Doctor Cabrillo said as we walked to the entrance; I will go with you to the correct ticket box. I don't know if you know this, but we Europeans depend on our trains for transportation. An automobile is a luxury for most Europeans because of the closeness of the countries. It is much more economical for the masses to travel by train. You will see some beautiful country, especially when you cross into the Alps. I wish we could go with you, but I must hire an architect or contractor to fix our home. Your train leaves at two in the afternoon. Magdalena and I will leave you here. I believe you change trains only once. God, bless you and we will continue to pray for you and success for your trip."

"Thank you ever so much for your hospitality. We are indebted to you for more than you realize. You will be in our prayers daily."

We hugged each other and said our good byes. I glanced at the large clock inside the station and saw that it was almost noon. The number of our train would be announced over the loud speakers. It would also be announced in English as well as German. We found a bench close to where we would board our train.

Bev leaned over and said; "Dear, see that man over there? He has been watching us for a long time. He has made eye contact with me on several occasions. He has smiled back at me. He is a very distinguished looking man. Do you think he is someone we need to watch?"

"Honey; at this juncture, I don't know----oh he is getting up and coming over to us."

The man said, "Forgive me for staring at you. I noticed by your mannerisms that you are Americans. Let me introduce myself. I am Professor Klaus Burger, from the University of Vienna. I am head of the Department of Archeology at the University. I am on my way home from a recent dig in the State of Israel. May I ask what part of the United States you are from?"

"It is our pleasure professor; this is my wife Beverly. I am Gregg Johnson former head of the FBI. These are our friends Mary and Burt Smith. We are from Washington, D.C., but live in the state of Virginia."

"May I be so presumptuous, but where does your journey take you?"

"We are on vacation and on our way to Austria. I understand it takes a couple of days to make the trip by train. Our accommodations are for joining compartments. We plan to rent a car when we get to Austria."

"Perhaps we can have dinner on the train together. I would be honored if you would be my guests?"

"Your very kind professor, we would love to join you, but why don't we buy you dinner?" I said.

"I insist that you be my guest's;" As he laughed.

Bev asked, "Do your trains run on time?"

"Yes my dear; in fact, we Europeans are very proud of our trains. They are very punctual." He said.

"Then it is settled, we will meet for dinner at seven PM." I said

CHAPTER 24

(Tuesday July 9th)

While we waited for our train to arrive I thought about the last thirty days, and their impact on me and my family. I decided to call the boys; then looked at my watch it was almost two here in Madrid. They would be getting up now, so I dialed the number and Mother Richards answered. "Good morning Gregg, I was just getting up. I just put the coffee on. How is the trip going? The boys are doing fine. James can do almost anything he could do before the accident, John is progressing rapidly as well, he will be fitted for a leg cast today and will be able to get around without the use of his wheel chair. They are both asleep, but I will tell them that you called. How are Bev and the Smiths doing?"

"We are all fine Mother. How is the Senator doing?"

"Gregg; I don't want to alarm you but he is not doing well. He won't go to the doctor, but I'm afraid his heart is not good. He will be seventy-seven in a couple of months. I was hoping he would retire so we can spend a few years together before the Lord calls us home. Perhaps when you return you can get him to see his doctor. I hear him coming, I'll let you talk with him."

"Hello Gregg; how are you son? Good to hear from you. James and I have been fishing a couple of times. I must say that he sure knows a lot of scripture by memory. He will make a fine Army Chaplain. John is ready to bust a gut. He wanted to go fishing with us, so yesterday we were able get him into his wheel chair and push him down to the pond. Anyway, how are you folks doing?"

I told him about the bombing and the attempt on Dr. Cabrillo's life. I told him what I felt the Lord was saying to me about going directly to Austria. I also asked him to check on the professor we had met. He said he would and that next time we called the boys would be on the line.

I hung up and told Bev about how the boys were doing. "Honey, what does your heart say about our new-found friend?"

She said; "I don't have a good feeling about him, but I may be too suspicious, but we need to keep our eyes on him!"

I started to say something when we heard our train number being called. Ironically, it was number thirteen, destination Austria. We waited for the conductor to open the doors. Our compartments were number nineteen and twenty. Ours was number twenty. The professor was in another car. Our bags were loaded by the porter in our overhead storage space. He said that there would be a dinner call at six PM.

Burt knocked on our door, "Gregg----I need to talk with you."

"Come on in Burt. What's up?"

"I just got done walking through the sleeper cars. Remember the gal on our flight? Well; she and a guy are in the same car we're in, it may be the same individual that you saw on the bike; he's dark skinned, could be Mexican or even Arab. I believe they are following us. We need to be on guard. If they are hit men for the Scorpion, they will stop at nothing to try and kill us."

"Why don't you go get Mary so we can talk strategy, and what our next step is? They would be less apt to try and hit us when we are all together. The way they operate we need to look for unorthodox ways that they would try and take us out. Now go; quickly I want both your opinions on this Professor Burger guy."

He went and returned with Mary:

"I think it best that we stay together." I said, "I wanted to get your input regarding Professor Burger. I am waiting for a full check on him from Senator Richards. My gut feeling is that he's not what he passes himself off to be. What do you guys think?"

Mary said; "He maybe an archeologist, but he has an air about himself that bothers me."

Burt said; "Amen to what Mary said. I don't trust the guy."

"Hush, for a minute, I thought I heard someone at the door." I whispered.

I motioned for them to keep talking. I pulled my Glock out and made my way to Burt's adjoining compartment. He motioned for me to wait at the count of six. We would both open our doors. While the girls continued to talk. We counted----then burst open our doors at the same time. We had caught the guy on the motorcycle listening at our door, and the women from the plane standing guard.

"Both of; you put your hands up, go into the compartment and sit down." I had carried handcuffs all my years as an agent, it turned out a good habit. I went over to where they were seated and handcuffed both together. Burt said he had bought a piece of rope yesterday during our shopping tour and tied them to the seat.

I rang the buzzer and waited for the porter to show up. I walked outside of our compartment and said to him, "We are agents of the Federal Bureau of Investigation, USA. We are on a highly classified assignment. We need to bring charges against this couple. I would suggest that you contact Interpol and have them meet us at our next stop. What is your name sir? Please."

"My name is Jose Armendez at your service. May I ask you what these two have done?"

I'm not at liberty to divulge top secrets, but trust me Senior Armendez, you are doing your Country and mine a distinguished service."

"Come, I will lock them in their compartment. I suggest we keep them locked up until we reach Zaragoza. We will arrive at Zaragoza around eight thirty."

"Thank you Jose. Let's go and get these vermin locked up so they won't do any more harm."

After we locked up the two would-be assassins, we went back to our compartment and resumed our conversation. About the time I sat down my cell went off. It was the Senator: "Gregg; I won't keep you very long, but I have the information you asked for. Be extremely careful with the guy who introduced himself to you as a professor. He is not; I repeat he is not what he says he is, he is a paid assassin. He generally travels with a man and women. The man's name is Antonio Hernandez----the woman's name is Elizabeth De Madrid. The so-called Professors name is Klaus von Berger, a defrocked MD. He is a student of Joseph Mengele who was a high-ranking Nazi doctor. He is highly sadistic. He will come on to women and has been known to forcibly rape them, but then will kill them. He is also wanted by Interpol. Be extremely careful and may God bless, and keep you protected, and please keep me posted."

I told the group what the Senator had said about our three killers. "Guys; I wonder how far the Scorpion's web stretches? He has a lot of help from Heilman and Fenneman. Money is not an issue with them.

They still want to dominate the entire world. They are not Socialist, but died in the wool Fascist. El Alacran likes being seen with them. It builds his ego, but if he deems a person is a threat to him, he will eliminate that person in an instant."

As I finished talking, there was a knock on the door, Mary got up and opened the door it was Dr. von Berger. "Forgive me for interrupting, but I'm sorry that I will not be able to keep our dinner date, I just received an urgent message. I must return to Madrid on the first train. Perhaps we will meet again in Innsbruck by the end of the week. Thank you for being so kind."

After he left, Bev said: "Somebody must have tipped him off. I no more think that he has to return to Madrid than there's a man in the moon."

Burt said; "After what I know about this pervert, no wonder I feel uneasy around him."

It was getting close to seven thirty, so we made our way to the dining car. We sat down to eat a good meal. We were looking over the menu when I heard a familiar voice.

It was Moshe Peres. He said; "what a surprise to see all of you on this train. I never would have expected to run into people who are dear to me. May I ask where you are going?"

I answered. "Moshe my brother----we are on vacation and headed for Innsbruck Austria. What brings you to this part of the world?"

He answered and said. "First, I'm sorry you are no longer with the agency, and second I'm on a special assignment. Do you happen to know a Nazi thug named Klaus von Berger?"

We all laughed when he said the guy's name, so I explained everything to Moshe, and that we had met the man. That he was on this train and told us he was getting off at the next stop to return to Madrid.

Moshe continued: "If you run into the creep, be extremely careful. He likes to kill people with a scalpel. He studied to be a doctor, but because of his sadistic tendencies, he was kicked out of his residency with only a year to go. Recently he has showed up at various diggings and passed himself of as an archeologist. He absconded with some very important documents that were unearthed from a recent dig in Israel. They are priceless, since the experts claim they are personal letters written by Paul to Peter the Apostle."

I hesitated as I started to say, "Moshe we are here for the Brotherhood, so what I tell you must not go any further than the table here"

He said, "My lips are sealed my brothers. Have you seen Rachel? When you do, tell her I send my love. I have never worked with a better individual and miss her expertise, but happy for her that she has found happiness."

Mary and Bev spoke up. "We see her on a weekly basis for bible studies. She and Cash are expecting another baby in the fall."

Bev said; "She is expecting in about seven weeks, and Cash is thinking about going into full time ministry. They seem to be very happy. Cash is like a young man with his baby and is excited about the new one on the way. Like all men, he wants a boy this time."

"What about you Moshe; are you seeing someone at present, or are you going to stay a confirmed bachelor?" I said.

Before he could answer, the waitress walked over and asked if we were ready to order? We all said yes----as she proceeded to take each of our orders.

After we ordered Moshe said; "Gregg you asked me a question

if I was seeing anyone, as a matter of fact I am. I never told you this before, Gregg, but I was engaged to be married once. She was killed by a PLO bomb, detonated by a suicide bomber that ran his truck into the bank she worked at. I am finally getting over this wanton act by a poor misguided soul. I pray to God each day that a great awakening would move through the Muslim people. I don't hate them; I blame the Imams for teaching violence and jihad. I pray that----"

There was a loud noise as the train shook and rattled as it came to a stop! The lights in the dining car went out. I had a pocket flashlight and found myself saying "Sit tight people till we find out what is going on." Finally, a waiter came to our table with a candle as he lit it, Moshe asked him in Spanish what had happened. He said it was likely a terrorist attack from the Basque people. They want their independence from Spain and will continue to plant bombs and do destructive acts to further their civil unrest. Moshe thanked him and asked him to find out when we would be underway.

After about half an hour the lights came back on. We continued with our small talk when they finally brought us our dinners. While we were eating dinner, a man came into the dining car who I knew. He was the bomb expert that had defused the bombs at Dr. Cabrillo's home. I was looking at him, but he acted like he didn't know me. I thought it was odd that he ignored me on purpose.

I asked Moshe; "do you know a young man named Ignacio Beto Vendrell de Ybarra?"

"Yes I do, why?"

"Gregg, we have a dossier on him, but nothing that we could go after him for. I personally think he sells himself to the highest bidder. For some strange reason, he always manages to show up where there is a bomb to detonate, or where one has exploded. Why do you ask?"

"I met him at the home of Doctor Cabrillo yesterday. As a matter of fact, he is sitting down at a table about four tables in front of ours. He didn't acknowledge me when He saw me. I think it rather strange that he would be on the same train we are on when it is bombed by extremist."

Burt responded, "Gregg, I know about this guy, like you----we met at the Doctors. Some of my friends believe like Moshe. They all feel that he is playing both sides. Tell you what; I'm going to pass by his table and pretend to slip, so I can get close enough to see if he smells like cordite, which is a dead giveaway that he has been around dynamite within the last forty-eight hours. I'll be back in a few minutes."

Burt returned in a few minutes and said; "the guy smelled like cordite, which only confirmed that he had handled explosives recently."

"Moshe, do you know any of the other people sitting with our suspect?" I said.

"Only one looks familiar to me, the only woman sitting at the table. She looks like----ah yes, it is her. Her name is Berta Miller. She is a known terrorist! She is not wanted here in Spain. She comes from a family of Nazi sympathizers. Her grandfather and great grandfather were SS troopers under Hitler. She is wanted in my country, but Spain will not extradite her. Franco's regime was Fascist and sympathized with the Reich. Perhaps Mr. Vendrell and his companions were responsible for what just transpired."

"I agree with you Moshe. If they wanted to destroy the entire train, I believe they could have. I think what stopped them was public opinion. Killing a lot of people would go against them and their cause."

It was after eleven when the train finally got under way. The engineer had stopped the train in time before it was derailed. Some rubble had to be removed and track had to be replaced. We all decided to go to bed, Moshe was in a different car than ours so Burt, Mary, Bev and I made our way to our car.

CHAPTER 25

(Wednesday July 10th)

We turned on the lights in our state rooms, but as I walked into the room the beds were all made up, but something wasn't quite right. I stopped, and said to Bev. "Honey stand still, there is something amiss. Burt, can you come here for a minute?"

Burt said, "What's wrong Gregg?"

"We need to check our beds and closet, very carefully. I specifically told the porter not to make up our beds, yet they are. Girls, help take each sheet and blanket off very carefully, then fold them up and place them on the table. Bev, you help me."

We began with the blanket, nothing out of order. Next we pulled back the sheets, wham----there were four Black Tail scorpions between the sheets. I could catch them with a magazine. I walked over to the toilet and flushed them one by one. I rang for the porter. When he came, I asked him who had made up the beds, he said he didn't. He had followed my instructions to the letter. I sent him for a couple of large flashlights, and went through both compartments and found one more scorpion in our compartment, but none in Mary and Burt's.

I went through my top coat hanging in the closet and found an envelope addressed to me. On the outside, it said; "To el Gringo." I opened the envelope very carefully with my gloves on. (I was glad

I had packed them for the weather.) I pulled out a paper with a message addressed to me. "Gringo, I didn't want you to think that I had forgotten you. I think you are now beginning to know how powerful my sting is. I left you a reminder. I'm sure you found them already. You have some information that would be beneficial to me. I know that you are on a quest, so am I. You will find it very difficult to achieve your goal. I am willing to pay you a lot of money for the information you have. Here is my cell phone if you are interested; 339-678-1212"

El Alacran.

I said; "the arrogance of the man, he wants to kill me, then he offers me money. I think he wants the letter that Victor Van Heisdorff has?"

Burt said; "Without a doubt he wants it, he didn't mention how much he would pay?"

Mary said. "He sounds like a very sadistic human being. I wouldn't trust him. I also believe that he is a man who has lost his soul."

"Bev said: How do we love a killer and a maniac. Jesus said that we should pray for those who persecute you and for those who spitefully use you. We need to pray that he has an encounter with Jesus our Lord. I suggest we start now by praying. Join me would you please." We all knelt and prayed that we would never let our sinful nature dictate how we feel about others. That we would put aside anger and malice towards those who were of a different faith and for those who were not believers, even our enemies.

We finally went to bed at two thirty in the morning.

We slept until almost nine, showered and dressed and made our way to the dining car and were surprised to learn that breakfast was still being served. We would be entering Austria and would see the magnificent beauty of the Alps. I thought of my love for history and about Hannibal when he and his entire army crossed the Alps. It was a spectacular achievement, today they can be driven by automobile within a few hours. We sat down and soon were joined by Moshe. We had stopped at two or three cities. I had slept through them all. I asked the rest of our group how they all slept?

Mary spoke up, "I slept very poorly. I kept thinking about those horrible scorpions that we killed last night. I finally drifted off after hearing a scuffle in our car. I think it was the Interpol police who came to pick up the couple that was taken into custody by Gregg and Burt. They were speaking German and Spanish both."

Burt said: "I heard the ruckus as well, but with my limited German I was still able to understand that those speaking German were Austrian secret police. They arrested the man and woman, then took them to Interpol headquarters."

Bev then said; "I had a frightening dream about a terrorist attack at home. I saw a group of men wearing stocking mask's shooting people running from the steps of the Capital building, when the bomb exploded and blew the building to pieces. Then I woke up. The last thing I remember was people searching the rubble. It was an awful dream."

I reached over and placed my hand on her shoulder and said, "Honey, the prophet Joel wrote that in the end times men and women would have dreams and visions. That they would prophesy so that those who heard the Lord would turn their hearts to Him."

We ordered our meals and sat in the dining car until it was almost time for lunch. Our waiter said not to worry that we could sit and enjoy the view of the Alps. We all commented on how majestic and wonderful they looked. I thought that they truly show God's magnificent sculpturing. I thought of Genesis chap. one that states, 'and God saw everything that he had created and said it was good.' With the snow, capped peaks reaching to the heavens; with the green fertile valley's sloping from the mountains to fill the rivers and streams as the snows melt, bright colored flowers filling the landscape, it is a sight to behold. I suggested we go to the club car and enjoy the scenery. They all agreed as we made our way to the glass roofed car.

I looked at my watch and saw that it was almost five in the evening as we approached Wien. We had changed our plans and decided to meet our contact man in Wien. We would spend the night at a local hotel, and meet with Victor Van Heisdorff at an address to be given to us by a fellow brother, a Twelfth Knight. He was to leave us a message where we could meet with him. He would personally take us to see Van Heisdorff. I had received an urgent message from Dr. Cabrillo, just before we went to bed the previous night. The conductor making his rounds said we would be arriving in Wien in about fifty minutes. We went back to our compartments and packed our bags. I made sure there were no surprises in our luggage.

As we pulled into the station there was a tall distinguished looking man that I instinctively knew was the man who was to meet us. He was searching those getting off the train, when he motioned to Moshe. Moshe in-turn looked around to me and signaled for us to come over to where he and the gentleman were standing.

As we approached him, Moshe, introduced me to the man. He was probably in his late sixties with a crop of brilliant white hair and an infectious smile. Moshe said; "Doctor let me introduce you to

Gregg and Beverly Johnson along with Burt and Mary Smith. Guys----this is Doctor David Gutierrez de Obregon Ph.D. His degree is in Criminal Behavior. He is here at the behest of my government on an urgent matter concerning national security."

"It is my pleasure to meet all of you and I am also a member of the Brotherhood, Christ is my Lord and Savior. Moshe telephoned me to meet him here and I must say I am blessed that I can fellowship with you all. I am fluent in Spanish and Austrian. I have contacts in Madrid and Barcelona. In fact, my grandparents are from the Barcelona area. I have some friends here in Wien. My wife and I are staying with them. I know my way around most of Austria. Come; we must be going, I have a car waiting for us, besides the hotel is not far from here----

It took us about fifteen minutes to get to our hotel. The bellhop came out and unloaded the car as we made our way to the front desk. Doctor Cabrillo had made our reservations for us. I think the name of the hotel in English translated meant Regency, or Regent. Dr. Gutierrez said he would see us later in the afternoon. Moshe could get a room across from ours. We said we would gather after we had all relaxed and refreshed ourselves.

Bev and I decided to take a shower, since the shower we took on the train was not adequate because of the problems we had on the train. Bev took hers first. While she was in the shower I turned on the local news. It was in German, but I understood a few words as they were showing a picture of Dr. Cabrillo. He and his wife Magdalena had been killed in a collision on their way home today from the hospital. She gone to the hospital as follow up to her wound. I was crushed by such shattering news. I knelt beside my bed and started to pray when Bev came over and joined me. She asked why I was praying as I had tears in my eyes. I explained to her what had happened to Dr. Cabrillo and Magdalena. We also prayed that if others were involved-—-they would be spared. We knelt there for several minutes holding hands---- asking God to bring those responsible to justice if it was not an accident. I asked Bev to contact Burt and Mary while I took my shower. I couldn't help feeling a sense of emptiness. A gentle man and a beautiful godly woman went to be with our Lord. Just as I stepped out of the shower, Bev came in and handed me the cell phone.

"Who is it honey?"

"It's the Senator."

As she handed me the phone, "hello Senator what's up? Sir, I have a feeling this call has to do with what we just heard awhile ago on TV, the death of the Cabrillo's?"

"Your right Gregg; it pertains to them, but a new problem has surfaced! The recent disappearance of your contact man; Victor Van Heisdorff, he was to contact you at your hotel. No one has seen him in the last seventy-two hours, but we have an alternate plan, you have met Dr. Gutierrez, a fine man and a fellow brother Knight. I just got off the phone with him. He also has a small portion of the map. But of course, Van Heisdorff has the entire map. I urge you to be extremely cautious with those you meet son. Oh----one more thing----I just received a letter from a close friend that lives in Caracas, Venezuela. He keeps tabs on Fenneman for me. He said that there has been a lot of traffic via the cell phone between the Scorpion and Herr Heilman. He said he intercepted a call yesterday, stating that the Scorpion was recruiting more men, especially those with expertise in assassinations. I can't emphasize enough to watch yourself. Also, don't be afraid to use Burt's expertise. He has been a covert op for many years. Make sure you fill him in as to what you and I have discussed. Before I hang up, your two sons want to say hi."

The boys took turns sharing with me how neat it was to have friends like the Richards. I asked how they were both doing physically. They were both praising the Lord for the quick healing in their bodies. We reassured them of our love as we said our goodbyes.

Burt and Mary came into the room and said;

"Mary and I have been talking about what has been going on. We don't want to be a burden to you guys, so we thought if we are a hindrance, we would leave you guys and go ahead and visit the original places we had planned on seeing."

"Look Burt, you're not a hindrance to Bev and I. We love you both very much. We would be highly disappointed if you left, I think we are safer if we stick together. I know it's a dangerous assignment we are on, but I am no longer employed by the United States Government. I must rely on God and men like you to protect Bev and me."

"Mary; we are on our own when it comes to protection, but both Burt and I are taking a big risk by putting you ladies in harm's way. I felt you both could handle anything tossed at us."

Bev spoke up. "Gregg is right, I think I could be a good agent. There is something about living on the edge that excites me. I used to be a big worry wart, not now----Gregg has shown me how to use a weapon and I will use it, but only as a last resort. I might add----this is the first time that I have felt what my husband has been through all these years. It has drawn us closer together. Again; it is your decision either to stay with us or go your own way, whatever you decide----we will still love you both."

Burt said. "We will have an answer for you in the morning. Now what was it you wanted to share with us?"

I told them everything that the Senator had said to me and the death of the Cabrillo's.

Mary said, "Can I say something? As you know my first husband was killed in Vietnam. Before he left for Nam he went through Special Forces training as a Green Beret. When he came home on leave he taught me how to shoot a weapon and how to disarm an opponent in hand to hand combat. He was worried that I couldn't take care of myself, so he rectified his fears by teaching me how to protect myself. As far as waiting for tomorrow for your answer to your question, we are staying together as a team. We started out together we will finish our quest together."

Burt said; "I guess this conversation is mute. Mary my love, this is one of the reasons I love you."

I said, "Let's go downstairs and meet with Moshe and Dr. Gutierrez.

We made our way to the main lobby; waiting for us were Dr. Gutierrez, and a very attractive looking older woman and Moshe.

Moshe said; "Folks this is Dr. Gutierrez's wife, Elena."

She said; "It is my pleasure; I hope and pray that our relationship will grow as true Christians." She shook everyone's hand and gave each of the women a big hug. She said, "I hope you are all hungry----my husband and I have chosen a very fine restaurant. I hope you like Austrian food?"

We all said at the same time. "We look forward to tasting our first meal of authentic Austrian cuisine." I don't remember the name of the restaurant, but it was very authentic, very Germanic and Austrian looking. The waiters and waitresses dressed in colorful local costumes. The head waiter came over to where we were standing. He recognized the Dr. and his wife, and said "Would you like a table up close to the stage Herr Doctor?"

"Yes by all means, Herman. There are seven of us. Four of them are from the United States. Moshe Peres is from Israel and of course my wife and I are from Spain"

"It is my pleasure to serve you and your friends Dr. Gutierrez. I have just the right table for you----you are in for a treat. We have a special entertainer, a young Violinist. A virtuoso from Spain, his name is Fernando De La Garza. He plays like an angel; you will soon see. Would you care for wine or a non-alcoholic beverage?"

Dr. Gutierrez said; "I think we will have the non-alcoholic, since I know that my friends do not drink alcohol, unless I am mistaken?"

Bev spoke up. "No we do not drink alcohol of any sort, we would all like a non-alcoholic beverage. We have also heard about your specialty----Wiener schnitzel----I have one question, what is it made of?"

The waiter answered. "Ah you have made a wonderful choice. It is originally an Italian dish----Costoletta Milanese----bread-crumbed fried veal escalope. We serve it with Erdapfel Salat: It is salad made with potatoes. You will enjoy the selection. It is our house specialty."

The rest of us said they would have the same. Mary said, "I would love a piece of your famous cheese Danish as well.

Prior to our main course being served, fresh hot bread with butter and Italian style garlic and vinegar was also served.

I ordered a cut of their famous apple strudel and a cup of coffee. The meal was superb. We sat there for almost an hour sipping our coffee and enjoying the evening----getting to know each other. One thing I can say about Europeans, they enjoy their meals by interacting with each other. I believe that as Americans we have lost this viable aspect of life.

The evening's entertainment started as we were in for a great treat. A young illusionist who was fantastic was first. Finally, the young violinist was introduced. I have never heard a person so gifted who played the violin. If heaven has an orchestra, this young man will play first violin when he gets there. The chief waiter brought him over to meet us after he finished his stint. He was a nice young man from Madrid. He spoke fairly good English and thanked us for coming to hear him play."

It came time for us to leave the restaurant. I wanted to pay the bill, but Doctor Gutierrez insisted he pay, since we were his guests. While we waited for the bill----I glanced around the room. All through our meal I had felt that I was being watched! My feelings were correct as my eyes settled on a familiar face. Beto Vendrell de Ybarra, the bomb expert. He acknowledged me by shaking his head, and started toward our table. I don't think he knew that we were on to him.

When he approached us, he said; "Hi Mr. Johnson. What a pleasant surprise to see you here in this part of Austria. I have family here, a cousin. Sorry I must go; I have someone waiting for me---- good seeing you again. Enjoy the rest of your vacation."

As he left, Burt spoke up. "I don't know what this guys up to, but I think we caught him off guard by seeing us here in Wien. I know a few people here. In the morning, I'll make a few calls and see if I can find out what he's up to."

"Good idea Burt, maybe we'll get lucky for a change. I see we are ready to leave, let's go."

Dr. Gutierrez said our car was waiting for us. We made our way to the front entrance as the attendant delivered our car. We headed back to our hotel. The Doctor said he would pick Burt and me up in the morning and get a copy made of the map. The map held the key to a lot of unanswered questions. We said good-night to the Doctor and his wife as we made our way to the front desk to get our keys.

Moshe came over to me and said, "Gregg, I have to leave in the morning. The assignment that I am on necessitates that I leave for Innsbruck. We've got a line on our friend Herr Berger. I wish we could work together. Who knows maybe our cases are tied together some-how. See you soon, my brother."

We hugged as he left. I was proud of my friend because he was willing to die for our Lord. We got our keys and made our way to the elevator and to our rooms.

I didn't realize how tired I was till after we showered and went to bed. I was sound asleep, when Bev shook me very gently and said "Gregg honey wake up, someone or something is trying to get into our----room"

"What; who? I'm awake, I put a chair in front of the door just in case. I was right about my hunch. Be very still I whispered, don't make a sound. I have my weapon handy." I slowly made my way to the door, not knowing what or who was on the other side of the door. I heard a woman's voice on the other side say, 'Heinrich; open the door.' I slowly pulled the chair away from the door with a swoop and turned on the lights and opened the door. There stood a very attractive young woman who had gotten the wrong room number. She apologized for the inconvenience and asked that I not say anything to the management. She was a prostitute, but I felt sorry for her and gave her a twenty-dollar bill as she thanked me. Bev had gotten out of bed and came over to the front door of the room and said to her if she knew Christ as her personal Savior, no but had been witnessed to by a group of college students. She said she was still thinking about what they had said to her.

After standing there in front of our door for about twenty minutes she said she would consider what we told her about the Lord. We closed the door and went to sleep and woke up when it was almost eight thirty.

CHAPTER 26

(Thursday July 11th)

After showering and dressing we made our way down stairs for breakfast. Burt and Mary joined us. The girls decided to go shopping, while Burt and I were to meet with Dr. Gutierrez later in the morning. We were excited about viewing the map where the robe and manuscripts mentioned by Paul were supposed to be. We ate our breakfast and talked about our Country. How it has become so politically correct, and how a select group of self proclaimed elitist----have taken over our Country.

Burt asked me, "what was the commotion outside our room this morning? It startled Mary and me. We wondered what she wanted----was she lost, or did she think you were her boyfriend?"

"She was a misguided soul a prostitute who had the wrong room number. We were able to witness to her."

Burt responded, "Europe is a very open continent when it comes to prostitution and drugs. I am amazed by what has happened to a continent that led the world with Christian missionaries, now less than ten percent of the population of Europe goes to church on a regular basis. Ironically Islam has grown at a fantastic pace and threatens the Europeans way of life. They believe that reproduction of children is how they will become the dominant religion and their initiating Shari a law where they live. The most recent terrorist attacks in Europe by this new group called Isis. Because of the unrest many in our country have canceled their European vacations."

Mary said; "As a Roman Catholic I am saddened by the state of Catholicism here, and in our Country. One of the abominations is abortion, killing a human life. They are willing to take the Holy Sacraments, yet see nothing wrong in aborting a baby. I sometimes get so disgusted I find myself praying that Jesus would come now."

Bev said; "I agree with Mary; I can't understand the mindset of some people. I suppose I never will, but my prayers are that our Lord will be merciful to those who have had an abortion."

I responded. "The Bible states that we will never understand the heart of man. Jeremiah the prophet said, 'The human heart is most deceitful and desperately wicked. Who really knows how bad it is?' 'But I know! I, the Lord, search all hearts and examine secret motives. I give all people their due rewards, according to what their actions deserve" (Jer. 17:9-10 NLT). Only God knows why some women choose to get abortions. They are sometimes coerced by their boyfriend or peers. I know that it's wrong to abort a child, but as a male I cannot put myself in a woman's place. If the Holy Spirit can't convict the women that it's wrong----how can I be her judge? Let's change the subject" as my cell phone rang. 'It's Dr. Gutierrez, he's on his way."

"I called you Gregg to ask of you a favor----Elena asked me to ask the girls if they wouldn't mind her tagging along on their shopping trip."

"I believe they would be honored, but let me ask them to make sure." I asked Mary and Bev and of course they said yes.

"It's all set Doctor, we'll see you in a few minutes

Dr. Gutierrez and his wife were in the lobby waiting for us. The girls said their goodbyes to us. We would see them later in the evening.

The Dr. said that he was double parked in front of the hotel and wanted to know if we were ready to go. We said let's go, and made our way to the front of the hotel. Out of the corner of my eye I saw a couple of guys that I knew were tailing us. They had been in the dining room earlier, but I acted like I didn't see them.

I've been asked by many people; how can I spot another agent or a hit man? Experience, with years working in the field teaches you to recognize subversives and other agents by their mannerisms. As a rookie agent at the academy you are taught to observe people, by their gestures. The way they walk and talk, the way they move their head and glancing behind and from side to the side. You are taught to observe the way they look at you as you make eye contact. A killer is harder to spot because he/she will in most cases not allow themselves to be seen, taking great precaution not to be noticed until they attack or kill."

"Doctor Gutierrez, may I ask where we are going." I said.

"We are on our way to a small village where a friend, a recluse ex-monk has the entire map. Heisdorff has the original. I never felt comfortable having it in my possession. He lives in an ancient castle that has been in existence since the crusades. Some of the crusaders came from this small mountain village. The castle is close to the town of Melk about thirty miles from here. I called him this morning and he is waiting for us. He is a Biblical language expert, especially Greek and Aramaic. He has been translating some of the writings on the map. He said he had a breakthrough in decoding some of the symbols. He also said that he had some exciting news to tell us."

"Do you think he has decoded the entire map?"

"I think so, he sometimes acts like a little child, but he is also a fellow brother."

Burt spoke up; "I don't know if you are aware of it, but we are being followed. It's a Mercedes and it looks like it can fly!"

The Doctor said; "There is a rest stop about five kilometers ahead of us, I will pull in; perhaps one of you gentlemen can drive. This car is equipped with everything modern to either outrun or engage in any attack. I unfortunately do not know how to drive it properly. I have a driver, but as luck would have it, he is on vacation."

I said to him as we pulled into the rest stop, "Sir permit me to drive. Just let me know ahead of time where we will need to turn off the main highway."

We all got back into the vehicle and sped away as the two guys from the hotel scrambled to get into their car. I started asking the Dr. what some of the buttons on the dash meant. The car was equipped with a turbo charger. It was even equipped with a rocket launcher and was bullet proofed. The "Brotherhood" had ordered the car for the Dr. because he was a Twelfth Knight and because of the recent killings.

I enjoyed driving a vehicle of this type as I pushed down on the accelerator to see how quickly the car would respond. It was a special built Mercedes and could fly, as I would find out. I looked in the rearview mirror and saw that we were outdistancing our two guys. I believe if there was a next time they would come at us in a chopper or a faster better equipped vehicle. I kept looking in the mirror, but there was no auto approaching us, thank God we had lost them.

The Doctor said; "Gregg, keep your eye out for a billboard on the left side of the highway. You will see a small gravel road about a kilometer past the sign. Turn right and go about four to five kilometers. The gravel road ends and becomes a private road. You will see a gate closed with a chain and lock on the gate. After we enter the private entrance we will go about two kilometers, then you will see the castle.

It is owned by an Austrian brother whose name escapes me now. The brother monk is waiting for us in the caretaker shack. You will find him rather strange, but a very loving brother."

Burt asked, "Dr Gutierrez; what is the brothers name?"

"I only know him as Brother Sebastian, but I am sure he has another name."

———— ————

We arrived at the gate as Burt got out and tried to open the gate, but found it padlocked. The Doctor got out of the car and walked over to a tree where there was supposedly a key. He came back without it as he said, there is something wrong here. Usually the chain is not padlocked, but it is rather strange that it is locked?"

I pulled out my weapon and fired at the lock and blew it off. I opened the gate as we all climbed back into the car and made our way to the Castle. Burt and the Doctor, laughed at my actions, but said nothing. As we approached the ancient edifice, I was overcome by the care that it had received. The grounds were well taken care of as you could see the rows and rows of fruit trees and vineyards of wine grapes. The grapes were starting to ripen on the vine since you could smell the fragrance in the summer air. Burt and I sat in the car for a few minutes looking and surveying the castle and entire grounds and its splendor, a stone monument over seven hundred years old!

I said; "gentlemen I suggest we split up and search the grounds surrounding the castle first, then we will meet back here in front. Let's say we get back here in twenty minutes. From the looks of the place, it would take a small army of men to check out the entire estate. Burt, you go to the left and I'll go to the right with Dr. Gutierrez, if that's all right with you?"

"Sounds good to me Gregg," he said. As he started walking he pulled his weapon. I un-holstered mine as well. The doctor and I started out as we looked behind bushes and shrubs, especially those close to the walls of the castle. We had worked our way about half way around the front and side when I spotted what looked like a body lying behind a large shrub. I motioned for the doctor to come over. When he saw the body of the man he knelt beside him and felt his pulse, saying; "Sebastian, Sebastian can you hear me? I feel a faint pulse; I will call the police. It will take about twenty minutes to half an hour for them to get here."

"That's great Dr, let me fire a couple of shots for Burt to come back. Burt was there before you knew it."

"What's all the shooting about? Oh, I see, you found our missing monk."

I said, "go ahead and make the call Dr. Gutierrez. Burt; while he's making, the call let's see if we can get our good monk to come out of it. I've checked him over and I didn't see any visible gunshot wounds or contusions on his head, but I think he may have been intoxicated to the point of passing out. I noticed the smell of alcohol on him and it wasn't the rubbing kind. I also noticed some motorcycle tire marks. I remembered it was a special tire brand found only in the USA. I believe he was poisoned, as well, but because he drinks so much the alcohol may have saved his life. Look here on his left forearm the marks of a sting from most likely the Fattail Scorpion. Notice he tried to scratch an arrow towards the caretaker's cottage, I think we need to go and investigate there first. Perhaps Dr. Gutierrez can stand watch for the police and ambulance to arrive. Doctor, is there a pathway that leads to the caretaker's house?"

"Yes; do you see that tile path that leads away from the orchard, go about fifty yards, you will then come to a fork in the path----stay left for another thirty or forty yards and you will abruptly come to it."

"Thank you Doctor, we will be at the cottage when the police arrive." We made our way on the path and followed his directions when we came upon the cottage. The front door was wide open. As we approached the entrance we again pulled our weapons and crept into the front room. I glanced around and knew instinctively that somebody was in the cottage that didn't belong there. I motioned to Burt to cover my back as I made my way into the back of the cottage. I heard some rustling of papers and pulling of drawers. I made my way along the wall to the last doorway as I noticed a light in this part of the house. I saw a familiar form, a guy in a biker's suit with a huge scorpion embroidered on the back. Out of the corner of my eye I saw Burt fire his weapon as the other intruders shot missed me by a few inches. The guy in the biker's suit jumped through the window and went running through the trees.

I picked myself up and walked over to Burt as he was kneeling feeling the woman's pulse, as he said, "I hit her on her left side in the back as the bullet went right through her heart. It's a strange MO, they work as couples to distract their crime or victims in this gang. I guess companion is gone. I heard the roar of the motorcycle as he left. I don't understand why they stuck around after I fired the shot at the lock on the front gate?"

"Yeah I did hear the bike, Burt. Thanks for saving my life, I saw her out of the corner of my eye as I was about to tackle the guy that got away."

"Gregg; did you see what she went after you with? This knife is as big as any I have ever seen. The blade has to be over a foot long and sharp as a razor."

"Listen Burt, when the locals show up we must explain what this is all about. Tell them as little as possible without lying. I wondered why the good monk pointed to his cottage. Let's go back into the living room and see if we can see what they were looking for?"

I said, "let me see the lay-out of the room, this is too easy Burt look at the wall over there, what do you see?"

"I see a knight's shield, hanging on the wall, a garment worn by a knight under his armor, and oh and a sword and a dagger used for infighting."

"Think Burt----what does a shield represent?"

"Protection, ah----now I see. The shield in-turn protects the body under the garments and the cross is the symbol of our Lord protecting his disciples."

"Burt; let's first look behind the shield."

I went over to the wall and pulled it down. There was nothing behind the shield. Then I walked over and pulled the swords and the garments nothing. I said, "that's odd, that we didn't find it in the knights clothing. Let me think----we need to think like a monk would think, It's right here in front of us. Burt, the Bible, there are only two places that it could be, either Ephesians Chapter six, or Revelation nineteen. My guess is Ephesians chapter six."

Burt was all excited when he opened the Bible to the book of Ephesians. Out popped a map that was very old, but had been preserved over the years. Burt handed it to me as he said; "Gregg how old do you think this map is?"

"Burt, it's hard to say, but my guess is that it goes back to the days of the Crusades. Listen I hear voices; we will look at the map when we are alone."

CHAPTER 27

(Thursday July 11)

I spoke up, "Dr. Gutierrez we are in here in the living room."

Dr. Gutierrez walked up with four men. Two were in police uniforms and the other two were in sport coat and ties. One of the men whom I assumed was the head of the investigators spoke up. In precise English, he said; "I am Captain Heinrich Krause of the Wien Police Department at your service, first gentlemen your names and your occupations and your business here in Austria?"

"I am Gregg Johnson former director of the Federal Bureau of Investigation of the United States of America. Here is my identification card along with my badge. My friend here is Burt Smith who is an agent of the CIA. We are both on vacation along with our wives. We came to the castle to meet Brother Sebastian. One of my hobbies is to collect religious artifacts. Brother Sebastian supposedly had found some relics that I might find interesting so we came to see them. When we got here we found Brother Sebastian unconscious's where you found him and the good doctor. We heard some noise coming from the cottage and decided to investigate. Not sure what we would find when we entered the cottage, our training as lawmen kicked in. Burt was to watch my back as I made my way along the wall. The next thing I hear is the sound of a gun going off. If Burt hadn't reacted so fast; I would be dead by now. You can see the knife is where the woman dropped it when she hit the floor, the other intruder got away. I suspect they were trying to steal some of the antiques that are in the cottage. I have no reason to believe otherwise."

"Thank you Mr. Johnson for your concise statement. How about you Mr. Smith? I thought perhaps you could add more to what Mr. Johnson said."

"It's like Gregg said. I did find it rather strange that the thieves took their time in ransacking the cottage. Perhaps they were looking for gold and silver antiques, as they bring more money, especially now that gold and silver are at an all time high."

The other man spoke up. "I am inspector Mueller; I have a question for both of you men. It is obvious that you both are carrying weapons, but I must remind you that unless you have an international permit you are breaking our laws. It came in handy today for self defense, but I would advise you to refrain from un-holstering your guns."

Captain Krause asked, "Does either of you gentlemen know this woman."

We both stated that we didn't know the woman, and it was the truth. I felt better not alerting all of Austria now with my personal suspicions.

Inspector; to ease you mind, Burt and I both have international permits for our weapons.

I said. "Captain Krause; I did hear the roar of a motorcycle as I went down, it sounded close to the orchard."

Captain Krause said. "We can leave the cottage now. Let our crime scene experts do their job. Let us walk back and see if our monk has revived enough to question him."

We made our way back to the Castle and found the ambulance

crew finishing up with Sebastian. He was sitting on the front edge of a circular fountain that had water spouting from a figure of a horse with a Knight mounted on the steed. Dr Gutierrez introduced us to Sebastian, but it was very noticeable that he was still very groggy. I attributed it to the alcohol he consumed and the scorpion sting. The inspector decided that he was in no condition to answer questions and it was decided that he needed to be transported to the nearest hospital for observation.

As the ambulance left, the crime scene people were rapping up their investigation while we allowed to leave. We made our way to Dr. Gutierrez's car and started back to Wien.

Dr. Gutierrez said; "may I see the map? Ah yes, it is very old. Perhaps you would allow me to take it with me so that I may translate the map into English."

"I don't feel comfortable letting it out of my possession, but perhaps we can sit down together as you translate the map. Maybe we can get together tomorrow, morning?"

"I am sorry Gregg, but I have some urgent business that will take me away for the day let's try for the day after."

"Dr. We must be on our way to Innsbruck this same day. We can catch a train after you translate the map."

"Gregg; I cannot do it in such short notice, but if I can keep it overnight I will have it back for you late tomorrow evening."

"Doctor, perhaps I can make a copy for you and keep the original; just in case something was to happen to the copy."

"Ah yes, tomorrow is fine. We should still try to authenticate the map by carbon dating."

I said, I will contact the hospital later. There are some questions I need to ask the good monk. You can reach me on my cell phone when you have translated the map."

While on our way back to the city, I pulled the map out and started looking at it. The symbols and writings were written in outdated French that was in vogue during the 14th century. I didn't have a clue as to what it said. Sebastian knew how to read and decipher the map. We would have to wait till either this evening or in the morning to contact the monk.

I turned to Dr. Gutierrez and asked him where they were going to take the monk?

"Wien General Receiving, it is supposed to be a state of the art hospital."

We arrived at our hotel and told Dr. Gutierrez to wait for me while I went to the front desk and asked to use their Xerox machine. I purposely modified the first copy and left some vital symbols and words off the map. I went back and gave Dr. Gutierrez the phony copy and said we would see him late tomorrow evening.

Burt and I went into the dining room and were surprised to see Mary and Bev sitting and drinking tea and eating Austrian pastries. I said----ah what a lovely surprise. Where is Mrs. Gutierrez?"

Bev said; "Hi honey we didn't expect to see you so soon, Elena dropped us off about an hour ago."

We sat down and joined the girls for a cup of coffee and some pastry. I said to Burt; "the reason I changed my mind to drive directly to the hospital, is I don't feel right about the good Doctor. My suspicions started when we were told where they were taking Sebastian. Remember I asked the Dr. if he knew any of the police officers? There was something about them that made me a little suspicious. First they would have impounded your gun as evidence.

They would have sealed the crime scene off so that no one could contaminate the scene. Not to mention that there were only two so called crime scene experts with two uniformed cops. Most crime scene experts do not dress in police uniforms, but in white smocks and wear gloves and are very fastidious about a crime scene. These guys were in a hurry to leave the grounds. The first thing they generally ask----did you touch anything in the room?" They should have blown a gasket for killing someone in their Country. It's illegal to carry a weapon here in Austria, other than a police officer.

At this point Burt said, "Gregg, don't you think you might be over reacting."

"Burt, why did Dr. Gutierrez have to take the original map? It would read the same on the copy as well----wouldn't it? I'm going to check the good doctor out."

I dialed Moshe's cell, after a few minutes of ringing. He answered. "Moshe; this is Gregg, sorry to bother you, but I need an answer to a question. 'How long have you known Dr. Gutierrez?"

"Gregg; I talked to him on the phone a few days ago and met him the same day as you, Why?"

"I believe the guy that we both met is an imposter. I'm going to contact the Senator and see if he can send me a fax picture of the real Dr. Gutierrez. Thanks' Moshe, Shalom. Oh----Moshe, I'll let you know if my suspicions are true."

Then I dialed the Senator, but was unable to reach him. His cell phone was not responding. I dialed one of the twins. James answered; "Dad, what an awesome surprise how's the trip going? The Senator and Maw Richards are not here. He had some event he had to go to in D.C. They will be back in the morning, by the way, John's doing great; the Dr. is amazed by his quick healing. He can walk without any help and uses one crutch for balance. Here let me have you talk with John----hey John catch."

"Hi; Dad, great to hear your voice, how are you and Mom doing? We just got up. It's five in the morning here. I'm able to walk with one crutch now, but still have a cast. When you and Mom get back, I'll be walking without any help. Thanks for calling Dad, we love you. See you soon."

As he hung up, I had tears in my eyes. My little boys were gone from the nest forever. They were men, with the knowledge of what they wanted out of life, to serve our Lord.

"The Senator was not home, but I was able to speak with my sons as you heard."

Burt said. "I know an Interpol guy right here in Wien. Let me get his phone number if he's listed. I'll be right back."

Chapter 31

(Thursday July 11)

Burt had been gone about twenty minutes, when he returned he was all smiles. "I was able to find my man. I asked him if he knew a Dr. Gutierrez, famous criminologist. He said he did, so I asked him to describe him to me. We have been had Gregg. He said that Dr. Gutierrez is a small man, with a receding hairline. He is in his late sixties and a scrubby white beard. He is about five feet eight inches tall, with a very distinct Spanish accent. He is married to Elena a very small petite woman. His hobby is ancient languages. He and his wife recently disappeared. He was teaching a class at Wien University, until one day he didn't show up for his class."

"Bingo, the people we are dealing with will stop at nothing to get what they want. They will kill without blinking an eye. Girls, Burt stay on the alert. I think they will try and kill our monk, he has become a liability. Perhaps he could have memorized the map and its symbols? I have an idea. There is the local University with an antiquities department. Let me call and see if they might have a person who could read the map in its original language. I got the phone number from the desk clerk.

I dialed the phone and asked to speak with their antiquities department. I got through right away and was transferred to the head of the department. "This is Professor Engels, whom may I ask is calling?" I introduced myself and told him what I needed someone who could translate the language on the map. I told him I needed it right away. He said he could see us right away, and that we were only a short distance. I thanked him and said we would be there in a few minutes. The girls wanted to come along, so we all went out front and had the doorman hail a cab.

———————

The cab dropped us off in front of the antiquities building. There was a map of the university in front as we got directions to his office and made our way there. We found his office and knocked on his door. The door was opened by a very tall slender distinguished looking man with a full head of graying blond hair. His glasses were on the tip of his long nose. He also had a mustache that needed trimming. "I am Professor Franz Engels. It is my pleasure to meet you all." We all introduced ourselves.

He asked, "May I see the map you have." I handed him the map, as he placed it under a microscope. "Ah yes; it is an authentic map and is written not in French, but Latin and some Aramaic. Based on the type of paper they used in the twelfth or thirteenth century. The map describes the area surrounding Innsbruck Austria and the location of what it was then. It is very undistinguishable from today's topography. I may have in my archives a map of the area during this time. Let me go look. He returned within a few minutes. "I found it right away. The map has a name on it by a Count Fernando J De La Cruz. I also believe that there is another part of this map or a letter that is not here. Do you have another part of this map?"

"No we don't. Why; do you think there is more to this map?"

"It was customary to send a letter explaining the map to the recipient. My guess is that the map is authentic and is telling the recipient where the item is buried. Notice the trail of three knights in full battle mode coming from the south on horseback. Most likely coming from the Holy Land, probably Crusaders. The trail will end at a small church, where there is a handful of grave sites marked with small crosses. There are some other symbols that only the writer of the map could decipher. I don't believe that it is treasure buried in the cemetery, but most likely some artifacts taken during the Crusades. There is also a legend written in colors. The map I think is a copy hand written from the original written on leather. One more thing, find the recipient and you will find the letter or the original leather map."

I said; "wow you have given us a lot of information, but we are lost as to what happened to the original and the adjoining letter or the other part of the map."

The professor replied; "I would venture to say that the small church depicted on the map is where 'Domkuche zu St. Jabok is or St. James Cathedral' is located today. Unfortunately, the original site of the little church could be the site of the cemetery where the current Cathedral now stands. There are rumors that some of the Knights were buried in the little cemetery. I have a book that may help make your quest much easier. Let me see where I put it. What a coincidence, I had a call a couple of days ago by a man. Oh, my, his name escapes me----oh yes a----Dr. Castro?"

Burt said, "do you mean----Dr. Gutierrez?" "Yes that was his name. It was a rather strange request, but he was asking for a copy of the oldest map of Innsbruck Austria, especially the area near the

Cathedral. I told him to contact the City of Innsbruck for such a map. He hung up very abruptly."

"I said: "Thank you ever so much professor, you have been a great help. If we had the time we would love to have taken you to dinner. God, bless you."

"Mr. Johnson; thank you for the thought, one more thing, do you know a Senator Richards we met several years ago at a convention in Innsbruck."

I said; "what a small world, he is like a father to my wife and I. Right now, my twin sons are staying at their home." I asked him if he was a Christian. He said "yes; I am a Messianic believer----Meshua is my Lord."

Mr. Johnson, "Can I ask you a question, is your quest taking you to Innsbruck for the so-called Pauline letters and the robe that may have belonged to Meshua?"

"Yes professor, why do you ask?

"I may know the person you need to see in Innsbruck. He can trace his family tree all the way back to the Crusaders. His name is Juan de la Cruz de Obregon. I will give you his number, here is the address and phone number. I'm sorry I must leave; I have an engagement committed too by my wife that I cannot miss; can I drop you off at your hotel? And please say hello to Senator Richards when you see him." We accepted his offer for the ride. We chatted and talked about how we loved Austria on our way back to the hotel.

We arrived at our hotel and saw what time it was, seven thirty. We all looked at each other and decided to eat here in the hotel as we made our way to the dining hall. I stopped at the front desk to check and see if I had any messages. The guy at the desk had an envelope for me. It only had my name written on the envelope in very poor handwriting. I stuck it in my pocket and would read it later.

I found the rest of my group sitting in the patio and sat down to a fantastic view of the city lights. We ordered dinner and while waiting for our food chatted about how the professor was a friend of the Senators and our trip so far. The waiter brought our dinner and we continued our conversation while we ate. I said that I was sorry that I had been duped by the phony Dr. Gutierrez. Even the waiter had been a plant where we had dinner at the fancy Austrian restaurant.

We sat and chatted about our children and how fast they grow up and leave the nest. I looked at my watch and said to Mary and Burt that we needed to go to bed. We had talked till almost eleven, so we all headed for our rooms.

CHAPTER 29

(Friday July 12th)

We had a wakeup call for seven thirty and got up and showered, dressed, then packed our luggage ready to take downstairs. Our train schedule was not a problem since they run almost hourly. We went down stairs to meet Burt and Mary for breakfast. I decided to order poached eggs on toast with a Danish pastry washed down with several cups of coffee. While eating, I remembered I had forgotten to open the envelope left for me at the desk. I pulled it out and read the short message. Dear Mr. Johnson. I was supposed to meet you in Salzburg a few days ago, but because of the threats on my life, I am in hiding. I will contact you further when you reach Salzburg. I have what you need to complete your quest, Respectfully Victor Van Heisdorff. I have your cell number and will contact you tomorrow."

I showed the letter all around to the group and said that it sounded authentic. I said we needed to check out and catch a train. We finished our breakfast and went to our rooms and had the bell-hop pick up our luggage. After paying our bill we caught a cab to the train depot.

We checked in at the train depot and bought our fares. We decided to stop in Salzburg and spend the night there. We boarded the train at twelve thirty and went directly to our non-sleeping compartment prepared to enjoy our trip to Salzburg. The Country side was gorgeous. After we had been on the train for about two hours, there was a knock on our compartment door.

I said. "Who is it?"

"Please open the door I have a message from Victor Heisdorff."

I glanced at Burt and motioned for him to hide in the bathroom in case the person on the other side was hostile.

I said, "Just a moment please," as I gradually moved to the door and hesitated to open it. As I slowly turned the knob and pulled back on the door, I was startled when I opened the door and saw that it was Professor Franz Engels. I was speechless for a few seconds, but could only stammer out; "Professor Engels what a surprise please come in."

As he entered, he motioned with his finger over his mouth to be quiet as he said "May I come in?"

"Please sir, come in. What do you have to do with the quest we are on? I am still surprised and confused, please sir enlighten us."

He said, "Let me put you at ease. As you probably know, I am Jewish, but a Messianic one, we have followed the teachings of Jeshua from our youth. Christ and my wife and two sons are my life. I came to tell you that your lives are in danger. The name I gave you, De la Cruz, he is dead. I know young Heisdorff of Hussein. He and I have been very close. The map he has maybe the missing piece to the puzzle"

"Excuse me Professor, did you say Hussein?"

"Yes; Victor Van Heisdorff of Hussein, but some call him Heisdorff. Anyway, he called me last night and asked about you and if you were who you said you were. I assured him that you were real.

The Senator called me a few days ago and told me to watch out for all of you. I also know where young Heisdorff is hiding. He will meet us in Salzburg this evening. He is anxious to get rid of the map. He thinks it is cursed. I have tried to convince him that there is no such thing as a curse unless from God."

Burt said; "Professor, why didn't you say this to us last night?"

"I wasn't sure about you, and wanted to make sure you were who you said you were. I also checked with Senator Richards. He sent his love. I must confess; that the deaths of all the Twelfth Knights has us all running scared. Please forgive me for my short comings"

We all chimed in and said, "we love you and forgive you."

Bev said; "why don't I order some refreshments, and please Professor take a seat."

As Bev rang the buzzer for the porter, I decided to ask Professor Engels a vital question. "Professor Engels have you been able to interpret the map."

"Please, all of you, call me by my given name Franz. I have always honored men and those with a title, but when it requires me to respond to my title, I have difficulty. I believe that the good Lord will deliver me from this idiosyncrasy."

I was about to say something else when the porter showed up and knocked on the door. He came in and took our order for coffee, tea and pastry.

After he left, I said. "Professor; I have to ask you a few questions. Have you figured out what the map says? You told us it is written in Latin and Aramaic?

"I said this to you last night when I wasn't sure of you? As to your question, no, it is written in Hebrew. The Map is older than we first thought. It goes back to the third or fourth century. The Crusaders trekked to the north in the twelfth century, but apparently, they followed a path made by Christians who were being persecuted. They were Jewish followers of Jeshua. I believe the map to be authentic. I also am a student of the Hebrew writings. I believe this map is a copy of the original map written in Egyptian the language of the Egyptian Pharaoh's. It is an ancient language, but some believe that some of the Egyptian's who converted to Christianity may have been the first settlers in what today is parts of Austria, this of course is only a hypothesis. There are also some inscriptions on the map in Latin. This is what makes it so fascinating."

I said, "how did you get involved with the 'Brotherhood'?"

"I was born in a concentration camp July the Fourth, 1944, after the allies landed in Europe. It was called Treblinka. My parents; my sister and older brother, we all survived the Nazi's camp. We somehow escaped the invading hordes of Russians and ran into a truck full of American GI's. They took us to an internment camp until we could come back to our homeland, here in Wien. My Father and mother both asked Jeshua into their hearts when they were in the concentration camp. They suffered from both the Nazi's and the Jewish people in the camp. My mother told me that the Jewish people held a funeral for all of us. As far as they were concerned; we were dead." He paused and wiped tears from his eyes.

He continued; "I didn't ask the Lord into my heart until I was in my late teens, while I was attending the university. I was introduced to the Brotherhood by one of my professors. He was a Professor of Religious Studies. He had come to know Christ as his Savior while doing his studies. One evening after class I asked him to share his testimony with me. It touched me so much, I asked Jeshua into my heart. I have never looked back since."

Mary asked; "why did the Jewish people shun your family so much? It seems to me that it is a strange way to shun people, because of their religious belief."

"Mary, I don't know the answer to that question. I pray for my people every day; perhaps one day." He stopped and looked ahead, teary eyed. We have a little over an hour before we get to Salzburg. Did you make reservations yet? If not; I know a small hotel out of the way, with a wonderful restaurant. Their pastries are known all over the continent. If you don't mind I will call ahead and make reservations for two more rooms."

I said; "No we did not professor please make the reservations for us."

After he called and hung up he started laughing. I asked why he was laughing, as he told me. "I must confess my cousin owns the hotel, but it is a fine hotel and the food is excellent."

We arrived at Salzburg and after gathering our luggage, while the Professor hailed us a cab. We arrived at a quaint small hotel. We checked into our respective rooms. After we freshened up a bit we made our way downstairs, and of course waiting for us was the Professor. During dinner, he said he had a confession to make. Again, he started laughing as he shared with us that the pastry chef was his sister. We found out that our new friend had a great sense of humor. After dinner, we all decided to go to bed and get an early start in the morning. As we got up from the table the Professor motioned for me to stay behind. Bev went upstairs to our room. "Gregg honey I'll wait up for you."

Professor, "my brother, what is so important you needed to see me in private?"

"Victor Van Heisdorff of Hussein wants to see us right away. He was sitting in the restaurant a few tables away. He wants us to meet him in his room. His room is on the floor above us. Let's take the lift, my legs don't move as well as they used too."

"Fine, let's go."

We knocked on his door, but no one answered. I touched the door and found that it was open. I looked at the professor as he gave me the let's go in sign. I had my hand on my Glock as I pushed the door open and stepped inside. The room was a shamble's as we inspected the room along with the bathroom. There was only one place I hadn't inspected and was not surprised when I opened the closet door and found Van Heisdorff slumped over, bound and gagged with no sign of life. I felt his pulse and found he was still alive. He was only unconscious as he started to wake up.

I told the professor to contact the local police while I untied Van Heisdorff. I went to the bathroom and got a wet towel and a glass of water. I gave him a glass of water and wet his forehead with the towel.

The professor said something in German then he caught him-self and started speaking English. "My boy what happened? Did you know the thugs who did this?"

He said, "Who is this man with you?

"I can speak for myself; I'm Gregg Johnson former director of the FBI and a fellow member of the 'Brotherhood."

"Forgive me brother, but my head feels very cloudy right now. As I entered my room somebody grabbed me from behind and placed a rag over my nose and mouth. I believe it was chloroform that they used, please help me up. They think they got the map, but all they got was a phony one. You couldn't find Salzburg with what they got. The real map is in a safety deposit box at the local train depot here in

Salzburg. I suggest that after the police leave, we head for the train depot and get the real map."

"May I suggest; that we send my friend Burt, whom our enemies don't know. He can retrieve it without being suspicious." Just as I finished talking the local police arrived.

The guy in charge asked us what we knew. We all said we felt that it was a robbery, but felt the robbers left because they didn't find but a few Euros in the jacket hanging in the closet. He asked us all what we were doing here in Salzburg. He also asked each one of us what had happened. I told him that Burt, Mary his wife and Bev and I were on vacation and that we had an appointment with Van Heisdorff. He said that no one was hurt and warned us to keep our doors locked while away from our rooms.

As soon as they left I called Burt and told him to come to Van Heisdorff room. When Burt got to his room, Van Heisdorff asked him if he knew where the depot was. He said he knew, having just arrived from there. He gave Burt the key to a locker. Burt said he would be back within an hour. After he left I called Bev and told her I would be awhile. She said she was playing a board game with Mary.

Burt returned with the envelope that held the map. He handed it to Heisdorff as he hurriedly opened the envelope and carefully took the map out of the envelope. We were looking at an ancient map in fantastic condition. I spoke up and asked Van Heisdorff where his father had it stored?

He said; "My father had it in a glass humidified case, in a vault in our home. He was murdered for the map, but the culprit or culprits did not find the secret room where he had it hid. I also had a copy of the map made in case the original was stolen or destroyed. As you can see it is very fragile, so I would suggest you just look at it without picking it up. The map you have is not as old as the one I have. We thought at first that there was a part of the map missing. Not so, we believe that the map you have is part of a bigger map of the ancient city of Innsbruck. The area shown on the map is where the current Cathedral is located. The map I have shows where the actual artifacts are. The map you have is where the catacombs are located right underneath the sanctuary of St. John's Cathedral. We will have a difficult time trying to get the Monsignor to let us do any digging or crawling around the grounds of the Cathedral. Time is of the essence; we must hurry because of those who would kill for the artifacts. There is an early train that leaves around eight thirty in the morning. I suggest we make that connection top priority."

I was about to say something when my cell phone rang. I punched the answer symbol and recognized the number immediately. "Short Stuff what a surprise my brother! Boy how I wish you were here with us. We are in Salzburg right now. What's up?"

"Gregg, I have some good news and bad news all at the same time. First I got into an argument with the commissioner and handed in my resignation. The bad news is one of my nephews died from an overdose of smack, heroin. You remember him, he was Tashanna's boy. He got to hanging around with a bunch of bums who turned him on to drugs. He was only thirteen years old. We had a wake and burial for him last night. His father is coaching at a local high school, and is beside himself. I called to let you know that I'm available to help you. I received a pretty good severance pay. My wife and I could join you in Austria. Where will you guys be Saturday?"

"Wow my brother oh yes please come. I'm also sorry to hear about your nephew and of course losing your job. We will be in Innsbruck tomorrow. Let me give you the name of the hotel." I gave him the name; he would call us when he got to the airport.

Burt said; "was that Short Stuff that called? What's going on with him?"

I said, "Yes that was him. He is now a private citizen, and will join us day after tomorrow. It will be great working together. He has a keen mind and will be an asset. Gentlemen; its late, so I suggest we go to bed and meet at the front desk in the morning ready to go at six thirty. We can eat on the train. We can get a cup of coffee or tea in the lobby. Victor; I suggest you hide that map some place safe until we are ready to leave in the morning. Gentlemen; I'll see you in the morning."

Burt and I made our way to my room, since Mary and Bev were together playing a board game. We said good night to the Smith's and would see them in the morning. I told Beverly I had a surprise for her. "Guess who is going to join us in Innsbruck?"

She said; "let me guess, it's not Rachel and Cash, it's not the Senator and Mother Richards. I give up."

"None other than Mattie and Short Stuff, late of the D.C. police department."

I told her the entire story of what had happened and why they were joining us, and of course she was elated that Matte and Short Stuff would join us.

CHAPTER 30

(Saturday July 13th)

We both showered and went to bed. I tossed and turned, something wasn't quite right. I think we had been had again. I sat up and got up and walked out on the balcony. I started running back in my mind what had happened last night. The story by the professor and then what Victor Van Heisdorff said about my map versus his map. They had been bought off by Fenneman and Heilman. At this point I didn't know what language the maps were written in. I trusted no one to examine the map, unless they were a friend.

Bev came out to the balcony and said; "Gregg, why can't you sleep."

"Honey, the people we have been traveling with are believers, or were, but they have sold out to our enemies. They used a ruse to look at my map, by showing us a phony map. If I were to go to their rooms right now, you would find that they are no longer here. They have flown the coop, and are on their way to Innsbruck. Sugar; do me a favor, and call Burt and Mary and tell them we need to check out right now. Tell them I will explain the early checkout to them when were on our way. Hurry dear, time is of the utmost."

We dressed in a hurry and made our way downstairs and asked the night clerk how we could rent a car at this hour of the night. He said he would arrange it over the phone and have a car within the hour. I handed him my credit card and true to his word the car agency delivered us a Mercedes supercharged sedan. We loaded our luggage in the trunk and said to the guy who delivered the car. Do you want to make a few extra dollars?

He said in broken English, "how?" I asked him if he would drive us to Innsbruck. He said, yes but he would have to get permission from his boss. He left and was gone about ten minutes. It would cost us an additional four hundred bucks for his services.

"I'll give you three hundred."

"He said he would do it for three hundred and fifty." I agreed.

I asked him, "Young man what is your name?"

"My name is Erick Miller. I am in my last year of studies at the University of Innsbruck. I am working on a degree in Criminology. I would like to earn a doctorate some day. We are on summer break, so I must work to pay for my tuition. My father died when I was eleven, so I have had to help my mother raise my three siblings. My father was a police officer here in Salzburg. He was killed by a deranged killer who was stopped by my father and his partner. The man who killed him shot him point blank through the heart. The ironic thing was they stopped him for a routine check because his tail light was burned out."

"Son; the two of us are both peace officers, I am the former director of the Federal Bureau of Investigation in the United States, Burt is with the CIA. We are sorry about your father."

"I am honored to be in your presence sir. I had to study about your agency, the CIA, and the United Kingdom's MI-6 and MI-5, and our own Interpol."

"Before we take leave, how long does it take to drive from here to Innsbruck?"

He hesitated, "normally it takes three to four hours. It also depends on the traffic and how fast you drive."

"If you get us there before----ah let me see. What time is it?

Bev Said. "Honey, it's almost five am."

"You get us there by eight and I'll give you a bonus of a hundred dollars."

"Sir; you are on, let's get going."

He revved up the engine as we all got into the big Grey Mercedes. It had a beautiful interior of handcrafted wood with hand crafted black leather seats and side panels. This car had been made for speed and comfort as our driver punched the accelerator as the turbo responded, heading for the Autobahn.

I leaned over and asked Erick where he learned to drive a car. He said he had taken lessons on Saturdays at a local open speedway.

He said, "it is in the blood of all Germanic people. One of our leading sports is motorcycle racing, next is auto racing. I love to drive fast and defy gravity. Watch how fast this car can accelerate as he weaved in and out of traffic. My great grandfather was a famous race car driver before the War. During World War Two he became a German paratrooper, but unfortunately he was captured by the Russians and was never seen again."

"I'm sorry to hear that. I suppose your father didn't have to go into the military?"

He said; "You are correct, but he did serve for two years, when his enlistment was up he went to the State University. I was very young when he died, but he was a good man."

"Erick, can I ask you a very personal question."

"You certainly may----sir."

"Has anyone ever told you about Jesus Christ?"

He said; "No, no one has ever told me about Him. Once I picked up a little booklet in a train station that stated something about salvation. It also stated that Christ was the only way to this salvation. I laid it down on the seat when I got off the train, why do you ask me this?"

"Erick, do you believe in eternal life after you die?"

"Forgive me, but I don't know what you mean by eternal life."

"Erick----we are all Christians who are riding in this car. We believe that man without a belief in God is doomed eternally. We believe that God the Father, the Son and the Holy Spirit are one Eternal God. Man, needs a Savior from his sins. God the Father sent his Son to die for mankind. Therefore, we celebrate Christmas, the birth of His Son the Savior of mankind. Due you follow me?"

He shook his head, signifying yes.

I continued; "We believe that the Bible is the written word of God, writings that give you a history of Gods plan for mankind's salvation. You must have faith to believe that what is written in the Bible is of God.

I used to be like you, but one day God spoke to me through His word and I fully understood why Christ died on a cross for mankind. I would encourage you to read the Bible. If you don't have one, I have an extra copy that I would be more than happy to give to you, would you allow me to do this?"

"Yes, I would like that very much. You have given me much to think about."

We continued our conversation about a lot of things. He wanted to know about our sons, and about West Point. He said he would like to come to the USA some day. For now, he had to focus on finishing his education. I finally leaned back in my seat and enjoyed the country side. Unless you have been to Austria; it is almost impossible to describe its beauty, especially the Alps. The rolling hills and country side showed the signs of summer with flowers all in bloom with their rich colors and fragrance, especially in the early dawn. The hum of the car's engine soon found me sound asleep.

I awoke to my wife shaking me very gently "have we arrived yet? Did you tell our former hotel manager to make us reservations for Innsbruck?"

"Yes dear to both your questions, we're about to arrive at the expressways in the city of Innsbruck. I told Erick to take us directly to our hotel. He said we would be there in about ten minutes."

"Thanks honey for being so efficient. I was dog tired; forgive me for having zonked out. I feel refreshed, it must be the weather. Oh, it's raining; I heard that we would get rained on, thank God it didn't snow?"

I said to Erick; "I see you made it on time, so I owe you an extra hundred dollars and a Bible. Open the trunk so we can get our luggage. Ah----there it is, my suit case." I opened it and found one of the extra Bibles I had brought along. I dedicated it to Erick and wrote my home address and phone number on the inside cover. "Dear Erick when you start to read the Bible, start with the Gospel of Luke. Then read the Gospel of John. It will give you an idea about how important it is to know Christ as your personal Savior. God, bless you and a safe return journey."

He said he was driving back right away and would stop and sleep a couple of hours in one of the rest stops along the way. He promised me he would read the Bible. And again, thanked me for the bonus and the Bible. As he left I prayed to God he would give his heart to Jesus.

While we were waiting for the bellhop to come out and pick up our luggage, we stood in front of the hotel and watched the people walking by and wondered where all of them were going. I thought how many of them had a personal relationship with Christ as Lord? While I was so engrossed in my thoughts, out of the corner of my eye I spotted a person that I knew instinctively that he was a henchman for the Scorpion. About the same time the bellboy came and picked up our luggage and took it inside as we followed him to the front desk to check in. Burt and I had to show our passports and a credit card before we were taken to our rooms. I told the desk clerk we would be here at least a week. It depended on how our search for the artifacts progressed. I asked if Mr. and Mrs. Butler had checked in and they said no, but that the shuttle had not arrived from the airport.

We went to our adjoining rooms and decided to splurge and order breakfast in our rooms. It was after ten in the morning when we finally sat down to eat. They had an American breakfast listed: A choice of Ham, bacon or sausage with German potatoes and eggs. Cooked to your choice, but for the light eater there was toast or German crêpes, a fancy name for pancakes; sprinkled with powdered sugar and lemon juice. There were other dishes offered on the menu, but the meals we ordered were based on our own custom. What we were used too.

The waiter had just delivered our breakfast, when in walked James (Short Stuff) Butler and his wife Matte. They walked into our room as we got up and hugged them both while our waiter called for a couple of workers to add another table to ours in our room. They said they had already eaten breakfast, but would join us and have a cup of coffee while we caught up on all the gossip from home.

"Ladies forgive me; but, I have to speak with Burt and Short Stuff as to where we are going this afternoon. Why don't you ladies play tourist this afternoon while us guys go and snoop around the Cathedral. We can compare the actual grounds with the maps we have. Perhaps we will get lucky and run into a friar who knows how to read Hebrew and Aramaic. We will meet back here at the hotel late this afternoon. Ladies select a nice restaurant you would like to eat at and we will make a night of it."

Bev said, "Honey, why can't' we go with you? Maybe we can help in deciphering the maps?"

"Dear, I insist that you let us go scout the place out first and then if we think it's safe, we will take you with us on the next visit----ok?"

Bev replied, "if you put it that way we will go shopping instead."

We got up from the table and started to make our way to St John's Cathedral as the ladies took off the other direction. I asked the desk clerk how far the Cathedral was from the hotel. He said it was walking distance from where we were staying. It's roughly less than three quarters of a mile. I thanked him for the info as we started to leave he said that they sold maps of the Cathedral and its grounds; and that one of the Friars would take us on a personal tour for a small fee. I bought the map and again thanked him for the information.

We were about two blocks from the Cathedral when Burt dropped to his knees and whipped out his weapon! A small foreign auto slowly drove by us as the windows opened, and a couple of weapons peered out simultaneously. They both fired at us; then sped away! Short Stuff and I had hit the pavement all within a split second of their first shot and fired back at our adversaries. I was thankful that our wives had changed their minds. Burt had emptied his weapon into the Blue British built Cooper as he hit one of the assailants. People walking along the streets ducked behind cars and some hit the ground. I thought I caught a glimpse of the guy driving. I would never forget Ignacio Beto Vendrell de Ybarra, the Madrid Bomber. As I got up I looked around to see if anyone was hurt. I barked out; "Burt, Short Stuff, are you guys ok?"

Burt and Short Stuff both responded simultaneously, "were fine Gregg. Did you get a look at the thugs?"

"Yes, but keep it down guys don't say a thing when the cops come. They will be here in a few seconds, say as little as possible."

The police pulled up within a few minutes of our small battle. I walked over to the officer I thought might be in charge. He said he was as I introduced myself. I told him I thought they were terrorist trying to make a statement in regards to their upcoming elections. He said perhaps you are right. He wanted to know if I remembered anything that might help in their investigation. He asked me how long we would be in Innsbruck. I told him a few days, but that our plans could change. He asked me if I caught the license plate numbers. I said I did, but thought that the car was probably stolen and the numbers were probably of no use.

He thanked me for the license numbers of the cooper and asked me if we were staying at the Dressler Hotel. I told him yes we were. He was very formal and since no one was hurt he said that it was a pleasure to have a peace officer of my stature here in his city and country and hoped we would enjoy our stay in Innsbruck.

"Burt; Short Stuff, "Do you guys think he bought what I just told him, that the people in the Cooper were local zealots?

Short Stuff said, laughingly, "if he did, I'm the Tooth Fairy."

"Guys we need to get going to the Cathedral. I recognized the driver; Beto Vendrell, the bomb expert from Madrid. I had a feeling he worked for the Scorpion, this incident proves it as my phone rang. I instinctively knew who it was. "Hello maggot; I was hoping you were in the car, but like the scum that you are, you let others do your dirty work"

The Scorpion laughed as he said, "you're talking tough doesn't cut it with me. But I'm in a good mood today, so listen carefully. 'El que sabe donde esta el pozo habre sus hojos en la oscuridad, hasta luego gringo."

"Guys; what do you think this guy meant by this riddle? I believe it has a meaning for us."

Burt said, "The translation means; 'He who knows where the cistern is, opens his eyes in the darkness.' I believe that it's a warning to us to watch our steps, especially in and around the Cathedral."

"Ok; let's go across the street and see what we can find out about where our Knight is buried. We made our way to an office that said, Rectory. I knocked on the door and heard some shuffling of feet, as the door was finally opened. There in front of me stood a man that if there was a Santa Claus, he was him. When he smiled, his face lit up the room. I was not disappointed when he opened his mouth. "Gentlemen; please come in. What can I do for you?"

I spoke up and said; "Good afternoon Friar, we are here looking for the tomb of a Twelfth century Knight. Perhaps you can help us?"

"You are the second group of men to ask to see the resting place of a fallen Knight. Sorry to say we had a cave-in, in part of the Cathedral that fell into a stink hole. But it turns out that under the Cathedral, we found ancient ruins and a fifteenth Century cemetery. This happened a few years ago. The area is roped off, but we haven't had the money to do any repairs and more investigation. Unfortunately, the city engineers have stated it is unsafe. I remember years ago when I was first assigned here, a man came to see the very tomb you seek. He was a very nice man. He said he was part of a group of Christians called the Brotherhood. That was over thirty years ago, I'm so sorry. There are legends and stories that there are some hidden artifacts some place here under the Cathedral that this Knight and others were bound by oath to protect. They had been Knights Templers at first but a rotten King was disappointed in how they had fought in Jerusalem so he set out to kill them. A few wound up here in Innsbruck, only to die as outcasts----so the story goes."

He continued, "I personally think that there is a lot of truth in the legends. I fancy myself as an amateur geologist/anthropologist. One states that there is a letter or note written by Jesus Himself to John His disciple when he would return, supposedly with the actual date. Can you imagine what could happen if this were true? There is no end to what an evil person would do with this information?"

I replied, "all of us are part of the Brotherhood. I am a Twelfth-Knight and was sent out by our Elders. We have sworn by the blood of Jesus to guard the items you referenced to, from unscrupulous men. Unfortunately, there are those who want to use the artifacts for control and power. We are on a quest to stop them. If we are successful we will keep the artifacts secret, and from falling into the wrong hands."

"How do we address you Friar?" I said.

"Please call me Friar Emanuel. I chose this name, when I dedicated my life to serving the Lord Jesus Christ forty years ago, I have never looked back. Would you like to take a tour of the underground city and see what is left of the original Village? What I will show you will certainly interest you? We will need torches, flashlights to you. I have personally been searching the ruins in secret. I'll be right back with what we need."

He wasn't gone very long and returned with four flashlights, a huge bundle of nylon rope, and four pair of leather workman's gloves. He passed them around to all of us. I noticed that we towered over him, but that smile of his was contagious.

I said; "Where do we start?"

"Behind the rectory is a garden and after you near the end of the garden, you will see another building. It is rather old going back to around the sixteenth century, they say, but I believe it is older. I believe this is because of what was directly underneath the building as you will see it in just a few minutes."

We made our way into the garden and soon saw the small building looking rather awkward as it leaned rather precariously to one side, like a ship about to capsize. We walked up to the front door as the Friar pulled out a bunch of keys and found the correct one that fit the padlock. I thought with all the other Cathedrals in Europe, how many had subterranean ruins under their structures, just waiting to cave-in and expose great history.

"Forgive me He said. I always have trouble opening this lock."

Short Stuff said, "Here; let me see if I can open it. Ah, I knew I hadn't lost my touch. You have to have come from the hood to open this type of lock."

We laughed except the Friar, as he said "what is this hood? Look my robe has a hood, perhaps I should wear it each time I enter here."

"Forgive me Friar my friend Capt. Butler meant that you have to come from a certain social status. The hood is a reference to black people who live in ghettos in our country."

"Now I know why you all laughed," as he began to laugh. He stopped just as he opened the door. He said; "gentlemen be careful where you step from now on, you will be amazed as to what you will see. Follow me and please close the door behind you."

We took about thirty steps when the Friar said; "stop here and turn on your torches directly in front of you."

We were astonished at what we saw. I asked, "how far down does the hole go Friar?"

He said; "it only goes about fifteen to twenty feet down, but we will enter some caverns further on. Follow me to the protruding ledge there is a ladder in place that we will be able to scale down." As he went over the side and started down, I was surprised at his agility for a portly short man.

We all made it down the ladder as he waited for us at the bottom. Soon a row of small lights went on as the Friar turned on some temporary flood lights. He again told us to stay close for we were about to start seeing grave markers and tombs. Suddenly there was a deep roaring sound in front of us. We all stopped as the Friar assured us that it was portions of the ancient Cathedral ruins tumbling down, exposing more of the subterranean catacombs. We finally ran out of lights and had to turn on our flashlights again.

The Friar spoke up. "From here on gentlemen we will be in the caverns. I want you to notice the door that will give us entrance to them. Please come closer so you can see some of the markings on the door."

I looked at the door and the first thing that caught my eye was the Cross of Loraine cut into a door made of iron and crumbling wood. I thought; was this the vault or tomb that we were looking for? My thoughts were interrupted by the Friar. Mr. Johnson, may I see the copy of your famous map for a second. Ah yes, this is the door. There are two other main doors leading to these catacombs, but my hunch was right. I don't know if you can see in this darkness, but I see on the map and the door a small letter at the left-hand corner of the cross of Loraine. Look at the bottom of the door notice the letter C, the same letter that's on the cross in the map. Now all we need is a crow bar which I brought along." As he pulled a crow bar from under his robe and said, I always carry one along you never know when one will be needed," as he laughed at his joke.

We all laughed at the way he said it, but it was rather funny. He tried to open the old rusty door, but was unable too.

Short Stuff stepped up and said, "Let me have a crack at it Friar. As you can see; I'm over six feet six inches tall, and weigh in at two hundred fifty pounds." As he placed the bar into the top right hand corner and began to pry the bar all the way down, clear to the floor. He retraced his steps and began to exert strength as the door began to screech and make cracking sounds, till it finally opened. Short Stuff was a powerful man, but gentle as a lamb.

The Friar said; "Gentlemen; as far as I know, this is the first time that anyone has entered these tombs in centuries. We suspected that they existed, but my government didn't want to spend the money to find out. I believe that the good Lord interceded somehow and caused the hidden underground cemetery to be discovered. I feel honored to be here with you gentlemen. I must caution you that the wood pillars are very old and rotting, so be very careful where you place your hands. Let us proceed."

Suddenly the Friar stopped as he said, "gentlemen do you hear running water?"

Burt Spoke up first and said, "I think I do. Why?"

I said, "Friar is there an underground stream or river here in Innsbruck?"

He said, "Yes, the In River is not far from here. Perhaps there is a tributary that empties into the river that at one time was part of the In. With as much snow and moisture as we get here in my Country, it would not surprise me. I don't know how wide it is near us, but perhaps God will show us the way."

CHAPTER 31

(Saturday July 13ᵗʰ)

As we continued our decent, I kept getting feelings of anxiety and premonition. I needed to ask Friar Emanuel a question.

"Friar, I need to know where you learned how to speak English? This has been bugging me ever since we met this morning."

He said; "My Father was a career military man from America, he and my mother met here in Innsbruck. He was recalled to the States where I was born and went to school in the USA. I went on to college at Fordham University, and gave my heart to Christ while I was a student. I became a Franciscan priest over thirty years ago. I majored in Geology and Anthropology, so that I could do the very thing we are doing right now. Oh! I might add; I also belong to the Brotherhood. I hope this clears things up for you. Let us proceed, time is not our ally. It will soon be dark top side. Be careful as we move slowly. We must examine each tomb. Look for the dates on each tomb.

As we drew nearer the sound of the running water Friar Emanuel stopped. "Gentlemen, we are at a crossroad. We have a choice to stay together or break up into teams of two. Mr. Johnson and I can go one way and Lt. Butler and Mr. Smith can go another way. I brought a compass along. We have been going due north. The water seems to be farther away. Let us search another hour then we can come back in the morning and do some more searching if we don't find the tomb, how does this sound to you gentlemen?"

I said, "It's a great idea Friar. If we spot a tomb with the cross of Loraine we will yell out to the other two. Let's get started gentleman!"

We split up and started to go on when the Friar stopped. "Mr. Johnson; I think I have found something that maybe what we are looking for, shine your light over here." I shone my light and saw a door to a tomb that was different than the others. There was a carving of a Knights Shield and sword into the rock. At the bottom of the shield was the name de la Cruz. (Of the Cross), the cross on the shield was the cross of Loraine. We both felt around and scraped the outline of an ancient type of door. The Friar took out the crow bar and started to dig into the dust and dirt. Within a few minutes we had the stone door outlined so we could move the stone. We would need help. I whistled for Burt and Short Stuff. They were with us within minutes.

As they walked up, I said, "Guys, we may have found what we are looking for, we need help to see if we can open the stone door. There may be a secret lock on the wall, what would it be? It would be something that they used in their day. Ah here it is. It is a simple design. Directly above the cross, over the door is a hole with a spring lock. To release the lock, you must hold the spring down. I will hold it down and the rest of you push in."

I no sooner said this when the stone door opened and led us into a large tomb. There were rats scurrying and spider webs all over the walls and other sarcophagus in the large room. There were several ancient torches on the walls so we decided to try and light them. Amazingly they all lit up the room so we could examine the entire room. There were ancient pieces of rusted broken swords and pieces of mail used for protection. Also, a couple of broken spears and one skeleton of a former Knight, still dressed in tattered mail and tunic. It was one of those times I wished we had a camera, until Burt pulled out his cell phone and started taking pictures.

"Gentlemen, we have been given a golden opportunity to view something that is rare. Few are given the opportunity to examine remains that go back almost eight hundred years. Imagine this tomb has been closed for the same time frame. Just think of the history that has been lived since these men and women walked the earth. Some of them were buried with their family members as you can see. A certain Knight was buried in these tombs perhaps what we are looking for is here in one of these tombs or maybe somewhere else. We need to focus on what our quest is, to find the tomb of Juan De La Cruz, Knights templar. When we find his resting place, we will have a lot of our questions resolved."

"Gentlemen, gentlemen, I think I may have found his sarcophagus." The Friar shouted in excitement.

We all cried out, "where Friar?"

"Come over here and see what I have found. Notice in the corner at the top, a small shield with the cross of Loraine and the C at the bottom. I hate to open the sarcophagus and find that it isn't him."

"We'll never know, unless we open it." I said.

The next thing we know the four of us are pulling at the stone coffin and finally could pull it out. We had to use the crow bar, but the lid moved without a lot of effort.

We were all so excited that we didn't notice that we had visitors, as one of them said, "thank you gentlemen. Please put your hands up and move to the other wall." There was enough light to see who our company was. It was Professor Franz Engels; Dr. Klaus Von Berger and Ignacio Beto Vendrell de Ybarra, the bomber and our dear friend Victor Van Heisdorff.

"Why do we owe the pleasure of your company Beto de Ybarra? You seem to have us at a disadvantage. You and your henchmen remind me of a bunch of hungry vultures ready to devour their kill."

A voice that I had heard before stepped into the tomb with a couple of goons; "Hey Gringo, you can thank me. Sorry to interrupt this gathering, but time is valuable. I'm so sorry that we must meet in such an eerie place. Gentlemen please continue with opening the sarcophagus. Gringo you and your three comrades may observe while my experts open the resting place of Count Juan De La Cruz. Raul, por favor, (Please) take their weapons. I don't want any distractions to interfere with our inspection of the coffin. Professor Engels---- would you please continue with your examination of the interior of the coffin."

Engels spoke up, "It is not here, the other part of the map is not here. All that is interred with Juan De la Cruz is his armor and sword and a crumbling leather belt with a few coins of the period buried with him. Perhaps it has all been a hoax?"

Beto spoke up. "I hope that you gentlemen are not hiding anything from me. I did not come halfway around the world to be told it was a joke, or perhaps a gigantic hoax, besides my boss would not like it. His sting is deadly"

I could tell by Beto's voice that he was agitated. As he shouted out orders to tie us up until he decided what to do with us. Finally, it was decided by him to blow up the tomb with us in it. When he had set the bomb to explode within twenty minutes enough time for them to exit the catacombs as they all left, they closed the tomb door. The

Scorpions number one man, last words were his heart felt sorrow that he would not be around to see our demise.

After they left, I said, "Do any of you have any suggestions how we can get out of this? One problem is they gave up on the search too easy. I thought he would torture us for more information. It was not like El Alacran's men to be so nice. We must stay on guard; they may be back later. The Scorpion is a very self centered man and does not like defeat and will kill his own men at the drop of a hat if he feels they failed him."

Short Stuff said; "I think the guy who tied us up was too easy on us, he left a lot of slack in the rope. Gregg, why don't you scoot over behind me and let me cut you lose with my handy blade. I hide it in the inside of my boot for situations like this. Besides; I always expect the worst on assignments." As he broke out laughing

After we were set free I said, "You never cease to amaze me big guy. Guys we still have a problem! A bomb is set to go off any minute?"

Burt spoke up. Guys you don't need to worry. When I first started with the Agency, I was assigned to a unit on how to disarm bombs. I've looked it over it's a piece of cake. Gregg, I watched the guy who armed it. It's very crude, but still very effective. Detonated it can raise a lot of havoc. Don't worry I'll be careful. It will take me a few minutes. Ah; let me see, it's done, but it's not a very sophisticated bomb. In my Jacket is an all-purpose Swiss Army Knife, I need to unscrew a couple of screws and cut two wires, black and white on this bomb. There that should do it, a piece of cake guys.

The Friar started laughing; "Ha, ha. I knew they were not smart enough to read the map properly. The ancient Knights where smart when it came to planning their demise. They knew that there would be grave robbers and thief's who would desecrate their graves. So, they disguised their graves by putting the real knight in the armor bearer's sarcophagus, usually below the Knights coffin, but in this case. I believe he is in the one above. Help me pull this one out."

We all helped the Friar pull the stone tomb out and again held our breath as we opened the lid. In it was a man who looked like he had recently died. We were amazed at how preserved he was. His uniform with the bright red cross of Loraine on a white background brightly lit up his mail armor. Even his boots were polished. His face showed that he was a man in his early sixties. His hair was streaked with grey which had once been jet black. Alongside his torso were some parchments rolled into scrolls. On the other side of his body was his sword, but the only thing that was missing was his helmet and shield. I thought of the book of Ephesians in the Bible. Paul's description of a soldier of faith came to mind, 'The full Armor of God.' We were all completely amazed at the preservation of the man and his garments. It took us all back in time.

I said; "let us say a prayer for this man and his commitment to our Lord, as we all knelt and prayed."

Friar Emanuel spoke up after we prayed; "Mr. Johnson, you have the maps in your possession, one we believe is a poor imitation, but the other one is authentic. We will be able to compare them when I unroll the two manuscripts. This is the tricky part, because of aging and the type of paper it's written on, we must be extremely careful. We must hurry; time is of the essence because when old paper is exposed to the atmosphere, it tends to become very brittle rather quickly. Let us put back everything as we found them, except for taking the map. Help me put the sarcophagus back in place----thank you gentlemen for your help."

I said; "Good, we need to get back to the ladies, they must think we were abducted or ran off. We will come back in the morning and do a further search."

We got back to the hotel and found our wives waiting in the lobby as we came walking in. They came over to us and asked what had happened to us. I related the whole story and our encounter with the Scorpions men. Friar Emanuel was busy at his office in the rectory unrolling the two ancient manuscripts.

Bev said; "We are all hungry, you promised us a good meal and a night out. It's almost nine pm, the dining room will close in about an hour let's eat here, and tomorrow you can take us to a fancy restaurant, is that ok with you girls?"

In unison; the other women said it's a date, as they all laughed while we made our way to the dining room. I explained to the ladies what had happened in the catacombs, and thanked the Lord for their safety. After dinner, we sat and chatted till almost midnight. Then we made our way to our rooms.

(Sunday July 14th)

I was awakened from a sound sleep by the ringing of my phone. I had picked up the phone in the room thinking it was ringing. I then grabbed my cell phone. "Yes; this is Gregg Johnson what can I do for you?"

"Dad; this is James and John. We started to worry about you guys since we haven't heard from you in three or four days. Are you and Mom ok?"

"We're sorry son, we're ok we just got caught up being tourists. How are you guys doing? Is John walking without his cast?"

"Dad we are both fine. John had his cast removed two days ago. I do have some bad news for you. The Senator was hospitalized yesterday with chest pains. They are running tests on him today to see if he had a heart attack. So far what they have done has come up negative. We are praying for him Dad. Here talk to John; I love you Dad, give Mom a big hug for me."

"Hi Dad; sorry to have to call you with bad news, but so far the reports about the Senator have all come back negative. As for me, I feel great. I will have a slight limp the rest of my life per the orthopedic specialist. It still hurts, but it will get better as I continue in therapy and trust in the Lord. All the doctors still can't believe that I'm up and walking already, but I know my Lord interceded for both James and I."

"Son, your Mom wants to say hi."

"So long Dad put her on bye, Dad."

I handed the phone to Bev. She talked with the boys for a few minutes. I glanced at the phone and saw what time it was. It was nine pm in Tennessee yesterday, but around seven in the morning here in Austria. I was concerned for the Senator and would call the hospital and check on his condition. Bev and I prayed for the Senator and Mother Richards and our sons. After we finished praying I called the hospital where the Senator was. I got through to his room as Mother Richards answered the phone and of course she asked how our trip was going. Had I spoken with the boys, and for us not to worry about them and their care. She assured me that they were in good hands. She handed the phone to the Senator.

"Hi Sir, how are you feeling?"

"Hi Gregg, I'm feeling fine son. I don't believe I had a heart attack. I believe it was a bad case of indigestion. I ate some fresh water shrimp that may have been tainted. Enough about me, how is your quest going. Did you find what you're looking for?"

"No sir, so far we haven't had any luck. We did find the tomb of Juan De La Cruz, Knights Templar. Sir you would have to see his remains to believe it. He is almost perfectly preserved; as if he was buried a few weeks ago. We found a couple of parchments that are being worked on as we speak to preserve them. I'll let you know just as soon as we find where Count Fernando is entombed. Sir; I must get going, I have an appointment this morning with an archeologist. Take care of yourself, before you hang up, let me pray for you." I prayed with him for a quick recovery, and said goodbye.

It was time for us to get up. As I started to get out of bed the phone rang. It was Friar Emanuel. "Mr. Johnson; I have great news; I was able to unravel the two manuscripts. I am amazed at their condition like they were written yesterday. Why don't I come over and have breakfast with you and we can look over the manuscripts together? One has a map that may surprise you. I'll see you in about half an hour in the lobby of the hotel." I said it was fine as he hung up.

We showered and dressed and made our way downstairs to the dining room. Ever vigil for the unexpected, I felt that each day brought us closer to a final confrontation with the enemies of God.

CHAPTER 32

(Sunday July 14)

Bev and I made our way down stairs, when my cell rang just as we entered the Hotel lobby. I motioned for the Friar to let me take care of the call. It was a call from Dr. Sergio Calderon. "Dr. Calderon, what a surprise. You must be working rather late. What can I do for you?"

"Gregg; I'm not at home, I'm here at a conference in Berlin, Germany. I arrived yesterday. The news I have for you is good. I isolated the mystery drug that has been laced into crystal meth. It is the poison of the black Scorpion found only in the near East. It was mixed with an ancient drug used by the Egyptians to treat people with sleeping problems. The problem is that in small quantities the scorpions poison does help with the other drug. I call it Zodak for its chemical makeup. In the proper dosage, it can help treat arthritis, when it is mixed with methamphetamine it becomes a highly toxic drug and lethal. While here in Berlin I will alert my Bio-Chemists. I have also notified your friend agent Vasquez, from DEA. Sorry it took so long, but thank God we had a breakthrough. Listen; I must go; my meeting is about to start. I'll talk to you soon."

After he hung up, I thought how dumb some of the people who are involved in illicit drugs are. Never knowing how the next dose may be their last. I walked over to where Bev and the Friar were standing when Short Stuff and Matte joined us. Burt and Mary decided to stay in their room, but would see us later at the Cathedral. I introduced the Friar formally to Matte and Bev. We all ordered breakfast and asked for coffee to be served. I filled in the Butlers about the Senator and the call I had just received from Dr Calderon.

Short Stuff said; "that's great Gregg, too bad we aren't going to help Manny."

"Perhaps we will my brother when we get back to the States. You might be surprised."

Friar Emanuel said. "Can I speak freely in front of the ladies?"

"Absolutely Friar, you can speak to all of us, but first let us pray for our food and this day and for our safety as we go back down into the Catacombs." I asked Short Stuff to pray.

After we prayed for breakfast, the Friar continued. "Let me show you the first scroll. It is a letter written by the First Knight, Count Fernando Joaquin De La Cruz. Notice what he wrote!

I said "I thought his name was Juan De la Cruz?"

The Friar said, "I thought so as well, but this may have been a God send. The Knight we exhumed is not the Knight we are looking for, but a guardian. It may help us understand what we are up against. Here goes."

"I; Count Fernando Joaquin De La Cruz, witnessed this day by my remaining son Diego De La Cruz do hereby accept his pledge to guard the secret manuscript and the robe belonging to our Lord. He has taken a sworn oath that he will give his life if necessary to guard these artifacts. They will be hidden in a secret vault at his discretion to guard its secrets after my demise. I believe that in the hands of the wrong person they could cause much harm."

"The letter instructs the son to carry on the Lords work while guarding the robe and manuscripts. Let me show you what else caught my eye. Let me see----ah yes; near the end of the letter. I have one last request my son, before I pass on from this life. I ask that you bury my remains close to where you store the artifacts. The robe and manuscripts are buried or stored near the burial place of Count Fernando Joaquin De La Cruz. Let me pose a question to you. He asked his son Diego to bury him near wherever the son would store the artifacts. My question to all of you is what was the one of things that most of the so called elite families desired?" Short Stuff said, "I'll take a crack at it. To be recognized by other clans or name recognition."

"Correct," cried the Friar. "They all had family crests made. Most Europeans were recognized by their family crest. Notice the letter was sealed by the family seal or crest. On the instructions to his son the Count was no different. The son Diego would have made sure that his father's sarcophagus would have the family crest carved somewhere on the sarcophagus. Gentlemen, look carefully at the crest. Now remember the tomb of the Knight that we uncovered. He did not have the family crest on his tunic. His tunic only had the cross of Loraine. I believe that he was a Knight, but not of the family of De la Cruz. He was a decoy buried to throw off grave robbers. I looked up the De La Cruz family crest and found that it originated in Castile, Spain. It has a large square; within the square is a smaller square with a red cross at the top. At the bottom is a green snake head. At the top of the larger square is a knight's helmet with feathers surrounded by red flowers. At the top of the yellow square is a yellow scroll on which is written the code of commitment. Then at the bottom were written the name Delacruz. The main color of the crest is red and yellow."

"This is what we must look for. I don't know if he is buried here in

Innsbruck. We must search the tombs under the Cathedral, but I have a feeling that he may have been buried in his home town of Castile, Spain along with the artifacts. This is my take on it."

Friar; I said. "If you are right, our enemy El Alacran may have found this out and is on his way right now to Spain. I still don't know why there was another letter which was supposedly written in Hebrew, which was the language of the Jews. The problem is that Hebrew is much older than our letters. I say we finish looking at all the tombs and if we don't find the De La Cruz tomb here, we go to Castile."

Friar Emanuel said; "I'm not sure if I can get away, but I will ask my superior and see if I can go. I will cross that road when I have too. I suggest we get going, we will be underground for most of the day.

We made our way to the underground entrance and found the door to the tomb we had opened yesterday. We found the tomb of the well-preserved Knight. I wondered why God had allowed this man's preservation. When we opened the door to the tomb we started looking for the De la Cruz crest on the other sarcophaguses. We reopened the sarcophagus where the preserved Knight was buried, and when we opened it we found that he was no longer so preserved, somehow he had aged like the rest of the other remains. I thought perhaps God had intervened so as not to have the media create a circus atmosphere in the tombs of those who were dead.

I asked the Friar, "What do you think happened to the Knight's remains?"

Is it a chemical reaction to the air or a supernatural change to age him overnight?"

"I believe it's a supernatural change, he answered. I believe that God wanted to show us how this man looked over five hundred years ago. We need to search every sarcophagus in here and the other two large tombs. Remember we are looking for the Delacruz family crest."

We were down to the last tomb with only a handful of granite blocks to investigate. Burt hollered out and said, "ladies and gentleman I think I may have found what we are looking for. Friar, can you come over here for a minute?"

The Friar said; "Gentlemen, I need some help in opening the sarcophagus. Here is the crow bar. Short Stuff, please help me open the lid."

Short Stuff said: "Friar, let me see if I can get that cover off. I think it is loose. Yes, it is loose. Here help me remove it. We need to be very careful that we don't break any part of the sarcophagus, or molest the remains of the individual who lies in rest. Gregg, Burt, give me a hand to pull the entire coffin out from the wall. On the count of three, one, two, three pull. Good guys----here it comes. Friar, will you do the honors."

He said, "My pleasure, as he was startled and he cried out its empty. There is something scratched under the lid in Spanish. It maybe a clue to where he is buried. It reads; 'sepultado circa de las flores en el jardin de dios.' In English; 'entombed near the flowers in the garden of God,' this is our only clue. I believe this is a great clue. The Spaniards loved to plant flower gardens. They would name them in honor of God. The Knight came from Castile, or what was called Hispania in those days. I believe that he is buried in Toledo, or close to the Alcazar Castle or Cathedral. Toledo was once the capital city of Spain then Madrid became the capital. During the Crusades, many Knights were commissioned to fight for God and Hispania. It is a wonderful place to see and has a lot of historical places to visit and study. The Moors conquered this high fortified city and made it a Moorish stronghold. It remained under Moorish control even after most of the Moors were expelled from Spain."

"I said; thank you for the history lesson Friar Emanuel. We must continue our search. Did you ask your superior if you could accompany us to Spain?"

"I asked him and much to my surprise, he said it would be good public relations if I went. We are finished here, let us close the tomb and leave."

"We can look further, but if my hunch is right; the Scorpion may already have this information. If not, he no doubt will be watching us to see where we are going next. I also believe that the ploy about blowing us up was just that. He's going to let us do the dirty work, then try to take it away from us. My friends, we need to be very vigilant as we are up against a very wily adversary. Let's go, as John Wayne would say; "we're burning daylight."

We got back to the hotel earlier than I thought, so I went to the front desk and asked the clerk when the next flight to Madrid Spain. He said that there was a flight leaving for Madrid at five. I called and made reservations for the seven of us.

I also called and rented a car in Madrid. Toledo is only a couple of hours away. I asked to see if we could rent a large SUV, an Escalade or something in that class. We lucked out, they had one that had just been turned in. It would be ready for us when we arrived. I looked at my watch and saw that it was after two in the afternoon. The Friar was going to go with us to Toledo. We decided to eat an early dinner. We went into the dining room of the hotel and sat down to eat. Our flight left around five PM. The girls were disappointed that our night out had been delayed.

The Friar was quite a historian. He filled us in as to the history of Toledo. He called it a Spanish Treasure. We were excited that we would see such a beautiful city with such a rich history. The Romans founded it, and then captured by the Visigoths, then the Iberians. The Moors brought a great change to the Spanish people as well. Spanish culture is rich in Christian, Jewish and Moorish culture. There were many famous people who were born or lived in Toledo. It is a city of close to seventy-nine thousand inhabitants. Two famous landmarks line the skyline, the Alcazar, is the Arabicized Latin word for palace-castile. In 1085 Alfonso VI of Castile re-captured Toledo and took direct control of the Moorish city. This era was called la Reconquista, (re-conquest.). Arabic books and Hebrew would be translated to Spanish by Arab and Jewish scholars; then from Spanish to Latin by Castilian scholars. This allowed the lost knowledge to spread throughout Christian Europe again. The decline of Toledo helped to preserve its cultural and architectural patrimony. Today; it is one of Spain's foremost cities, receiving thousands of visitors yearly. I have been there on sabbaticals and if my hunch is right, we will find our Knight in the Cathedral."

"Friar Emanuel; thank you for the valuable information about Toledo, it is so rich in history and has played an important part of American history. We can thank the King and Queen of Spain for allowing Christopher Columbus to visit our shores. He opened the United States for exploration along with Fernando Cortez who explored Mexico. Sadly; Cortez ravaged Mexico because of his lust for gold. Men like Cortez think wealth gives them power, in most cases they reap what they sow." I said.

Short Stuff spoke up. "I look at my people who were brought to our country by Spanish slave traders. I have heard it referred to as the black ivory trade. They were one of the last ones to stop slave trading.

Ironically there is still slave trade being done in certain parts of the world."

Matte said. "My great, great, great, grandmother died at a hundred and four years of age. She had been born on a plantation a slave, but praise-be to God she lived to be set free."

Bev said. "Most of us can't relate to what a slave had to go through. People who live under a totalitarian form of government are slaves to the dictator who subjugates his people. One of my favorite passages in the Bible is where Paul and Silas are incarcerated in Philippi. They were chained to the wall worshipping and praising Jesus, when an earthquake hits and frees them, yet they witnessed to the jailer. They were rewarded by the jailer by releasing Paul and Silas and giving his heart to Jesus, along with his entire household. What a gracious God we have that turns a bad scenario into a positive one." (See Acts Chap. 16)

We were interrupted by the Assistant Manager stating that our shuttle to the airport was here. We went to our rooms for our luggage. As Bev and I went to our room I noticed out of the corner of my eye a couple of men that got up at the same time. Instinctively I knew they were tailing us. The Scorpion hadn't forgotten us. He was watching for a more opportune time to strike again. After getting our luggage brought down to the front desk, I glanced around ever alert on guard in case I was called on to react immediately. I noticed the same two guys as I made eye contact with one of them. He was trying to stare me down. He was not very tall, perhaps five feet eight or nine. What caught my attention was how powerful he is built, he reminded me of one of those men who compete in the Ironman competition. His shoulders and neck were huge, along with his brutish arms. He looked like he could lift several hundred pounds with ease. You could see all this by the way his suit fit him. I thought, if he wanted to he most likely could flex and tear his suit jacket. I prayed to God I would never have to wrestle with him.

Short Stuff said "Gregg; did you notice the little bull and the other goon with him? We need to be very careful with these two guys, especially the guy built like a small tank. Here comes Burt and Mary. I think we can be on our way."

"Your right my brother, as to the two guys who are tailing us, I agree with you. I think the Scorpion is planning something for us all. Let's go, I see my wife waving for us to go to the curb."

We all piled into the hotel airport shuttle and made our way to the Innsbruck Airport. The flight would take no more than three hours. We would spend the night in Madrid. Then drive to Toledo in the morning where we had made reservations close to the Cathedral. I glanced out the back window and saw our two shadows get into a supped-up Mercedes, as we pulled away from the curb.

Chapter 33

(Sunday July 14)

The flight to Madrid was easy without any glitches. We arrived in Madrid close to eight PM and took a shuttle to our hotel. As we were leaving the airport walking to the shuttle a man brushed me as he went by. I checked my coat for any cuts and found that I had a slash above the pocket of my sports jacket. I looked under the jacket and found that the cut did not penetrate my shirt, but it had cut my pocket Bible. I was lucky this time. It was a warning from El Alacran. I remembered what had happened in the D.C. mall a few weeks back.

Tired and sleepy we went to our rooms. We said goodnight to the others and made our way to our respective rooms, showered and hit the sack.

(Monday July 15th)

After breakfast, we went to the car rental to pick up our SUV for our drive to Toledo. Friar Emanuel offered to drive us to Toledo, since he knew the roads, especially his way out of Madrid. Toledo is only about seventy km from Madrid, but because a major part of the trip is winding mountain roads, it takes almost two hours to drive.

As we went along I said to the Friar, "Can you see the dark sedan that has been behind us since we left the hotel?"

He said, "Yes; as a matter of fact, he has stayed back when he had plenty of time to pass us if he intended too. They definitely have malice in their hearts towards us."

"Good, we are on the same page. I understand that we will be hitting a steep grade in a few minutes. I think he will try and ram us off the road when we get there. Here's the pull out ahead. Pull over and let me slide over to the driver side. All of you fasten your seat belts, I think we will be in for a very rough ride."

As I pulled away from the pull out here comes our tail and starts hitting us from behind. The SUV I was driving was a Cadillac with a supercharger. I decided to wait till we got to the steepest climb before we descended into the town of Toledo. We had about two miles to go when he again revved up his speed and rammed us a couple of times. I felt that the person who was driving was a novice. A pro would have hooked us and tried to spin us around and hit us broadside. As I punched the accelerator and pulled away from the sedan and started our descent, I knew he was not used to ramming cars. He was a rank amateur because he let us get away.

I looked in the mirror and saw that he had pulled over and was arguing with another person, a woman. A woman I knew along with the man she was arguing with, Augustine and Rebecca Villalobos. I had forgotten that they lived in Toledo and of course they had to work for the Scorpion based on what they had just done. We drove directly to the hotel and checked in and unloaded the van as the clerk took our luggage to our rooms.

I didn't know how long we would be in Toledo, so I told them at the desk we would be here for at least three days; perhaps longer. I signaled for the Friar to come over to me. I told him I wanted to speak with him concerning where he felt we needed to start our search. He said that we should go to the Cathedral and start our trek there. He said that he and I should go and talk to the fellow brother who was knowledgeable about the history of the Cathedral. I concurred with him. I told the rest of the group that the Friar and I would be checking out the Cathedral. We needed permission from the local head Friar to search the tombs. We would be back in a couple of hours. Friar Emanuel said he knew the Friar in charge who would allow us to explore the Cathedral; with its twenty chapels where Knights and former dignitaries of Spain are entombed.

We hailed a cab to the Cathedral which was about ten minutes from our hotel. I said to the Friar. "The guy that rammed us was a person that we met at Dr. Reynaldo Cabrillo's home. The good doctor was also a Twelfth Knight. Unfortunately, he was killed a few days ago. The man who tried to kill us was a guest of Dr. Cabrillo's. His wife was the woman who got out of the car. I believe they work for the Scorpion, and live here in Toledo. I wanted to alert you that they may go to great extremes to try and kill us." We arrived at our destination.

We made our way to the rector's office, ever alert; especially now with thousands of tourists walking the halls of this great Cathedral. We approached the rector's office and knocked on the door. We heard a voice respond in Spanish, "come in." We opened the door and were greeted by a very distinguished looking man in his late fifties or early sixties, with jet black hair graying at the temples. He responded by saying; "Emanuel, what a great surprise my brother. What brings you to Toledo? How many years has it been since you and I last saw each other?"

"It's been almost four years, when the reigning Pope was installed. As for what brings me to Toledo, let me first introduce you to Gregg Johnson, former head of the famous FBI. He is here with some other people on a quest ordered by the Brotherhood. We are searching for the burial place and remains of Count Fernando Joaquin De La Cruz, former Twelfth Knight."

I'm sorry, but I didn't get your name?" I said.

"My name is Friar Miguel from Cordoba. It is an honor and a pleasure to meet you Mr. Johnson and to know that you are a fellow brother. What makes you think he is buried here in Toledo? I understood that he was buried in Innsbruck."

Friar Emanuel said; "We found his tomb, but when we opened it we found it empty. We also found this written under the lid of the sepulcher where he was entombed, 'sepultado circa de las flores en el jardin de dios,' or in English; 'entombed near the flowers in the garden of God'. Brother Miguel, do you have any idea where he could be buried?"

"I had the same request a couple of days ago. He said he was head of the, oh I forgot. Let me see the entry book, ah here it is. He signed it Professor Franz Engels Director of Antiquities Wien University. He claimed he was a member of the Brotherhood. It was the way he said it that made me suspicious, so I told him that I was unsure if this Knight was buried here. Our records go all the way back to the thirteenth century when this place was being built. It was built on the site of where the Great Mosque of Toledo stood. A Visigoth Church replaced the mosque in 1226 and was completed in 1493. There are several Knights buried here in the Cathedral.

Let me review some old manuscripts and books tonight then I will contact you. What hotel are you staying at?"

"We are staying at the Alcazar named after the Old Castile." I said.

He said. "It's a good hotel. I will call you as soon as I find something important. I have a tour to do in a few minutes, so I must go."

We left and went back to the hotel and decided to visit some of the local tourist shops and foundries where they still make swords of the famous Toledo steel. Bev wanted to buy some kitchen knives that she had always wanted. We also visited some of the glass blowing shops and were totally amazed at how they can make such beautiful glassware and vases. All of us were completely enthralled with the local artistry. We also visited the Alcazar that has a rich history of Moorish conquest. It is a very historical fortress.

We returned to the hotel and had a couple of calls from Friar Miguel. I asked Friar Emanuel to call him and see what was so important. He called him and got right through to him. "Brother Miguel! This is brother Emanuel, what is so urgent?"

"I found something of interest but there is a hitch. Would you give me the name of the Knight you are looking for?"

"We are specifically looking for the sepulchral of Count Fernando Joaquin De La Cruz. His youngest son was named Diego De La Cruz. These are the names that we have, but there could have been a miss-spelling Delacruz, or such as De La Cruz."

"Ah; my brother, you have cleared it up for me. There are two ways of spelling the last name, and the records show a Juan De La Cruz de Obregon. He is a relative of the Count, also a Knight and most likely the one buried in Innsbruck. Now the tricky part is; how do we interpret the riddle 'sepultado circa de las flores en el jardin de

Dios,' or in English, 'entombed near the flowers in the garden of God.' I remembered that when it was a Visigoth church there was a garden and a cemetery with several family tombs close to the garden of God. Why don't you come back this evening and perhaps I will have some more information for you? I have an old book full of drawings and maps of what is under the Cathedral, perhaps I will find some clue to what you are looking for."

As Friar Emanuel finished speaking with Friar Miguel he explained to me what was going on. We would wait for his call. We decided to have dinner as Friar Emanuel told us about a fantastic Spanish restaurant close by that was walking distance from the hotel. Burt and Mary decided to stay and eat at the hotel. Mary wasn't feeling that well and felt she would be a burden to the rest of us.

The walk to the restaurant was about three blocks. As we made our way to the restaurant I caught sight of two men tailing us across the street. Since we were here at the height of the tourist season the two were trying to blend in with sidewalk lookers. I alerted Short Stuff so he and Matte could back us up. I was praying silently to myself that they wouldn't try anything because of the women. We came to a large department store. I motioned to Matte and Short Stuff to follow into the store. I wanted to buy a few gifts for the boys. I noticed that there was an elevator so we went upstairs where they had a shop for younger men. As the elevator door closed, I caught a better look at our tails and saw it was the same guys from Innsbruck.

Bev said after we got into the elevator; "Gregg, I saw the same two characters who were following us earlier in the hotel. I don't think they will try anything with all the people walking around. I told you that we would be in constant danger. Just tell us when to react, ok Dear?"

"I'm sorry Dear; I forget that you have taken some classes in martial arts and know how to defend yourself. It's my nature to protect those who are in danger. I'm sure even Short Stuff does the same? Am I right brother?"

"Yes, Matte knows how to take care of herself as well. We met at the police academy. She was a good cop, and tough. I would advise people not to mess with her."

Matte responded; "You bet don't let me lose my cool, or you will see Wonder Woman in action."

We all had a good laugh, but as we went back down to the main entrance. We made it a point to purposely pass by the two men. They looked surprised as we walked out the door.

We made it to the restaurant without incident and enjoyed a wonderful dinner of Paella, and an Authentic Gazpacho soup that is served chilled. It is made of tomato stock or juice and contains chopped raw vegetables. They served us antipasto, several different chesses and assorted cuts of ham and great French bread. We topped it off with a great dessert of Spanish pastries and strong Spanish coffee.

We had just ordered more coffee when my cell rang. It was Friar Miguel. He said; "sorry to bother you Mr. Johnson, but I have that item we discussed earlier. When can you get here? I will be in the rectory, just knock on the door. I have found some interesting data that will help us locate the Knights in question. I'll see you soon."

"That was our friend Friar Miguel. He said he found what he was looking for. We are done with dinner so if no one objects, let's go."

We walked outside into the early night air and decided to catch a cab to the Cathedral. I felt this might throw our adversaries off track. I didn't see them, but felt their menacing presence as we got into the cab. I told Friar Emanuel to tell the cab driver to lose those following us. The cabby turned around and said; "Mr. Johnson, the senator sends his regards. He is all right he's in excellent health, but at the advice of other fellow Knights, he feigned that he was sick and went into hiding for protection. I also belong to the 'Brotherhood' the two that were following you are sleeping comfortably in their car near the Alcazar in a parking lot. My name is Gustavo Mesa. Here is my card, God speed." We had a safe short ride to the Cathedral.

We thanked him and wished him well in his duties as a fellow brother as he drove off; we wondered if we would see him again?

CHAPTER 34

(Monday July 15)

We walked over to the rectory and knocked on the door, but to no avail. I tried the door and found it open. There was a small light at the back of the front room where Friar Miguel said he would be. I tried the door and found it open. I said to the rest to be quiet as we made our way to the back room. I looked at the desk and saw a form of a man slumped over on the desk. I asked Friar Emanuel to find a light switch and turn on the overhead lights. The form at the desk was not Friar Miguel but another man. The man at the desk had been hit on the head and was knocked un-conscience. He was starting to come around when we heard a sound in another room.

We made our way to the other door and opened it. It was the living quarters of the Friars who are assigned to the Cathedral. We found the room that said Friar Miguel and opened the door. We found the light switch and turned on the lights. There was a small single bed, a night stand and a small desk and a book shelf with loads of books on antiquities and ruins. There was also a book on ancient burial sites in Spain and other parts of Europe. There were some older leather bound books that were hand written and very old. I opened one and saw a piece of paper with some recent writing and the name of our Count, Fernando Joaquin Delacruz underlined. Everything was written in Spanish and Latin.

I called out; "Friar Emanuel can you come back here for a moment. I'm in Friar Miguel's room."

He came running with Bev; while Short Stuff and Matte were trying to revive the Friar, who had been knocked out. I heard them say he was coming around. "Friar Emanuel, what do you make of these notes that Friar Miguel wrote."

Friar Emanuel said; "He has done some searching, but it looks like he was looking for the ruins of the Visigoths. His notes are in Spanish, but the map he is looking at; is in Latin. They are symbols of a cemetery that once was part of the original grounds. There are traces of it all over the Cathedral grounds. Remember he asked to be buried close to the garden of God. There must have been a garden in the days when the first crusades took place. There would have to be a symbol, one that his son Diego would have known to fulfill his Fathers request. There are twenty Chapels in the Cathedral. Ah yes, why didn't I see this before? There is a Chapel, one of the twenty that is named Capilla de Santiago or the Chapel of St. James. They were named in memory of the Knights of Saint James. Some of them are buried behind the Alter. Perhaps we will be able to examine the vault. We know that our Knight will have his family crest on the front of the tomb. I think if we locate where Friar Miguel is we can get started."

"Let's go back see what happened to the Friar who was knocked out. Perhaps he can shed some light on what happened to Friar Miguel." I said.

We walked back into the outer part of the rectory and met Friar Antonio. Short Stuff said, "this is Friar Antonio. He has a good size lump on the back of his head, but can only tell us that he and Friar Miguel were doing some research for us, when in walked these four men. They all spoke Spanish and wanted to know what the Americans wanted. They took Friar Miguel with them and said to Friar Antonio not to call the police. The next thing he knows, he sees me trying to wake him up. He said he remembers one of the men hitting him over the head with a pipe or leather looking object. He said that Friar Miguel had told him that we were looking for a tomb of a dead Knight."

"Do you speak English Friar?" I said.

"Of course I do. I also speak German, French and Italian. Here help me up."

"You said that the men who hit you on the head were Spaniards?"

"No their accents were from Mexico or Central America. I remember one of them had a tattoo of a scorpion with the name; 'El Alacran.' His tattoo was clearly visible because he had his coat off. He did most of the talking. One of the men called him Beto. I hope and pray that they didn't harm Brother Miguel. Forgive me Sir, I need to know if Brother Miguel told you about the new discovery we made a few weeks ago?"

"No he didn't mention anything to me about a new discovery, why?"

"You asked me where I learned my English. I majored in English, at the University of Madrid, but got interested in archeology one summer on a sabbatical to the Holy Land. I volunteered to help a brother Friar who had a doctorate in Archeology. I was fascinated at what lies underneath our feet here in our Cathedral. We discovered a well-preserved portion of a small village underneath parts of the grounds. I was looking at some writings in one of the many Chapels when the flooring gave way under me. I went tumbling down under the floor. We found a small portion of a garden, next to a sepulcher. There are several tombs where Knights are buried facing the cemetery. I would love to show you the ruins. Now would be a great time, but for one thing; Brother Miguel."

"Do you think he showed the ruins to the people who took him?" I asked.

"I don't know Mr. Johnson. I don't think so, knowing Brother Miguel."

The rest of the group said "let's go. It will be fantastic seeing something that has been buried for centuries."

No sooner did we get the words out of our mouths when in walks Friar Miguel. He had been roughed up a bit, but was alright.

I asked Brother Miguel if he was ok! Did they threaten him if he said anything to the authorities?

He had answered yes to both of my questions, but he told them that God was more powerful than the misguided leader they followed. "I told them I would pray for their souls. They were looking for the same Knight that you were seeking, but with one error, they had the wrong name as you had, Juan de la Cruz de Obregon We have all made the mistake because of the way this name is spelled two ways. When they figure it out; they will be very upset. Upset that I sent them on a wild, how do you say Chicken chase?"

We all cracked up when he said this.

"I believe that they were going back to Innsbruck. The last I saw of them was the tail-lights on their car.

Brother Miguel, we are deeply sorry that they hurt you. Now what are we going to do? Did you tell them about the new find you unearthed?" I said.

"Yes to your question about the new archeological digs. And we are all going down to see what they look like. We are all ready with flashlights and lanterns. We are waiting on you." Said, Friar Miguel and Brother Antonio will show us the way."

CHAPTER 35

(Monday July 15ᵗʰ)

We made our way into the Cathedral as the Friars led the way. We were all so impressed by the magnificence and beauty of the structured art-work. The historical artifacts that make up the Cathedral here in Toledo and throughout Spain gave us the history of this great country. They don't need museums since most of their national treasures are showcased in their Cathedrals.

Friar Antonio broke the silence by saying; ladies and gentlemen, let me caution you. From here on be very careful as you walk. Parts of the old flooring may give way. This is how we discovered the underground ruins. Please follow me in a single file. Notice the roped off area. There is a ladder going down to the next level, which is circa thirteen or fourteenth century. Below that is another floor, which we have recently started to explore, which goes back to Roman times. We believe between two hundred and three hundred AD. I will go down the ladder first then Friar Emanuel then the ladies and the then the rest of our group. Friar Miguel will bring up the rear. Again, let me caution you! Please watch your steps. Oh; one more thing, we are behind the chapel named after the apostle Saint James; in Spanish, Capilla Santiago."

As he disappeared below we each followed him down the ladder into the ruins. We went down about fifteen feet as I shined the light around to see what we were exploring, when all at once a bunch of flood lights went on. Now you could see very clearly as to what had been unearthed. There was an old alter and Catholic artifacts and a large crucifix of our Lord made in marble. On the floor were grave sites of important people who had died during this period. We were looking for a sarcophagus with the De La Cruz crest. What amazed me was, how some of the colors were still so bright and vivid. This place was an Archeologist dream to find a dig so well preserved.

Friar Antonio said; "Ladies and Gentlemen, again let me remind you, be careful where you step. As you can see, we had another collapse from this level to the next. It is my opinion as well as Brother Miguel's opinion that the resting place of Count Fernando Joaquin Delacruz, or De La Cruz is buried pointing eastward. The request he made to his son was, he wanted to be buried near the place where the artifacts, the robe and manuscripts were stored. We need to put our heads together. Please come closer to me."

As we all gathered close to him, I said, "Let us pray and see if God will show us where the Knight is entombed."

Friar Antonio said, "Mr. Johnson why don't you pray that the Holy Spirit will give us insight where to look."

"Thank you Brother Antonio for asking me it is an honor. 'Dear Holy Spirit we come before you to ask your blessing in finding the resting place of Count Fernando Joaquin De La Cruz. Lord we also pray for protection and the integrity of the Knights pledge, to guard with his life! The resting place of the things entrusted to him, so long ago. May we in our zeal not disturb or destroy his earthly grave. Give us insight dear Holy Spirit where we can look, I thank you in Jesus blessed name. Amen!"

After I finished praying I said, "Do any of you have any clue or idea where the tomb is?"

Friar Miguel said; "I think I have an idea, let us look for a large painting or a fresco covering a wall depicting the Garden of Eden"

We all started looking on the walls of the ancient chapel. Matte and Bev were the first ones to say something. Bev said; "Gentlemen come over here. There is on the wall a painting of some sort but it has been covered over with a painting of the village and the country side."

Friar Antonio went over to the wall and started peeling off layers of what was used in those days for covering over an existing painting. It was a crude form of plaster. It would take several hours of careful work for us in order not to destroy what was underneath. Was it what we were looking for? Only pains-taking work done by an expert would uncover what we were looking for. Removing the crude paint and plaster that was hiding what was underneath, we had reason to believe it was the mural of the Garden of the Lord.

Friar Antonio said; "What the ladies have discovered maybe what we are looking for. It is on the east wall. In those days' people believed to look to the east for the return of Christ mentioned by Him in the scriptures. He said they can discern the weather, but not the times of His return. If all three friars who are experienced in archeology will concentrate on cleaning the wall, perhaps they can expose enough of the wall to see if it is a painting of the Garden of Eden. Let us also continue to look for the resting place of our fallen Knight. It is now almost midnight and we need our rest. Let us go back to the rectory and we will resume our quest in the morning say at nine am. Ok; let us go."

We made our way back to the hotel and enjoyed the night air. We decided to stop and have some Spanish pastries with Spanish hot chocolate. We spied a small place called El Nuevo Toledo that was still open. The name meant the New Toledo. We weren't disappointed with the hot chocolate. Spain is noted for its chocolate and fine pastries. We just sat and talked about a lot of things, when I remembered it was a good time to call the boys. I excused myself from the table and dialed the number. Mother Richards answered the phone. She said everyone was fine including the Senator. She said that the boys were out fishing with Sheriff Duckworth. They had been gone for about an hour. I told her I would call back later and to give my love to the boys, the Senator and Sheriff Duckworth. We finished our midnight snack and went to our hotel.

(Tuesday July 16th)

We finally made it to our room and I decided I needed a shower. My wife joined me in the shower and of course we did what most husbands and wives do. It was about five AM when I was awakened by a familiar rolling and a shaking and rumbling sound. It was an earthquake. It wasn't of the magnitude that I had experienced in Rome a few years back, but it was enough to wake us both up. Then it got quiet and then the eerie sound of sirens in the distance. Earthquakes are not uncommon in Spain, but I was praying and hoping that the new archeological discoveries were not affected. We decided to check with the Friars. So, we got dressed and went downstairs to the lobby. Burt and Mary were already there along with Matte and Short Stuff. They had been awakened by the earthquake as well. Like us, they were worried what could have happened to the ruins? We were all concerned at what we would find?

We decided to have some pastries and coffee before we left for the Cathedral. The coffee shop was about to open so we all sat down and enjoyed our small breakfast. After we finished we hailed a cab. It was our brother in Christ, Gustavo Mesa. "Good morning" he said. "Did the rolling and shaking wake you up? I thought so. By the way tell Friar Antonio and Miguel that the four assassins were arrested and dispatched to Interpol. They were out to get you three men, but the Brotherhood interceded. I want to warn you that El Alacran has been seen here in Toledo. He has a Hacienda in Madrid and has people in his organization all over the world. We know that he has established a lucrative business of selling illegal drugs here in Spain. He has a lot of ties with Spanish politicians. The Brotherhood are here to back you up, but still be on the alert. Perhaps I will see you later. Keep the faith and remember the Brotherhood."

"I wonder why the Scorpion is so set on going after the artifacts. Some would say it is a wild goose chase. Unless he has positive proof that what we are looking for is real? We don't have proof the artifacts are authentic and the robe belonged to our Lord. Heilman put up some of his billions for the Lords robe. Some of his Nazi sympathizers have been offered a reward for the robe. Just think; if the robe is authentic. Heilman, could then recoup his money by marketing the robe as authentic. I personally pray that it's not." Ever since the first century, fraudulent artifacts have been hawked.

Short Stuff said, "Gregg, you have a good point. I believe that the Scorpions hatred stems from his being born Hispanic and white. He suffered discrimination at the hands of racial zealots. He has tried to kill you and anyone who has anything to do with you."

I responded; "In other words, your saying he could give a hoot about the robe and manuscripts, He is using Heilman and Fenneman because they are financing his drug wars. He has a lot of competition with the other drug cartels. He has alienated some of the European Cartels as well. I think when he introduced Euphoria he miscalculated its lethality. He didn't realize that the chemical makeup would kill rather than cause the user to be addicted. One of the last reports I read as Director was the information I just shared with you. I also believe that he and Heilman are at odds. I believe that he is trying to cover up his mistakes. He also underestimated the Russian and Italian Mafia. There were some killings in D.C. that were made to look like the Scorpions killings, but they were done by the Mafia. The Mafia in the States is pushed out of shape because of the death of kids."

Burt spoke up; "Jesus said, 'a house divided against itself cannot stand.' We need to figure out how we can drive a further wedge between the Scorpion and Heilman. After we find what we are looking for we can focus on doing just that."

I said; "We need to find out what happened at the Cathedral. Let's go directly to the rectory and see if we can roundup the Friars. Sounds like the great Tenors, Pavarotti, Placido Domingo and Cabrera. Ours are Antonio, Miguel and Emanuel." Everyone got a great laugh as we made our way to the rectory.

We knocked on the door and within a few seconds the door opened and there stood Friar Miguel. He apologized for taking so long to open the door. "Please come in. I'm sure you felt the temblor this morning. Brother Antonio is down in the digs checking to see if there was any additional damage to the site. He will be back in a few minutes. If all is well, we will go and complete the work we started. He always sings when he is thinking. He has such a beautiful tenor voice, I think, I hear him now."

We all started laughing, because of what I had said earlier. I decided to explain to the Friar why we were laughing and he also thought it funny so he burst out laughing.

Friar Antonio said, "Good morning my friends. I just came from making an extensive inspection of the site. I am blessed to say, that I believe the good Lord interceded for us. Much to my amazement what I thought would take us all day to do, was done by the earthquake; the outer wall over the fresco came tumbling down. You will see one of the most beautiful murals ever seen and paintings of the Garden of Eden. Now what we need to do is find our Knights burial place. If we are ready to go let us proceed."

CHAPTER 36

(Wednesday July17)

We made our way to the ruins through the Cathedral. The Chapel of St. James was closed to the public because of repairs, so we would not be bothered by tourists. We went down the ladder and were totally taken back at what we saw. The entire East wall was a painting of the Lord's Garden. The colors and hues were blended into deep greens and blues. The light was illuminated by the brilliance of the Lord's presence. He was depicted as walking along with Adam and Eve. The tree of the knowledge of good and evil was depicted as a tree with different types of fruit with the shape of the serpent wrapped around the trunk. The tree of life was painted with brilliance and hues of light. The plants and animals were all shown in natural colors. They were so realistic it was hard not to want to touch the images. It looked three dimensional without the special glasses

Friar Antonio said; "It is the most realistic depiction of the Lord's Garden I have ever seen, it is if God painted it. I can see why the Knight said he wanted to be buried facing the wall. Now where would Diego De La Cruz bury the manuscripts and the Lord's robe?"

We all stood looking and studying the painting. Where would the Knight have buried these vital artifacts? I said; "The letter the Count left said to bury the artifacts in a vault, he said to bury him facing the garden of the Lord. Where would be the least suspected place, a Catholic has access too?"

Mary spoke up. "I would think that it would be on the Altar. The most restricted place to parishioner's, is the Altar. The writings and the Lord's robe are considered sacred. Much more in those days, only a priest could approach the Altar. The sacred place on the Altar is where the chalice is stored. If I were going to hide it, I would place the artifacts behind where the chalice is. I think the box where the cup and bread for communion representing the host are kept. We should look their where I believe we will find the burial place of the Knight."

All three Friars concurred. Friar Antonio said; "let me see if I can move part of the Altar away from where the host is kept, while some of you see if there is a space behind the Altar."

Short Stuff and I found that you could go behind the entire Altar. We made our way behind and noticed the crest of the De La Cruz family about the middle of where the crucifix is placed. At the feet of where the crucifix is aligned was the outline of a small vault. I thought it would be easy to open, until I tried to pry it open. It had been sealed with mortar and brick. I went over and started to chip away at the mortar.

Short Stuff said; "Gregg, there has to be a secret lock let me see if we can find it. Push on the bolts on the four corners."

We tried that, but nothing happened. I looked at the crest and saw the snake. I pushed in on the snake and it started to open, but because of the age it didn't open all the way. I asked for a crow bar and Bev brought it over to me. I pulled it back and found a small room behind the door. It was large enough to hold us all, if we crammed ourselves.

I called Friar Antonio over along with Friar Miguel to come and enter the vault.

Both came over highly excited. Friar Miguel entered first, then Friar Antonio. They asked me to enter as well. In the center of the room was a sarcophagus. It was the tomb of Count Fernando Joaquin De La Cruz. We needed to open the sarcophagus and because I had the crowbar in my hand, I inserted the bar and started prying.

Friar Antonio said, "Be careful. Place a handkerchief over your mouth and nose. It is well known that many of the tombs opened in the past excreted body waste or poison. Go ahead Mr. Johnson, finish prying the lid off."

When the lid came off, we were dumb founded at what we were looking at. It was a man who had been mummified, yet had been entombed with his entire Knights armor. Within the sarcophagus was a large sealed jar. I thought; these must be the manuscripts. Under the head of the Knight was a folded ancient fabric. As Friar Antonio carefully lifted the blanket or robe and started to unfold it, it turned out that it was a robe. What amazed us was that it was in fantastic condition. It also had what looked like blood stains on it. Could this have been the robe that our Lord wore?"

"Gentlemen, are we holding in our hands what some believe is the Lord's robe?" I said.

Friar Miguel said; "This find must be reported to our government authorities, as well as to the Papal authorities. We cannot keep this secret to ourselves. Even though I am a Christian first, I must follow my conscience as a moral principle."

"Brother Miguel I concur, but we who are of a different belief other than Roman Catholic are faced with a conundrum. If it is the robe of Christ, the Catholic Church will most likely not allow others to examine it or even see it? They will most likely treat it like the Shroud of Turin. Very few people can view the Shroud. Because of the condition of this robe, they may allow others to examine it. I don't know if I am willing to negate my sworn statement, that I would guard these artifacts with my life."

Mary spoke up; "May I interject something, as a Charismatic Catholic I believe that far too many people venerate icons within the Catholic Church. I'm afraid that this will happen to the robe. We haven't examined the manuscripts yet either. Perhaps they are writings of the Lord Himself, or Paul the Apostle. If we are going to release these artifacts, then we must allow all leading Biblical scholars and religious archeologists to examine them. That's my opinion on the matter."

I spoke up. "I recently was ordained as a Twelfth Knight and was assigned my first quest. To find out if the artifacts existed, and if they did to care for them until they were secured in a safe place. I took an oath to give my life if need be to protect the integrity of the things of God."

Friar Antonio said, "I concur with Mr. Johnson. My vows were not to protect artifacts, but to protect the teachings of our Lord Jesus Christ. I belong to the order of Saint Francis of Assisi, a vow of poverty and compassion. Brother Miguel belongs to the order of Jesuits. Brother Emanuel is of the same order as I. I think I can speak for him as well. Let us pray until tomorrow and perhaps the Holy Spirit will give us guidance as to which way we should go. In the meantime, we should guard these artifacts with our lives if need be."

I said; "I think brother Antonio has spoken with authority, we all love the same God who died for our sins. Where will we store the artifacts until tomorrow?"

Friar Emanuel said, "Why not just leave them where we found

them. One more day won't disturb them. We can seal the vault and place an undisturbed seal on the vault door.?"

"I think it's a great idea, and if anyone here thinks we need to guard it overnight; I am willing to stand with that person or persons." I said.

I had a feeling that one of our Friars was not what he said he was, so I needed to be on guard for my friends and the artifacts. We placed the artifacts back in the coffin and placed the heavy rustic iron lid on the sarcophagus. For those of us who had opened the sarcophagus we climbed out of the vault and closed the vault door and replaced the seal. All three Friars volunteered to guard the tomb.

"Gentlemen, why don't we take turns; it is now around ten in the morning. Let us pray for guidance first, then come back tonight at six o'clock. I don't think anyone here would take other measures. The public is not allowed in here yet. So, if anyone came in here it would be one of us."

Friar Antonio said; "I concur with Mr. Johnson; he is right we need to go about our daily routines. Besides there are only two other Friars here and one of them is not into archeology. There are a couple of Priests assigned here, but they are involved with the daily Mass and church polity. They know we are working in the new dig, but again are not involved with this area of the Cathedral."

"It's settled then, we will return tonight at six and select teams for guarding the tomb. Keep fervently in prayer and seeking God's Will for what He wants us to do with the artifacts, let's go." I said.

CHAPTER 37

(Wednesday July 17)

We made our way back to the surface and felt rather good to breathe the clean mountain air rather than the stale musty air that had been in the tombs. I asked Bev what day this was and we both had to look at our calendars. It was July sixteenth. We had been gone almost three weeks. We decided to have a late breakfast and an early lunch combined. We left the Friars at their rectory since they had to dispatch their duties at the Cathedral. Friar Emanuel decided to stay with the other two, which turned out later for the best.

We found a small out of the way café that advertized deep pan potato pies. It is like an American omelet, but made like a pie and baked in the oven. We all decided to have the same dish, along with ham and cheese and hot rolls and butter. They also advertised as one of their specialties Spanish Hot Chocolate. I felt it would be a great change from their strong coffee. We were not disappointed with our meal. While eating Mary and Burt said that they were thinking of going on to the Holy Land. They had never been there and had never had a honeymoon. They said they would be leaving our group in the morning. We were sorry they were leaving us, but we wished them well.

After eating, we made our way back to the hotel. I checked at the front desk to see if I had any messages. I had three, one from the Senator and one from Mauricio Grabaldi my friend from Interpol. There was also a note from Manny Vasquez my brother in Christ from the DEA. I wondered what they wanted. I told Bev that I would make the calls from our room.

When we got back to our room I looked at the messages. I opened the Senators note first. "Gregg; pray that you and Bev are doing well. Reason for the note, I am under wraps; because of death threats. I am fine, so don't worry about me. Mother Richards is fine as you well know. If you need to get in touch with me contact my friend Calvin Duckworth. You have his number. Your boys are fine, and are both doing well. Mother Richards is spoiling them, and they love it. Keep the faith and let me know how you are doing with your quest for the Lord. Your brother in Christ: T. Richards."

I showed the note to Bev and she said; "I sense there is more to his note than he is saying. Perhaps I should fly back and see how Mother Richards and the boys are doing. I had a dream last night that concerned me. It related to the evil man the Scorpion. He somehow had stolen the artifacts and you and Short Stuff were chasing him, but Matte and I were not along. We were on a flight heading home. Then I woke up."

"Bev honey; I want you to feel comfortable, but I know this hasn't been what you expected. Hindsight is always better than foresight. I have thought about the danger we have been in, but truthfully, I have worried about you more than ever because I have seen your reaction during times of stress and danger. I don't like putting you in danger."

"Sweetheart if you don't mind let's see if I can catch a flight back tomorrow if it's ok with you?"

"Honey; one of the things that I love about you, is your willingness to give up your comfort for others. Come here and let me give you a big hug," I held her in my arms for a long time. She seemed so fragile in my arms. I felt her tears seep through my shirt. This was a moment that I would cherish the rest of my life. We sat on the bed for what seemed like hours. We were brought back to reality when there was a knock on the door.

"Who is it?" It was Short Stuff and Matte. "Come on in," As I opened the door to let them in.

Bev said, "Hi guys what's up?"

Short Stuff said, "We have a problem, we just got a call from my Mom. Matte's mother was rushed to the hospital. The first report is she had a stroke. We don't know how severe it is, but it sounded like she was critical. Matte is going to fly home tomorrow. She wants me to stay here and be your backup."

I smiled and said, "Forgive me Matte, but I am terribly sorry about your mother. I smiled because of Bev. She is going to try and fly home tomorrow and be with Mother Richards. I'll let her tell you about her dream."

Bev retold the entire story about her dream and seeing Matte flying home with her on the plane. When Bev had finished, we all held hands and began praying for one another and Senator Richards and Matte's mother. When we finished praying we decided to eat an early dinner and would eat at a restaurant near the hotel. We had an appointment with the Friars at six.

Before we left the hotel, I excused myself so I could make my two calls. I called Mauricio Grabaldi first.

He answered the phone; "Gregg my brother, thank you for your quick response. How is your wife and family and your friend what's his name; ah yes----Short Stuff and of course Burt, Cash and Rachel."

"They are all fine. Cash and Rachel got married and Burt and Short Stuff are here with my wife and I. Burt will be leaving in the morning with his wife. My wife and Short Stuff's wife will be leaving as well. I'm here on a case for the Brotherhood. What can I do for you my brother?"

"My call is twofold. One, it involves a terrorist Friar who has turned rogue. Senator Richards contacted us and wanted to know about him. He calls himself Friar Emanuel. His real name is Peter Fenneman. He is related to the oil baron. I understand he is a nephew of the Sr. Fenneman. He was born in the United States, but lives in Austria. He claims he is a Franciscan Friar, although he has been involved in some sexual affairs with rich women. We are still trying to prove if he is a genuine Friar. He is also an amateur archeologist and has a degree in European history. He is also known for his expertise of the Crusades and the Knights of that era. He is a hired assassin and extremely dangerous. Be extra cautious. One more thing, when are you coming to Italy again? I want to show you my country and meet your lovely wife. One closing thought, I am sorry that you are no longer with the FBI. Why don't you come to work for us here at Interpol, we could use people like you? Think about it my friend, I must hang up. I have another call. Please keep in touch."

As he hung up, I thought about how I could have missed my suspicions. All along I thought it was Friar Miguel, because he was a Jesuit. I had one more call to make and then go down and have dinner with the group. I saw the note from Manny Vasquez; that sounded urgent. He wanted me to meet him in Madrid tomorrow afternoon at the Madrid airport. He gave me his international cell phone number.

I dialed his number and got his voice mail. I decided to leave him a message, a message of urgency concerning our quest and chase of our adversaries. I confirmed a time that we would meet in the late afternoon. I had a lot to think about as I made my way downstairs.

When I got off the elevator I spotted my group, but one was visibly missing, Mr. Peter Fenneman, aka Friar Emanuel. I asked the rest of my group if they had seen our esteemed Friar. The guy at the front desk overheard our conversation and said that he had checked out a couple of hours ago. I said; "People, we need to go to the Cathedral right away, I'll explain later."

When we got to the Cathedral we went directly to the rectory where we found both Brothers, Friar Miguel and Brother Antonio sitting and praying for the soul of our rogue Friar, Emanuel.

Friar Antonio said, "My friends----all is lost. Our brother Emanuel and a couple of thugs overwhelmed us and tied us up, then hit us over the head with some sort of weapon as we just now came too. He absconded with the artifacts and the robe. Whatever possessed Friar Emanuel to do such a thing we couldn't understand? We were praying for his soul."

I said, "How long ago did this all happen?"

Brother Miguel said, "Shortly after you left. He said that he had left something inside the vault while the four of us were examining it. He said it was a valuable formula for decoding ancient writings. It made sense to us so we went back to help him retrieve his formula. While in the ruins these two men armed with weapons said they would kill us if we didn't comply with them. So, we did what they asked; that was almost five hours ago."

I asked him, "Where do you think they were headed? Did you hear something that might give us a clue?"

Brother Antonio said: "Let me think; ah yes. He said uncle Fenneman would be pleased. Does that help Mr. Johnson? I was so set on examining the manuscripts."

"Brother Antonio and Brother Miguel you don't know how much you have helped us. We know where Brother Emanuel is headed. One more question. Was one of the other men a small distinguished looking man that spoke with a very distinct accent?"

Brother Miguel said; "There was a man that they kept calling Dr. von Berger."

"His full name is Klaus von Berger. He is a defrocked MD. He was a student of the famous German Doctor Joseph Mengele. What about the other man was he tall, and much younger? Both Friars said yes. I suspect that it was Augustine Villalobos. He spoke excellent Spanish and made you think he spoke very broken English, he speaks almost perfect English.

Friar Miguel said, "How did you know that it was these two?"

"I just put two and two together and they added up to four. I'm not trying to be flippant, but we have had our conflicts with these two already. Gentlemen we must leave you. We need to check out of our rooms and drive to Madrid. God, bless you both for your help. Oh; and if someday I get the artifacts back, I will let you examine them."

We went back to the hotel and asked the desk clerk to bring our rented car around so we could be on the road to Madrid. There were no flights out of Madrid for South America until late in the evening tomorrow. We still had time to catch our crooks, but once they got to Venezuela they would be lost to us. I would check with Interpol when we got to Madrid.

While I was paying my bill, my cell rang. I looked on the small screen and saw that it was Manny Vasquez. "Manny, I'm glad you called. We were on our way to Madrid. Things have gotten out of hand. The items we were looking for we found. One of the people who we trusted was a mole and split with the items. Get this; he is the nephew of none other than Mr. Fenneman." I said.

"Sorry about that, but I can get you to Barcelona ASAP. Remember I told you that El Alacran had a hacienda near Madrid? I came because we got a break on how he is bringing in illicit drugs. He uses his own Yacht. The guy you dealt with was not him. It was his double, but unfortunately he was killed in a shootout early this morning before we could catch him. His ego really shows what a maniac he is, when he renamed his Yacht."

"Let me guess. El Alacran, with most likely a picture of a black scorpion painted on the sides. Before you go on Manny; you said that the guy we ran into in the tombs was his double? Now I know why he didn't kill me while he had the chance. Go ahead Manny finish what you started."

"Well as I said; he has this gorgeous yacht so we followed him from the U.S. in a government yacht, it used to belong to one of the Mexican Cartel leaders so we confiscated it. This boat is state of the art in design, purposely outfitted by its former owner to outrun anything on the open seas. It's unmarked and has been modified for our use. I know that our man will not stay long in Barcelona. He likes to keep on the move. I have a private plane ready to pick you up when you get to Madrid. If the mole who stole the items is headed for Venezuela, he won't have to go all the way. His uncle and Heilman are in Barcelona on their yacht, called El Aquila, English meaning the Eagle. I can be there in a couple of hours."

"Manny; I have one problem; my wife and Short Stuffs wife are headed back to the states. They were going to leave tomorrow. I know there are flights out of Barcelona for the States. Do you have any room in you plane for them?"

"Gregg; this is a converted Boeing 727 that used to belong to a South American drug lord. Yes, we have plenty of room, and they can catch a ride back to the states when they drop us off. Its set then, what time will we pick you up?"

"Great Manny; why don't you pick us up at nine tonight, barring any incidents we will see you in a few hours."

I said to the rest of group, "You heard most of the conversation I'll fill in the blank for you as we drive back to Madrid."

The desk clerk came over and said to me, "Sir we have a slight problem. The car that you had rented was taken by the Friar who was with your group. He must drop it off in Madrid. We can have another car in the morning for you. I am terribly sorry."

A tall light brown skinned man with a crop of white hair and his wife stepped up and said, "we have a car that we were going to turn in. I see the auto desk is closed, but if you drop it off at the Madrid airport under my name, Dr. D. Contreras and explain to them what happened, they will take it back. They can call me here at the hotel to verify what happened. How many are in your group?"

"It's very kind of you Sir; you are a life saver. We started out with seven, but there will be six of us on our way back to Madrid. How can we ever repay you?"

"You can repay us by keeping the faith and continue to honor the Brotherhood."

I started to say something else, but he and his wife were gone. I told the rest of the group that we needed to get going. After we loaded the Chrysler 300 we headed for Madrid. It was a late evening drive as we headed almost due west. I also explained to them about the Scorpions yacht and the Boeing 727. Bev and Matte were ecstatic that they would be home much sooner than they thought. Burt and Mary still planned to visit Barcelona and depart from there to the Holy Land.

CHAPTER 38

(Thursday July 18ᵗʰ PM)

When we arrived in Madrid we had to find our way to the airport, everyone watching for the Avion (Airplane) signs. After finding our way to the airport, I went directly to the return car rental. The young woman was all smiles as she said that Mr. and Mrs. Contreras had called and explained what had happened. She had a bunch of papers that needed to be filled out and signed which took us almost an hour, but it was worth it. I asked the young woman if the stolen car had been turned in yet. She said that they had reported the auto stolen when it was explained to them by the management of the hotel what had happened.

After signing the papers of the rental and paying what we owed, we made our way to the terminal where the D&A plane would be. It would take us a few minutes to get to the terminal. As we made our way to our terminal we had to pass the Barcelona gate. While passing; I heard a familiar voice, it was Peter Fenneman aka Friar Emanuel, but in street clothes. He was surrounded by a group of men, talking about a new find. They didn't notice us as we passed by in the transport vehicle. We were ready for action if they spotted us. I was satisfied that we would get to Barcelona before they did. Our plane was ready to leave when we arrived at our terminal. The commercial flight was scheduled to depart in a couple of hours.

When we got to our gate, Manny was waiting for us. He escorted us to the airplane and within minutes we were air-born on our way to Barcelona. We would be there in less than two hours. We had made reservations through the hotel in Toledo for lodgings in Barcelona for one night.

Manny came over and sat down next to Bev and me. He asked me what we were doing in Toledo. I decided to tell him everything about the artifacts and robe. I explained to him why it was important that we recover the artifacts. He sat their almost mesmerized. Then he said; Gregg what you have told me sounds like a story out of Indiana Jones movie. It would make a great movie, but how many people would think that you are nuts?"

"Manny; what I have told you, is the entire truth and does sound like something Hollywood would produce, but it is factual. Let me propose something hypothetical to you. Suppose the robe is the garment that Jesus wore and does have healing powers. If this guy Heilman, who supposedly has some form of condition that limits him from being out in the sunlight. What would happen if he got his grubby hands on it? And was healed instantly? He and Fenneman are one world order government advocates, and of course they want to be in charge. With the robe, they could manipulate billions from sick people. I believe they would use the robe to set themselves up as leaders of the world. It's all predicated on the robe's authenticity?"

Manny said; "A man like Heilman would use the robe for his own purposes, but would God allow this all to happen?"

"God says he is no respecter of persons, this may apply, but in the book of Acts chapter eight, Simon the Sorcerer wanted to buy the power of the Holy Spirit from the Apostles. This same scenario could also apply. Just the mere thought that it has healing powers could cause massive civil unrest with people trying to get to it. The rich trying to buy it for themselves"

"You raise some good points Gregg. I don't want some nut like Heilman trying to use the robe for his own personal gain. In fact, I think we should not let people know that the robe exists. I remember a scripture in the Gospel of John when he rose from the dead and appeared to the Apostles in the upper room. Our Lord said to Thomas, 'Then Jesus told him, "Because you have seen me, you have believed blessed are those who have not seen and yet have believed" (John 20:29 NIV). We are blessed because we have faith in Him, not in artifacts or some icon. I believe that faith is what generates the power of the Holy Spirit and it's by this faith we accept and believe."

We finished talking as the plane was preparing to land. It was a good smooth landing. We were told the plane would be leaving early the next morning. The women had to be back to the airport by eight, as they were required to go through customs, but the pilot a DEA employee said that he would make sure the ladies went through customs without any glitches.

We went to our hotel, checked in and went straight to our rooms. We left a wakeup call for six. After Bev and I prayed for safety and God's will to be done in the case of the stolen artifacts. I decided to read my Bible for awhile. I noticed the clock and finally turned off the light at one in the morning. For some reason, I placed my Glock 7mm under my pillow.

CHAPTER 39

(Thursday July 18th AM)

I was awakened out of a sound sleep because of a sense of danger. I slowly released the safety from my weapon and looked around the room. Someone was in our suite in the front part. We had been given the suite because it was the last room they had. I got up slowly and noticed that there was movement where we had left our luggage. I reached for the light switch and startled the intruder. I was not surprised it was none other than Augustine Villalobos. "Augustine" I shouted, "put your hands behind your back." I grabbed my handcuffs out of my suit case and cuffed him. "Do you realize I could have blown your head off? Did you place a bomb or a tracking sensor in my luggage? I want a direct answer and don't play stupid with me, saying that you don't understand English very well."

"I no speak English Bueno, as well."

I decided to play a bluff, when Beverly came into the front room. "Honey; contact the local police when I give you the signal."

"Ok dear."

I continued my interrogation. "Augustine; I had you checked out, and your English is as good as mine. You graduated from VMI with a Doctorate in physics and a Masters degree from Columbia. Now tell me who are you working for? I'll give you thirty seconds to answer and if I don't get a true answer I'm going to blow your head off and make your wife a widow. One, two, three, four;" As I clicked the safety on and cocked the automatic all the while counting. When I got to ten he said "All right Mr. Johnson, I'm working for Mr. Heilman and Mr. Fenneman. I got into trouble when I graduated from VMI. I went to work for Mr. Fenneman working in his research lab. I started gambling and got in over my head and soon was in debt so deep I could never pay it back. He said if I did some jobs for him, he would pay off my debts. He has never paid them off. So, he said if I could blow up certain houses along with you and Dr. Cabrillo's house, he would release me from all my debts. Instead, he had the Mafia visit me and they reminded me that I owed the money to them; since Heilman had sold the IOU's to them. I was instructed to look and see if you had any more information concerning the artifacts and the robe. Honest Mr. Johnson this is the truth, I swear by the grave of my mother what I told you is the truth."

"Why couldn't you have borrowed the money from your family?"

"Sir; there is one other thing, I got an underage girl in trouble and they threatened to expose me and ruin whatever I had left of my reputation. But if I asked my father for the money he would want to know why? And knowing he would feel disgraced by my actions. Honor is very important in my family."

"Ok, I believe you Augustine. I know for a fact that Mr. Fenneman and Mr. Heilman are here in Barcelona on Mr. Heilman yacht. Perhaps you can be of use to me. We need someone to get us on board the Heilman ship. You can get us a schematic of the ship. I also need to know when they plan to leave Barcelona, along with why they are here and where they plan to go when they leave here. I will not press charges against you if you do what I say, but if you cross me and alert them, I promise I will do everything in my power to place you behind bars. I have influential friends in Interpol and within many law enforcement agencies in the free world."

You could see he was frightened when he answered. "I don't know how to thank you. I remember the evening we spent with you at Dr. Cabrillo's home. You were talking about your faith and how important Jesus Christ is in your life. How can I believe the same? I see a strength in your eyes that at times seems almost supernatural. How do you get this assurance and belief?"

"It starts with believing that Christ is our Savior from eternal damnation for our sins. If you can believe this and that He died for your sins and believe that He rose from the dead, without any doubt, confessing your sins to Him verbally you are born again. If you want to be secure of your salvation, repeat the sinner's prayer after me."

"Mr. Jonson I want to know Christ as my Savior.

"Please kneel in front of me."

As he knelt he started to say the sinner's prayer with me and soon the flood of tears started to flow. I knew that what was happening was real. A soul had been won for Christ. I leaned over and hugged him for his new birth in Christ.

After we finished praying I said, "Augustine you are now a part of the Brotherhood and a celestial home awaits you. Start reading the Bible daily, start with the Gospel of Luke, then the Gospel of John and when you go home to Toledo to your wife, find a church where they teach from the Bible."

"Sir; I no longer live in Toledo, we moved to Barcelona with my wife's sister Christina and Domingo this past week. They started going to a church that meets in a hotel. Rebecca is expecting a baby and she has been asking Christina questions about the Lord. We're staying with them until I can get set free from Fenneman and Heilman."

"Young man; you were set free. With your help, we can put Fenneman and Heilman behind bars. Here is my cell number, call me when you get the information I need. I will also try to find out how much money the Mafia will settle on as to what you owe, now get out of here and God speed."

As he left, Bev and I sat down to pray for the souls of Augustine and Rebecca. After we finished praying, Bev said, "Honey, I think you did the right thing with that young man. I believe that his conversion was sincere and real. We have to place our faith in the Holy Spirit that he will not slide back into the world."

"Only time will tell honey if he truly is born again. Remember a couple of weeks ago we planted seeds. Those seeds produced fruit. The quality of the fruit will depend on his continuance in reading and hearing the word of God."

Gregg Honey; I wanted to tell you how much I love you and your zeal for the Lord, I thought about being here with you. Wondering how I was going to tell you that I felt that we were too large a group and that we were hindering your assignment. God worked it out so I could accompany Matte and go home. I know that later we will be able to have a few weeks to ourselves. I love you my Gregg."

"Sweetheart; I can't thank God enough for you, next to God you are the most important being on this planet. I don't want to see you go home, but it will make my mission a lot easier. It's almost five am; we might as well stay up and get an early breakfast, give me a hug and a kiss." We both reached over and hugged each other and thanked the Lord for our life together. We got dressed and went down stairs to an early breakfast. We found the rest of our group couldn't sleep either and had decided to have an early breakfast as well. Burt and Mary joined us because they wanted to say goodbye to us all.

It was time for Short Stuff and me to take Matte and Bev to the airport. Manny had arranged transportation for all of us. The plan was to drop the ladies off at the airport then Short Stuff and I would take our luggage to the DEA yacht and store our gear on board. We made it to the Barcelona Airport and said our tearful goodbyes to our spouses. We stood for a few minutes, seeing our women fly west back to the States.

Short Stuff was the first to speak. "Guys; I always find it difficult to say goodbye to my lady, but I feel safer now that she will be at home with family and some of my friends. How about you guys?"

Manny said, "My wife is constantly telling me to get out of the DEA and get a job working for some low profile investigating corporation. What about you Gregg? You no longer work for the Bureau?"

"Until I get through with this assignment and have those artifacts in my hands, I truly haven't given it much thought. I have a couple of options, but since I'm a career lawman, I don't know any other way of life."

Manny said, "Guys, I hate to break it up. I am enjoying our conversation, but we must get aboard the yacht. We have a perfect location where our yacht is berthed. It's very close to where Heilman and Fenneman are berthed. By the way, you will find it hard to believe the size of their yacht, it should be called a ship, because of its size."

While we were driving to the wharf my cell went off. I barely recognized the voice on the other line. "Mr. Johnson, this is Augustine. I have the schematic of the Heilman, Fenneman yacht. I went to the records department and found out that it had been made here in one of Barcelona's yacht builders. One of the reasons they are here is to inspect it for corrections needed. Where are you so that I can personally deliver the blue prints to you?"

"Just a minute Augustine, let me ask Manny. Manny will give you instructions as to where our yacht is berthed."

"Yes, this is Manny tell me where you are right now?"

"I'm at the Barcelona Maritime Commission."

"Stay where you are. I know where it is. We'll pick you up within twenty minutes. As he hung up many said, Gregg, he said he was afraid that he might be found out so he preferred that we pick him up. He thought that he was being followed. I know a short cut that will save us some time."

As Manny finished his sentence, he punched the accelerator as we felt the turbo kick in. One thing for sure, the DEA spared no expense of confiscated drug money to buy and lease state of the art equipment for their agents!

While we were traveling to pick up Augustine, I felt that we were being watched. I thought with all the new technology available it has gotten easier for the underworld to battle us. We keep introducing new weapons as well as tracking devices, but it seems that the drug cartels and people like Fenneman and Heilman spend billions to keep abreast of us. Spy satellites can read your license plates and even read newspaper print from outer space. Laser science is being developed so that you can point a laser beam into outer space and blind a pilot flying a 747 Jumbo jet at an altitude of thirty-five thousand feet.

Drones is a new device that can be as small as a bumble bee, used for spying, with the larger ones carrying bombs.

I was brought back to reality when we arrived at our destination. Augustine was waiting outside of the building when we drove up. When he got into the car I introduced him to the others. I also shared that he was a baby Christian, not even a day old.

Augustine responded, "I told my wife about my new-found faith and she asked Christ into her heart this morning. We both read the Gospel of Luke together. She was touched by what she read. We are looking forward to spending time with Domingo and Christina in studying God's word. Here is the blue print of the yacht. I will fill in where they have installed state of the art detection alarms and weaponry. I can do it as we drive to the berthing docks."

"Fine, when we get to our destination you can go over the entire layout with us. We must be accurate as to where certain sensors are and alarms that would give us away. We plan on boarding the yacht, oh before I forget did you happen to see a yacht called El Alacran?"

"As a matter of fact I did. Yesterday, this yacht pulled in next to the Fenneman yacht. They just changed the name of the ship to the Aquila with a strange looking Eagle."

I said; it most likely looks like the one the Nazis used on their standards." I started to laugh and said, "Now why did I know this." Short Stuff and Manny both started laughing as we all enjoyed a good laugh."

I continued. "It was almost laughable because of the dedication to a philosophy and ideology that almost destroyed the entire world. Our country is flirting with Socialism. Our way of life at this very moment is in danger of slipping into this horrible form of government. As a Representative Republic, we enjoy many freedoms that unfortunately some of us take for granted. We must ask ourselves, what price are we willing to pay to uphold freedom? Sorry guys, but I love my country too much to see her fail; and would give my life for her."

Short Stuff started to say something when we got to our dock. Manny said that we had arrived. Short Stuff said, "We need to continue this conversation later."

CHAPTER 40

(Thursday July 18th)

We made our way to where the ex-drug cartel yacht was berthed. There was a full cadre of DEA agents on board. The yacht could sleep comfortably twenty people, but in a pinch, you could add another half a dozen. We were led to our respective rooms. Short Stuff and I would be bunk mates. I had asked Augustine and Manny to get together with Short Stuff and me in about half an hour. Manny said we could use the conference room equipped with a large map of the world. There was also state of the art equipment to formulate high level strategy sessions.

We made our way to the board room and met Manny and Augustine. One of the aids who ran the equipment was prepared to show the blue prints of the Heilman yacht. She flashed it on the screen as Augustine began to explain where the crew slept and where the living quarters were for Heilman and Fenneman. The yacht was almost two hundred and fifty feet long, the size of a modern-day destroyer. It had a crew of about twenty. He didn't know how many it slept, since he had only been on the ship three times. He wasn't allowed to meet Heilman, but did meet Fenneman. He noticed that there were guards posted at each stairwell that went below two decks. He said he overheard them saying that the engineer and crew slept in a third deck below. All this was being shown on the blue prints.

I asked; "Where do Heilman and Fenneman have their living quarters?"

"I saw Fenneman go to an upper deck that stated off limits to ships personal. Only those approved by Mr. Fenneman will be allowed past this point."

Short Stuff said; "It looks to me that we have a major problem, gentlemen. How are we going to get past the posted guards? I also have another question. Since this is Spanish soil and their sovereignty, we can't do anything until they set sail and are past the international limits which I believe is twenty-one miles. We can't risk alienating the Spanish government and create an international embarrassment for the United States."

I said; "This is in Manny's court, Manny what do you say?"

"The plan is to wait until they get out to the twenty-one-mile limit. At this point we expect to board the ship. It is no longer a yacht, because of its size, it's a ship. I have notified my superiors and they are asking the Spanish government to storm the ship and seize the cargo. We know for a fact that there is close to half a billion dollars' worth of cocaine on board. The guards have the latest weapons available, and will use them if needed. Our element of surprise is our best offensive weapon. Any questions thus far?"

"None, continue Manny." I said.

"Thanks Gregg, the guy we want the most right now is El Alacran. He is the main supplier to the Fenneman and Heilman partnership. We want him away from the Spanish coast. We think that he is reloading his yacht on the high seas. We have been monitoring and counting the number of people he has coming and going. With his crew and fellow henchmen there are about two dozen men and women, plus El Alacran and his women. If we must run them down

at sea we have the edge, but if we must act here in Barcelona; I don't
know if the Spanish government will go along with us? We may have
to play a wild card."

About that time Manny's cell rang. "Manny here" he said, "go
ahead." He turned the volume to max so we could hear the call.

"Manny; this is agent Helen Morgan our bird just went aboard
the Fenneman ship, along with Fenneman' nephew. They were met by
Fenneman himself. The Scorpion didn't look very happy. He was using
profanity at Fenneman for some reason. I heard a name shouted about
Gregg Johnson and how he had slipped through their grasp. That's all I
have Lieutenant Vasquez; I'll check back right away if the bird moves."

Manny said, "We must be on our toes if we wish to capture these
thugs. That's all they are----thugs trying to hide behind the guise of
respectability. A thought occurred to me, since I don't have enough men
to board both ship and yacht at the same time we are faced with a very
difficult decision, which group do we go after if they decide to leave at
the same time. Fenneman and Heilman have hundreds of operatives all
over the world, not so with the Scorpion. Gregg has the more difficult
decision. He is after Peter Fenneman first because of the artifacts. My
people were deployed to catch El Alacran so it is much easier for me."

"Manny, I no longer work for the government, but let me ask you
a question. Which is the lesser of the following: a legend that the robe
of Christ maybe in the hands of two megalomaniacs, or drugs that are
destroying families and human life? I will choose the latter and pray
that God will intervene supernaturally on the other."

"Gregg; I thought you would say that. If we play our cards right,
perhaps the Lord will give us all three fish. As to the plan we have for
El Alacran, I cannot include you in officially, but I can't stop you as
a citizen who wants to help. If you get my drift?"

"Manny, can I borrow some scuba gear I just had a thought?"

"You sure can Gregg, why may I ask?"

"I have an idea. I know that all ships have scuttle plugs, but I don't know where they are located on his yacht. My guess is it's like the Eagle. Let's Look at the blueprint of the Eagle, ah----there near the fan tail, one on each side."

"Gregg I believe that all yachts are equipped with a plug or plugs of some sort for when they take them into dry dock or are attacked by pirates. The Scorpions yacht should not be any different, but just in case it doesn't have plugs we have some explosives with timer devices we can set that will work even better," as Manny responded.

"Manny you have just given me a better idea. The timers can be set either by day, month, or both. Let's set the device so that when the Scorpion decides to leave, we can trip the on button to the time we have it preset. Our on-board equipment will let us know when they pass the 21-mile limit. Then we blow the devices and the yacht starts to sink, you and your men will be close enough to answer his S.O.S."

Manny said; "Gregg, I get your drift, we can board the yacht, but then under the guise of helping them, we arrest them. It sounds like a feasible plan, but what about Fenneman and Heilman? What about the artifacts and the robe?"

"God must intervene supernaturally at this point."

Short Stuff said, "It's settled then. Our plan is to wait and see when they decide to leave, but what if they decide to pull out tonight. You need to place the small charge now to scuttle the yacht."

"Gregg; Short Stuff is right; we need to do it right now. Come on let's get the gear. Short Stuff and Augustine can act like they're fishing, while Gregg and I place the device."

CHAPTER 41

(Thursday July 18th pm)

Manny and I climbed into a small dingy in full scuba gear, while Short Stuff and Augustine had fishing poles in their hands and would pretend to be fishing. The Scorpions yacht was berthed about a quarter of a mile from the DEA yacht. Our yacht was birthed closer to the Eagle. We moved away from our yacht and proceeded to run the dingy out about a mile from shore to act like we were going to go snorkeling and scuba diving along with some fishing. It had been a few years since I had been scuba diving. The boys and I used to go at the lake when they were young teens. I had shown them how to be good trust worthy divers, I had been taught well by a collage friend.

We arrived at our predetermined spot so that we had a good view of the vessels.

I said, "Are you ready Manny?" He nodded his head as we went overboard. I was swept with a feeling of euphoria as it all came back to me how much I liked it. It is a wonderful sight to see under water in most places, but we found the water in the Barcelona port murky which would make it more difficult to see. We had one advantage, the current was very slow and did not hinder our movement. We soon saw the shape of berthed boats so we decided to surface and see how far we had missed our target. We barely got to the surface when we were totally surprised that we were off about two yachts away from the Scorpions yacht. We swam the few feet away from where we had surfaced and again resurfaced after finding our target.

As we broke water; I thought to myself Bulls Eye, we were right next to the Scorpions yacht. Manny must have been thinking the same thing when he broke water about the same time I did, as he said "Bulls Eye." I motioned for him to be quiet. I also motioned for him to follow me under the yacht. It was dark underneath and we needed our lights. We didn't want to sink this beautiful yacht if we could help it. We set the timer to start automatically after it reached the twenty-one-mile limit. It would explode when we remotely set the signal. We were just about to start back to the dingy when we heard the props on the Scorpions yacht start up. Had our plans been ruined? We swam away past two boats and resurfaced. We looked and saw that they were running the engines to use their bilge pumps. After placing the two devices next to the drain plug we said a small prayer to our Lord, for watching over us and that He would intercede that no life would be hurt or lost when the two small charges exploded.

We made it back to our boat without any mishaps and decided to eat something. It was late afternoon and an early dinner sounded great. The yacht had a fully stocked galley and a full-time chef to run it. Not only did it have a fully stocked pantry, but I decided to take advantage of what was on the menu and ordered a steak with a baked potato along with a dinner salad and hot rolls. The rest of the guys ordered the same.

Augustine declined and asked if he could be released to go home. I warned him not to say anything to anyone, not even his wife or any member of his family. I told him I would be in touch with him, and told him to say hi to Domingo and his lovely wife Christina. As he left I knew he was going to be all right. I also made a mental note to contact a Mafia individual who owed me a favor to drop the debt Augustine owed. I liked him and felt that he would stay on course with the Lord. As we were about to order dessert, Manny's phone rang. It was his stakeout people telling him that the Scorpion was back in his nest. Perhaps they were preparing to get under way.

"Guys let's see what our thug is doing right now. Let's go you can have the Ice Cream later when we get back."

"Manny how far are your people from his yacht?" I asked.

"Gregg, we are right next door to his yacht. We have a couple of agents who are playing tourist as newlyweds in a rented yacht. They are young and both good looking. They have been there since the Scorpions yacht has been berthed. It will take us a few minutes to get there."

Manny had a car in the parking lot. We didn't want to be seen by walking to the berth, so we rode in the car for cover. It was late in the day as twilight was being swallowed up in darkness. We decided to stay in the car which had state of the art listening equipment. Just as we pulled up and parked in a nearby vacant car lot, we heard gunfire that muffled by a silencer. We felt that the worst had happened when we tried to contact the two agents. Perhaps the Scorpion had found out that we were staking-out his operation. The Scorpion had started his yacht and was pulling out of his berth. We ran to the rented yacht and saw both the agents slumped over where they had been killed. I knew instinctively they had been executed by a tiny arachnid. I told Manny that they had been stung to death by a Fattail Scorpion. Manny called his people and told them to crank up the engines as we would be under way to chase the butcher, El Alacran!

Manny also had to contact the locals. He would assign a couple of agents to report the shootings. We had a golden opportunity to catch a crafty drug Lord.

⁂

We decided to walk back and left the car for the two agents who would guard the crime scene. They would stay with the two dead agents to answer any questions from the local police. There were other agents watching the ship of Fenneman and Heilman. Manny called and checked in and asked his agents who were watching Fenneman and Heilman if there was any sign of them leaving? They said that they hadn't heard a thing. We would find out later why.

As we started to go to the DEA yacht, I had a hunch and told Manny. "Look, we have a tracking devise along with two small explosives set to explode when we detonate it. With this high-speed yacht, we can chase the Scorpion and run him down. He will not get away from us. I'm not sure, but perhaps you have a double agent on board that will alert us if he changes yachts. I have a premonition about something. I want to check out the Eagle ship? I think the artifacts are still on board."

"This one is your call Gregg, because of the location and the security that this part of the yacht club provides for its rich clients. I don't know how many guards are on board."

"Thanks Manny, I think we can get on board without setting off a bunch of alarms. I noticed something about the Eagle. I believe that they are in port to stock up on supplies, and are getting ready to set sail. They also must unload their cargo of cocaine. There are two gangplanks, if my hunch is right they will be allowing caterers to come and go aboard as they wish. Also, they will be unloading their drugs at the same time. We can get on as caterers, which will give us access to the entire ship without them paying much attention to us."

Short Stuff said; "Good plan Gregg. We stop a caterer and we use a little persuasion for their uniforms for getting us aboard and snatch Heilman and Fenneman, along with that phony Friar Emanuel. I'm ready let's get going."

Manny concurred as he alerted his people to what we would be doing.

When we got to the Eagle and saw what a gorgeous majestic looking ship it was. I couldn't help think how it reminded me of a small version of one of the many luxury liners that people take their vacations on. I couldn't imagine how much it cost, but it was well into the millions.

"Guys we are here, but where are the vendors and caterers? The ships doors are open. Notice the handful of crewmen sitting and mulling around. I'm going to play a bluff. None of us has any law enforcement authority, but let's see if we can bluff our way. Just follow my lead!" I said.

We walked up the gang plank like we owned the ship. When we got to the top, one of crew members came over and asked us who we were. I flashed my badge and said FBI.

He said, "Who are you looking for sir?"

"I am looking for a Mr. Fenneman who I understand is owner of this luxury liner."

He said, "I didn't know that the FBI had authority here in Spain. I don't know, you'd better wait here while I get an officer."

He was gone for a few minutes and came back with a guy who said he was the first mate. The Captain was not available right now. He said, "What can we do for you sir?"

"I told your seaman that I wanted to see Mr. Fenneman. It has to do with being in international waters giving aid to terrorists."

He said, "I guess it's alright, follow me. I haven't seen him today, but he had some visitors this morning. We were told to get ready to set sail. Watch your step as we go upstairs to his quarters. Its ok guys lower your weapons; these men are FBI agents here to see Mr. Fenneman." As we passed the entrance to Heilman and Fenneman private quarters the First Mate guided us through their security. We continued. "Captain Kruger said it was ok. Here we are gentlemen." He knocked and knocked several times. He opened the door and went in crying out, Mr. Fenneman we have some important people to see you sir."

We looked around and saw that something was not right. I proceeded to cry out; "Mr. Fenneman; this is Gregg Johnson head of the FBI; we need to talk to you." Nothing, there was no response. I said, "First Mate why don't you look in the bedroom?"

We walked over to one of the three bedrooms and opened the door. We were not prepared for what we found. The first Mate said, "Mr. Fenneman are you okay? as he approached the bed and saw that his throat had been cut along with his wife! Both killed with a large knife of some sort. We went to the next bedroom and found who I thought would be there, none other than Peter Fenneman the nephew, lying on the floor in a pool of blood!

I asked the First Mate. "Are there other people living here?"

"Yes, there is a daughter. I believe that the third bedroom is hers."

Manny walked over and opened the door and walked into the room and yelled out, "There's the body of a middle-aged woman who had the same fate. Looks like she was killed the same way, with her throat being cut"

"First Mate, what is your name? I am tired of calling you by your rank." I asked.

"My name is Olaf Thorson. I just hired on a few months ago so I can get my masters license."

"Olaf, we better check Mr. Heilmans stateroom as well."

We started out the front door and made our way down the same corridor to Heilman's quarters. We went through the same scenario and no answer to our knocking, so we opened the door and walked in. The lights were almost nonexistent. Olaf said that Mr. Heilman lived alone with a male nurse and occasionally had a visitor by the name of, ah what was his name, yes it was a Matthew Hopkins. I understand he used to work for your agency."

"Where is Mr. Heilmans bedroom?" Olaf, I asked.

"That door over there. There is a dark light like you would grow marijuana with. You know he has a skin condition that requires him to stay out of direct sunlight."

As he opened the door he cried out. "My God what fiend would do such a thing? He is dead along with his male nurse. Look for yourself."

We walked over to where his body was laying. Next to his body was an unfired gun, with a lot of blood on the gun and his wheel chair. The only person I could think of that had that much rage was El Alacran. Manny came over and said to me we had better contact the locals.

"The Bible tells us that a house divided cannot stand. These people tried to rule the world and look what they gave up; their lives. Olaf please call the local authorities concerning the carnage we found. Before you do though, I need to search for a bag that has some of the information we came here to find."

We started searching and went through the entire apartment except for a small alcove between the two bedrooms. We found a safe behind a picture of Adolph Hitler. I walked over to the safe and thought what would be the code. It was a letter type safe, after typing several names with no success I typed in A D O L P H-H I T L E R and nothing happened. Then I punched in some other names, finally I punched in "Mein Kompf" and it popped open. Inside was what I was looking for. I took the duffel bag with me and told the guys. "Gentlemen; we have seen the good Lord intervene with our enemies, but we still have a job to do.

"Brothers, the killer of these men is still loose. We need to stay here until the locals arrive. Olaf, you need to get your Captain in here so we can fill him in as to what has happened."

"Mr. Johnson, the Captain is an alcoholic and we could not roust him. I will go and see if I can sober him up."

While he was gone, I told the men to give the same story to the locals, that we suspected Heilman and Fenneman of drug trafficking, and specifically not to mention the duffle bag. Also, not to mention anything about the Scorpion, he has influence here in Spain with high ranking politicians. I didn't want them snooping into his being a drug lord and compromise Manny's operation. What a butcher I said, 'a man willing to kill other human beings almost for pleasure. I personally think he is a sadist and insane."

Olaf came back out of breath. "The Captain has also been killed the same way the others were. He was a brutish man, besides being a Nazi, which bothered me. What will happen to us and the crew? How will I get my masters papers?"

I said; "It's up to the local authorities, they will want to question each one of you.

"How many crew members are on board?"

"Some of the crew hired on here in Spain and said they would not return. There were around forty to fifty, not counting the guards. The guards are from Venezuela, there are twelve regular army soldiers, headed by a Captain Montoya. He is on leave here in Spain along with half of the soldiers. I believe some of the crew-members are also mercenaries, but most are from Venezuela and will want to return home."

"I have a couple more questions for you Olaf, where are the rest of the guards? And what happened to Matt Hopkins the close friend of Mr. Fenneman?"

One of the crew members came up to Olaf and said something in Spanish to him. I only picked up the gracias (thanks in Spanish).

"Mr. Johnson, a crew member found the rest of the crew; they were locked in their quarters tied together and gagged. As to your question about Mr. Hopkins, he got off in Tunisia for some reason. That's all I know."

"Thank you Olaf I will speak with the police when they get here about your cooperation. One final question for you, have you met a man they call El Alacran, or the Scorpion?"

"Yes, as a matter of fact he was here late this afternoon with a couple of his men. I saw them leave about an hour before you boarded. He has a second in command named Beto. He is a brute of a man, not to mention the way he treats people. That's all I know, except that when I saw the Scorpion he was angry and screaming at Mr. Fenneman."

"I want to thank you Olaf for being so honest. You will get your masters papers serving on a good ship. I will recommend you to some people I know in the States, just leave me an address where I can get in touch with you. I see the local police are coming on board. I have a favor to ask of you. Please don't tell the police that you and I had this conversation. Ok."

The police approached as I recognized one of the men I met in Rome when we were assigned to protect the Pope. His name escaped me as we exchanged pleasantries. I told him we were trying to break-up a drug ring and knew that this ship had a billion dollars' worth of cocaine on board. We spent three hours answering questions finally they let us go. We returned to our yacht, thanking God that two of the world's worst criminal were dead, but saddened that they were doomed to hell. I thought where did Matt Hopkins fit into this scenario?"

Chapter 42

(Friday July 19th am)

We were under way as fast as our vessel could go. The Scorpion had almost seven hours' advantage on us. His craft was also a state of the art high speed craft and almost as fast as ours. While thinking about what had just happened, I thought back to three weeks ago when we embarked on this mission, as it neared its completion.

I couldn't sleep so I walked up on deck to take in the cool late night breeze and do some praying and thinking. It was a beautiful summer night with the moonlight shining on the Atlantic waters. I felt a familiar presence suddenly overwhelm me. I knelt by the railing of the boat and asked God to forgive me for the anger I had felt towards the cruel sadistic killer the Scorpion. I asked God to allow me to be what He wanted me to be. I prayed for the welfare of my wife and our sons and for the health and welfare of my adopted parents; Senator Richards and Mother Richards. I included Short Stuff, Matte and Manny along with Burt and Mary.

I started to say amen when I heard a voice next to me. It was Short Stuff. He had been praying along with me. We both had a hardy laugh. I knew instantly what David and Jonathan felt for each other. We both knew we would die for one another if asked to do so.

I looked at my watch and saw that it was almost two AM, when my cell phone rang, Gregg Johnson speaking."

"Honey, don't you know your wife when she calls. I thought you would be asleep. How did things work out? I want to know all about it? Where are you right now Honey?"

"Sugar, first I love you and miss you. Second I'm on the yacht with Manny and Short Stuff. We are on our way in pursuit of the Scorpion. He had a seven hour jump on us. And lastly; I'm tired and need to go to bed, but before I hang-up how are Mother Richards, the Senator and the boys?"

They are all fine. Senator Richards is in the next room along with Mother Richards and the boys are at Lords Land. They are going fishing with Sheriff Duckworth in the morning. We are in a secret place until certain people are apprehended. You didn't tell me about Fenneman and Heilman, what about them?"

I told her the whole story, but for reasons I didn't want her to know about; I left out that I recovered the artifacts and the robe. They were safely hidden in my luggage. "Honey, I miss you deeply and wish you were here with me. We will finish our vacation and make my decision about the two job offers when I get home. I love you very much and miss you being at my side. Good night dear."

One thing still bothered me. Who was responsible for killing the Twelfth Knights? I had a hunch, but would have to check it out when this trek was finished. I wasn't sure it was the Scorpion and ruled out Heilman and Fenneman because of their deaths by the Scorpion.

(Friday July 19ᵗʰ am)

I awoke to a siren going off and quickly put my clothes on and went to the top deck. I saw Manny standing at the rail, so I asked him what was going on.

"Gregg; this is standard procedure; we have to drill the same as the Coast Guard. We are under the same laws as them when we intercept drug dealers off our coastlines. We are about four hours behind el Alacran. We should be able to catch them by this time tomorrow. They don't know we are in pursuit of them. Thank God it's to our advantage in making up time."

"What time is it? I left my watch next to the bunk."

Manny started laughing; "Bro as they say, it's almost noon Spain time, but the further West we go we gain time. How about something to eat, you should be hungry by now. I haven't eaten either, let's go down to the galley and have a late breakfast."

"Sounds good to me my brother, have you seen Short Stuff this morning?"

"As a matter of fact I haven't. Somebody told me he was seasick and that he was in his bunk. One of our Medics aboard gave him some motion sickness pills. I'll have one of my men look in on him.

As we made our way to the mess hall the Holy Spirit spoke to me about something I had to do. I turned and asked Manny if we stopped at the Azores? He said we normally would, but that we were going to bypass them and try to gain on our prey.

He said; "If it's important we can make a short stop to refuel only, and take on water."

"Manny it is very important that I return to Europe with Short Stuff."

"Gregg, we will be there about two o'clock or even sooner. I'll tell the Captain to speed up."

When we got to the mess hall Manny called the Captain and set it up. We would stop at the Azores.

When we sat down to eat the Captain came over and said; "Lt. Vasquez, we just received a coded message from our man onboard the Alacran and it seems that they have changed course. He said he thought they were headed to the North West African coast. We lost contact with him. If they get there before us they can ditch their cargo and are home free to return to South America. My guess is they are headed for Columbia or Venezuela."

Manny said; "He has ties with the Columbian Cartels, so I think that's where they are headed."

The Captain produced a map and showed us if we headed for the Cape Verde Islands. He said; we could be waiting for them. Our tracking device is still working fine. I need to know within the next half hour if we turn due south or continue on course to the Azores?"

"Manny, I want this guy just as bad as you do" "Cape Verde Islands here we come. I can catch a private plane, or fly out of the capital of Mauritania. Captain, can I see that map a minute. What are these Islands off the coast of Western Sahara?"

"They are called Las Palmas de Gran Canarias known by us as the Grand Canaries. They could pull in here and berth the yacht in one of the many marinas and hotels open for the tourist trade. Again; our tracking device will let us know where they are so we won't lose them."

"Great Captain; it's all set, change course for the Gran Canaries and parts unknown." I said.

Short Stuff finally joined us as he was starting to feel better. I filled him in as to what was going on in our chase and that he and I would be returning to Spain, most likely tomorrow or the day after and then home. I had one call I needed to make, to my friend Mauricio Grabaldi.

I excused myself from the group for a few minutes and found a place where I could get a clear signal to Italy. I reached Mauricio and filled him in on what was happening with our chase. I told him about the favor I needed and he said he thought he could handle it. He would call me back later to confirm. I walked back to the table where Manny was sitting enjoying a great meal of ham and eggs, along with some fantastic muffins. Short Stuff had ordered some toast and coffee as he felt better. I had ordered the same as Manny, a meal I thoroughly enjoyed.

I said; "Guys, I have an idea concerning the Scorpion. I received a memo from the CIA and another from Interpol confirming the subject. The Scorpion developed the drug Euphoria so he could sell it to the other drug cartels in Mexico. He did this so that he could blame the other cartels and start a war between the different factions, making him like a Mafia Don. Some of the drug was inadvertently released to his distributers in the States. Therefore, he killed Fenneman and Heilman. He was being blamed by them for this blunder so he wanted them out of the way, another test to his ego. Now why was he headed to North Africa? I believe he is coming here to pick up his pets the Fat Tail Scorpion. They are native to this area. What does it cost him to pay some of the natives to set traps for his little beauties? You saw the outcome of their sting in Barcelona. They are deadly and unless you are near anti-venom, you're dead! He also has to have venom on hand for use against some of his enemies within the drug cartels."

Both Manny and Short Stuff agreed with me as they said, "We agree Gregg."

"Manny" I said. "What time do you think we will get to our destination?"

"It depends on the ocean currents, but most likely tomorrow in the late morning or early afternoon. We are cruising over forty knots. This baby will exceed fifty knots or better. The top speed is classified so I can't say. Listen guys, I've got to send a report to my boss, but I have to write it first, I'll see you later at dinner."

I told Short Stuff I was going top side and take in the hot sun. He said he would join me in a few minutes. I made my way to the top deck when it hit me. Who would profit from a change in the directorship of the FBI? Matthew Hopkins. He was never charged with anything when he was assistant director, but what was he doing involved with Heilman and Fenneman? He was an opportunist. He always wanted my former job. The current President placed my successor as the Interim Director only. I would check it out when I got back to the States. I picked out a lounge chair and decided to try and get a quick tan and nap. My last thoughts were how this puzzle would work out?

I was interrupted by the yacht having to make some evasive maneuvers. I hit the deck as I heard a rat-tat, rat-tat as a plane made a pass at us trying to sink us. As I lay there feeling helpless the Jet fired rockets at us and machine gun fire. I thanked God that our Captain knew how to handle our assault by a plane. I knew then we had a Scorpion agent on board and this confirmed it. There was no reason why a foreign government would try to sink us. As far as they were concerned we were a private corporation on board a yacht enjoying the summer cruise. It had to be a drug cartel as he finally flew to the West after he emptied his shells on us.

I found the Captain and asked if everyone was all right? He said everyone was Ok. No one was injured. No fatalities. I said to him that we might have a Scorpion sympathizer on board who may have alerted the Scorpion. He said he would review the files of all on board and get back to me.

————————

I had sunbathed and napped most of the day. It was around seven in the evening, so I decided to make my way to the mess hall. They had set a table for us with the yachts Captain. Manny was already sitting down along with Short Stuff as I sat down. The Captain would be there shortly. One of the crew members came over to me and asked me what I wanted to drink. I decided on a glass of iced tea, as he handed me the menu. I decided on some roasted chicken, mashed potatoes, string beans, a large dinner salad, and hot dinner rolls. We all talked mostly about our families and spent a long evening playing dominoes. It was almost midnight when we decided to go to bed. We said goodnight as Short Stuff and I made our way to our quarters.

The Captain pulled me over and said he had some good news for me. He had a name for me, a guy with a tattoo saying "El Gato Negro."

"Thanks Captain; this guy is one of the Scorpions Top Aides. Arrest him and place him in irons. We will deal with him in the States, thanks again and good night."

————————

(Friday July 19th am)

"I was awakened by the pitching and rolling back and forth of the yacht. I glanced at my watch and realized it was after eight in the morning. I looked out the porthole and saw that we were in a summer tropical storm. It would pass shortly. I shaved and showered and went top side and found Manny and Short Stuff talking with the Captain as the yacht continued to roll and pitch, but not as bad as earlier.

"Good morning guys, what's going on?"

Manny said, "We have arrived off the coast of the Gran Canary Islands. We need to find an open marina close enough where we can visibly see the Scorpions yacht."

Why don't we try Las Palmas De Gran Canarias; I understand it is a tourist attraction by Europeans. It has several marinas where we can berth our yacht. It's located on the North/East side. I think this guy's ego will direct him to where there are plenty of women who like to party, especially the European rich."

They all agreed with me as the Captain made his way to the island that we could see from a distance. It would take us a couple of hours to reach one of the marinas in Las Palmas.

Manny came over to us and said, "Gregg, my boss contacted me and said that I had to return at once to the States. I haven't told the Captain but when we put into port we will get some sorely needed stores. He said we can't do anything here because of the nations we might offend. I believe that we will get another crack at the guy, but not this trip. Gregg, I'm sorry."

"Hey brother, don't feel sorry. In a way, we are indebted to our Sr. Alacran. He took out two of the evilest men I have ever encountered in my lifetime. You know it's kind of exciting to play cat and mouse with this guy. Like all evil people, they somehow get their reward. I think God allows them to destroy themselves. I think of men like Hitler and Mussolini. A lot of good men died because of them. Stalin was another butcher, but eventually succumbed to age. All through the history of mankind God has allowed us humans to accept his rules or a far more horrific punishment awaits those who disobey Him. A constant torment of their souls in hell is reserved for them. The Bible is clear on this. I wouldn't want to have been Heilman and Fenneman when they came face to face with God Almighty."

I continued. I am concerned about Heilman and Fenneman about deaths. I think we missed something. All the deaths that have been attributed to the Scorpion have been due to a bite of the Fat Tail Scorpion; right? The deaths of the people on board the ship the Eagle was caused by their throats being cut. It's not the Scorpions MO. What do you think Manny and Short Stuff?"

Short Stuff said, "I think you could make a good case Gregg. In fact, who would profit by saying he was responsible for doing what the international courts have been unable to do?"

"They would be indebted to this person or persons that they knew and trusted. I think it is an individual close to the Scorpion. Anyway, we need to be on the alert. Short Stuff when you and I get to Las Palmas we need to catch a flight back to Spain. I have something special that I have to do."

———————

We made port ahead of our nemesis and his gang of thugs. I kept thinking about Matt Hopkins or was he the one that had Fenneman, Heilman and his henchmen killed? I would find out much later.

When we got to port, we checked into a hotel and asked at the desk if they could book us a direct flight to Rome or if we had to take a commercial flight back to Spain, then to Rome. We were in luck there was a flight that went directly to Rome once a day. It leaves here in Las Palmas at one PM. We booked our flight for the next day and rented one room with two beds.

(Saturday July 20th am)

We got up and had breakfast in the hotel. Manny and his men had left for the U.S. yesterday evening. I picked up a local newspaper as an interesting article caught my eye. It seems that there was an explosion on a pleasure yacht a hundred and fifty miles from port! All the people on board were rescued by a British destroyer on maneuvers. I started to laugh and told Short Stuff as we both had a great laugh. We ate our meal and then checked out of the hotel, caught a cab and made our way to the airport. I thought how great God is. He intervened and caught our nemesis. I thought about a scripture, "Do not be deceived, God is not mocked; for whatever a man sows; this he will also reap" Amen! (Galatians 6:7 NASB) The Scorpion reaped what he sowed.

The flight would take about four to five hours depending on the headwinds. We would be met by Mauricio Grabaldi my friend from Interpol. I would fill him in about my suspicions on the deaths of Fenneman and Heilman's people. I knew that there were other family members related to both Heilman and Fenneman. I wondered if they were Nazi's as well. I thought; who would take over their vast empires of wealth?"

After a pleasant flight and talking with Short Stuff about what he was going to do since he and I were no longer employed, I asked him if he would consider teaming up with me if I took the offer from President Blankenship? He said he would pray about it and talk it over with Matte. I was also considering the offer from the Senator, but I wasn't sure this was what God wanted me to do. All this would require me praying and fasting for direction.

When we landed, I spotted Mauricio standing at the terminal entrance. He waved us over and helped us get our luggage loaded into his car. We would be staying with him overnight. We would be catching a flight home the next evening. Mauricio's wife had prepared us an authentic Italian dinner. While our drive took us out of the city, I called my wife to see how things were going and everything was great. I told her, barring the second coming of our Lord, we would be home late tomorrow night. I wanted her to pick me up and we would stay at our home in DC.

We ate everything that Natalia placed before us. It was the best Italian food I had ever eaten. The selection of pastas and Italian sausages, with all the spices and herbs you could imagine. The Italian meatball soup and all the breads we ate were baked and cooked by her. It was a meal fit for a king. She knew that one of my favorites was Chapino, so she made it especially for me.

Mauricio said, "I was able to get you both an audience my friend. He will see you at ten o'clock Monday morning. I had to pull some, how you say----rope."

Both Short Stuff and I laughed when he said rope. He asked why we were laughing, so I explained that we were not laughing at him, but that the word strings should have been used instead of rope. After much laughing and having a fun night of exchanging stories and talking about our children we finally went to bed. Short Stuff never asked me who we were going to see and for what? I called Bev and told her about our change in plans. She was sorry, but understood and expected me late Monday night.

We spent the weekend taking in the local sights. We went with Mauricio and his family to a Charismatic Mass. It was the first time we both had ever been to a Mass, let alone a Charismatic one. The presence of the Lord was fantastic, and the message was very good. The theme "Who is my brother? It was in Italian, but Mauricio interpreted for us.

CHAPTER 43

(Monday July 22nd am)

We got up Monday morning and after showering and shaving I
packed my bag and went downstairs to enjoy an Italian breakfast.
Natalia again blessed us with a great Italian Torte made with potatoes
and Italian sausage along with strong hot steaming espresso coffee and
fresh baked Italian bread.

We were on a tight schedule so we said our goodbyes to Natalia
and Mauricio's two lovely daughters, Angelina and Maria, who were
both trying to get into college. I thought of my boys and hoped
that they would find two wonderful young ladies like Mauricio's
daughters.

We made our way in and out of traffic as the trip would take us
about thirty minutes. Shortly after we got on our way, Short Stuff
finally asked me "Gregg where are we going and why all the secrecy?"

"I thought you would never ask me, we have an appointment with
a very influential man."

"That's it, a very influential man? Hum!"

We sat in the car in silence when I said, "Mauricio; when do, your
daughters enter college?"

"They are trying to get what you call in your country as exchange
students. They are both interested in working in the diplomatic field,

in fact they have applied for a grant to go for a year to a college in the States. They have not heard anything yet, but they are praying that the Virgin Mother will hear their prayers."

"I know some very influential people in my country perhaps I can intervene----if you like?"

"I would be eternally grateful my friend. Ah; we have arrived."

Short Stuff shouted out, "Man who are we going to see, isn't this the Vatican? Don't tell me we are going to see the Pope?"

"I don't know, perhaps!"

Mauricio said, "Let's go the man will be waiting."

We made our way to the private entrance to where the Pontiff lives. It was a long walk and everywhere you could see the Vatican guard. There were Priests rushing here and there, busy men who have dedicated their lives to serve God and mankind. I noticed the Nuns with the old-style garb that they called habits. As I saw them I thought of a Godly woman who gave her life to the people of India serving the untouchables in the slums; Mother Teresa. We arrived at the door where two guards were posted guarding the Vicar of Christ. Roman Catholics believe that he speaks for God here on Earth.

We were ushered into a large official looking office and were asked by a young priest to take a seat. He said that His Holiness would be out in just a minute. Shortly the Pope appeared as we stood.

He came over to the three of us and addressed Mauricio by his first name. He asked, "How are Natalia and your two daughters, Angelina and Maria?"

"Your holiness; thank you for asking, they are all fine Sir."

He came up to Short Stuff and extended his hand as Short Stuff kissed his ring due to protocol. Then he came to me and I did the same. But when he extended his hands, I noticed that he had a Gold

Ring with a Ruby and crested with a gold cross of Loraine. I knew he was a member of the Brotherhood and a Twelfth Knight. I bowed and kissed his ring. I was overcome with a feeling of being in the presence of a true man of God.

We sat and talked about our work as law enforcement men. He wanted to know how it feels to be in a dangerous situation and thanked us all for the job we had done in saving his life almost three years earlier. I told him that the two main zealots were recently dispatched to hell. I told him I felt God had intervened supernaturally.

Then He stood up and asked Short Stuff and Mauricio if they would mind stepping out into the outer office and wait for me. He thanked them for coming and before they stepped out of the office he handed Short Stuff a small gold cross and chain, as a token of his love and devotion for his service.

'Guys, I'll see you both in a few minutes."

The Pope said to me. "Please sit down; Gregg, I have wanted to thank you personally for what you did a few years ago. When Mauricio called, and spoke with my assistant that you wanted to have an audience with me----I was honored. Now; what was so urgent and a matter of world consequences that you needed to see me? Oh; before you answer, I almost forgot tell Senator Richards that I send my love and regards to his wife. Go ahead my son, I am sorry I interrupted you."

"Well Your Holiness, I need to start from the beginning. I was asked to take on a mission for the 'Brotherhood'. Little did I know that it would lead to Your Holiness! By the way I see your ring is like mine. I assume you are a member of the 'Brotherhood?'

"I have been ordained as a Twelfth Knight, and saddened by the death of my fellow Nights. Do you know who is murdering them? I'm sorry go ahead----please continue."

"Your Holiness in answer to your first question, we not only caught the murderers, but in answer to your second one, we feel we know who the murderers are. They are disgruntled men who want to re-establish the Nazi Party. We will catch them sooner or later. The quest to find the ancient artifacts has taken most of my time. We believe the artifacts may have belonged to Paul the Apostle. We have a copy of a letter supposedly written by a Twelfth-Knight in the thirteenth century, stating he was commissioned to guard for life, some ancient artifacts. 'The Brotherhood' believes that the original letter is authentic. These same Nazi zealots tried to thwart every move we made. We believe they are also involved in killing the Knights. Our quest led us to Innsbruck, Austria where we found the clues that led us to the Cathedral, in Toledo, Spain. Some friars recently discovered the ruins of a church that was under the Cathedral."

"We were blessed to see a wall size painting by an unknown artist that is almost so beautiful that you feel you are in the real Garden of Eden. Your Holiness should try to see the painting for yourself. It is indescribable your Holiness. It covers the entire wall where the old church stood below the Toledo Cathedral. Facing the mural, we found the tomb of the first Twelfth Knight. Count Fernando Joaquin De La Cruz. In his coffin, we found a robe, some manuscripts and parchments and the original letter written to his surviving son. I'm sure you have heard legends of the robe of Christ. Some believe what we found; maybe that very garment. It was almost new and had not aged. The parchments and letters are very ancient. One of them is written in Coptic and none of the people with us knew how to decipher it. Unfortunately, we had a fake Friar who stole them. We were only able to recover the 'robe' the other artifacts were stolen, but we have a lead as to where they are." I paused----then the Pope said "please continue Gregg".

"I was on my way home to deliver the robe to some of the people from the 'Brotherhood,' but while I was in prayer the Holy Spirit spoke to me and told me to return it to a secure resting place. I thought far too many people knew of the robe and where it had lain all these years. I thought where is the safest place in the world where it would be among other ancient artifacts that are not for the masses. As you know sir; I am a Protestant in my beliefs, but I embrace my Catholic brothers. I also believe that the artifacts and especially the robe are genuine, based on 2 Tim. 4 where Paul instructs his beloved Timothy. 'When you come, bring the robe that I left with Carpus at Troas, and my scrolls, especially the parchments' (2 Tim. 4:13 NASB). I was called to protect them with my life, but I also have a private life. I thought, how much better than to have the Vatican and the Pontiff protect the robe. I know that you are a man of integrity and a fellow brother, I place it into your hands." I opened the satchel and took out the robe and handed it to the Pontiff.

He sat there not saying a word. After awhile he spoke; "I thank you My Son that you showed wisdom; if this garment is authentic, in the hands of the wrong person it could cause riots throughout the World. People wanting to get healed like the woman with the blood flow. Her faith made her well. I believe that the Christian World owes you a tremendous number of thanks, for keeping this out of the hands of ruthless greedy people. I must caution you that this meeting between you and me never took place regarding this subject. If asked; tell them I wanted to reward you for what had taken place almost three years ago. I'm so sorry, but my time is limited. I wish I could offer you and your friend lunch and just chat, but I want to give you something instead. Unfortunately, I have another commitment I must keep."

He opened a gold crested long box. When he opened, it he said; "This item was given to me by a great man when I was a young seminary student, one of my mentors. It is very old. It supposedly belonged to Joan of Ark. It is the dagger she used when she fought against tyranny. Keep it as a reminder that God has use for warriors. He has chosen you as one of many to protect us. The dagger is a symbol of that choice. Go son with the Lords eternal blessings."

He asked me to kneel as he placed his hands on me and prayed for me and my wife and family. He also prayed that God would always protect me in being a guardian of the faith. He also gave me his private number and said I could call him anytime I needed too. I walked out of his presence knowing I would cherish this day the rest of my life!

———————————

I walked out into the outer hall and saw Short Stuff and Mauricio waiting for me. They both wanted to know what was so important that he would only speak to me in private. I told them that it was a personal thank you for the protection I had given him during the attempt on his life a few years ago. He also prayed for me as a warrior of God of my special calling and gave me this dagger belonging to Joan of Ark. He said he was sorry that we could not have lunch together, and for all of us to go with His blessings.

"Mauricio, I said; Lets go directly to the Roma airport, I am tired and want to go home to my wife and family. I pulled my cell phone out and dialed my wife. She answered with that great sultry voice. "Hi honey, when are you coming home?"

"Sugar; I'm on my way, see you soon." As we weaved in and out of traffic, I reflected on what had transpired over the last two months. The attempted killings of my wife, my twin sons and me. I know that God was always with us. I felt secure in Him, but always alert because of the profession I had chosen. I thought about all the other men and women, who have taken an oath to give their lives to protect our masses. That is why we can sleep at night knowing that we have men and women who wear a badge; a symbol of protection.

I leaned back in my seat totally exhausted after boarding the plane and prayed----dear Lord, please forgive me for not telling the Pope that I had the other artifacts. This way the artifacts will always be in the hands of scholars whom we know and trust, who knows what the next Pope will do? I thank you for giving me strength to carry on your work. I will share the find with the Senator and Dr. Isaiah Hamilton as the hum of the engines lulled me to sleep.

EPILOGUE

We had been home for over a week. One day while puttering around the garage, my cell-phone rang. I didn't recognize the number, but it was a D.C. call. I said; "Gregg Johnson speaking what may I do for you?"

"Gregg, this is Gloria Blankenship. How is your vacation going? I hope you are rested up. I was wondering if I could meet with you. I want to up the ante to my former proposition to you. I have some time this coming Friday, could we meet, if it fits your schedule?"

"Sorry; my wife and I are leaving this afternoon for our cabin for a few days. Another two couples will be joining us as well; Madam President."

"Gregg; it's a matter of National Security that is so urgent! Perhaps I could meet you at your lake in the woods say around ten in the morning?"

"It would be an honor Madam President. It is a very crude cabin, but one of the most peaceful settings in all of Virginia. Let me give you the directions."

"That won't be necessary Greg, my staff knows where it's located. See you Friday."

As she hung up, what went through my mind, what was so

important? Why all the urgency? Bev came out to the garage and said, "Honey, who was that?"

I said, "it was the President. She wanted to know if I had thought over the offer of being the head of the quick response team she wants to start. I told her I hadn't made up my mind yet. She also will be here with her National Security Advisor this Friday at the cabin."

Bev said, "Gregg honey what do you think she really wants? I wonder what Short Stuff, Matte also Manny and his wife will think. It will be an interesting Friday morning. It's almost noon come on into the house and have lunch, then we can go on up to the lake."

I walked into the house well engrossed in my thoughts about what could she want. I wasn't ready to give her my response about the unit she wanted me to head up. I hadn't given it much thought. I was still suffering from jet lag and a tremendous emotional letdown along with doing a lot of praying.

Friday morning came early at the lake as we all sat down to an early breakfast waiting for the great Lady to arrive. The girls had joined in and prepared a fantastic breakfast of ham, sausage and eggs, gravy with fried potatoes and hot biscuits. We were just finishing up breakfast when we heard a couple of powerful boat motors. Manny, Short Stuff and I walked outside to see what the commotion was? It was the Presidents entourage pulling alongside of our dock barely large enough for only two boats. Then we heard the whoomph, whoomph, whoomph, of the helicopters rotors that hovered over our small three-bedroom cabin, then one of them touched down in a small clearing. Then the chopper with the President landed. As she disembarked from the copter flanked and surrounded by her advisors and secret service, she made her way to where we were standing

The two boats carried several Marines who after jumping out of the boat made a large perimeter around the cabin to protect the President. They were running through the woods and along the lake shore, ever vigilant as they were trained to do.

The girls came out as the President made her way to the front porch. She approached me and said, "Good morning ladies and gentlemen. I know the men, but I don't know the ladies." As she shook hands with Manny, his wife Estrella (Star) along with Matte and Short Stuff, and at last she came up to Bev and me and said; "And you must be Greggs wife, Beverly. Nice to meet you all, we will only be here for a few minutes. I need to meet with Gregg in private, can you and I go inside Gregg?"

"Of course Madam President please go on in."

We went inside with no other advisors or watchdogs, we were alone. She took a seat at the breakfast table. And said; "Let me get right to the point, I want to start a special unit that answers only to me, but with the approval of Congress. I believe that far too many of our CIA, FBI and our Secret Service agents are being corrupted. Corrupted by our current system and hindering our ability to get information. I can't get Congress to restructure our Homeland security so that's its leadership is under a career law enforcement person, the way it is run today by a homeland security Czar----a political appointment, leaves a lot of loop holes. I have some information that a former FBI agent has formed a Nazi type group of people who plan on destroying our form of government.

I interrupted her; "Madam President the man you are talking about is our former assistant FBI director under my former boss,

Mathew Hopkins. Sorry Madam President, please continue, as you were saying.

Where was I, Ah yes. I want you to head up this unit. I don't need an answer today, but I do by next week. The unit I want is one that can respond immediately when we are threatened here at home and abroad. They will work closely with the other agencies, but won't have the red tape to hinder them. They will be completely autonomous. Finally let me interject one more thing, you will find that I am not as liberal as you think. I am a born again Christian in a male run World so I must play the part of a masculine type woman. Being the first woman President I am under constant scrutiny."

"You will be able to work out of your home or a small front office in D.C. Your pay will be at the same rate as it was as director. Talk it over with your guys and I expect to hear from you by no later than the middle of next week, unless you can give me an answer now. God bless Gregg"

I had heard the same pitch prior to leaving for Europe, except the part that she was a Christian. As she walked out, I knew I had a lot of praying to do. I now knew what had happened to Matt Hopkins, he was involved with the small group of Germans we met in Europe in our recent quest.

As to the Scorpions fate or call, he was released by the British. I believe that somehow God intervened in his demise. He was playing his favorite game, arm wrestling with a live Scorpion tied to the table while the two combatants wrestled over the fatal sting awaiting the looser. He underestimated his opponent as the guy beat him at his own game. He died within a few hours. It was rather strange that there was no anti venom aboard his craft. Ironically I understand that his number one man beat him. Good old Beto! Ah sweet Jesus, in a way he reaped what he sowed.

As to the artifacts; they are in a secret vault and location that only three other men besides me know the location. Senator Tyree Richards, Calvin Duckworth and Dr. Isaiah Hamilton.

One final note! I believe Beto the scorpions number one man was the man who killed Heilman and his cohorts. It's something to think about. Peace!

I certainly had a lot to think about and pray about! Amen.